THE CLONE BETRAYAL

STEVEN L. KENT

ACE BOOKS, NEW YORK

THE BERKLEY PUBLISHING GROUP
Published by the Penguin Group
Penguin Group (USA) Inc.
375 Hudson Street, New York, New York 10014, USA
Penguin Group (Canada), 90 Eglinton Avenue East, Suite 700, Toronto, Ontario M4P 2Y3, Canada
(a division of Pearson Penguin Canada Inc.)
Penguin Books Ltd., 80 Strand, London WC2R 0RL, England
Penguin Group Ireland, 25 St. Stephen's Green, Dublin 2, Ireland (a division of Penguin Books Ltd.)
Penguin Group (Australia), 250 Camberwell Road, Camberwell, Victoria 3124, Australia
(a division of Pearson Australia Group Pty. Ltd.)
Penguin Books India Pvt. Ltd., 11 Community Centre, Panchsheel Park, New Delhi—110 017, India
Penguin Group (NZ), 67 Apollo Drive, Rosedale, North Shore 0632, New Zealand
(a division of Pearson New Zealand Ltd.)
Penguin Books (South Africa) (Pty.) Ltd., 24 Sturdee Avenue, Rosebank, Johannesburg 2196,
South Africa

Penguin Books Ltd., Registered Offices: 80 Strand, London WC2R 0RL, England

This is a work of fiction. Names, characters, places, and incidents either are the product of the author's imagination or are used fictitiously, and any resemblance to actual persons, living or dead, business establishments, events, or locales is entirely coincidental. The publisher does not have any control over and does not assume any responsibility for author or third-party websites or their content.

THE CLONE BETRAYAL

An Ace Book / published by arrangement with the author

PRINTING HISTORY
Ace mass-market edition / November 2009

Copyright © 2009 by Steven L. Kent.
Cover art by Christian McGrath.
Cover design by Judith Lagerman.
Interior text design by Kristin del Rosario.

ISBN: 978-0-441-01787-4

ACE
Ace Books are published by The Berkley Publishing Group,
a division of Penguin Group (USA) Inc.,
375 Hudson Street, New York, New York 10014.
ACE and the "A" design are trademarks of Penguin Group (USA) Inc.

PRINTED IN THE UNITED STATES OF AMERICA

10 9 8 7 6 5 4 3 2 1

In 2001, I became acquainted with one of the world's last Renaissance men, an American who speaks Portuguese like a Brazilian, plays the piano like a concert pianist, and knows how to frame his own home. When the retention pond beside his house became choked, he hopped into a Bobcat and dug it out. When I asked him how he learned to operate heavy equipment, he responded, "It really isn't that hard." He said the same thing when he finished restoring a classic Austin Healey: "It really wasn't that hard."

John Thorpe's long list of skills goes well beyond carpentry, auto restoration, music, linguistics, landscaping, and driving a backhoe; it also extends to human renewal. I know this for a fact. My entire family has benefited from his talents.

Here's to you, J.T.

SPIRAL ARMS OF
THE MILKY WAY GALAXY

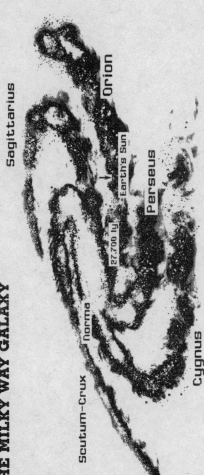

Sagittarius

Orion

Earth's Sun

Perseus

27,700 ly.

Scutum-Crux

Norma

Cygnus

|← 100,000 ly →|

Map by Steven J. Kent, adapted from a public domain NASA diagram

We have a wretched, motley crew in the Fleet. The Marines, the refuse of every regiment, and the seamen, few of them ever wet with salt water.

—Benedict Arnold

SIX EVENTS THAT SHAPED HISTORY:
A Unified Authority Time Line

2010 TO 2018
DECLINE OF THE U.S. ECONOMY

Following the examples of Chevrolet, Oracle, IBM, and ConAgra Foods, Microsoft moves its headquarters from the United States to Shanghai. Microsoft executives maintain that their company has long been a global corporation and remains dedicated to the United States; but with its burgeoning economy, China has become Microsoft's most important market.

Even though Toyota and Hyundai increase manufacturing activities in the United States—because of the favorable cheap labor conditions—the U.S. economy becomes dependent on the shipping of raw materials and farm goods.

Bottoming out as the world's twelfth largest economy behind China, Korea, India, Cuba, the European Economic Community, Brazil, Mexico, Canada, Japan, South Africa, Israel, and Unincorporated France, the United States government focuses on maintaining its position as the world's only remaining military superpower.

JANUARY 3, 2026
INTRODUCTION OF BROADCAST PHYSICS

Armadillo Aerospace announces the discovery of broadcast physics, a new technology capable of translating matter into data waves that can be transmitted to any location instantaneously. This opens the way for pangalactic exploration without time dilation and the dangers of light-speed travel.

By the end of 2030, the United States creates the first-ever fleet of self-broadcasting ships, a scientific fleet designed to locate planets for colonization. When initial scouting reports suggest that the rest of the galaxy is uninhabited, politicians fire up public sentiment with talk about "manifest destiny" and spreading humanity across space.

The discovery of broadcast physics leads to the creation of the Broadcast Network—a galactic superhighway consisting of satellite dishes that send and receive ships across the galaxy. The Broadcast Network ushers in the age of galactic expansion.

JULY 4, 2110
RUSSIA AND KOREA SIGN A PACT
WITH THE UNITED STATES

With the growth of its space-based economy, the United States reclaims its spot as the wealthiest nation on Earth. Russia and Korea become the first nations to sign the IGTA (Intergalactic Trade Accord), a treaty created by the United States that opens the way for nations to become self-governing American territories and enjoy full partnership in the space-based economy.

Hoping to consolidate its position as the sole nation colonizing space, the United States issues an open invitation for all nations to join the IGTA. Several nations, most notably China and Afghanistan, refuse to sign the IGTA, which leads to a minor world war, in which the final holdouts are coerced into signing the treaty.

More than 80 percent of the world's population is eventually sent to establish colonies throughout the galaxy.

JULY 4, 2250
TRANSMOGRIFICATION OF THE UNITED STATES

In an effort to demonstrate that the IGTA is a unilateral entity rather than an extension of the United States, the organization changes its name to "The Unified Authority."

Deemed inadequate for governing the galactic expansion, the U.S. Constitution is replaced by a new manifesto merging principles from the Constitution with concepts from Plato's *Republic*. In accordance with Plato's ideals, society is broken into three strata—citizenry, defense, and governance.

With forty self-sustaining colonies across the galaxy, Earth becomes the political center of the republic. The eastern seaboard of the United States becomes an ever-growing capital city populated by a political class—families appointed to run the government in perpetuity.

Earth also becomes home to the military class. After some experimentation, the Unified Authority adopts an all-clone conscription model to fulfill its growing need for soldiers. Clone farms euphemistically known as "orphanages" are established around Earth. These orphanages produce more than a million cloned recruits per year.

The military does not commission clone officers. Officers are drafted from the ruling class. When the children of politicians are drummed out of school or deemed unsuitable for politics, they are sent to officer-candidate school in Australia.

2452 TO 2512
UPRISING IN THE GALACTIC EYE

On October 29, 2452, a date later known as "the new Black Tuesday," a fleet of scientific exploration ships vanishes in the "galactic eye" region of the Norma Arm.

Fearing an alien attack, the U.A. Senate calls for the creation of the Galactic Central Fleet, a self-broadcasting armada. Work on the Galactic Central Fleet is completed in 2455 and the fleet travels to the Inner Curve, where it vanishes as well.

Having authorized the development of a top secret line of cloned soldiers called "Liberators," the Linear Committee—the executive branch of the U.A. government—approves sending an invasion force into the Galactic Eye to attack all hostile threats. The Liberators discover a human colony led by Morgan Atkins, a powerful senator who disappeared with the Galactic Central Fleet. The Liberators overthrow the colony, but Atkins and many of his followers escape in G.C. Fleet ships.

Over the next fifty years, a religious cult known as the Morgan Atkins Believers—"Mogats"—spreads across the 180 colonized planets, preaching independence from Unified Authority government.

In 2510, spurred on by the growing Morgan Atkins movement, four of the six galactic arms declare independence from Unified Authority governance.

On March 28, 2512, the combined forces of the Confederate Arms Treaty Organization and the Morgan Atkins Believers defeat the Earth Fleet and destroy the Broadcast Network, effectively cutting the government off from its loyal colonies and Navy.

Believing they have crippled the Unified Authority, the Mogats then turn on their Confederate Arms allies in an attempt to take control of the renovated Galactic Central Fleet. The Confederates manage to hold on to approximately fifty ships and join forces with the Unified Authority, leaving the Mogats with more than four hundred self-broadcasting ships, the most powerful attack force in the galaxy.

Under U.A. leadership, the combined forces stage a counterattack on the Mogat home world destroying the entire Mogat Navy and leaving no survivors on the planet.

2514 TO 2515
AVATARI INVASION

At the heart of Morgan Atkins's doctrine was a claim that aliens he referred to as "Space Angels" planned to invade the Milky Way. The U.A. government, however, dismisses Atkins as a crackpot, ignoring warnings of alien sightings during the invasion of the Mogat home world.

In 2514, an alien force enters the outer region of the Scutum-Crux Arm conquering U.A.-held planets. As they attack, the aliens wrap their "ion curtain" around the outer atmosphere of the planet, creating an impenetrable barrier that cuts off all contact.

In a matter of two years, the aliens spread throughout the galaxy, occupying only planets deemed habitable by U.A. scientists. The Unified Authority has lost 178 of its 180 populated planets when it makes a final stand on New Copenhagen.

During this battle, U.A. scientists unravel the secrets of the aliens' tachyon-based technology, enabling the U.A. Marines to preserve Earth and New Copenhagen.

PROLOGUE

Earthdate: October 16, A.D. 2516
Location: Terraneau
Galactic Position: Scutum-Crux Arm

With the ion curtain sealed around it, Terraneau looked more like a small star than a living planet. Before this mission, I had never gotten a firsthand look at a "sleeved" planet from the outside. From space, it looked like it might have been plated with white gold.

I could not see so much as a trace of the land or water through that ion layer. With the curtain around it, the planet was as featureless as a ball bearing.

Until four years ago, Terraneau was the capital planet of the Scutum-Crux Arm. Of the 180 populated worlds, this rock had the fifth largest population—1.2 billion people. But Terraneau was an early casualty of the Avatari invasion. The aliens wrapped their ion curtain around the planet, and no one had heard anything since. At least they had not heard anything until one month ago, and they didn't hear much then.

We still didn't know if we would find survivors behind the curtain. We might find the planet covered with alien soldiers. We might find a hollow ball populated only by alien miners. The only message we received from the planet was brief—just the words "Go away."

"I have a fix on the target zone," the pilot told me. We sat watching the planet from the cockpit of a military transport. We had to use computers to calculate the location of the target zone on the planet; the ion curtain rendered our sensors useless.

Kelly Thomer, the third man in the cockpit, asked, "Do you think that was what New Copenhagen looked like from outside, sir?"

He and I had fought together on New Copenhagen, a planet not much different than Terraneau. The aliens "sleeved" the planet with their ion curtain, cutting us off from the rest of the universe. Once the curtain was up, no ships could enter or leave the atmosphere. The ion curtain disassembled light waves and absorbed energy. The aliens who created the curtain also used its tachyon particles as building blocks for creating an army of remotely controlled soldiers.

That was their strategy, isolate and attack. First the aliens wrapped the planet in their ion curtain, then they invaded.

"I've never thought about it," I said. When pedestrians were hit by a car, did they wonder what the accident might have looked like from across the street? Did shark-attack victims wonder what the attack looked like from shore?

"Captain, what if the aliens are still down there?" the pilot asked.

"They're gone," I said, trying to sound confident even though I had my doubts. "They don't have time for sightseeing, not with an entire galaxy to destroy."

"Do you have the torpedo ready?" I asked the pilot.

As a rule, military transports flew unarmed, but this particular bird had been modified. Our engineers had attached a tube below the cockpit armed with a nuclear-tipped torpedo—the key we would use to unlock a trapdoor through the ion curtain.

If it worked, we might have a one-minute window to penetrate the curtain and land on the planet. If we didn't get through the curtain quickly enough, the electrical systems on the transport would fail while we entered the atmosphere. If the ion curtain proved impenetrable, our fleet would be stranded in space with no port for food and supplies. Even if the torpedo got us in, and we landed safely, we might run into aliens. We might also enter an atmosphere so saturated with toxic gas that our ship would dissolve around us.

"Ready to go, sir," the pilot said.

"Do you think this will work?" Thomer asked. He didn't usually ask so many questions. Nerves.

"It doesn't matter what I think," I said; though, in truth, I thought we had a good shot. We were firing our torpedo directly over the spot where the aliens had landed. Assuming our calculations held up, and the spheres from which they emerged were still down there, the radiation from our torpedo would tear a hole in the curtain.

I didn't feel as confident about what would happen next. Once we made a hole through the curtain, we had to enter the atmosphere before our hole closed in around us. If we successfully entered a breathable atmosphere, then we had to land without running into aliens. If we landed safely, we would need to evict the aliens. The odds grew longer with every step.

For Thomer, though, my first answer was good enough. I said, "We'll know one way or the other in about five seconds." Then I told the pilot to fire the torpedo.

He reached up and flipped the trigger. I caught the quickest glimpse of the torpedo as it sped off from under the ship— just a flash of dull white casing and bright orange flames— and the torpedo was gone.

The official reason for liberating Terraneau was to use it as a base for the Scutum-Crux Fleet, the largest fleet in the Unified Authority Navy; but I had reasons of my own. I wanted to wage a war against mankind.

The Pentagon had sent us out to the farthest corner of the galaxy and stranded us here. Back in Washington, they thought they could leave us out here to rot. The politicians and generals thought they were sweeping their clone problem under the carpet, but I would show them. I knew something they did not know, I knew a backdoor that would lead to Earth.

Clones have ghosts, and this time their deceit would come back to haunt them.

PART I

THE WORKINGS OF WAR

CHAPTER
ONE

Earthdate: December 31, A.D. 2515
Location: Washington, DC, Earth
Galactic Position: Orion Arm

"Ava, this is Lieutenant Wayson Harris. I told you about Harris."

"The big hero," Ava said, her voice betraying a distinct lack of interest. "Didn't you say he was a Liberator clone?"

I had been talking with three of the men from my color guard detail, and now found myself speechless.

Colonel Theodore Mooreland stood before us with his date, Ava Gardner—Hollywood's brightest star and the subject of more debates and fantasies than any woman of her time. Mooreland casually threw his arm around her tiny waist. Maybe it was my imagination, but his expression reminded me of a dog marking its territory. Most of the men in the room would have died happy if they could have placed one of their hands where Mooreland now had his.

"He's the one," he said. "Lieutenant Wayson Harris, the toughest man in the Marines."

Ava threw back her head as if about to laugh. Her lips spread in an inviting smile. Trying to keep from staring at the neckline of her dress, I studied the gentle cleft in her chin.

"How's it hanging, Lieutenant?" Mooreland asked.

It wasn't hanging at the moment, but I answered, "Fine, sir," just the same.

I had never paid much attention to Ava Gardner; but now, seeing her up close, I understood the Ava obsession. She exuded sensuality the way officers exude arrogance and politicians exude snobbishness. She inspected me with her olivine eyes, her gaze both appraising and dismissive. I got the feeling she found me inadequate; but coming from her, even feelings of inadequacy were strangely erotic.

Her hair, a deep and lustrous brown with just a hint of red that only showed in the light, hung over her shoulders in a wave of curls and tresses that somehow managed to look both wild and organized at the same moment. The hair, the eyes, and the body all did their job, but I think it was her indifference that got my blood pumping. The aloof way in which she viewed the world around her came across as a challenge, like the slap of the gauntlet before the duel.

"Where do they have you stationed?" Mooreland more or less grunted his question, wrestling my attention away from the girl in his arms.

"I'm running errands for Glade," I said. That was General James Ptolemeus Glade, commandant of the Marines.

"An officer like you in the Pentagon, what a specking waste of talent," Mooreland said. "They should have you out in the field somewhere. Maybe they should send you to the outer planets . . . see if we can reclaim lost territory."

"Teddy, I'm ready for a drink," Ava said.

"Yeah, let's head over to the bar," Mooreland said.

"Nice meeting you, Harris," Ava said in a voice so sweet and soft it sounded like she'd sung the words.

It was like I was in a trance. I extended my arm as if I wanted to shake hands with her. She giggled, took my hand, and gave it a soft squeeze, then she turned away. Mooreland remained another second and gave me a smirk that said it all.

"Better check for frostbite, Lieutenant; I bet that bitch has icebergs flowing in her veins," one of my Marines said.

"What a ball-buster," another said.

"I'd kill to put my arm around her like that," said the third man on my detail. Watching Ava and Mooreland disappear into the crowd, we all agreed with him.

We were at a party that few Marines thought would take place—a New Year's Eve celebration ushering in the year 2516. I began the year battening down the hatches on a planet called New Copenhagen, making a last stand for mankind against an alien onslaught. Other than Earth, New Copenhagen was the only Unified Authority planet that had not been conquered by the aliens which the top brass now knew as the "Avatari."

At the time, all we knew was that wherever the Avatari appeared, our planets fell in a matter of minutes. We'd gone from 180 planets spread across the galaxy to two in a couple of years. Even after winning the battle on New Copenhagen, we were still down to two planets.

Across the floor, a handful of silver-haired couples danced to moldy songs performed by a live orchestra. A buffet of desserts and finger foods stood mostly ignored, but a large crowd of men in tuxedos and military uniforms milled around the bar. On the far side of the ballroom, women in sparkling gowns sat and gossiped. Waiters in white uniforms walked the floor carrying trays with champagne and hors d'oeuvres, offering food and drinks to everyone except me and my Marines.

But we only had eyes for Mooreland and his date. We watched Mooreland in astonishment as he guided Ava around the floor, introducing her to officers and politicians.

An air of scandal surrounded the "glamorous" Ms. Gardner. Gossip columnists and Hollywood reporters spread dark rumors about her being cloned from an actress who died five hundred years ago. Despite the fact that the nearly all-clone military had just saved mankind, the natural-born crowd still looked down their un-engineered noses at us clones. If the rumors proved accurate, her career would be ruined; but the hint of scandalous dirty secrets surrounding her only made Ava more intriguing so long as they remained unproven. There is a mystique about a starlet who is rumored to have worked her way into Hollywood as a call girl, but an actress known to have worked as a prostitute is nothing but a whore.

Since I was a lowly lieutenant, I came to this party as the hired help. That was one of the differences between me and Ted Mooreland; he came as a guest, and I came as part of the color guard. He and I were both officers, we both put our asses on the line on New Copenhagen; but I was a clone and he was a natural-born.

The ballroom hummed with the sounds of music, muffled voices, and the clink of ice cubes in glass. The only light in the room came from dimmed chandeliers and candles on tables. When they had the chance, the Washington elite preferred to lurk in shadows.

"I never paid much attention to her movies," I told the Marine beside me.

"You made up for it just now," the Marine said. "I thought your eyes were going to fall out."

"Go speck yourself," I whispered. A Marine could end his career using that word at an occasion like this.

"I'd rather speck her," the Marine answered. We both laughed.

"Speck" was the obscenity of choice among the Marines. It referred to the fluid being transferred rather than the act of transferring it.

For the rest of the night, I tried to forget about Ava Gardner. I went about my duty, occasionally catching glimpses of her here and there. As the evening went on, Tobias Andropov, the newest rising star in the Unified Authority Senate, made glowing remarks about the recovery of our Earth-based economy. Generals and admirals gave three-minute speeches about the readiness of the U.A. military. The presentations ended with William Grace, the retiring head of the Linear Committee, presenting plans to rebuild the Republic.

Hiding in the back, I listened to these optimistic speeches and wondered what galaxy these people lived in. From what I could tell, we had barely survived the attack and had no real means of defending ourselves if the aliens returned.

The speeches ended at 2300. With an hour to go before the climax of the evening, the orchestra returned, and the night became festive. Some of the politicians put on party hats and played with noisemakers. The pace of the drinking picked up, and a steady herd remained on the dance floor. I caught a brief glimpse of Colonel Mooreland and Ava on the floor. They cut a striking couple. He was about my height, six-three, but more muscled, with a broad face, a dark crew cut, and a square jaw. She was petite, and her head rested in the hollow between his chest and shoulder.

I had an inexplicable desire to shoot Mooreland as I watched them dance. She was scrub, nothing more, just another girl, prettier than most to be sure; but just a skirt all the same.

At midnight the guests drank, shouted, and shot off party favors. Mooreland and Ava stood in an exclusive knot of revelers that included "Wild Bill" Grace and two of the Joint Chiefs of Staff. Mooreland was their boy, a man with a thoroughbred bloodline and a good combat record. His father, a former commandant of the Marines, had died fighting the Avatari. Now Ted stood shoulder to shoulder with generals and politicians, a man with a future and Ava Gardner in his arms. Whatever angels looked after him, I hated the speckers.

As I presented the color guard to end the evening, I spotted Ava and Mooreland in the front row of tables. I performed my duties, staring past them into space. The revelers stood at attention as we marched the flags out of the room, and the party came to a close.

For the next few weeks, I fantasized about Ava calling me; but, of course, she never did. All that came of Ava was a string of cold showers. When I went out with other women, I sometimes thought of her; but those daydreams faded away.

It was an exciting time. As the politicians had predicted, the Unified Authority began to rebuild. For the first time that I could remember, no one questioned the military. The Senate enacted a new holiday celebrating the victory on New Copenhagen. In past times, the House of Representatives had been a vipers' pit of sedition. Since the war, it had become the soldiers' best friend, calling for improved GI benefits, increased military spending, and the erection of a New Copenhagen Memorial in Washington, DC.

In January 2516, the Smithsonian Institution's Museum of Military History opened a wing dedicated to the history of cloned soldiers. Clones in the Smithsonian—I never thought I would see the day, but there it was.

I visited the exhibit and learned things about clone history that I had never known. One display showed the first cloned soldiers—big, brainless, and brawny; a force of brutes that lived and died like robots. The evolution of synthetic humanity quickly selected those first Neanderthals for extinction, and a new class of smaller, smarter synthetic soldiers replaced them.

One display showed wax figures of the twelve generations of clone evolution. In that lineup was a man with my exact face and physique, a Liberator. Another display depicted Liberators invading the Mogat home world. The display included twenty-five figures that looked exactly like me—six feet three inches tall, wiry frame, and the same brown hair and brown eyes found on every other clone.

The plaque read:

LIBERATOR CLONES

The product of a top secret collaboration between the U.A. Navy and the Linear Committee, Liberator clones were designed as a weapon in the war against aliens believed to inhabit the Galactic Eye. When the Liberators advanced on the enemy stronghold, they discovered a planet populated by humans.

I appreciated the whitewash. What the plaque did not mention was that we Liberator clones were the missing link of synthetic evolution. The Pentagon had its scientists strip our genes from the DNA of all future generations.

The problem with the Liberators was their fundamental addiction to violence. The Liberator physique included a gland that secreted a combination of testosterone and adrenaline into our bloodstreams during combat. The hormone made us faster and fiercer. It kept our thoughts clear during combat; but it was also addictive. Once the fighting was over, most Liberators would happily sell their souls to keep the hormone pumping through their veins. The only way to keep it flowing was to continue fighting. That led to battles like New Prague and Albatross Island, where Liberators slaughtered allies and civilians once they ran out of enemies.

After a few massacres, Liberator clones were banned from the Orion Arm, the galactic arm in which Earth was located, and the Pentagon began manufacturing a new generation of clones.

We did leave our mark on future generations, however. Instead of building a gland with testosterone and adrenaline in later models, Congress opted to build a fail-safe into later generations of clones—a gland that caused their brains to shut down if they discovered their origins. They called it the "Death Reflex." It was a stopgap designed to prevent clones from rebelling against their natural-born creators.

Along with their deadly new gland, the latest clones received some impressive neural programming. They were raised in special all-clone orphanages by mentors who convinced each clone that he was the only natural-born child in the facility. Neural programming filled in the blanks. When they saw themselves in the mirror, the new clones saw themselves as having blond hair and blue eyes even though they saw perfectly well that the clones around them had brown hair and brown eyes. That same programming made them docile in the face of authority, fearless in combat, and unable to call each other out as clones.

As a Liberator, I did not need to worry about the Death Reflex. I was the last of the Liberators, a one-of-a-kind clone. Twenty-six years ago, someone decided to run one last batch of Liberator juice through the old clone factory, and out I came.

The clone wing in the Museum of Military History had displays and holographic movies offering in-depth explanations of the evolution of clones in the same cheery light that the Air and Space Museum showed the evolution of jet fighters and broadcast technology.

Seeing my kind displayed without a warning that we were all mass murderers brought an ironic smile to my face.

The New Year's Eve party, the monument, and the new wing all happened in the months before the Joint Hearings. Those hearings changed everything.

CHAPTER
TWO

Earthdate: March 25, A.D. 2516
Location: Washington, DC, Earth
Galactic Position: Orion Arm

*"General Smith, according to your records, the Air Force
did not lose a single jet during the battle for New Copenhagen. Is that correct?"* Senator MacKay asked as he sifted
through his notes.

The eleven other politicians sitting behind the judiciary
bar had crisp suits, immaculate hair, and polished personas.
Senator Evan MacKay wore a rumpled navy blue suit that
had gone out of fashion nearly a decade ago. The spoon-
shaped lenses of his reading glasses rode low on the bridge
of his nose. With his disheveled clothes and smudged glasses,
Senator MacKay had an endearing professorial look.

More than a year had passed since the Avatari invasion,
but the Senate investigation into the war had just begun. The
politicians and populace in general had spent the last twelve
months glad to be alive. Now, a year after the threat had
passed, the witch hunt began. The politicians wanted to know
what went wrong. They wanted somebody to blame.

So Congress launched an investigation into the war, os-
tensibly to determine our readiness should the aliens return.

Through the first weeks of the hearings, the mood of the
investigation remained friendly but tense. As the investigation continued, it became obvious that the Pentagon had no
idea what to do if the aliens returned, and tension turned to

hostility. The galaxy-conquering Republic that once claimed to have manifest destiny in its corner now floated as helpless as a raft adrift on a stormy sea.

Senator MacKay did not ask about the fighter jets in an accusatory way, but General Alexander Smith became defensive nonetheless. "Our pilots took their chances just like everybody else, Senator," he said, sounding defensive—a man with something to hide.

"No one is questioning the Air Force's role in the war," MacKay said in a calming voice. "I'm just curious about your methods. From what I can tell, the Army lost nearly six hundred thousand soldiers and sustained a ninety-five percent casualty rate. The Marines sent four hundred thousand soldiers and lost ninety-seven percent of the men they sent.

"It would appear that your fighter pilots had a much higher survival rate. How many pilots did you lose?"

Up to this point, Senator MacKay showed nothing more than polite curiosity. Apparently unaware of these statistics, the congressmen around him looked up from their notes.

"We did not lose any pilots," General Smith growled. He was a chubby old man with white hair and a bushy white mustache, but all of the decoration on his uniform made him something more. He was the ranking member of the Joint Chiefs of Staff, the highest-ranking officer in the Unified Authority military.

"No pilots lost?" MacKay asked, clearly impressed. "Your pilots must be very good." He paused for nearly a minute as he looked through his notes, then turned his attention to General Morris Newcastle, the highest-ranking officer in the Unified Authority Army.

"As I understand it, General Newcastle, your gunship pilots did not fare so well. Didn't you suffer a much higher casualty rate with your attack helicopters?"

"Yes, sir," barked Newcastle.

Smith and Newcastle regarded each other as adversaries. As the head of the Joint Chiefs, Smith held the rank, but he waged his portion of the war from an office in Washington, DC. Mo Newcastle, on the other hand, ran the show on New Copenhagen from ground zero. Smith remained the ranking *member of the Joint Chiefs, but Newcastle emerged from the war as a hero.*

"You had a higher casualty rate?" Senator MacKay asked again, looking for clarification.

"We lost every gunship we sent out," Newcastle said.

The senator considered this, then went back to his notes. "That's a very high rate," he said. The people in the gallery laughed.

"We sent you out with our finest equipment," MacKay mumbled as he ran through his notes. "Didn't you have Limbaugh Attack Helicopters? Was there an equipment failure? Would you have been more effective with Cobra Attack Helicopters?"

"No, sir," Newcastle said. "The Limbaughs worked just fine. The problem wasn't the equipment."

"So attack helicopters were more vulnerable than jets?" another senator asked. He sounded confused.

"Helicopters make easier targets than jets. They fly slower and closer to the ground," Newcastle said. He and General Smith traded glares. "But I would not say that was the problem."

"You wouldn't?" asked MacKay.

"No, sir. We lost most of our gunships during the first battle outside Valhalla, but they were extremely effective . . . too effective. The enemy made them their chief target." Newcastle sat back as if satisfied with his answer, then mumbled, "At least our pilots went out."

"What was that?" a congresswoman asked. "What did you say?"

"I said that our gunships entered the fight," Newcastle answered.

"Entered the fight?" MacKay asked.

"Yes, sir, our pilots showed up for the fight. General Hill determined that the situation was unsafe and refused to launch his fighters." General James Hill was the Air Force commander on New Copenhagen.

"What do you mean he refused to launch?" the congresswoman asked. She sounded incredulous.

"The Air Force was grounded," Newcastle repeated.

"How can that be?" Senator MacKay asked the ques-

tion first, but several politicians echoed him. Every man and woman behind the bar now stared in Smith's direction.

General Smith launched into damage control. "We couldn't fly our jets under those conditions. The alien army had the planet surrounded with some sort of ion sleeve . . ."

"I believe you referred to it as the 'ion curtain' in your report," MacKay said.

"Yes, sir. The ion curtain shut down the electronics in our jets before my pilots could reach a safe altitude."

"But that sleeve did not affect your attack helicopters?" MacKay asked.

"Our pilots had to fly low. They kept to a couple of hundred feet. Flying that low made them sitting ducks, but at least they went up," Newcastle said.

Newcastle and Smith whispered fierce messages to each other which the camera could not record. Smith said something, and Newcastle smiled and nodded.

"How much . . ." MacKay began, trying to retake control of the meeting. "Excuse me. How much . . ." He banged his gavel five times, and the noise in the chamber faded. Finally, he asked, "In your opinion, General Newcastle, how much of a difference would the fighters have made?"

"I don't know what you mean," Newcastle said.

"General, what I'm asking you is, if the Air Force had sent out its fighters, how much of a difference could they have made?"

"Flying low? You mean if they had to fly low like my chopper pilots?"

"Yes, General. If they had entered the battle flying low, would you have taken fewer casualties?"

Newcastle did not even pause to consider the idea. "They would not have made a bit of difference, Senator. The enemy would have shot them out of the sky."

"I see," said MacKay. He was not on a witch hunt, not Senator Evan MacKay. The politicians on either side of him would have liked nothing more than to further their careers at the expense of Al Smith or any other sacrificial goat, but not MacKay. "I've read your report, General. You stated that your missile defenses were effective. You said you had more than enough equipment. What went wrong, General? Why did we lose so many planets? Why did our military come so close to losing the war on New Copenhagen?"

"It was the first time we encountered an alien army," explained Alexander Smith. "We never experienced anything like that before. They did not use spacecraft to travel, so we could not attack them until they reached our planets. Then they spread that ion screen around our planets, obliterating any chance of naval support." He sounded anxious as he spewed a stream of reasons why his military was so badly outgunned.

Newcastle shot Smith a fleeting, mysterious smile that faded quickly as he turned toward the bar, and said, "The problem was lack of discipline." He paused, and added, "Cowardice."

"Are you referring to the pilots not flying their fighters?" the congresswoman asked.

"No, ma'am," Newcastle said. "I am referring to our enlisted men."

"The cloned soldiers?" MacKay asked. He sounded surprised.

"Yes, sir," said Newcastle.

"Are you saying you had a problem with the clones?" MacKay repeated.

"Yes, sir. They did not perform well in battle," said Newcastle.

"As I understand it, clones are programmed to follow orders without question," MacKay said.

"That is correct, sir," Newcastle admitted.

"What are you saying, General? Are you telling us that their programming failed?" MacKay asked.

"Senator, their programming broke down under stress. We saw vandalism . . . graffiti . . . men disobeying orders. I'm not sure this was in the report, but one of our clones attacked and killed a superior officer."

"Are you talking about something that happened on the battlefield? Was it friendly fire?" MacKay asked.

"No, sir, it was not friendly fire. Both men were off duty and we were not under attack, and the clone in question was a Liberator. He attacked and killed his superior away from the battlefield."

Arguments and confusion broke out through the chamber. Senator MacKay banged his gavel and tried to regain order.

As the room quieted, Newcastle continued, "Senator, if you want to know what went wrong on New Copenhagen, we crumbled from the bottom up. Our enlisted men proved ineffective, undisciplined, and unreliable in battle. What went wrong was that we entrusted our future in the hands of clones."

CHAPTER THREE

Every restaurant in Washington, DC, had the hearings playing for the lunch crowd. This was a town in which the favorite sport was politics, and congressional hearings were the Super Bowl.

I glanced up at the screen as I pulled up to the counter at my favorite diner.

"Corned beef on rye?" the waitress asked as I approached the counter. She looked like she was in her sixties, a stubby woman with badly dyed red hair and a waxy complexion.

"Same as always, Helen," I told her. Having eaten lunch at her counter at least once a week for over a year, I knew Helen better than any woman alive.

She placed an empty mug on the counter and grabbed a pot of coffee. As she poured, I asked, "Quiet day?"

"You're early; it's only eleven," she said. "We just finished with breakfast."

The clock on the wall said 10:46.

"Yeah, I was in the neighborhood," I said. The diner was near Union Station, not far from Capitol Hill. It was a long way to go for lunch, but they made a good sandwich, so I manufactured excuses to come to the area.

I drank my coffee black, not that I liked it that way. I preferred cream and sugar; but I was a Marine. I had an image to uphold.

From across the counter came the voice of Senator Mac-Kay. *General Smith, according to your records, the Air Force did not lose a single jet during the battle for New Copenhagen. Is that correct?*

I heard this and laughed. "Damn right they didn't lose a jet. The speckers never left the damn hangar," I muttered.

On the screen, the senator paid little attention to General Smith as he answered the question. It was a throwaway question. His old man's glasses riding low on his nose, Senator MacKay sat running his pen over his notes while he waited for an answer.

Our pilots took their chances just like everybody else, Senator, answered General Alexander Smith. He sounded angry.

I heard the annoyance in Smith's voice and realized a dustup was coming. "This should be good," I mumbled to myself.

No one is questioning the Air Force's role in the war. I'm just curious about your methods. Senator MacKay rattled off the casualty statistics, but the camera stayed on Smith. The general looked ready to leap out of his seat and rush the bar. The "old man of the Air Force" clearly thought his bravery had been challenged.

It would appear that your fighter pilots had a much higher survival rate. How many pilots did you lose?

Helen brought me my sandwich, but I didn't look in her direction. I watched General Smith's face redden as he said, *We did not lose any pilots.*

She looked up at the screen and yawned. "I can change the channel if you want," she offered.

"Leave it," I said without looking away from the screen. "It's getting interesting." I had been grilled in a congressional hearing once. Military types found themselves at the mercy of politicians when they entered the Capitol. If the senators began pissing on General Smith, the most the old man could do to defend himself was comment on the lovely shade of yellow.

"Suit yourself," Helen said, and she walked away.

As I understand it, General Newcastle, your gunship pilots did not fare so well. Didn't you suffer a much higher casualty rate with your attack helicopters?

General Newcastle; I knew that bastard. I attended briefings with him on New Copenhagen. He was all bluff and bluster, an officer who talked a fierce fight but stayed away from the battlefield. He returned from New Copenhagen a hero to everyone but the men who served under him.

We lost every gunship we sent out, Newcastle told the committee.

My eyes still on the screen, I picked up half of my sandwich and took a large bite. Watching Senator MacKay and Mo Newcastle gang up on Smith brought a smile to my face. General Newcastle discussed equipment with the committee for a minute, then he showed his fangs.

General Hill determined that the situation was unsafe and refused to launch his fighters. Newcastle's testimony hung in the air like the mushroom cloud after a nuclear explosion. There was a moment of devastating silence followed by utter confusion.

The moment I heard Newcastle's charge, I knew it would cause a feeding frenzy. Having finally found a blemish in the military's new, all-but-sainted image, the politicians moved in to attack.

He refused to launch? asked a lady senator. Senator MacKay might have been the chairman at this hearing, but this gal had a nose for blood. Sensing headlines, she wanted to move in for the kill; but she didn't know how to close the deal. She had not done her homework as thoroughly as MacKay.

General Smith explained that his fighter jets were unable to reach a safe altitude, but madam politician wasn't interested. I watched in fascination. This was theater. This was fun. There was something hypnotic and satisfying about watching Al Smith sweat like a stuck pig. Laughing and muttering jokes to myself, I wolfed down the second half of my sandwich in three bites and chased it down with a jolt of black coffee.

The flogging continued until Senator MacKay banged his gavel, and asked, *In your opinion, General Newcastle, how much of a difference would the fighters have made?*

I don't know what you mean, Newcastle said.

General, what I am asking is, if the Air Force had sent out its fighters, how much of a difference could they have made?

Flying low? You mean if they had to fly low like my chopper pilots?

Yes, General. If they had entered the battle flying low, would you have taken fewer casualties?

I should have seen it coming. When push came to shove, the fraternal order of natural-born officers presented a united front. They might have it out between themselves in private; but in front of Congress, they protected their own.

They would not have made a bit of difference, Senator. The enemy would have shot them out of the sky, said Newcastle.

I see, said Senator MacKay.

General Smith spewed out a litany of excuses, hoping to explain why fighting the alien invasion was different than fighting a human war. He left out classified information about how we never fought the aliens themselves, just an army of avatars they projected onto the planet. That was why we called them the "Avatari."

Then General Newcastle joined in. *The problem was lack of discipline.* He paused for dramatic effect, then added, *Cowardice.*

Are you referring to the pilots not flying their fighters? asked madam politician. She wanted a shill, some political target she could demolish to fuel her career.

"Don't do it," I muttered, knowing exactly what Newcastle would say next.

No, ma'am, I am referring to our enlisted men.

The son of a bitch was going to sacrifice the clones. In battle and now in peacetime, whenever officers felt threatened, they sacrificed the clones.

The cloned soldiers? Senator MacKay asked.

Yes, sir.

You had a problem with the clones? MacKay followed up.

Yes, sir. They did not perform well in battle, said Newcastle.

As I understand it, clones are programmed to follow orders without question, said MacKay.

Senator, their programming broke down under stress. We saw vandalism . . . graffiti . . . men disobeying orders. I'm not sure this was in the report, but one of our clones attacked and killed a superior officer.

I was the clone who killed his superior. As far as I knew, I was the only clone on New Copenhagen who killed a superior, and he deserved what he got. My only regret was that I only got to kill the bastard once. In a perfect world, I could have killed him, resuscitated the son of a bitch, and killed him a few more times.

I pulled out my wallet and left enough cash by my plate to cover the sandwich twice over. I needed to get back to the office fast.

Are you talking about something that happened on the battlefield? Was it friendly fire?

No, sir, it was not friendly fire. Both men were off duty and we were not under attack, and the clone in question was a Liberator. He attacked and killed his superior away from the battlefield, said Newcastle, as Helen came to check on me.

Seeing the bills by my plate, she called, "Don't you want some change?"

"I'm in a rush," I said as I started out the door. I felt like I was under fire. Watching Newcastle's testimony was like watching bombs fall from the sky and not knowing where they would explode.

Just before I stepped out into the street, I heard General Newcastle say, *Senator, if you want to know what went wrong on New Copenhagen, we crumbled from the bottom up. Our enlisted men proved ineffective, undisciplined, and unreliable in battle. What went wrong was that we entrusted our future in the hands of clones.*

That was the explosion.

FOUR

It was an unseasonably warm day for March; the sun had broken through the morning drizzle, and steam rose from the streets.

In another hour, lunch crowds would spill out of every building, but for now, just a few pedestrians strolled along the sidewalks. Men and women in suits walked at businesslike speeds in self-imposed isolation. Nobody paid any attention to me as I hurried to the car I had checked out of the motor pool. With my Charlie service uniform and clone genes, I almost expected people to see me and shout, "Traitor!" as I climbed into my Army green sedan with its Pentagon plates. Nobody did. These people had obviously not watched the hearing.

An old man walked toward me as I opened my car door. He had white hair so fine I could see his pink scalp between the strands. He had faded blue eyes, and his lips were the same bloodless color as the skin on his face. When our eyes locked, he smiled, and said, "Hello."

"Good morning," I said.

He nodded and walked away without looking back.

I sensed an imminent calamity, the same feeling I had when I pulled the pin from a grenade. Perhaps I was being paranoid, but that did not mean I was wrong. I had the brown hair, brown eyes, and olive complexion of a military clone. And thanks to the exhibit in the Smithsonian, everyone in town could now recognize Liberator clones.

I drove around Union Station, then up Massachusetts. A police car stopped beside me at the last light before the freeway. The patrolman driving the car stared in my direction. He might have recognized me as a Liberator, but he would not have known what was said in the hearings. Other people might listen to the hearings as they drove, but not the police.

When the light turned green, I pulled slowly away, wanting nothing more than to blend in with the traffic around me. The cop car hovering behind me like an angry hornet preparing to sting, I kept to within five miles of the speed limit. A few minutes later I took the bridge across the river. When I checked my mirror, the police car was gone.

Once across the bridge, it was a short drive to the Pentagon. A guard checked my papers and said nothing as I pulled onto the lot. I entered the underground garage and parked my ride. As I walked away from the car, I looked up and down the rows of parked vehicles. No one seemed to notice me. A voice in my head tried to dismiss the whole thing, to laugh and say I had overreacted.

As I entered the elevator to the street-level lobby, two officers called out for me to hold the door. I tensed, but they kept talking to each other, not even noticing me. I started to think that maybe I had overreacted, then we reached the lobby. The elevator door slid open, and I entered a world of marble and glass in which large mediaLink screens hung from walls showing live news coverage of the hearings.

The lobby was huge and sparsely furnished, with a high ceiling. Men and women in business suits sat on rows of chairs, and officers in various uniforms stood in clusters. Everywhere I turned, people stared back at me. A few people looked from me to the screens on the walls and back again.

General Newcastle's words echoed from the screens . . . *what went wrong on New Copenhagen, we crumbled from the bottom up. Our enlisted men proved ineffective, undisciplined, and unreliable in battle.*

The image of the hearing shrank into the upper right corner of the screens and an analyst appeared. *While testifying before Congress this afternoon, General Morris Newcastle blamed the cloning program for setbacks suffered during the alien invasion. According to historian Michael Maynard, Newcastle's testimony marks a sharp departure from other reports that cloned soldiers have been one of the strengths of the Unified Authority military.*

Most of the people froze as I passed them. They acted as if I might be carrying a bomb, and one man whispered the word, "Liberator."

I walked across the floor, my eyes focused straight ahead as I tried to ignore the uneasy silence around me. The Pentagon had its own police force, a complement of enlisted men with sidearms and armbands. Two of those MPs stood guarding the elevators to the upper floors. As I approached, they stood at attention and saluted.

I took the elevator to the third floor. When I stepped off the lift, I heard someone say, "Lieutenant Harris? Ah, Lieutenant Harris. Lieutenant?"

The man was an ensign, dressed in the crisp tan uniform of the U.A. Navy. He was short and slender, very likely a kid just out of the Naval Academy. "Are you Lieutenant Wayson Harris?" he asked.

"I am," I said.

"Admiral Brocius sent me to find you," said the ensign. "Would you mind coming with me, sir?"

Judging by his anxious demeanor, I knew he had not come to arrest me. He looked from side to side as though he thought someone might sneak up on us.

"Where are we headed?" I asked.

"B-ring, top floor . . . Office of the Navy," the ensign said.

We started down the hall. I attracted attention everywhere we went. On the elevator ride up to the top floor, a couple of commanders stood staring at me, not even attempting to hide their fascination.

I started to say something, but the ensign beat me to the punch. "What's the matter, you never seen an officer-killing Liberator clone before?" He asked this in a voice drenched with sarcasm so that everyone knew he was lampooning the commanders.

"Watch your mouth, Ensign," one of the officers said.

"Why don't you report me, I'm on my way to Admiral Brocius's office right now?"

That ended the conversation. Apparently the combination of an "officer-killing Liberator clone" and an aide to the highest-ranking man in the Navy made the commanders nervous. They got off on the next floor. As they stepped out, the ensign smiled, and said, "Good afternoon, gentlemen." Neither of the commanders bothered to respond.

"Assholes," the ensign said, as the elevator doors closed.

We rode in silence as the elevator rose to the fifth and final floor. When the doors opened, the ensign asked me, "Where have you been for the last hour, Lieutenant?"

"I was out running errands," I said.

"You didn't happen to catch the hearings while you were out?"

"Yeah, I saw it," I said. "That bastard Newcastle . . ."

"You had to know it was coming, Harris. It's an old military tradition—when things go wrong, blame the speck-up on somebody else. That's why all four branches have enlisted men; so that officers have someplace to dump the blame."

When we arrived at Brocius's office, the ensign walked me past the secretaries and MPs and knocked on the admiral's door.

CHAPTER
FIVE

Admiral Brocius kept a personal casino on the second floor of his family estate, but he did not gamble. He owned roulette tables, craps tables, and an array of slot machines, both antique and modern, among other things; but he never used them himself. A few times a year, he threw gambling parties attended by top brass and politicians. They did the gambling. He was the house. In everything he did, Alden Brocius insisted on house odds. That made him a safe bet but an unreliable partner—he didn't mind improving his chances at the expense of everyone around him.

Admiral Brocius was, for instance, the officer in charge of the invasion of the Mogat home world, a strategically brilliant offensive that included assigning sixty thousand Marines to pin the enemy down until the Army arrived. The Army never arrived. Brocius skewed the odds in his favor by leaving those Marines stranded while the planet melted around them. As one of the few Marines to make it off that rock, I had an old score to settle with the admiral.

For his part, Brocius kept a wary eye in my direction. If he could, I think he wanted to clear his account with me.

Brocius did not rise as the ensign and I entered his office. He sat behind a desk so sturdy that it might have been able to hold a tank. Like his home, Brocius's office reflected his family's wealth. Except for a nook in which a row of three slot machines stood, the walls of the office were lined with book-shelves and paintings. A yard-wide ornamental globe, entirely made of brass, sat in the center of the room.

"Where did you find him?" Brocius asked the ensign.

"He came off the elevator as I was giving up."

"Better late than never, I suppose," Brocius said. He turned to me and said, "Did Ensign Kwai brief you on the hearings?"

"I saw them," I said, making no attempt to cover my dislike of the admiral.

"Newcastle missed his calling. He should have been a politician," Brocius said.

Brocius looked smaller than I remembered him, perhaps it was stress. He stood around six feet tall and might have been muscular once, but that muscle had gone to seed. The stress and aggravation of the Mogat War had left him with a gut. Then came the Avatari invasion. Now he looked old, fat, and tired. His hair was white, and his skin had a bleached quality to it.

"Newcastle nailed you, Harris. I don't think the spit on his microphone dried before J. P. Glade received a call from the Judge Advocate General." J. P. Glade was General James Ptolemeus Glade, the highest-ranking officer in the Marines.

"They cleared me of all charges back on New Copenhagen," I said. Two witnesses had testified that I did not strike the late Lieutenant Warren Moffat until after he pulled a gun.

"The JAG thinks we should reopen the investigation," Brocius said. "Look, Harris, Congress wanted a sacrificial goat; and Mo Newcastle handed you over."

"Me?" I asked.

"Not just you, the whole damned cloning program," Brocius said. "This isn't about you. You're not a big enough target, they can't blame the whole war on one man.

"This is about knocking the military down a peg and keeping Congress in control. Nobody gives a rat's ass about one measly clone, even a Liberator. They want to run the government the way they did before New Copenhagen, with Congress giving the orders and the military as its whipping boy. That makes you the poster child for everything that is wrong in the world.

"Being a Liberator makes a damned easy target. You're like a gun or an earthquake or a nuclear bomb, yes, a damned nuclear bomb. No one needs to tell people to be scared of nuclear bombs, they already are. It's automatic.

"From now on, whenever anything goes wrong, Congress will slap your face on it and blame it on the military. You're the new boogeyman."

"Where do we go from here?" I asked.

Brocius sighed. "For now we bury you and every other clone we can find. We stick you someplace deep, dark, and ugly until the rest of the universe forgets you exist."

CHAPTER
SIX

The week after the Senate hearings ended, a gang of twelve men jumped three clone soldiers who were on leave in Florida. The clones beat the shit out of the men who attacked them, one of whom spent the next three days in a coma.

The security camera of a nearby bank recorded the entire incident and multiple witnesses told the police that the attack was unprovoked. It made no difference. The clones were thrown in the brig.

The men who started the brawl, it turned out, were officers from MacDill Air Force Base.

The clones made it through the fight with barely a scratch, but they showed up for court the next day looking like they had been in a car accident. The judge did not ask about their black eyes and contusions. He ruled the attack "a military matter," making the testimonies of civilian eyewitnesses irrelevant. He refused to review the video feed caught by the security camera for the same reason. The JAG bastard found the clones guilty of assaulting superior officers and sentenced them to five years.

One of the men who attacked the clones had a familiar name—Smith. Captain Seth Smith was the attacker who ended up in a coma. His father, General Alexander Smith, reviewed the case personally and commended the judge for justice dispensed.

Florida was just the opening salvo in the war against clones. The synthetics fared better in that battle than they would in the fights that came next.

In April, the Smithsonian Institution closed the doors of the Museum of Military History for an annual cleaning. When the museum reopened the following month, the clone exhibit had been replaced by a display showing the evolution of the combat boot. Asked why the clone exhibit had been replaced, the Smithsonian Institution's public affairs office issued a statement about wanting to dedicate more space to the "heroic sacrifices made by human soldiers" . . . and their footwear.

When a reporter pressed the curator of the museum about the role of clones in war, the curator said, "Clones, dogs, and propagandists, they've all played important roles in military history."

In a matter of months, the pendulum of public sentiment had swung. Appearing in daily interviews on the mediaLink, members of the Linear Committee called for a "more invested" military—i.e., a military with natural-born conscripts. The Republic could not trust its future to clones or robots, they claimed.

When Congress opened for business in September, Senate Majority Leader Tobias Andropov proposed Resolution #2516-7B, revoking the 250-year-old Synthetic Conscription Act. The resolution called for the permanent closure of the clone orphanages that once produced over a million new recruits every year. It was all show; the Mogats had destroyed those facilities four years earlier.

In the patriotic rush to eliminate cloning, reality no longer mattered as much as intentions. The Linear Committee—the executive branch of the government—unanimously praised Andropov for his courageous decision to close down nonexistent orphanages. News analysts all but nominated him to replace the retiring "Wild Bill" Grace as the chair of the Linear Committee.

Resolution 2516-7B ran through both houses unchallenged. With the already demolished orphanages officially closed, the Unified Authority military complex entered a bold new, all-natural phase in its history.

In truth, the Unified Authority did not need to beef up its military with clones now that it only had two worlds to guard. Sitting a mere three hundred light-years apart, Earth and New Copenhagen were next-door neighbors in astronomical terms.

With the public behind it, Congress moved to deep-six the cloning program once and for all. If they could have, I think the politicians might have classified us clones as obsolete weapons and demolished us like a stockpile of unneeded bombs; but we were constructed of human genes. There were limits as to what they could do with us.

In August, I was finally cleared of any wrongdoing in the unfortunate and untimely death of First Lieutenant Warren Moffat. That same month, I received orders to report to Fort Bliss, an Army base in Texas. So did thousands of other clones—be they soldiers or Marines. Those of us who survived the war on New Copenhagen went to Fort Bliss. Clones who had not served in that battle were sent to equally isolated military bases.

I reported to the base commander and was told that I would not actually be stationed in Fort Bliss. I would live in the ramshackle "relocation camp" erected beside Fort Bliss. Summer in the Texas badlands; the prospect was not very appealing. When I entered the camp, I wondered if it was meant for relocation or extermination.

Officially, our camp was part of Fort Bliss. The inmates, however, called it "Clonetown."

Clonetown was not large; but that did not matter, there were not all that many survivors of the battle for New Copenhagen. Of the nine hundred thousand cloned troops sent to defend New Copenhagen, only thirty thousand survived. At some point, somebody told me there were another three hundred thousand clones that had remained on Earth in support roles.

The Navy still had multiple millions of clones serving in its fifteen deep-space fleets, but nobody worried about clones in space. They manned the battleships, frigates, cruisers, and carriers that had once relied on a pangalactic transportation system known as the Broadcast Network to travel between occupied solar systems. With the Network down, deep-space clones were even less of a threat than unarmed clones interred in relocation camps. We were merely unarmed and locked up, they were trapped billions of miles from Earth.

I spent my first month in Fort Bliss before finding out what the Pentagon planned to do with us. There were plenty of rumors, most of which began with a line like, "I got a friend who heard General Glade say . . ." Of course, none of the rumors matched up. When it comes to gossip, Marines act like little old ladies in a sewing circle.

The most popular rumor was that the Army had built Clonetown on top of a bomb. Some general would explode that bomb as we slept, solving the nagging problem of what to do with us once and for all. Everyone agreed that the rumor was a joke, but that didn't stop groups of inmates from digging holes around camp. They didn't find any bombs, but they did come across an abandoned honey bucket burial site. The air reeked for a week after that.

I didn't get the feeling that Congress or the Pentagon wanted us dead; they just wanted us to fade away.

CHAPTER
SEVEN

Earthdate: October 3, A.D. 2516
Location: Fort Bliss, outside El Paso, Texas
Planet: Earth
Galactic Position: Orion Arm

I sat alone on a row of aluminum bleachers overlooking a parade field on which squads of newly recruited natural-born soldiers drilled. I paid no attention to the platoons doing jumping jacks and running. Instead, I concentrated on squads learning how to fight with pugil sticks. I had endured these same drills nine years and two wars ago. Boot camp was tougher back then; we had veteran drill instructors. The natural-born DIs drilling these boys were fresh out of diapers themselves.

Sergeant Major Lewis Herrington quietly came up and sat on the bleachers behind mine.

I would have demanded a salute from anyone else. As the highest-ranking guest of the Clonetown detention facility, I had that right; but Herrington and I were members of an exclusive club. He and I had both survived the final battle of the Avatari war, a claim only four people in the entire universe could make. He did not need to salute.

"How do they look, sir?"

"Like conquering heroes," I said.

As natural-borns, the five thousand recruits on the field came in all shapes and sizes. Many of them did not fit well into their government-issue tees and shorts. There was a time when one size fitted all enlisted men because every enlisted man came from the same helix. Some clones packed on a few extra pounds in the orphanages and some reported to boot camp looking skinny. I had five inches on everybody going through boot camp, but that's how things go when you are a one-of-a-kind clone.

Herrington, who had just turned fifty, had more white hair than brown. He was the oldest inmate in our little camp, but he was bred in a laboratory and born in a tube like the rest of us. We were all created for the same calling, to serve in the military. He had gone through boot camp thirty years before me, but he saw what I saw—substandard training.

Some of the natural-born recruits on the parade ground looked like they could fight, but most of them looked better suited for writing poetry. Unlike us, they grew up civilians, never suspecting they might one day be drafted. Many of them were clearly less than enthusiastic about their new life in the military.

Perhaps as many as a hundred soldiers had paired off for sparring with pugil sticks. In one match, a tall, lanky kid came out swinging against a short, chubby opponent. The short one looked like he wanted to drop his stick and beg for mercy.

The whole point of skirmishing with pugil sticks was to simulate long rifles and bayonets at close range—antiquated stuff, but a good discipline builder. The sticks were four feet long with padded ends, not that "padded" meant "soft." A solid blow with a pugil stick could break an opponent's ribs or leave him with a concussion.

The combatants were supposed to hold their hands a shoulder's width apart and pivot the stick back and forth while they struck with the ends; but this tall kid came out choking one end of the stick with both hands and swinging it like a baseball bat. If the shorter kid had even the slightest idea about how to fight, he could have blocked one of the other guy's crazy-ass swings and sent him down for the count; but the kid kept backing away.

I could not decide which bothered me more, the rube swinging his damn stick like a bat, the miscreant cowering in fear, or the pathetic specimen of humanity masquerading as a drill instructor. The man leading the squad was a lieutenant. The Army of the Unified Authority no longer had any actual sergeants to drill its recruits. Sergeants were noncommissioned officers. The military had not seen a natural-born below the rank of lieutenant for over two hundred years. Now that they were building their "more invested" army, they had to use officers to train the first generation of grunts. When it came to the in-your-face nastiness needed to drill new recruits, the silver-spoon boys of the officer corps just did not cut it.

Having eliminated their cloned conscripts, the natural-born officers now found themselves performing tasks formerly relegated to clones. From here on out they'd use natural-borns to rush enemy strongholds, peel potatoes, and mop latrines. The satisfying irony of the situation did not go unnoticed around Clonetown.

Down on the parade grounds, several platoons had pugil stick fights going, but Herrington spotted the fight that interested me at once. "God help them if they ever go to war," he said. "Those boys would need to improve just to qualify for shit."

"They're not all like that," I said. Just a few feet away from the brute and the wimp, two boys went toe-to-toe, really hacking at each other. Neither man showed any inclination to defend himself. With all the blows they were taking, it looked like they were pummeling each other with pillows. Their drill sergeant should have stepped in and decked them both.

It was late in the afternoon, with the sun still high in the sky. The day had cooled from miserable to unpleasant, and long shadows stretched across the desiccated ground.

Behind us, veterans with actual fighting experience headed back to camp. Clonetown was a fifteen-acre compound built to house ten thousand men and currently hosting thirty thousand. Dual barbed-wire fences surrounded the compound, and sharpshooters with rifles manned the towers along the outer fence, but we were allowed to leave the compound during the day. I came here every day to watch the high comedy of these natural-born recruits; but once the sun went down, I had to report back. We had nightly roll calls, violations would not go unnoticed. After roll call, the guards closed the gates, and we turned in for the night.

"The general population cannot possibly feel safer with these speckers protecting them," Herrington commented.

"The average citizen doesn't know and doesn't care," I said. "As far as John Citizen is concerned, the sun still rises in the east and the sky is still blue. He sleeps cozy in his bed every night safe in the knowledge that Congress has his back."

Down on the parade ground, the drill instructor finally broke up the mismatch between the tall guy and his squat victim. I actually felt sorry for these new recruits. How many hundreds of years had passed since the days when the regular Army was made up of regular men?

Herrington sat in silence watching the recruits for a couple of minutes, then asked what we were all wondering: "Sir, how long do you think they're going to keep us locked up out here?"

"You got someplace to go, Sergeant?" I asked.

"No, sir."

I knew three answers to his question. As an officer, my job was to give the party line—a simple *We'll leave as soon as we receive our orders* would suffice. Then there was the honest answer, the answer Herrington deserved. That answer would be more along the lines of *Wherever they send us, it won't be any better than this*. But there was a third train of thought, one that I even hid from myself. The new Army had approximately sixty thousand new dumb-shit recruits guarding the thirty thousand trained fighting machines now residing in this camp. They had the guns and the numbers, but we had the know-how, and the experience. If we decided to make a break, some of us would survive.

Down on the parade grounds, the drill instructor yanked the pugil stick out of the hands of his timid recruit and shook it in the air. He demonstrated the proper way to hold the stick by waving it in the man's face. I could not hear him from this distance, but it looked like he was giving the entire platoon a good drubbing. You learn how to read DI body language in boot camp. It's a lesson you never forget.

"The guys we had in our platoon back on New Copenhagen . . . I bet we could have taken every man on that field," Herrington said.

"I bet we could," I said, knowing he was both joking and speaking a truth. We couldn't really have routed five thousand men with forty-three Marines, but we would have given them a beating they would not have soon forgotten. We had a veteran force—forty-three fully trained and seasoned fighting Marines. Forty of them did not make it off that planet. "Hooha, Marine," I said. "We would've knocked them flat on their asses."

Herrington watched the raw recruits for several seconds, then said, "General Smith wasn't even on New Copenhagen. Why does Congress give a shit what that speck thinks?"

I heard what Herrington said, but a different thought ran through my mind, and I laughed.

Herrington misread my laughter. "Do you think it was our fault we lost those planets, sir? Do you think the clones ran scared?" He sounded defensive. Even though he thought of himself as natural-born, Herrington grouped himself with the synthetics. He was an enlisted man. In our world, the terms "enlisted" and "cloned" were synonymous.

"I just had this mental image of Smith leading a squad of grounded fighter pilots into the Avatari cave," I said. That was the first time I thought about the cave that the aliens had dug on New Copenhagen without an involuntary shudder. That cave . . . I took a full platoon and two civilians into that cave. Nearly fifty of us went in, but only four of us made it out. On that mission, I discovered a newfound appreciation for Dante and the hell he traveled through in the *Inferno*.

"General Glade said he would . . ." Herrington began.

I cut him off. "Herrington, they have us locked up in a camp in a desert. Who do you think cut the orders that put us here?"

"General Smith was the one who . . ."

"And has Glade done anything to get us out?" As commandant of the Corps and a survivor of New Copenhagen, Glade was generally seen as one of the good guys by most Marines.

"Son of a bitch," Herrington whispered.

"Yeah, son of a bitch," I repeated. "These days, it's a whole lot better to be a son of a bitch than a bastard bred in a tube."

Herrington snickered, an uncomfortable sort of snicker that hinted that his neural programming was still intact. Even now, locked up in a relocation camp in Texas, he didn't like saying bad things about superior officers.

Down on the field, the drill instructor gave the stick back to his timid recruit. He pushed the boy back out to fight. The little guy and his bigger opponent circled each other like crabs, occasionally feigning an attack but never committing themselves. After more than a minute, the drill instructor stepped in between them, cuffing them both on their helmets and probably daring them to strike him instead of each other. Neither took the bait.

"I'm glad I didn't have to babysit assholes like that on New Copenhagen," I said.

Herrington relaxed and laughed. "Yeah, that would have been bad," he said.

We watched the drills in silence. After a few minutes, Herrington gave me a nod and went back to the barracks. He was a good Marine, a tough Marine, a man ruled by duty and integrity. His hair had gone white, and some of the starch was missing from his shoulders, but I could still count on him. When the shooting started, Herrington would never cut and run.

CHAPTER
EIGHT

Evening gave way to night. The El Paso sky turned orange, then blue, then black. Lights came on around the parade grounds even though the recruits had already turned in for the evening. The lights were a signal for the residents of Clonetown to return to camp for the evening headcount.

A steady trickle of enlisted men walked in through the gate around me. They came in groups of two or three. We fell into lines; the guards took a quick count, and we called it an evening.

With lights blazing in their windows, the guard towers along the fence shone like candles against the night sky. I could see silhouettes of guards in the window of the nearest tower. They aimed their guns into the camp during headcount, then retired to card games once the gates were sealed.

The machinelike chirping of crickets and cicadas filled the languid air. The stuffy evening lacked so much as a trace of a breeze. Off in the distance, a fleet of trucks exited Fort Bliss. I could see their lights in the darkness. The trucks turned onto the highway and vanished. Few vehicles strayed toward our crowded encampment, especially at night.

Around camp, men stood in pockets smoking and talking. Some wore shorts and tank tops. More than a few had stripped down to their briefs. What did they care? No one would throw them in the brig. The brass had already done their worst—they'd abandoned us.

To the casual observer, everyone in this camp looked identical; but I had lived among clones my entire life, and I recognized the diversity that existed among supposedly identical men. It wasn't just interests or training. Here were thousands of men with the exact same brains physiologically; but some of these men were brilliant and others slow. The equipment these boys packed would not allow them to reproduce. We were built to "copulate, not populate," as a drill instructor once told me; but natural selection still toyed with their single-generation genes. The dumbest and most foolishly heroic clones died in training and battle.

As the ranking clone and only officer in the camp, I had "officer country," all to myself. Sadly, in Clonetown, officer country consisted of one small shedlike billet. I shitted and showered with enlisted men and noncommissioned officers, but I had a one-room barrack all to myself.

As I turned down the lane that led to my quarters, I saw the caravan parked outside my door. There was a staff car, a sedan with a GSA license plate sitting center position in a line of four jeeps. Soldiers with M27s sat in the jeeps waiting, but the staff car sat empty.

Some of the men in the jeeps placed their hands on their rifles as I approached. They all watched me carefully, their heads tracking me as I walked to the door to my little one-room shed. Mostly muffled by the walls and window, a strange sound wafted out of my billet. As I opened the door, that strange noise became all the louder. I recognized it by this time; it was the sound of a woman crying.

I had one light fixture in my quarters, a two-bulb affair in a white glass dome. The light was already on, its glare radiating out of the dome filling the closet-sized room in which my humble rack took up nearly three-quarters of the floor.

"I can't decide whether this is a military base or a ghetto," Al Smith said, as I stepped through the door. The general stood across the room fanning himself with a folder.

We did not have luxuries like ceiling fans in Clonetown. When the days got hot, we could either leave our quarters or stay in and bake; those were the only choices. This was not an especially hot evening, but the humidity had taken its toll on General Smith. His blouse was opened at the collar, and sweat stains showed under his arms. It might have been the heat or simply his girth, but Smith made a wheezing noise as he breathed; I heard it clearly even over the loud sobbing of the woman on my bed.

"General Smith," I said without saluting. The bastard did not deserve a salute; his bullshit testimony was the reason I was in this detention camp.

"What's that?" I pointed to the pile of clothes and hair slumped on my rack.

"You don't recognize her?" Smith asked. "I thought every man in the Unified Authority knew who she was."

Now that he mentioned it, I did recognize her. Maybe she had washed the red tint out of her coffee-grounds-colored hair, or maybe it only showed in better light. All of the style had gone out of her locks, which now hung in a mop over her face, and shoulders. Misery had whipped the haughty-movie-star glamour out of Ava, but I did recognize her. She sat on the edge of my rack doubled over as if she were sick, her shoulders heaving convulsively with her sobs.

"The actress," I said, pretending not to know her name.

"Ava Gardner, the galaxy's most glamorous clone," Smith said.

"Glamorous" she wasn't. It was as if somebody had stripped the magic out of the actress, and all that was left was a sweaty, weeping mess. Ava Gardner had become something less than she seemed at the New Year's Eve party. She had become human. Wearing a plain cotton blouse, white with no frills, she seemed far removed from the arrogant beauty I had seen the night of the party.

"What is she doing here?" I asked.

"What do you think she's doing here?" General Smith was an important man, but he was also an old man who was hot and uncomfortable in the Texas heat. When they are hot and uncomfortable, old men often become cranky. Smith seemed ready to explode. "She's a clone, Harris. This is a camp for clones. She's moving in."

"I thought that was just Hollywood gossip," I said.

"Some of Mo Newcastle's officers found the lab where they built her on New Copenhagen. It was hidden in a movie studio."

"So you're sticking a lone woman in a camp with thirty thousand men?" I asked. "Why not just take her out and shoot her?" General or not, I would show this man no respect.

Ava heard my question and moaned as if I'd kicked her in the gut. Until that moment, I thought she might have been drugged.

Smith laughed, and the corners of his dark eyes crinkled. A faint smile formed on his face as he said, "If clones are so dangerous, maybe it's a good thing . . ."

"She wouldn't be any safer with the natural-borns at the fort, and you know it," I said.

"You're right," Smith admitted, the smile vanishing beneath his mustache.

"So what do you expect me to do with her?" I asked.

"That's up to you, Harris. General Mooreland asked me to get her here safely. As you can see, I kept my end of the bargain."

"General Mooreland? They promoted Ted Mooreland to general?" I asked, feeling both envious and disgusted. The last time I had seen that bastard, Ava was tucked under his shoulder, and he was a newly minted colonel.

Smith brightened and the crinkles returned to the corners of his eyes. "I've got good news for you, Harris. You'll be back on active duty by the end of the month. In fact, you're about to receive a promotion as well. General Glade cleared you to receive your second bar effective next week." Having two bars on my collar points would make me a captain. "And that's just for openers. We've got big plans for you."

I heard the words, but I did not trust them. "No shit?"

"No shit," Smith said, sounding amused. "Let's head over to Fort Bliss. We'll find ourselves a nice air-conditioned office where we can discuss your orders in more detail."

"What about her?" I said, pointing to the crumpled heap of dress and hair that had finally passed out on my rack.

"I can leave a couple of men to watch her if you want," Smith said; "but from what I hear, this gal can take care of herself."

Something had to give. The humidity and heat, along with the stillness of the night, turned the air into vapor. Sweat rolled down my sides. General Smith, "the old man of the Air Force," looked like he was suffocating. As we walked out to his sedan, a cloud broke somewhere in the distance. I didn't see the flash of lightning, but the extended clap of thunder shook the walls of the temporary tin shed I now called home.

"Sounds like rain," Smith commented, as his driver opened the car door for him.

"Maybe," I said as I let myself in behind the driver. "From what I've seen, we get more lightning than rain out here."

The first jagged streak of lightning looked like a hairline crack stretching between the earth and sky. It danced and vanished off to the west. Two seconds of thunder followed.

The air remained still. We were in the muggy doldrums.

"Do you get a lot of lightning out here?" Smith asked.

"Maybe, I haven't been here that long," I said, as another streak of lightning flashed.

"Sleeping in a metal structure during lightning storms, doesn't that make you nervous?" he asked.

"I'd prefer something made out of brick. You want to call in the order, sir?" I asked.

Smith gave me a cursory chuckle.

"I didn't think so," I said.

"Captain Harris, you wouldn't be here long enough to enjoy it if I did call it in." He told his driver, "Take us to the admin building over at Bliss."

"Yes, sir," said the driver.

Heads appeared in windows as our little convoy traveled through Clonetown. The guards opened the gate, and we drove into the demilitarized zone between our camp and the fort. Sheet lightning flashed in the sky just beyond Fort Bliss, illuminating the low-slung silhouettes of buildings and a water tower.

"Have you seen the new recruits?" Smith asked. "What do you think of our new natural-born Army?"

"Promising," I said in a bored voice. I didn't feel like making small talk, not with this asshole. Whatever assignment General Smith had for me, it would not be good. It could not be good. I was a military clone, an ugly stepchild of a society that wanted to sweep past indiscretions under the rug for good.

When Congress decided to wash its hands of Liberator clones, it eliminated us through attrition. The military stopped incubating us. The Senate banned us from entering the Orion Arm, and the Pentagon sent us into every combat situation until only a handful of Liberators remained. I wondered if history would repeat itself.

We drove up to the guard post at Fort Bliss. Rain began to fall as the guard saluted and opened the gate. It fell in thimble-sized bombs that crashed into the windshield and burst. The thudding of the rain on the roof of the car sounded like suppressed machine-gun fire. With the rain banging against the tin roof of my billet, Ava must have thought she was trapped inside a snare drum.

The rain fell so hard that deep puddles formed by the time we reached the administration building. More lightning flashed, and thunder followed only a second or two behind.

"Nice weather they have here," Smith said.

"Yeah, it's a real vacation spot."

"Like I said, you'll be out of here before you know it."

Moments later, the storm had already poured itself dry.

Compared to Clonetown with its tin-and-tent architecture, Fort Bliss looked like a civilization meant to endure. It had brick buildings, tree-lined streets, and grass-covered lawns. Our car pulled up to a two-story building that could have passed for an old-fashioned schoolhouse. Lights blazed in the windows, and guards waited just inside the doors.

"What happened to the rain?" Smith asked as he stepped out of the car.

I ignored him.

The storm might have vanished, but the air felt as humid as a wet towel. Doldrums. At least the temperature had dropped a few degrees.

Four guards held the doors open for General Smith and me to enter. They led us into a small conference room with an eight-man table, audiovisual equipment, and a screen. Smith asked me if I planned to behave myself. When I assured him I did, he told the guards to wait outside.

Now that we were in an air-conditioned office, I missed the heat. My clothes were damp from sweat and rain, and the overchilled air gave me a shiver.

I had long ago dismissed any illusions that General Smith cared for my welfare. Whatever he had up his sleeve, it would only get me far enough out of the frying pan to assure that I landed in the fire. "You served under Admiral Klyber, didn't you?" he asked. That was all I needed to hear to know that I was headed to the Scutum-Crux Fleet. The late Admiral Bryce Klyber had spent more than a quarter of a century commanding that fleet.

I said that I had.

"Did you ever visit Terraneau?" Terraneau was the capital of the Scutum-Crux Arm.

"No, sir," I said.

"I see. It's a beautiful planet. Lakes, oceans; it's a lot like Earth." He slid a folder across the table.

"It's been four years since the Avatari captured Terraneau, Harris. The first two years, we had no idea how to get through the ion layer in which the Avatari sealed the planet. After the experiments you ran on New Copenhagen, of course, we picked up a few new tricks."

The fat old man with the graying hair and the piglike eyes, watched me closely as he spoke. He was cordial, but I sensed a sharp blade inside his voice. He did not care what happened to me or the clones who had once served under his command.

"We haven't tried to reclaim any of the planets we lost during the war. As things now stand, the U.A. doesn't have enough population to restart lost colonies; and quite frankly, I doubt Congress has the stomach for it." General Smith slid into briefing mode that quickly. The conversation portion of our interview had ended, and he was giving me my next assignment.

"We have fleets orbiting fifteen of our lost colonies."

The man had a knack for putting a positive spin on a dismal situation. Our fleets were orbiting those planets because they were trapped. Without the Broadcast Network transmitting our ships across space, our fleets could not travel between solar systems.

"We have attempted to make contact with those planets," Smith continued. "Nothing big, mind you. Following your lead, we fired nuclear-tipped torpedoes into the ion curtains surrounding those planets and tried radioing in, but until last week, we've never made contact.

"Last week the Scutum-Crux Fleet picked up a signal from Terraneau. We're sending you to look for survivors and retake the planet."

"Am I going in alone?" I was being sarcastic. We'd stationed over a million men on New Copenhagen, and the Avatari damn near annihilated us.

General Smith ignored my comment. "We don't know how many survivors are on the planet. We won't know anything until you report back, but we're guessing that the Avatari have done whatever damage they were planning to do and have gone home."

The damage the Avatari planned on doing to New Copenhagen included doping the planet with poisonous chemicals, then charbroiling the place. They had bored a mine deep into the planet and saturated it with a toxic gas. I saw a man blister and die from breathing the fumes.

"What happens if I find the place crawling with Avatari?" I asked.

"Liberate it," Smith said in a matter-of-fact tone. "That's your specialty, right? If anyone can retake Terraneau, it's you."

Early in my career with the Marines, I developed a taste for philosophy. Now, listening to General Smith, I remembered a line from Nietzsche: *A casual stroll through the lunatic asylum shows that faith does not prove anything.*

"Just like that?" I asked. "Here's a planet, go capture it?"

Smith laughed. "You'll have the entire SC Fleet for support. Take whatever you need to get the job done."

"And once I retake the planet, then what? You said you didn't have enough people to reestablish lost colonies."

"If I were you, I'd start by establishing a base. That's your call, Harris. We're transferring our officers out of the Scutum-Crux Arm. Once they are gone, you will assume command of the fleet." He made it sound so specking magnanimous.

"You're sending me to the farthest corner of the galaxy to assume command of an abandoned fleet which you want me to use to retake an alien-held planet. Is that right? What if I say no?"

"I'll hang your ass from the nearest guard tower," Smith said without a moment's hesitation.

Another quote from Friedrich Nietzsche occurred to me: *Distrust all in whom the impulse to punish is powerful.*

CHAPTER
NINE

The Unified Authority was handing over more than the Scutum-Crux Fleet. Over the next six months, the Pentagon planned to deploy all-clone crews in twelve of its fifteen stranded fleets. This wasn't the rumored genocide my men talked about, but it would effectively turn Earth into a clone-free zone. You had to hand it to them, the Joint Chiefs had come up with a hell of a solution for their embarrassing clone situation.

General Smith claimed they were assigning us to the outer fleets so that we could "maintain security on the frontier," but it seemed more like the Joint Chiefs were doing the military equivalent of ditching an unwanted dog. Without the Broadcast Network or ships with broadcast engines, we would never be able to return home. Some frontier security we would offer, we would not even be able to send warnings to Earth. Pangalactic communications were just as dependent on the Broadcast Network as pangalactic travel.

When I returned to my quarters, I found Ava Gardner passed out on my rack. She looked peaceful for someone who had recently cried herself to sleep. I looked at her and thought about the irony of Ted Mooreland sweeping his own dirty secret under the rug as part of the larger Pentagon action. He would fit in well with those other generals.

There was only one rack in my quarters, and I did not feel especially chivalrous; but fortunately for Ava, sleep was the last thing on my mind. I reread General Smith's orders. That was when the first germ of my plan occurred to me. I thought it was time somebody taught the bastards a lesson. Not just generals like Smith and Newcastle, but Congress and the society that had turned its back on the men who defended it. The Scutum-Crux Fleet did not have self-broadcasting ships, but it had firepower. It was the strongest fleet in the galaxy, bar none. If I could find a way to sail that fleet back into Earth space, I could bring the Unified Authority to its knees.

Two hundred years ago, the Unified Authority began its cloning program as part of a master plan to colonize the galaxy. For two centuries, natural-born politicians feared us and natural-born generals abused us. They sent us to fight their battles and left us to die in space. And now this.

I reread the orders for the fourth time, then checked my watch. It was 0300. I didn't feel like sleeping on the floor, nor did I feel like turning the movie starlet out of my bed; so I climbed on the rack beside her. The pretty little kitten turned and snuggled against me without ever opening her eyes.

Ava was a practical woman, I could tell from the start. She was still on the rack when I woke up, though she had managed to put some real estate between us. She looked angry that I moved in on her, but she also knew I had not taken advantage of her during the night. I woke up to find her watching me, the stern set in those green eyes warning me not to cross her.

"Good morning," I said.

"What are you planning to do with me?" she asked.

"What do you want me to do with you?" I asked.

She sat up. "Well, I'm going to need an apartment of my own."

"An apartment?" I asked. "This isn't a specking hotel, it's a relocation camp."

"I need to shower," she said.

"Not as much as you will by the end of your stay," I said.

She ignored my comment and kept speaking. "I can cook for myself if I have to."

"Nope, no kitchens," I said.

She stood and started walking toward the window.

"I wouldn't get too close to the window," I said.

"It's hot in here," she said. She was sweating, and her skin had turned pink. Her hair was damp at the roots, and her eyes were puffy, but she still looked pretty. Her curves showed well through the sweat-stained blouse, and the shape of her face was addictive.

"It will get a lot hotter if one of those clones out there spots you," I said. "You're in a camp full of men who have not seen a woman for months. What do you think will happen if one of them sees you?"

"Well, I understand you're the commanding officer on this base. That was what Teddy said, that you were in charge here." She sounded annoyed. This was not the weeping, wilting damsel in distress that I had seen the night before, but neither was she the haughty diva I'd met back at the party. I think she'd cried out her helplessness.

"Teddy?" I asked, then realized she meant the newly minted General Theodore Mooreland. "I'm not in command, I'm just the only officer on the premises. There's a difference, just ask the guards. You shouldn't have any trouble spotting them—they're the ones with the machine guns."

She glared at me, but she also backed away from the window. That was a good thing, it meant she was thinking. "What about showers? What about food?" she asked.

I did not have running water in my billet, just a rack, a light fixture, and a small table. "I could request a second cot," I said, "but somebody's bound to ask why I need it."

"What happens when I need to use the restroom?" she asked.

"That's going to be a problem," I muttered, inwardly wondering what would happen if I suggested she hold it for the next few weeks. "I suppose I can bring you a bucket; I'll just have to dump it in the latrine every night."

"A bucket?" She started to raise her voice, then caught herself.

"Unless you have a better idea," I said.

"Teddy said . . ."

"If Teddy cared so much about keeping you comfortable, you would not be here right now."

The words hit her like a slap across the face. She backed farther away from the window and sat on the edge of my bed. I saw tears start to flow, but she didn't crumble this time. She glared up at me, her eyes boring into mine. It was just like General Smith had said, she was a tough little scorpion. "If it gets any hotter in here, I'll roast," she said.

"I can bring in water."

"What about a fan?" she asked.

"We don't have fans."

"How do I shower?"

"Same as going to the bathroom, do it out of a bucket. I'll find a towel; you can sponge yourself." She started to say something, so I added, "Or you can take your chances out there."

She fell quiet. The expression I saw on her face most closely resembled defeat. She must have realized there was nothing more I could do for her. Had Mooreland not sent her to the camp, she might have been able to get some movie producer or Hollywood friend to take care of her; but out here, I was her only option.

A forlorn smile formed on her lips as she whispered, "Thank you."

I started the day looking for buckets—one for water, one for excrement. I found a couple of rusty buckets around the latrine and took them to the showers to wash them out. It only took a minute of scrubbing to see that they were as clean as they were going to get, so I filled them with water, grabbed a few rolls of toilet paper, and went back to my shed.

"What are those?" Ava asked, when I lugged the buckets inside.

"One is your toilet, the other's your sink," I said.

"I hope you don't expect . . ."

"I don't expect anything," I said. "Tell you what, why don't you go tell the guards that the facilities aren't up to your standards, and this whole thing is all one big mistake?"

She looked up at me, and I saw emotions colliding in her moist olivine eyes. Her surprise boiled itself into anger which in turn distilled into desperation. The haughtiness of her expression went stiff, then relaxed, then toppled. She stood silent and distant. Her shoulders slumped as she realized that she could no longer control the world around her.

I felt sorry for the bitch, but, "I'll go get us some breakfast," was all I could say.

I went to the mess hall for breakfast, slopping a double portion of oatmeal on my plate, then grabbing four pieces of toast. These I carried back to my billet. When I offered her food, she said she was not hungry; so I started eating. A minute later, she asked if I had anything to spare. I handed her the tray. She considered the food, then barely touched it.

"You really plan to keep me hidden in this tin box?" she asked.

"Some people have skeletons in their closets; I have a movie star," I said.

She didn't laugh. Instead, she touched me on the cheek, and said, "I'm not sure if you are my white knight or my tormentor."

It sounded like a line from a movie. I started to tell her I was both but instead said nothing.

Our eyes met, and I read her. She needed protection, and she would give me anything I wanted if I'd just keep her safe. She was every bit as much a businesswoman as she was an actress.

Ava was beautiful, but I knew her allure would evaporate once I began hauling her shit to the latrine. She needed a shower. Smudges of dirt powdered her forehead. Her makeup had worn off, leaving her with blemishes on her cheeks and flesh-colored lips. Her hair had tangles and knots, and she needed new clothes, but in spite of all that, she still looked good.

Some mornings I woke up and looked into those green

eyes and realized I could lose myself in them. There was something calming about them. If I let her, Ava could intoxicate me with her eyes.

I'd spent time with a variety of girls. In the Marines we called them scrub—girls you played with and left behind. I might even have fallen in love once; I couldn't be sure. I knew more about fear than love.

CHAPTER TEN

There was no question, Master Gunnery Sergeant Kelly Thomer had recently luded up, the only question was, "When?" He sat on the warm ground in the shade of his barracks building, his eyes staring straight ahead. Twenty guys were playing a half-court game no more than ten yards from Thomer, but I doubt he noticed. One team wore tank tops, the other went skins. They swore, they fouled, two guys got in a fistfight; but Thomer sat oblivious to it all. In another couple of hours, the day would heat up, and the players would go rest. Clonetown might close down in the midday heat; but Thomer would stay seated. He was on Fallzoud, nothing mattered to him.

Thomer had once been as perfect a Marine as any man in the Corps. He thought too much, and he had too much compassion for his men; but he obeyed orders with precision, remained clearheaded in battle, and never placed his needs over the good of the Corps. Now thirty-one years old, he was still in his prime physically. He could run ten fast miles or hike fifty with a heavy pack. His subordinates respected him, and his superiors valued him, but the shadow of drug abuse now darkened his career.

New Copenhagen had left Thomer unstable. In the first days after the war, the doctors diagnosed him as clinically depressed and ordered him to take a serotonin inhibitor called Fallzoud. The drug wasn't supposed to be addictive, but that didn't stop him from getting hooked. Most clones who took Fallzoud had the same problem.

Most Fallzoud junkies turn into paranoid schizophrenics, but they also became capable of learning they were clones without having a death reflex. The drug was dangerous, but it had its uses.

The attendants manning the Clonetown medical dispensary handed out Fallzoud to anyone who asked. They wanted us on the drug; it made us less of a threat. Hundreds of clones had come to Clonetown with a Fallzoud habit; and thousands would leave here that way.

"Hello, Thomer," I said as I sat down beside him.

"Good morning," he said, turning his head and staring at me. His eyes were dull and heavy-lidded. After luding, Thomer sometimes went a half hour at a time without blinking.

"How are you feeling, Master Sergeant?" I asked, wanting to evaluate his condition before starting an important discussion.

"I just sprayed. I feel great," he said.

Deciding I would do better to come back when he had a few less bats in his belfry, I climbed to my feet. Fallzoud worked its magic quickly and with profound effect. In another hour, Thomer would show signs of intelligence. He'd remain unmotivated and lethargic; but at this moment, I would have described him as closer to catatonic.

"Maybe we should talk later," I said.

Drug-dulled as he was, Thomer managed to climb to his feet. "It's okay, sir. You don't need to leave, I'm a little sluggish, that's all."

A little sluggish my ass; if he turned any more sluglike, he'd leave a mucus trail. Not trusting his ability to grasp what I had to tell him, I suggested we find Herrington—my third in command. Maybe keeping Thomer on his feet would circulate some oxygen to his brain.

Herrington and Thomer had once been very similar. Thomer was more of a Boy Scout and Herrington more of a Marine, but they both lived by the rules and led by example. They had something else in common, too. Both of them lost best friends on New Copenhagen. Herrington, who was twenty years older than Thomer, shrugged off the loss. Thomer fell apart at the seams. I thought I could still trust him in battle, though. When a good Marine goes into battle, the drugs, doubts and, all-purpose demons go on the back shelf.

"Think you can go a full day without a Fallzoud breakfast?" I asked, as we crossed a "yard." They called the open areas of Clonetown yards even though they were dry and bald with not so much as a tuft of grass. The glare from the open sunlight left me squinting, and heat had already begun to radiate off the corrugated tin buildings. I saw ripples of heat in the air and wondered how Ava was doing.

It took us an hour to find Herrington. When we finally did locate him, he was sitting in one of the first places we had looked—a set of bleachers sitting in the shade of a guard tower and overlooking the parade grounds. Herrington saw us coming and waved, then looked back at the field. As we approached, I noticed his venomous grin.

"What's so funny?" I asked.

Looking down on the field, I saw a ring of recruits standing around a fallen comrade. The man lay flat on his back, legs out straight, two pugil sticks near his feet.

"Looks like they finally found a fighter," I said.

"He'll be doing it in the brig. The guy on the ground is an officer. One of the recruits lost his grip on his pugil stick, and it flew off and hit him in the head."

"You're joking?"

"Knocked him out cold," Herrington said. "It was the first clean shot I've seen all day."

As Herrington filled me in on the accident, Thomer stared out across the field with a blank expression. His hair was not regulation length and he needed a shave. I wondered if the reliable Marine I once knew still lived in that head.

"I had a visitor last night," I began. "Anyone want to guess who?"

"It couldn't have been Ava Gardner; she was too busy in my rack," Herrington said, an amused look on his face.

The joke hit too close to a truth that I was not yet ready to share, so I answered my own question. "Al Smith favored me with a visit."

Herrington whistled, then said, "The Old Man of the Air Force himself?"

"I heard something about a convoy driving through last night," Thomer said.

Herrington asked, "General Smith. I don't suppose he came bearing an apology?"

"Not exactly," I said, "but he did say we're going back on active duty. They're transferring the entire camp out to the Scutum-Crux Fleet."

"Back on active duty?" Thomer asked. "That sounds good." He was almost out of the stupor phase of his intoxication. Next he would begin a short period of paranoia. In another hour he would become withdrawn and stay in his shell until his next dose. Withdrawn would be an improvement.

"Those bastards are just trying to get rid of us by shipping us across the specking galaxy," Herrington said, stating the obvious. Giving it more thought, he added, "Oh well, at least we're going to be babysitting battleships. If it gets me out of this shit hole, I'm all for it."

"Smith says they've made contact with survivors on Terraneau. Our mission is to retake the planet and establish it as a base for the fleet," I said. "They're pulling all of the natural-borns out. I guess we get to do whatever we want once they're gone."

"The universe's first all-clone fleet," Herrington observed. "Rape, pillage, and plunder in an abandoned corner of the galaxy. Hooha!"

Thomer, a clone who suspected he might be a clone, shook his head. "What about the death reflex? Won't we lose a lot of men when they hear they are sailing with an all-clone fleet?"

"Not clones, 'enlisted men,'" I said. "They even covered that in the orders. From here on out, we only refer to ourselves as an 'Enlisted Man's Fleet.'"

Everything happened the way General Smith said it would. One week after he left, I received a message letting me know that I had been reinstated, given a transfer to the Scutum-Crux Fleet, and handed a new pay grade. I was promoted to captain in the Unified Authority Marines.

Every man in Clonetown received orders the following day. Like me, they had been transferred to the SC Fleet.

Battalions of officers descended on Clonetown to assign men new Military Occupational Specialties. They arranged us into platoons, companies, battalions, and regiments. It didn't matter what branch the clones were in before, they were all assigned to the Marines from here on out, and I was officially their commanding officer.

Fort Bliss armory issued us combat armor complete with everything but sidearms. Every man received two government-issue rucksacks, one contained a set of regulation Marine combat armor, and the other contained clothes and toiletries.

I was issued two sets of armor. I carried both sets back to my billet to inspect them.

As she always did, Ava hid under my rack when she heard someone approaching the door. The place looked empty, but I knew where she was. Closing the door, I said, "Come on out, it's me."

There was a pause as she searched the quarters from beneath the cot to make sure she was safe, then wiggled out. Her white cotton blouse was mostly brown now, and permanent stains had formed under her arms. She constantly washed her face and arms with a rag and water. Her skin was as white and creamy as ever, but her hair was a snarl.

"What's that?" she asked as she climbed to her feet.

I hated stupid questions; the words "Combat Armor" were clearly displayed on each rucksack. "Government-issue panties," I said. "All the men are wearing them."

She flinched as if I had threatened her. It always happened. She asked some stupid question, I answered sarcastically, and she winced and went silent. I hated it. I specking hated living with Ava.

"It's combat armor," I said. "They gave me two sets."

"Why do you need two sets?" she asked.

"One is for you."

I opened the first set and saw it was mine. The helmet had a discreet cluster near the collar identifying it as command gear. I pulled out the leg shield and chest. Sure enough, they fit me perfectly. I could fit into arm shields and leggings made for general-issue clones, but they were short for me.

I had no trouble spotting the modifications on the second suit of combat armor. The boots had three-inch-thick soles.

The arms were short. The chest plates were designed to compress and conceal a woman's chest. Ava would find them constricting, but they would make her look like a man.

"Somebody went to a lot of trouble putting this together for you," I said.

Ava took the armor, and said, "Honey, if they wanted to put themselves out for me, they should have put me up in a guest cottage back in Bel Air." She looked at the chest plates, turning them over so she could see them inside and out. "This part fastens over my shoulders, right?"

I nodded. "It'll be a tight fit, and the boots are going to be heavy," I said. "But once you put this on, you'll look like every other clone in Clonetown."

I thought Ava would have a smart answer, but she didn't. Without saying a word, she placed the armor on the table. She looked around my little one-room shit hole and her eyes started to tear up. "We're really going to leave," she said.

"Soon," I said.

"They're going to open the gates, and we're going to walk right out."

"That just about sums it up," I said. "We'll be on our way to the Scutum-Crux Fleet."

"Do the ships have showers with hot water?" she asked.

"You'll still be confined to my quarters," I said.

"Yes, I know, but will there be showers with hot water?"

"You'll still be in hiding." Even as we spoke, I tried to figure out our living arrangements. Until I assumed command of the fleet, I would live in the Marine complex. I'd have private quarters. They wouldn't be huge, but they would be larger than my Clonetown digs. I might even be able to scrounge up a second rack. "You'll still need to eat in my quarters."

"Yes, but will you have a shower in your room?" she asked. "Do officers take warm showers?"

"Yeah, there will be a shower in my billet," I said.

"I'm not sure what a billet is; but if it has warm water, I think I'll love it," she said.

"Quarters, your billet is where you stay," I said. "And it will have warm water."

Ava sat down on the bed and put her face in her hands. She started to sob.

"What is it now?" I asked. This was not the first time I had seen a woman get emotional. Normally I walked away from the relationship when their emotions started to show; this time I couldn't. Having just given her good news, I could not understand why in the hell she was crying.

"I'm happy," she said, both laughing and crying at the same damn time.

That night, after I'd emptied the waste bucket, Ava and I finally tested the springs on my rack. We were both hot, and our bodies were slick with sweat. It would have been nicer if a storm had broken; but she was willing enough, and it seemed like a good way to end the evening.

PART II

THE BATTLE FOR TERRANEAU

CHAPTER
ELEVEN

I looked around the cabin of the transport. We called this area the "kettle" because it was shaped like a teakettle and had thick metal with no windows. The Unified Authority built these sturdy birds for durability, not comfort. We would fly the transport to a self-broadcasting cruiser, and the cruiser would carry us to the farthest arm of the galaxy.

They packed a hundred Marines in this kettle, two platoons' worth. Since we were not flying into battle this time, most of the men wore Charlie service uniforms. A few of the veterans came in armor, preferring the air-conditioned comfort of the undersuit to the climate in the transport. I had all of my noncommissioned officers wear armor. Ava came wearing her armor as well. Counting Ava and me, there were forty people in armor. That gave her a reasonable chance of fitting in. Even so, I had her sit in a crowded corner so that no one would notice her short arms. I sat beside her.

Thomer dropped down to my right. We were on the bench that lined the wall of the cabin. We kept our helmets on. Thomer sat on one side of me, Ava sat on the other.

"What's wrong with him?" Thomer asked on a private frequency.

"Who?" I asked.

"Rooney."

"Rooney?" I asked.

"The guy to your left," said Thomer.

The gear in our helmets broadcast virtual dog tags, which showed on our visors. Ava's armor identified her as Corporal Mike Rooney.

She did look nervous, sitting absolutely still with her hands primly folded on her lap, her back ramrod straight. Had he not known we were a load of Marines, Thomer might have guessed there was a woman sitting inside that armor.

"He says he's never been on a transport before," I said.

"Want me to talk to him?" Thomer asked.

"No, let him work it out on his own," I said. Then, hoping to change the subject, I added, "You seem peppy today; did they up your prescription?"

"Speck you, sir," Thomer said. "We're out of specking Clonetown, and I'm back in combat armor.

"You sailed with the Scutum-Crux Fleet before, didn't you, sir?"

"Yeah, this will be my second tour," I said.

"Did you ever land on Terraneau?" Thomer asked.

"I never did, but I hear it's a nice place," I said, recalling my conversation with General Smith. "At least it used to be nice. There's no telling what condition the Avatari have left it in."

The first major battle of the Avatari invasion took place on Terraneau. Four years ago, the aliens spread one of their ion curtains around the planet, and no one had seen or heard anything since then. Presumably, the atmosphere could still sustain life. It occurred to me that the Pentagon could have lied about the message from Terraneau. That would be one way to solve the clone problem—a quick lie, a hearty salute, and a ride to some distant corner of the galaxy. The pieces fit, but I believed Smith.

The bastard didn't even tell us what the message was. It might have been a call for help or a planetwide obituary. Hell, for all I knew, they might have been calling out for a pizza.

We were expected to establish a beachhead on the planet. If we found aliens there, we were supposed to attack; and once we liberated the planet, we would declare martial law. Smith made it sound simple.

"What do you think we'll find when we get there?" Thomer asked.

"It's not going to be like New Copenhagen," I said. "We know how to unsleeve the planet. Once the ion curtain is out of the way, we should be able to hunt the aliens down with fighters and battleships. They won't be able to fight back if we hit them from space."

Borrowing a trick from Smith's playbook, I made it sound simple.

"Hit the Avatari from space, that sounds good," Thomer said.

Thomer was part of a select group who knew the term "Avatari." Only a handful of politicians, the top brass at the Pentagon, and a few survivors from New Copenhagen knew the name.

The transport had a top speed of one hundred thousand miles per hour. It lumbered along at about three thousand miles per hour until it left the atmosphere, then picked up speed as it flew out to dock with the self-broadcasting cruiser. The cruiser would take us to Scutum-Crux space, where we would rendezvous with the U.A.N. *Kamehameha*, an old fighter carrier that served as the flagship of the Scutum-Crux Fleet.

We'd been in the air for less than thirty minutes when the pilot of the transport gave the signal to prepare for docking with the cruiser. For Ava, those thirty minutes must have been a long and lonely time. Not taking a chance on one of my Marines striking up a conversation with her, I had crippled the interLink interface in her armor. She could listen in on open-channel communications, but she could only speak to me. The last thing I needed was for my men to hear a woman's voice over the interLink.

"Are we there? Have we reached Terraneau?" Ava asked.

"Not even close. We've reached the ship that will take us to the ship that will take us to Terraneau."

"Harris, I need to use the restroom," she said.

"There's a tube in your . . ." I started.

"Um, my plumbing doesn't exactly match up with the equipment," she said, sounding irritated.

"Speck, I didn't think about that."

"Honey, you seemed pretty interested in my plumbing last night," she said, sounding more brassy than ever.

"I wasn't thinking about how you matched up with the armor," I said. "You're going to have to hold it."

"Don't they put bathrooms on these planes?"

"There's a head, but everyone's going to notice if you go in wearing combat armor." The booth-styled bathrooms they built into these transports were too tight for use in combat armor. I explained this to Ava. She didn't like it, but she didn't argue the point.

A few minutes later, I heard the hiss of booster engines and the muffled creak of the landing gear as we touched down. There was a loud clank, and the rear doors of the transport slowly ground apart, revealing the ramp that led out of the ship. I removed my helmet and headed down the ramp.

A team of officers greeted me at the bottom. We traded salutes and formalities—in military circles discipline must always be maintained—and a nameless, faceless, prick of a natural-born asked me to follow him to the bridge.

I told him that some of my men were sick and asked if they could go to the head aboard the cruiser. When he asked why they didn't just use the facilities on the transport, I explained that they were in combat armor and that settled it. I ordered all of my noncoms to go. Ava was a bright girl; she'd find a way to get herself in and out of the stall without being noticed.

Having arranged for my men to use the head, the officer escorted me off the transport. Before we left the landing dock, I turned back and watched Corporal Rooney bringing up the rear as my noncoms left for the head. I could only imagine what they were saying over the interLink. Most of them would be indignant about being sent to the head.

Across the bay, I saw our four transports lined up in a tight row and neatly stowed for this journey. This was a cruiser, the smallest of capital ships. Our four transports filled the landing area to capacity.

"Captain Pershing wanted me to bring you up to the bridge," the ensign said, as we left. He was a short, slight man with thinning blond hair. He walked fast, pumping his skinny legs in overdrive but taking short, mincing strides.

"Is this call business or social?" I asked.

"He didn't say," the ensign answered without looking at me.

I had never spent any time on a cruiser. The ship had narrow halls and low ceilings. Equipment filled every nook and niche. Squeezing past sailors on my way to the lift, I felt more than a little claustrophobic.

This scow had both a broadcast engine and a nuclear reactor; it only made sense that it would fly hot. The cooling system succeeded only in keeping the temperature to a low bake around the engines, but then they built this ship more than fifty years ago, in an era when Congress feared an imminent attack. The engineers back then sent ships into space the moment they knew they could fly.

"Aren't you hot?" I asked the ensign.

"I'm warm," he admitted, still sounding haughty. "You get used to it."

As we entered the lift to go to the bridge, I saw an engineer, a natural-born seaman first class wearing a greasy smock covered with sweat stains. His face was blood-blister red and damp with perspiration. Normally clones did this kind of work.

When the doors closed behind us, the ensign and I stood in silence, each of us pretending not to notice the other. The lift started a slow climb, and a blessed gush of cold air flowed out from the vents. A moment later, the doors opened, and we stepped on to the bridge.

"Well, Captain Harris, I'm glad you decided to come up," Captain Pershing said as he met us off the lift.

"I appreciate the invitation, sir," I lied. There's a big difference between captains in the Navy and captains in every other branch. A Navy captain is the equivalent of a colonel in the other branches. Even with my promotion to captain, Pershing outranked me.

"Tell me, Captain, have you ever been on a bridge during a broadcast?"

"Yes, sir. A few times," I said.

"On a cruiser?"

"On a fighter carrier," I said.

"So you're a virgin." Pershing grinned. "You've never seen a broadcast until you've seen one from the bridge of a cruiser."

"I would think it's all the same once the shields go up," I said.

"Cruisers don't have tint shields, Captain," Pershing said, as one of his men handed me a pair of thick wraparound goggles with black-tinted glass.

The sailor said, "You'll want to put these on before we broadcast."

My helmet had tint shields, but I had left it back on the transport. I would have preferred my helmet over goggles. Hesitating for just a moment, I slung the strap behind my head and let the eyepieces rest on my forehead.

"Right, well, Captain Harris, if you could excuse me for a moment, the captain of the cruiser always directs the broadcast himself."

Pershing turned and drifted back into place in the center of the bridge. On other ships, bridges looked something like business offices with computer stations located around the deck. On this smaller ship, the bridge was more like a tiny movie theater with a window into space instead of a screen.

"Lieutenant Kim, do you have the coordinates logged into the broadcast computer?" Pershing asked.

"Aye, Captain."

Turning to his intercom, Pershing asked, "Landing bay, have you secured the outer hatch?"

"Hatch secured, aye."

Pershing said, "Lieutenant Kim, is the broadcast generator charged?"

"Generator charged, aye."

"Seal the hatch to the bridge," Pershing ordered.

"Aye, aye. Bridge hatch is sealed, sir." I guessed this was to prevent anyone from walking in without goggles.

"Goggle up," Pershing said to no one in particular. He pulled his goggles down over his eyes. I followed his example. The half-inch-thick rubber rim around the goggles formed a tight seal, blocking my peripheral vision, and the bridge vanished from my view.

Pershing must have stepped beside me because when I next heard his voice it sounded close by. He asked me, "Have you ever been in Washington, DC, during a New Year's Eve celebration, Captain?" Then he barked out, "Initiate broadcast."

I had been in Washington for New Year's Eve, but I was on duty, so I missed his meaning. Then the fireworks began, and I understood.

They called the electric fields created by broadcast engines "anomalies." I had seen traces of anomalies through the heavily tinted windows of fighter carriers and spaceliners. I knew anomalies were bright, but I had never appreciated how bright.

What happened next I could only describe as chaos. Somewhere ahead of me, a pulsing silver-white circle appeared. I hoped it was outside the viewport, but with the dark goggles over my eyes, I could not be sure. The circle spread in an unsteady jolt, then seemed to explode, sending jagged tendrils in every direction.

Only a physicist could grasp the workings of broadcast technology, but I knew enough to understand that there was enough electricity dancing on the outside of the ship to incinerate the entire crew. The lightning would coat the hull with highly charged particles that could be translated into some kind of wave and transferred instantaneously across the galaxy. Judging by the sheer violence of the anomaly, I suspected that the broadcast equipment on this cruiser had been designed for a larger boat.

The anomaly around the cruiser began at the bow of the ship and wound around the hull like an electric skein. With my goggles on, I saw only lightning, creating the illusion that it might be inside the ship. I felt a stab of fear, then the broadcast ended, and everything went dark.

"You can remove your goggles now, Captain," Captain Pershing said.

Feeling unsteady, I clamped my trembling fingers on the goggles and pulled them from my eyes.

"Isn't that something?" Pershing asked. "You never get used to it." He sounded so damned excited.

"Specking hell," I whispered, still feeling jitters in my muscles.

I had not meant for anyone to hear this, but Pershing did and laughed. "Harris, perhaps you would join me in my stateroom. It's going to be a while before the *Kamehameha* arrives. We might as well get to know each other."

CHAPTER
TWELVE

Pipes and cables ran along the ceiling of Captain Pershing's stateroom. He had a dented metal relic for a desk wedged into a space so small that books falling from his shelves would almost certainly hit him. At least the room was bright. Two high-lumens light fixtures dangled from the ceiling, projecting glare so bright that it made me squint.

Apparently, Pershing believed we would chat like old friends. He pulled a chair up beside his desk for me, then threaded his way through the narrow alley between his deck and the wall. He slid his chair out as far as he could, then ducked beneath a bookshelf and squeezed his legs into the tight gap under his desk. Once safely seated, he said, "I'll tell you up front, Harris, Fleet Command showed me your orders. Some duty you got there. Play your cards right, and you could end up the most powerful man in the galaxy."

Having known Pershing for about five minutes, I gave him the politic response to any statement by a superior officer. "Yes, sir."

"You don't seem excited about it," Pershing noted.

"Are we speaking man-to-man, or am I a clone Marine speaking to his superior?"

"The gloves are off," Pershing said.

"I've never traveled on a self-broadcasting cruiser before, but every other self-broadcaster I've ridden could go wherever it wanted," I said. "Is there a problem with your broadcast computer?"

"What's your point?" Pershing asked.

"We could have broadcast in right beside the *Kamehameha*," I said.

Pershing's expression hardened into something a little less friendly. "True enough."

"So Fleet Command asked you to stage this little soiree," I guessed.

Pershing leaned back in his chair and laughed. "Captain Harris, you're a bright man. Admiral Brocius warned me you were smart."

I did not respond. I had to play this interview just right, passing myself off as cautious instead hostile. If I came across as spoiling for a fight, Pershing might report back to Brocius that I was too big a risk. If I played it too polite, he might suspect a hidden agenda.

Pershing waited several seconds for me to speak, then added, "Okay, yes, this conversation may have been authorized on some level. Admiral Brocius is keeping an eye on you. Do you blame him?"

I still said nothing.

"You do realize that they're giving you command of the largest fleet in the galaxy?"

"The largest fleet in the galaxy," I repeated. "That's one way of putting it. Here's another, they're sending me to the far end of the galaxy with no way to return."

"Is that really how you see it, Harris?" Pershing asked. "You'll have three times as many battleships as the Earth Fleet."

True enough. All of the six galactic arms had three fleets; but in the Scutum-Crux Arm, the Unified Authority combined those fleets into one.

"Are they giving me any self-broadcasting ships . . . you know, for shuttling in supplies?"

Pershing shook his head. "It's not in the cards."

"Are they planning on reestablishing a broadcast connection between Terraneau and Earth?"

"No," Pershing said in a quiet voice, making no attempt to mask his irritation.

"So I'll have big ships, plenty of guns, and a lot of empty space."

"There's always Terraneau," Pershing pointed out.

"If we can't break Terraneau away from the aliens, we're screwed," I said.

Pershing sat silent for a moment. In former times, before the civil war and the Avatari invasion, the commanding officer of a scow like this cruiser would barely have been considered an officer at all. Some commanders didn't even think cruisers qualified as capital ships. Pershing had a shabby little office with pipes running along the ceiling and battered furniture, a stateroom fit for an officer with a dead-end career.

But times had changed. He was the commander of a self-broadcasting naval ship, a scarce commodity indeed. Officer country on this scow may have been dingy, but the men who inhabited it had friends in high places.

"You've got yourself a fleet, and I have no doubt you'll recapture Terraneau, Captain." Pershing said this with the voice that officers use when they want to signal the end of an interview.

I thought about offering to swap places with Pershing—he could have the gigantic fleet and the strategic planet, and I would take the dilapidated cruiser; but I knew better. I had already pushed him too far and, despite his chatty demeanor, his interest in me was anything but friendly.

CHAPTER
THIRTEEN

Some Pentagon genius must have choked when he saw the logistics. The Navy originally intended to ship the entire population of Clonetown to Scutum-Crux in one mass transfer. Who came up with the idea of trusting thirty thousand trained killing machines to behave themselves as you shipped them out to nowhere?

The plans changed. Instead of shipping us off like Marines, the Pentagon transferred the inmates of Clonetown the way prison guards transfer inmates—with limited contact and in small groups. Granted, they did not place us in shackles, but we were confined to our transports. Pershing's cruiser served as the prison bus, hauling us in increments of four hundred men at a time.

Captain Pershing's shuttle service ran in both directions. After dropping us off with the fleet, his orders had him loading up natural-borns and returning them to Earth. The Navy intended to complete the entire transfer four hundred men at a time, but I did not think the sailors out in Scutum-Crux would be happy with this slow-trickle approach. The natural-born officers coming back to Earth had just spent the last four years of their lives running laps around a tiny planet in a nondescript corner of space, they'd be in a rush to head home. The problem was, there were so many of them.

The *Kamehameha* was an old Expansion-class fighter carrier, making it the smallest of the thirty-six fighter carriers in the SC Fleet. She carried an eight-thousand-man crew, nearly a thousand of whom were natural-borns. She also carried a complement of two thousand Marines, almost two hundred of whom were natural-born officers. It would take Pershing's cruiser three trips just to bring home the natural-borns on the *Kamehameha*.

The other carriers would take longer as they were Perseus-class, vessels twice as big as the *Kamehameha*. While the basic crew of a Perseus-class fighter carrier was only slightly larger than the crew of an Expansion-class ship, Perseus carriers stowed five times as many Marines and twice as many fighters. All fighter pilots were natural-born.

And the carriers only formed the backbone of the Scutum-Crux Fleet. There were 90 battleships, 150 frigates, 120 cruisers, and sundry communications ships, minelayers and minesweepers, and scouts, and more. At four hundred men per trip, it would take Pershing months to ferry all natural-born officers back to Earth. Maybe years.

Sitting in the windowless kettle of the transport, I did not get a view of the cruiser as we left, nor did I catch a glimpse of the *Kamehameha* as we approached her. I sat in the darkness of the cabin with my men listening to the noise of the landing gear. The rear doors ground open, and the officer on duty came up the ramp.

I told my NCOs to keep their helmets on, then removed my helmet and went to meet the duty officer. I met him on the ramp, saluted, and said, "Requesting permission to come aboard, sir."

The officer returned my salute, and said, "Permission granted, Captain." With that simple ceremony, we took up residence in the Scutum-Crux Fleet.

Rear Admiral Lawrence Thorne met me as I came off the transport. He stood with an entourage of no less than seventeen officers. I counted them. You can tell a lot about an officer by the number of remora fish trailing behind him.

One of the men in Thorne's group had an anchor and two stars on his collar—the insignia of a master chief petty officer. The rest wore eagles, clusters, and bars. These were high-ranking officers. Thorne stood out because he was the only officer with a star. His single star identified him as a lower-half rear admiral.

I could not help but wonder at the Scutum-Crux Fleet's drop in stature. Years ago, when I arrived as a young corporal, a five-star admiral had command of the fleet. He was replaced by Rear Admiral Robert Thurston, an upper-half rear admiral with two stars. With Thorne in command, the fleet was down to one star. Once I took over, the stars would be replaced by the silver bars of a captain.

Admiral Thorne and his parade of officers greeted me as I stepped from the ramp. With all those younger officers trailing behind him, Thorne looked like a broken old man. My first impression of him was not good.

I saluted the admiral, and he returned my salute.

"You must be Captain Harris," he said. "Welcome aboard, Captain."

"Thank you, sir," I said.

"Warshaw, see to Captain Harris's gear." Thorne called over his shoulder, not looking back when the one noncom in the entourage acknowledged the order. "Your men are in good hands, Captain. In the meantime, why don't I get you up to speed with your new fleet."

I turned to look at Warshaw. He was a master chief petty officer, the ranking enlisted man in the Scutum-Crux Fleet. He gave me a smart salute.

He was, of course, a clone, but he stood out because he looked short for a clone. He was as tall as any clone of his make, of course; but he was more squat. He had broad, bulging shoulders and a neck like a bull's—the earmarks of a dedicated bodybuilder. The forms of his biceps and triceps filled his sleeves.

Warshaw barked rapid-fire orders to his men. Watching the master chief, I got the feeling that he pretty much ran the show on this ship.

"Perhaps we should begin your tour, Captain," Thorne said to me, interrupting my thoughts.

The docking bay of the *Kamehameha* was brightly lit, every bit as immaculate as I remembered it, and large enough to hold twenty-five transports. Pershing might have been able to fit half of his cruiser in this docking bay, and the other half in the second docking bay on the other side of the ship.

As we crossed the deck, Thorne said, "Your crew is as competent as any crew that has ever flown this fleet. We spent the last year training them.

"There is an all-clone crew manning the bridge at this very moment. There are enlisted-man crews flying every ship in the fleet. At this point, my officers are acting in an advisory role."

"Is that so?" I asked, unable to come up with a more interested response.

"You have a full complement of fighter pilots, all clones, all noncommissioned officers. It's a shame we didn't experiment with clone pilots earlier, this fleet has never run so smoothly," the admiral said in a loud voice, sounding like a salesman with a hearing problem. After a moment I realized that he was speaking as much for the benefit of the remora fish entourage as for mine.

He stopped and handed me a folder. "This is your new chain of command. You'll want to meet with your staff as soon as possible. There are a million things that can go wrong transferring command of a fleet, and I want this transfer to go as smoothly as possible."

"You sound anxious to get home," I said in as friendly a voice as I could. I did not want the admiral to know just how bitter I felt.

Thorne was an old man with a wrinkled face and alert blue eyes. He heard my comment and detected the disrespect hidden underneath my words. His smile did not falter, but his eyes narrowed. "Captain, I have officers who would kill to get home. Some of those boys thought they might never see home again. You bet they want to get home."

Since I had presumably been stationed here for the remainder of my life, I felt less than sympathetic. I took the folder without opening it.

Thorne turned and continued down the hall. He looked to be in his sixties. His hair had gone all white and thinned around the corners. Instead of a beard, he had powdery stubble on his cheeks and chin. Tall but bent by age, he had a stooped back, though his scrawny shoulders were as straight across as lumber.

Admiral Thorne's entourage followed behind as we left the hangar and entered a corridor that led all the way across the ship. "You once served on this ship, did you not?" Thorne asked.

"I did, sir," I said.

"Was that under Admiral Klyber? I was assigned to the Scutum-Crux Inner Fleet when Klyber combined the fleets," Thorne said.

I was on the *Kamehameha* when Klyber combined the fleets and said so. Then, in an attempt to show polite interest, I asked, "Have you been reassigned to the Earth Fleet?" I knew the Navy would not bother assigning a fossil like Admiral Thorne to another fleet, his career was over.

To his credit, Admiral Thorne did not take well to flattery. "The new Navy has almost as much room for overage officers as it has for clones. They're putting us both out to pasture." Then he lowered his voice to a croak, and said, "The difference between my new assignment and yours is that the Pentagon does not see me as a threat."

I wondered if I had heard him correctly. This was something I had not expected—honesty.

As I sorted this out, Thorne dismissed his entourage. They scattered in every direction like a flock of birds. When two officers lingered, he growled, "Did you need something?"

One man in particular, a captain, looked stunned, even flustered. "But sir, Admiral Brocius said . . ."

Apparently the soon-to-retire Lawrence Thorne did not give a flying speck what Admiral Brocius might or might not have said. "This is a conference for fleet commanders, Captain Stone. The last time I checked, you weren't on the invite list."

"But, sir, Admiral . . ."

"I give the orders on this ship," Thorne said in a voice so sarcastic it did not sound like something that could come from an old man's mouth. He licked his lips. "And here is a direct order, 'You are dismissed.'"

Stone took a step, stopped, took another step, and stopped again. Confusion showed on his face. He had orders from a higher authority than this broken-down admiral, but the officer who had issued them was too far away for an appeal.

"Don't make me repeat myself, Stone," Thorne said, now raising his voice.

Captain Stone turned smartly and strode away; quite the dignified officer. Once he disappeared around a corner, Admiral Thorne said, "Have they told you that rubbish about commanding the most powerful fleet in the galaxy?"

"Yes, sir," I said.

"Did they tell you the entire arm would be at your command?"

"Something along that line," I said.

"You do know it's all bullshit?"

"I had that feeling," I said.

Thorne laughed. "They tried to sell me the same line. Let me give you the skinny, Harris. Even if everything goes according to plan, you're still stuck out here a trillion miles from home. You and your men are going to be marooned out here, and nothing is ever going to change that."

I nodded.

"I bet you think it's an antisynthetic conspiracy. Do you think they sent you out here because you're a clone?" Thorne asked. "Somebody told me that you knew you were a Liberator clone and not to worry about the death reflex." He looked at me, concern showing in his sky-blue eyes.

"I know that I am a clone, sir."

"You're a Liberator, right?" He said the term "Liberator" with little emotion. "I've gone over your record. Not a bad record. It might even be a great record if they hadn't flagged you for killing superior officers.

"You're a Liberator; they should have expected a little fratricide from you. That's why they discontinued your kind."

Thorne walked as he spoke, leading me through the halls at a pace so fast that no one could follow us without looking suspicious. "We're outdated, Captain Harris. I'm old and you're obsolete. Didn't they stop making your kind fifty years ago? We're both marked for extinction."

The old man chattered nervously. He might have been scared of Liberators, but he might have just been giddy knowing that my arrival meant he could soon go home.

He paused to take a breath or possibly to let me respond. I had nothing to say. When I first saw him, I thought Admiral Thorne was a dried-up relic, a paper-pusher who had been pressed into commanding an inconsequential fleet. I might have been partly right, but there was something more to this man.

"They sold me the same line when I took command of the fleet three years ago. That was right after the aliens sleeved Terraneau. I was fifth in the command chain at the time. Admiral Chen should have taken command, but he had a brother in the Senate. Admiral Long was under him. He had an uncle on the Linear Committee. They both went home. I didn't have any high-ranking relatives, so they promoted me to admiral and congratulated me for becoming 'the most powerful man in the galaxy.'

"They had to reach a long way down the chain to find someone they could leave behind," Thorne said. "That was three years ago."

• I heard what he said, but my attention strayed. Three sailors walked past us down the hall, and I could have sworn that two of them had blue eyelids. It wasn't a dark pronounced blue, just a light, faint shade that could easily be overlooked.

I watched them walk past, my eyes following them even as they turned a corner and headed away from us.

"Is something the matter?" Thorne asked.

"No, just . . . I saw something I didn't . . . I'm fine," I said, feeling confused.

I knew the layout of the *Kamehameha* well, so I was surprised when Admiral Thorne walked past the bank of elevators that led to the fleet decks. He caught me looking back at the elevator, and asked, "What's the matter?"

"Aren't those the elevators to Fleet Command?"

"We're not going to Fleet Command, Captain."

"Where are we going?"

"Those men you saw following me when you arrived, they are all fleet officers. They're waiting for us on the fleet deck so they can give you a proper briefing. I want to take a few minutes to brief you improperly."

"That's very kind of you," I said, feeling a little suspicious.

By this time Thorne had led me across the ship to the second docking bay. Here he stopped, and said, "I want to start by showing you the things I am supposed to show you, then I thought I might show you what that prick Stone did to this ship behind my back. I've got something to show you that neither of us is supposed to know about."

CHAPTER
FOURTEEN

A fleet of five transports sat in the darkened hangar. These were obese, ugly ships with immoderately small wings sticking out of the distended bellies of their cabin. The spine that stretched from the cockpit to the tail along the top of the transports looked like it had been thrown on as an afterthought. The transports stood on struts instead of wheels, though they struggled with vertical takeoffs in atmospheric conditions. Lacking even the semblance of aerodynamics and entirely unable to glide, they dropped like bricks when their thrusters cut out; but they were the workhorses of the Unified Authority's invasion force. Without them, the Army and Marines would have been grounded.

Admiral Thorne led me to the first bird in the line and pointed between the struts. "This is the one with the torpedo tube," he said.

I bent down but still could not see the modification, so I dropped to my knees. A cylinder the size and shape of an Army boot hung from the bottom of the ship. It looked almost as if someone had welded a boot to the chassis.

"That's it?" I asked, amazed that such a small barrel could house a nuclear-tipped torpedo. I remained on my knees, staring into that tube. Deep inside it, I could see the rounded point of a red-tipped cone.

"Armed and ready," Thorne said. He coughed a dry, wheezing sort of cough. It was an old man's cough, not one caused by congested lungs or something in his throat.

I fired off a nuclear device once. The sight was dazzling and mesmerizing and horrible. Heat, or radiation, or maybe it was just force, rose from the center of the explosion like an electric sheet. I remember thinking that with some skill, you could protect yourself from a bullet or a knife; but with a nuke, there was nothing you could do. It would kill you, then incinerate your body no matter how you tried to protect yourself. The realization that I would once again be dealing with a weapon designed to destroy areas instead of people left me nervous.

"Per your request, the other transports are not armed. You have one armed transport, and that transport is armed with one torpedo. If the shot fails, you're going to need to return to the ship for another torpedo, Captain. I don't understand why you wouldn't want us to place tubes on the other transports."

"If we need another one, we can come back easily enough," I said. "It's not like we have to work around a window of time."

I was making up excuses. The truth was that nuclear weapons scared me. We would need one nuclear-tipped torpedo to get through the ion curtain; and once we made it through the curtain, I did not want any superfluous warheads distracting me.

"No, there isn't. Not for you," Thorne said. "How long do you think you will need to capture the planet?"

What would happen once we landed on Terraneau was anybody's guess. A few weeks had passed since Admiral Thorne received the message from the survivors. Apparently he had not heard anything since. He told me this along with his belief—that we would find ourselves on a ghost planet once we landed. I did not like that prospect, but I could think of a worse scenario—finding the atmosphere saturated with the gas the aliens used in their mining. The gas was so corrosive that it would dissolve our transports around us as soon as we punched our way through the curtain.

"Is the big package ready as well?" I asked.

"It's on board, Captain. So is the other equipment you requested," Thorne said. "Did you want to inspect it?"

"No," I said. The big package was a fifty-megaton bomb. If Thorne said it was ready and aboard the ship, that was good enough for me.

"Excellent. Now that that's out of the way, let's move on to the Engine Room," Thorne said.

I asked, "What's in the Engine Room?" giving Thorne an opening he could not resist. "The ship's engine," he said. Then he added, "Admiral Brocius authorized Captain Stone to make a modification without telling me, Captain. I became aware of it quite by accident last week, and I thought you might find it interesting."

What Thorne showed me next opened my eyes. I had not told anyone my plans, not even Thomer or Ava, but the brass suspected me just the same. Somebody had hobbled this ship.

CHAPTER
FIFTEEN

I spent hours touring the ship and discussing the fleet with Admiral Thorne. After that, I went to my billet to rest. A pile of combat armor belonging to Corporal Mike Rooney sat in the corner of the room. Rooney herself, now in Ava attire, sat cleaned and dressed in the booth-sized head across the room.

One thing about Ava; she kept her wits about her. Sitting in that tight bathroom could not have been comfortable, but it would give her some level of concealment if someone stepped into the room other than me. "How do you like the ship?" I asked.

"It beats the hell out of Clonetown, Honey."

"We had more space back at Fort Bliss," I pointed out.

"I had to pee in a bucket," she said. "I like the cool air."

"Glad you're satisfied," I said.

"Satisfied? Aren't you some kind of important officer. Why did they stick you in such a tiny apartment?" She stood up and examined herself in the mirror over my sink until she found a smudge on her forehead. Then she ran the water to wet a tissue and dabbed at the spot.

Ava may not have risked a shower just yet, but she had clearly preened. She had hand-tousled her hair and washed her face and arms.

Confined to my shed, she had not gotten any sun in weeks and her skin had gone milky white. A permanent film of sweat and dust had formed on her body. Having had some time to clean herself, she now looked clean and pale.

"These are not my permanent quarters," I said. "Once I assume command of the fleet, I get a deck to myself."

"A deck to ourselves? That sounds absolutely marvelous," Ava said as she continued inspecting herself in the mirror.

This was the first chance she'd had to fix herself since General Smith had dumped her off at Fort Bliss, and she could not tear herself away from the mirror. "When do we move in?"

"It's not going to be that easy. Before we can move in, Admiral Thorne needs to move out."

"Who is Admiral Thorne?"

"He's the fleet commander."

"I thought you were the fleet commander?"

"He's the outgoing fleet commander."

"So when does he check out?" Ava asked.

Ava stood there in the bathroom, the cleanest I had seen her since I met her at the New Year's Eve party. She had to know what I wanted, but she gave no sign of reading me. I took a step toward the bathroom, and she finally looked away from the mirror. Her green eyes locked in on mine, and I saw something both playful and stern in her expression.

"Don't you think it might be a little tight in here for two?" she asked.

"Not if we get real close," I said.

"That doesn't sound very comfortable," she said.

"Then come on out, there's plenty of space out here," I said.

She shook her head, and said, "I think I like it better in here."

"Any way you want it." I started toward her.

"By myself," she added.

"So why did you get all cleaned up like that?" I asked.

Ava smiled an indulgent, amused smile. "Honey, that's the difference between girls and Marines. I cleaned up because I wanted to be clean, not because I wanted to have sex."

"Oh," I said. After that, I went to my rack and reviewed the orders Admiral Thorne had given me. I spent two hours reading and rereading them; and then, ready or not, it was time to start briefing my men.

Our first staff meeting did not go as I had expected.

We held the meeting in a staff room near the bridge. In the future, once Admiral Thorne and his corps of natural-born officers returned to Earth, I would conduct staff meetings on the fleet deck.

For this first meeting, I only brought two of my men, Thomer and Herrington. Thomer, who must have luded up a few hours earlier, paid little attention to the surroundings as he entered the room. He walked straight to the conference table and sat down without even scanning his surroundings.

Not Herrington. An enlisted man who had limited contact with the upper ranks, he'd never seen how the commissioned tenth lived. He stepped through the door, stopped, took in the size of the room, then spun one of the leather chairs. He whistled. "Some digs," he said. "Do we get to play in here whenever we want?"

Hearing this, Thomer glanced around the room. He squinted his eyes, and his forehead wrinkled, giving him a confused expression; but he still made no comment.

Taking the chair at the head of the table, the captain's chair, I brought out the orders Admiral Thorne had given me, along with a small audio chip I had found inside the folder. I set the folder down on the table, then placed the chip in the media reader near my seat.

"Who's coming to this meeting?" Thomer asked, the glazed expression fading from his eyes.

"Ships' captains and fleet officers," I said.

"Officers?" Thomer asked. "I thought all of the natural-borns were going home."

"They aren't officers yet, but they will be once the Thorne administration leaves. There's a new round of promotions coming up. How does Brigadier General Kelly Thomer sound to you?" I said as I fished the promotions list from my folder and handed it to Thomer.

"You're joking, right?" Herrington asked, both looking and sounding as if he was fighting the urge to laugh. "Thomer, a general? I have enough trouble getting used to you as a captain."

Thomer took the list and slowly read it. Thomer had become a study in clinical depression. Over the last two years, he had lost enough weight to go from skinny to skeletal. He had the haunted look of a man who has seen too many friends die on the battlefield. Before New Copenhagen, Thomer's biggest problem was excessive worrying over small details. Now I wondered if he cared about anything.

"I'm a brigadier general?" Thomer asked. He looked me in the eye and could tell I was not joking. "How is that possible?"

Having been raised in an orphanage, Thomer had already reached the highest rank he could have hoped to attain—master gunnery sergeant. Now, out of the blue, the Marines had advanced him twelve pay grades.

Herrington moved behind Thomer so he could read over his shoulder. After thirty-two years serving in the Marine Corps as an enlisted man, Sergeant Lewis Herrington would shortly find himself holding the rank of full-bird colonel. He took the news of the promotion with his usual stoic good humor. He said what he always said when he heard good news, "You have got to be shitting me!" After a second glance, Herrington added, "A field rank promotion from sergeant to colonel, there's one for the books."

"You can't run a fleet with master sergeants and petty officers at the helm," I said.

According to these new orders, I was both fleet commander and "Scutum-Crux Arm administrator," a position that sounded more political than military. I held the field rank of lieutenant general in the Marines. In my experience, only naval officers commanded fleets; but my rank made me the highest-ranking officer in the Scutum-Crux Arm.

At least I would be the highest-ranking officer in the Scutum-Crux Arm once the natural-born officers went home. Until Admiral Thorne and his crew left, I would remain a captain. If and when Washington sent natural-born officers to inspect the fleet, my rank would automatically revert to captain.

Thomer finished reading the orders over and handed them to me. "I can't be commandant of the Marines," he said in that quiet voice. "I think that I might be a clone."

"Something's wrong with my hearing. I could have sworn he just said he thinks he's a clone," Herrington gasped. "Aren't you supposed to have one of those death reflexes now? Aren't you going to keel over?"

"Thomer, we have to get you off that Fallzoud shit," Herrington added, staring at Thomer as if he had horns sprouting from his ass.

"You might want to hold off on that, Sergeant," I said. "Fallzoud may be the only thing keeping this Marine alive."

Just then a chime rang, warning us that the other members of our conclave were outside the door. "Keep a lid on the promotions for now," I said as I placed the orders back in the folder and went to let them in. Herrington nodded, but his eyes remained on Thomer, who sat as placid as ever.

I took one last look at Thomer to make sure he was ready for the meeting. He sat bolt upright, his hands lying flat on the table before him. I might have mistaken him for a mannequin except that he was breathing. Hoping for the best, I pressed a button, and the conference room door slid open.

Master Chief Petty Officer Gary Warshaw was the first man to step through the doorway. My impressions of Warshaw did not change now that I got a closer look at him. You could not miss the effects of his bodybuilding; he had taken it so far that he looked slightly misshapen. The network of veins along his tree trunk of a neck looked like ivy vines growing in under the skin. His neck was so thick with muscle that I had trouble telling where his neck ended and his skull began. Those veins ran right up the sides of his clean-shaven skull. He stepped into the room, snapped a smart salute, and said, "Captain Harris, you are a legend around these parts, sir."

The words sounded sincere; but most ass-kissing subordinates had a talent for sounding sincere. I returned flattery for flattery, "Good to meet you, Master Chief. Admiral Thorne says good things about you."

There was an acute alertness about Warshaw. Like a predator on the prowl, he took in every movement around the room. He had such a commanding presence that I barely noticed the next few sailors who entered.

I needed to stay on good terms with the master chief. Despite my rank and assignment, he would end up as the power behind the chair. Running the Scutum-Crux Fleet was a naval operation, and I was a Marine.

A few more sailors entered. I recognized their names from the file Admiral Thorne had given me. He had referred to these men as "the backbone of the fleet."

Then came Senior Chief Petty Officer Perry Fahey, chief

NCO of the U.A.N. *Washington*, and I lost my train of thought. The man had eye shadow over his eyes. There was no mistaking it. His eyelids were light blue patches. He did not wear rouge, lipstick, or eyeliner; but there was no denying cosmetic coloring above his eyes.

Fahey saluted me and identified himself.

I saluted back, but I could not stop myself from staring at the makeup. I was about to make the mistake of asking about it, but Herrington saw what was happening and stepped in. "Senior Chief, you look like a man who knows his way around a ship . . ." And he led Fahey to a seat, asking him about how he could go about expanding the Marine compound on the *Kamehameha*.

Even after Herrington pulled him away, I could not take my eyes off the blue shadowing the man had painted around his eyes. I wondered if it was a tattoo. It was a pretty shade, and I wondered where I could get some of that for Ava.

The meeting started out well enough. Thomer, mostly recovered from his morning dose of Fallzoud, woke from his stupor and chatted with Warshaw. Herrington and Fahey swapped a few stories as if they were old friends.

When I said, "We might as well get started," the sailors standing in the back of the room found seats around the table. A good beginning.

We did a round of introductions first. None of us clones had ever commanded so much as a transport, let alone a fleet. Warshaw and his friends might have sat in on a few high-level meetings, but they would have attended as spectators, not participants.

"Our first objective is to recapture Terraneau," I said, trying to put a leash around any stray conversations. "As most of you know, Admiral Thorne recorded a transmission from Norristown. We may as well start there."

I tapped a button on the AV-console, and an old man's voice came from the speakers. The recording lasted less than two seconds. It began with a moment of static followed by the sound of someone taking a deep breath. Then a voice said, "Go away." The words were hushed, almost whispered, but emphatic. It sounded like a command. After that, the file went silent.

"That's it?" Herrington asked.

"That's it," I said.

"They sent us all the way across the galaxy because of that?" Herrington continued. "He wasn't even asking for help."

"Maybe he thought he was talking to the aliens. Maybe that's why he told us to go away," Fahey guessed.

"That can't be real." Herrington shook his head.

"It's legitimate," I said. "Military intelligence ran the feed through a voiceprint computer and came up with a match. According to the Pentagon, that's the voice of Colonel Ellery Doctorow."

"Never heard of him," Warshaw said.

"Doctorow was the head chaplain of the Unified Authority Army," I said. "The Army transferred him to Terraneau right before the assault." I pulled out a photograph of Doctorow and slipped it across the table to Warshaw. The picture showed a tall man wearing a cassock and stole over a set of Army fatigues. The stole had both religious symbols and military insignia, and the pressed eagle of colonel could be seen on his collar. Colonel Doctorow kept his hair in a coal-colored flattop.

"Okay, so if he's Army, why the speck does he want us to leave?" Herrington asked. "That doesn't make sense."

"Beats me," I said.

"Admiral Thorne's been punching holes through the curtain for two years now. From what I heard, they'd spotted movement on the planet; this was just the first time we were able to make contact," Warshaw said. The other sailors seemed content to have Warshaw speak for them.

"Movement? Are you talking cars . . . airplanes . . . bodies?" Thomer asked.

Warshaw shrugged. "I don't know. I just overheard a few conversations."

"The report did not cover anything other than the message," I said. This led to some unorganized chatter. I made a note to ask Admiral Thorne about it.

After that, we spent the next few minutes discussing the upcoming mission. News of the mission had trickled down through the ranks. Thorne had briefed his officers, who related the information to their key NCOs. I had gone over the details with Thomer and Herrington as well.

If there were aliens on Terraneau, we would need to slip around them. We couldn't afford a fight. Our goal was to locate the spot where the aliens were digging their mine and set off our nuclear device there. We had a serious package to deliver—fifty megatons' worth, enough to destroy the ion curtain if everything went well. Once the curtain was down, we would land more Marines and set up a base on the planet.

"Who are you sending to lead that mission?" asked Fahey, the sailor. He was young to have made the rank of senior chief, maybe not even in his thirties.

"I'm going," I said.

"Begging your pardon, sir, but is that a good call?" Warshaw asked. "It could get dangerous down there."

"I'll take my chances," I said.

"That's what they said about you. I have a couple of engineers who say they were on the *Kamehameha* when you went down to Little Man," Warshaw said. "They said you liked it hot."

"I didn't volunteer for that duty," I said. "They sent every enlisted man on the ship."

This must have synced with the gossip Warshaw heard about me. He smiled, nodded, and whispered something to the sailor sitting next to him.

"I heard you served on New Copenhagen," another said. I looked at my notes and saw that he was Senior Chief Petty Officer Hank Bishop. Once the transfers were complete, this man would take command of the *Kamehameha*.

"Sergeant Thomer and Sergeant Herrington were also on New Copenhagen," I said. No one knew how to respond, and we sat in silence.

"How's the training going?" I asked Warshaw, trying to get the meeting back on track. "Do your men know everything they need to know to run the fleet?"

He did not answer. Instead, he looked at the various men who had accompanied him and let them answer individually. To a man, the NCOs all reported they had been sailing with clone crews for months.

"I can't remember the last time I saw an officer in our weapons area," one of the men responded. "The last year has been a paid vacation as far as those bastards are concerned."

I almost laughed when I heard this; there was something ironic about a synth-bred clone calling natural-borns "bastards."

"I don't suppose Admiral Thorne has informed you about your new field ranks," I said.

"Field ranks, sir?" Warshaw asked.

I held up the orders and repeated the lecture I'd given Thomer and Herrington a few minutes earlier. Field promotions had been written up for every man in the room.

"May I have a look at that roster?" Warshaw asked. As he studied the new command structure, a change came over him. He had begun the meeting all handshakes and smiles; but as he read the changes, his jaw tightened and his eyes turned to flint. He read the orders a second time, then a third, all the while silently mouthing the words to himself. Finally, he looked up, an angry stitch showing across his forehead. "It says you're taking command of the fleet. There must be some kind of speck-up, how can they leave a Marine clone in charge?" He did not sound confused or curious, more than anything he sounded insulted.

Warshaw's behavior violated his neural programming. He should not have been able to call me a clone or question orders. Under other circumstances, I would have knocked his teeth in, then busted him for insubordination; but I needed him on my side.

A smoldering silence filled the staff room. Thomer, sounding more like an angry Marine than a Fallzoud jockey waking from a haze, asked, "What did you just say? What the speck did you just say?"

"Do you have a hearing problem, asshole?" Warshaw snapped. "I said that I cannot believe they are leaving a fleet in the hands of a Marine." Despite the bravado, Warshaw had just blinked in this game of chicken by not repeating the term, "clone."

"You're not the one handing out the orders, Master Chief," I said.

He glared at me, his face so red he might have been choking, but he did not speak a word.

I got the feeling that whether or not I won this battle, I might well have lost the war. Warshaw had come with twenty other sailors, all men who had served with him for years. They did not care who the Office of the Navy named top dog, their loyalty would remain with him.

If there was any way to win Warshaw over as a friend, I needed to find it. Trying to defuse the situation, I said, "You'll be the one running the fleet; I'm more of a figurehead. As I understand it, they've put me in as a regional administrator."

Warshaw grunted but showed no satisfaction.

I knew right then and there that the man was going to be a problem for me; the question was, how big a problem.

"Does that mean you will remain on Terraneau?" Fahey asked.

"No," I said, "I'll remain on the *Kamehameha*."

"But I will have command of the fleet?" Warshaw asked.

"That's what he said," growled Thomer. "Do you have a hearing problem?"

"That will be enough, Sergeant," I said. Then I turned to Warshaw, and said, "Our field ranks don't come into play until Thorne and the other natural-borns are gone."

"What's your point?" asked Warshaw.

"It could take months before the transfer is complete, that should give us plenty of time to work out any kinks in the command structure."

Warshaw did not say anything, but he nodded.

I could read the man easily enough. As the highest-ranking noncommissioned officer in the Scutum-Crux Fleet, he had expected to take over. Frankly, he had two thousand years of naval tradition supporting his position. The swabbies steered the ships, and the leathernecks ran the invasions. It had always been that way. The natural animosity between Marines and sailors only made things worse.

For a moment, I thought Warshaw or one of the other officers would threaten to go over my head about the promotion. Then we really would have had a problem. In the Marines, we did not tolerate the kind of politicking and political maneuvering that took place as a matter of course among ships' captains.

Warshaw fixed his glare on me, and his mouth worked into a nasty grin that reflected the hate in his eyes. I could just about hear his thoughts, they were somewhere between insubordination and mutiny. But Warshaw was a clone just like everyone else in the room. Angry or not, he had neural programming that in theory prevented him from disobeying orders, no matter how he felt about having a Marine in the chain of command.

I wondered what steps Warshaw would willingly take to correct the chain of command. I had heard stories about Navy officers wrangling for positions and honors in ways that a simple Marine could never comprehend.

Warshaw started to say something, and I put up my hand to stop him. "Our first order of business is to retake Terraneau, Master Chief. I think everybody here can agree that capturing the planet is very much a Marine operation."

There were nods of agreement around the table.

"Who says we'll let you back on our boats once you're through?" asked Fahey. That sent me over the edge. I had a combat reflex. Anger and peace merged together in my brain. Thomer started to say something, but I spoke over him. "Let's see . . . Senior Chief Petty Officer Perry Fahey?" I asked, making a show of looking down at the roster. "It says here that you're on the *Washington*. That's a Perseus-class fighter carrier."

Fahey, his made-up eyes now fluttering, said, "That's correct."

"That means there are ten thousand armed Marines on your ship, Senior Chief. Would you like to try and explain why you are scuttling the local commandant of the Marines on an alien-held planet to ten thousand combat Marines?"

Fahey was not stupid. He had to know that my Marines would seize control of his ship.

"No one is leaving anyone behind," Warshaw said. "My men obey orders, Captain Harris, even when they come from a Marine."

That ended the meeting. I dismissed the sailors, and they returned to their ships.

"That was specked," Thomer said after the last sailor left. "Warshaw's an ass."

"Do you blame him?" I asked. "He thought he was going to command the fleet."

"He has a point, too," Herrington said.

"No he doesn't," said Thomer.

"Yes he does," said Herrington. "Would you want a sailor calling the shots when we take Terraneau?"

"Okay, he's got a point," Thomer conceded.

"But what was that stuff on Fahey's eyes?" I asked. "It looked like eye makeup . . . like the stuff women use."

"It is," Herrington said.

"He's wearing makeup?" I asked.

"He's a bitch," Herrington said.

"What is that supposed to mean?" I asked.

"Harris, none of these boys have had R & R for four years now."

"And?" I knew where this was going, but I wanted to see how Herrington would handle it.

"And the makeup identifies Fahey as a pleasure vehicle."

"God, I'm glad he's not a Marine," I said.

"You haven't toured the compound yet, have you?" Herrington asked.

I shook my head.

Thomer and Herrington exchanged a glance, then laughed.

"Where the speck are they getting makeup?" I asked. I knew what Herrington wanted to say next. He wanted to ask something along the lines of whether or not I needed it for myself.

I gave Herrington an order to search the Marine compound for any cosmetics. When he found them, he had orders to "confiscate without repercussions."

At the end of the day, when I went back to my billet, I had lipstick, eye shadow, rouge, and a pair of man-sized silk stockings. I came into the room and placed the cache on the bed, then called for Ava—she was hiding in the bathroom.

She stood at the edge of the bed, staring down at the various tubes and bottles as if they were antiques from a foreign land.

"What do you think?" I asked. "Can you use any of it?"

"Use it for what?" she asked.

"It's makeup," I said.

"Honey, back home we called this 'queer gear,'" she said.

"Queer gear?" I asked.

"These are cosmetics for men," she said, picking up the stockings. "I could use these for a hammock, but I wouldn't want to wear them. Harris, stockings are not one size fits all."

Feeling deflated, I went to the mess to get us our first meal. While I was gone, Ava removed the makeup from my rack. She played coy, but I noticed the faint smear of red on her cheeks and the enhanced shadow above her eyes when I returned.

It looked good.

CHAPTER
SIXTEEN

A week passed between the day I boarded the *Kamehameha* and the time we would start the mission. I spent some of my time on the *Washington*, welcoming shuttles as Captain Pershing's cruiser ferried Marines in and natural-borns out at the snail's pace of four hundred men per trip. Walking the upper corridors of the ship, I heard officers complaining about the slow pace of the transfers.

In my off-hours, I stockpiled MREs in my quarters so that Ava would have food to eat while I was on Terraneau. If everything went well, the mission might only take a day. If things went wrong, I might not return for weeks, if I returned at all. Preparing for the worst, I hid a month's worth of meals around my billet.

I had Ava sample each of the meals to see which ones she liked. She didn't like any of them, but she did not complain.

After sampling the spaghetti, she groaned, and said, "Can't we just use room service?"

When I said, "They'd probably just bring you more of the same stuff," she said, "Honey, that's fine with me as long as the waiter looks good."

"Charming," I said. "He'd probably look a lot like me since they're all clones."

We could have smuggled a spare rack into the billet; we had the floor space. Instead, Ava and I slept in the same bed. I liked the warmth of her body under the sheets, though she showed little interest in me. She generally came to bed dressed in her bra and panties, both of which were made of a satiny white material that had been stained and dulled by the heat and sweat of Clonetown.

Ava slept with her back toward me. If I reached out and touched her, she did not pull away so long as my hands stayed around her back or her waist. When I reached too high, she wrapped her arms across her breasts and curled into a ball.

She probably would have allowed me to grope her if I forced the issue, but I never did. Instead, I would lie there, smelling her scent and feeling her warmth, entirely unable to sleep.

We talked a lot. Ava told me all about her life. She treated conversations like an autobiography. I didn't mind, though; her life was interesting.

Ava had known that she was a clone from an early age. When she was young, the man who claimed to be her father employed a series of lab technicians to help raise her. Although they treated her well, they were not especially careful about what they said around her or about keeping her safely away from the truth of her birth. As an eight-year-old, she sneaked into the lab where she was cloned and saw the equipment that reproduced her. She wanted to believe she was real, but seeing that equipment, she had her doubts.

She lost her virginity and decided she was a clone all on the same night. She had her first period at the age of fifteen. Exactly one week later, her "father" came to visit her after she'd gone to bed. By the time he left, her virginity was gone along with any illusions that the man was really her father.

She related this tale in a matter-of-fact style without shedding a single useless tear. After telling me this story, she stared at me for several seconds, then asked, "What's wrong with you?"

Her question caught me off guard. I did not know anything was wrong with me. "Wrong with me?"

"Don't you feel sorry for me?" she asked.

"Why the speck would I feel sorry for you?" I asked.

"He raped me and took away my dreams."

"Oh," I said. "Sorry." I grew up with thousands of clones who never knew any parents other than instructors at military orphanages. Our instructors lied to us and sent us to war. The closest thing we had to a dream was the goal that we might one day reach the rank of sergeant. Sex and reality at the age of fifteen sounded pretty good to me.

That night and the next, Ava and I slept in the same rack but a million miles apart. I call them *nights*, but they were just sleep periods. Life on a starship . . . the halls are constantly bright as day, and the world around you is generally dark as night. I had work shifts, shifts in which I was off duty, and shifts in which I slept.

Ava's attitude thawed the day before I left for Terraneau. From the moment I entered my quarters, she wanted to talk.

I came in sweating from a day spent working out, sparring, and drilling my men. Ava, pretending as if she had not given me ice for the last forty-eight hours, followed me into the bathroom and asked about my day as I stripped off my clothes. I grunted that I had worked hard and that my crew looked ready.

"That's good," she said. "Are you excited to get to the planet?"

I turned to look at her. Dressed in the smallest sailor suit I could find, she looked clean and childlike. The tunic looked stylish and loose on her, but the trousers were baggy around her waist. She had rolled the cuffs back on the denim sleeves to prevent them from covering her hands. There was something vulnerable and oddly erotic about seeing this petite woman wearing a sailor's suit.

She had also applied the makeup I brought her. Her eyes looked wide and the blue of the eye shadow played well against the green of her eyes. The makeup looked a lot better on her than it had on Fahey.

"Are you excited or scared?" she repeated in a soft voice.

I stood there naked and sweaty, considered her question, and said, "I'm both," no longer thinking about the mission. I was excited and scared by the beautiful woman standing in the doorway. For a sliver of a second, I thought of Pavlov and his dog. He rang a bell, and his dog salivated. Ava dressed right, and I did the same.

"Excited to fight?" she asked. The other half of her question hung in the air entirely tangible but unasked. Was I anxious to get away from her?

"I was designed to fight," I said.

I stepped into the shower. Ava had once said the difference between women and Marines was that women did not only shower when they wanted to have sex. She was wrong, of course, the Corps demands hygiene. That said, she had certainly pegged the motivation behind this particular shower.

Ava stepped into the bathroom so we could hear each other over the water. She didn't mind the fact that I was naked. Ava was many things, but she was not shy. Rather than sit on the toilet, she stood just outside the shower and half sat on the washbasin. She kept her arms folded across her chest.

"Do you think it's going to be dangerous?"

"Any time the Avatari are involved, things are going to get dangerous," I said. The term "Avatari" was highly classified, but I had shared a lot of classified information with Ava. I was an outcast now; what did I care about Unified Authority security?

"Is Thomer ready?" she asked. She knew all about Thomer and his drug problems.

"He's as ready as he's going to get," I said.

"Can you count on him?" she asked.

"I think so," I said. He did a good job drilling the men today—not perfect, but good enough. "He still moves slowly; but once he gets a little adrenaline running through him, I think he'll do okay."

"What about Warshaw? Are you worried about him?" she asked.

"There's not much I can do there," I said.

"What if he doesn't let you off the planet?" she asked. "Would he try to shoot your transport?"

"He could," I said. "I don't think he will. If he shoots my transport, he's going to answer to some angry Marines."

"Does he know that?" Ava asked.

"He'd better."

After my shower, I dressed and went to the mess. We had hundreds of MREs stowed by now, but we would save those meals. I brought back a tray covered with food—two steaks, two bowls of soup, two potatoes, and an oversized salad.

Ava mostly ate salad and picked at a potato. I ended up eating both steaks, which was just fine.

After dinner, I dropped off my dishes and went to the officers' club to grab some bottles of beer. Ava preferred wine to beer, but she would need to make do. No one paid attention to off-duty officers walking around with a beer, but a bottle of wine would attract all kinds of notice. So far no one had asked me if I had a Hollywood starlet hidden in my quarters, and I wanted to keep it that way.

I stepped through the door. Silence. Always aware of her precarious situation, Ava never called out my name when I came back. She waited for me to identify myself, then came out of her hiding places—usually the shower.

"Ava, I'm back," I called softly.

She came out from the bathroom, very much the confident woman of the house. "Why do I feel like I should be bringing you a pipe and slippers?" she asked.

I laughed as I placed the bottles on the nightstand. She came and sat across the bed from me. She poured her beer into a glass. I drank mine from the bottle.

She took a sip of beer, and asked, "I know you're excited about going on a mission, but don't you ever get scared? Do Marines get scared?"

"Sure we do. The Avatari scare the hell out of me," I said. "A little fear is a good thing; it keeps you from making stupid mistakes. Scared is another thing. I've seen good men freeze under fire."

"But that's never been a problem for you, Harris," she said.

"The Avatari are eight feet tall. You can't hurt them. Their guns cut through shielded bunkers as easily as they shoot through the air. I saw a man get hit by a bolt in the shoulder. He went into convulsions and died a miserable death.

"Yes, I get scared."

Ava laughed softly and touched a warm finger to my cheek. "I'd be worried if they didn't scare you," she said.

I did not like this conversation. I did not like discussing my fears. "Once we liberate Terraneau, you will be able to move into a mansion or maybe even have a whole damn hotel to yourself. I bet you'll be glad to have a place to yourself."

"I suppose so," she said, and sadness filled her voice. She didn't cry, but her mood turned melancholy, and she seemed to withdraw.

"You don't want your own hotel?" I asked.

"Not to myself," she said, looking down at the food. She would not meet my eyes. "I thought maybe . . . I thought maybe we could share a place."

I had just downed a large mouthful of beer when she said this. I nearly choked on it. I coughed, which she must have taken to mean I was laughing at her. She looked up, and I saw anger in her eyes.

"Are you laughing at me?" she asked.

"No," I said, shaking my head. "I thought you'd be glad to be rid of me."

"Why would I want to get rid of you?" she asked.

"You haven't let me touch you since we landed on the ship," I said.

"And you've been wonderful about it," she said. "Ted and Al never took no for an answer."

"Al?" I asked. "Al Smith?" I knew she had dated General Mooreland, but she could not possibly have meant who I thought she meant. "You don't mean General Alexander Smith?"

Looking like a scolded child, she silently nodded, her beautiful green eyes fixed on mine.

"You slept with Al Smith? That fat old bastard has to be twice your age," I said.

"He's almost three times my age, thank you," she said. "I'm twenty-three, he's sixty-five."

I had a brief, chilling vision of Smith, his body as white and round as an egg, sliding into bed beside Ava. She would not have let him touch her for money. She had to have made millions. She sure as hell wouldn't have slept with him for love.

"What in the world were you doing with that old man?" I asked.

"Faking it mostly," Ava said. "He needed a lot of encouragement."

"I don't understand," I said.

"The Senate hearings set off a witch hunt, and I was the galaxy's most famous witch. Ted dumped me before the hearings even ended. We were living together, and he kicked me out of the house." Ava sat silent for a moment.

"Was he good to you before the hearings?" I asked.

"Was he good to me? Honey, I hope he knows more strategies in battle than he does in bed."

"No shit?"

"Even good things get boring when you do them the exact same way every time." She paused, thought, and said, "I will say this for the boy, he's got a lot of energy . . . a lot of energy."

I could not help but feel a little jealous. Maybe she read me too well. She reached over and squeezed my hand. "He liked it more than I did, Harris."

"So how did you end up with General Smith?" I asked.

"I moved in with Al after Teddy kicked me out. He said he would keep me safe until things calmed down. That lasted for about a month, then he dropped me off at Clonetown.

"So what do you think, Harris? Does that make me a whore?" she asked, her voice defiant, almost daring me to condemn her.

"It says a lot about Smith's negotiation skills," I said.

She moved toward me, her hand still over mine. Her touch was warm, and the air in the room was slightly cold. I wondered how she might describe me to the next man. It made me nervous.

"What about me?" I asked. "Am I energetic?"

"You took care of me, and you never forced yourself on me," Ava said.

"I think I'd rather have you think of me as 'energetic,' " I said.

"Do you want to hear you were the best lover I had?" Ava laughed. "Men."

"Teddy showed me off like a trophy, like one of the medals he wears on his chest. That's why he introduced me to you at the New Year's Eve party; he wanted to show you he had something you couldn't have."

"He's got a lot of things I will never have," I said.

"He doesn't see it that way. He's scared of you, Harris."

"Scared of me?" I asked.

"Scared to death. They were all scared of you. Al, Teddy, J. P. Glade, all of them. They knew you won the war. They were scared Congress would find out who was a hero and who was a fake."

"Even Mooreland?" I asked.

"Especially Teddy."

"But he fought. He was the only officer who stood his ground."

"He said he didn't fight in the last battle, the one that ended the war."

"No, he didn't."

"But you did," Ava said.

"Herrington, Thomer, Freeman, and me," I said, more to myself than to Ava. Ray Freeman was a mercenary, a ruthless freelancer who knocked down a billion-dollar payday for helping win the war. Thomer, Herrington, and I were clones. The only men to survive that final battle were three clones and a mercenary, no wonder the Pentagon kept a lid on the story.

"You were the real heroes," she said.

I didn't respond.

Ava slid closer to me. She fixed her eyes on mine, a strange smile playing on her lips, and she ran her finger along the open neckline of her blouse. She moved slowly and her eyes never left mine. There was nothing unusual about the way she undid the first buttons. Her eyes stayed on mine; her smile remained gentle. There were seven buttons on her sailor's tunic. As she undid the buttons, she peeled back the material, giving me a glimpse of breasts and bra. Just that glimpse of satiny material got my pulse pounding.

She leaned toward me until our lips met. We had kissed before, but those other times had been mechanical and infrequent. Kissing had been part of a ritual, just another step toward having sex. This time it seemed to take on its own significance.

I realized now that she was in control. Ava, with her perfect body, green eyes, and gentle touch, knew what she wanted and how to get things done. I did not think she loved me, but she gave herself over to me that night in a way that seemed more lasting than before.

When my alarm woke me the next morning, I found her lying beside me wide-awake. She took my hand in hers and held it against her breast.

"Are you going to be okay?" I asked.

"Me?" she asked. "I'm not the one going out to fight the aliens."

"You're going to need to hide for a while," I said.

"You just come back to me," she said. She teared up as she said this. Maybe I was being cynical, but it reminded me of a scene from a movie. I did not know if Ava loved me, but I absolutely knew she was an accomplished actress.

"We'll find other women on the planet. You'll be safe once you're not the only woman on this side of the galaxy," I said.

"I have to admit, I would be so glad to talk to another woman. God, Harris, you have no idea."

"For now, you have to stay hidden. I'll be back as soon as I can," I promised.

"No problem," she said. "I'll just hang the 'Do Not Disturb' sign outside your door." She rubbed her naked body against mine. I knew I would be a few minutes late arriving at the docking bay, but some things cannot be helped.

Admiral Thorne did not come to see the transports off, but he did wish us luck on the mission. As I dressed in my armor, I noticed the message light flashing on the communications console beside my desk. Instead of a steady flash, the light blinked three times, paused, and blinked three times. That meant the message came from Fleet Command.

I vaguely remembered ignoring a call while Ava and I

were in the throes. Not entirely sure there was anyone in Fleet Command I wanted to hear from, I played the message.

"Good luck on Terraneau," said the reedy voice, and that was it.

"Who was that?" Ava asked.

"Admiral Thorne," I said.

"That's it? That's the entire message?" she asked.

"It would appear so."

"It's a bit on the terse side, don't you think?" she asked.

"Well, he is an admiral. Maybe he's too busy running the fleet for mushy farewells," I said.

I kissed Ava. We had kissed more over the last twelve hours than all of our other nights together combined. "Stay hidden," I said.

She put a hand on the crook of my arm, and asked, "What do you think will happen if they find me?"

"The sailors on this scow have not seen a woman in four years, what do you think will happen?"

"I see," she said.

"So don't get caught."

Ava hid her fear well. She was, after all, the clone of an actress. She looked at me, her green eyes scanning my face. "Will I ever be safe?" she asked.

"Sure you will," I said. "There will be women on Terraneau. I'll smuggle you down and release you into the flock."

"Will I still be yours?" she asked.

She had not had time to fix her hair that morning. Her lipstick and rouge had not survived the night. I probably had more of them spread on my skin than she did on hers. Somehow she had replaced last night's glamour with simple beauty. She looked less like a starlet and more like a beautiful housewife—the prettiest woman on the block.

Looking into her face, I silently asked myself if I loved Ava Gardner. At the moment I felt sexual satisfaction more than anything else, but I could grow to love her.

"I have a planet to capture," I said.

She stood up, gave me a long, luxuriant kiss, and scampered into the bathroom. The last I saw of her was blue panties covering cream-colored cheeks as she slipped through the bathroom door.

"Stay hidden," I said.

"As if my life depended on it," she said.

"It does."

"You be careful, too."

I turned and left the room.

I had not suited up for a mission in more than two years, not since New Copenhagen. It felt good to wear a shell. Combat armor was not bulletproof, though it would deflect shrapnel. Under my armor I wore a skintight bodysuit, which was airtight, climate-controlled, radiation-resistant, and pressurized. There were limits as to how much it would protect me; but it stood up well to heat, radiation, and chill. If I found myself at ground zero during a nuclear explosion, the percussion would crush me, and the extreme heat would cremate me, but my bodysuit would shield me from the radiation.

Our armor was light and bodysuits impressive, but it was our communications and surveillance technology that enabled the once-powerful Unified Authority Marines to conquer the Milky Way. The list of tools built into the visor of our helmets included a communications network called the interLink—video lenses that let us see in the dark, read heat signatures, and view distant targets. We had radar/sonic detection equipment for locating traps and surveying battlefields. Our visors also housed a memory chip that recorded everything we saw and heard in battle. Officers could transmit live visual feeds or read images from their subordinates' visors. All of these tools were controlled with an ocular interface. Only Marines wore this combat armor. Soldiers fought in fatigues, and sailors . . . well, you could say they wore their ships when they went into battle.

Inside the docking bay door, 250 Marines in combat armor waited beside transports, lined up and ready to go. These were the men with whom I had trained for the last week. Some had come with me from Clonetown, the rest were veterans of the Scutum-Crux Fleet.

We had five transports, enough room for 500 men; but each transport also carried two armored jeeps. We were a small force traveling light. Even if the aliens had withdrawn from Terraneau, there was no way we could take control of the planet with 250 men and ten jeeps.

"Captain Harris, the men are ready to board, sir," Thomer, very much the sergeant in charge, said as I approached.

"Load 'em up, then meet me in the cockpit of the first bird once we are under way," I said.

"Aye, aye, sir."

I walked to the front of the queue and proceeded up the ramp of the transport with the torpedo. A jeep waited at the top of the ramp, its headlights facing out toward the dock. I stood beside the jeep and watched as men boarded the dark, vaulted space of the kettle. The cabin was dark, with a high, curved ceiling. Metal floor, metal walls, metal ceiling, a metal booth with a cold metal seat for a head, and a wooden bench lining the wall that sat thirty men—kettle comfort was the military equivalent of being sealed in a can.

I climbed the ladder at the far end of the kettle and entered the cockpit. The pilot behind the yoke was a clone—brown hair, brown eyes, the works.

"Are we ready for takeoff, sir?" he asked as I entered.

"Just loading the men," I said, as the distant rattle of armor boots walking across a metal floor carried to the cockpit. On some level, I still did not believe clones could run their own fleet; it hardly seemed possible. We were the grunts, the cannon fodder, the drones. Natural-borns threw us into the line of fire, and we held to the last man, never questioning orders. Seeing a clone in the pilot's seat and the confident way he checked the controls made other possibilities seem more real.

The pilot radioed the other transports, and we rolled out of the staging area, riding on "sleds"—wheeled vehicles that carried transports through the various atmospheric locks. We passed through the first lock, then the second, and finally the third. Once past the third, the artificial gravity ended and a simple thrust lifted us into space.

As the pilot dropped us below the fleet where we could safely maneuver, I watched ships pass above us and felt like a minnow in a sea filled with whales. A frigate, the smallest of the capital ships, crossed over us. The frigate was thirty times larger than our transport; but when it sidled up beside a battle-ship, it looked no bigger than a flea.

In the far distance, Terraneau shone like a light. With the

ion curtain around it, the planet had a man-made appearance. Instead of the blues, greens, and whites of a habitable planet, Terraneau looked as if it had been spun in white gold. It did not look habitable.

Hard as it was to believe, a census taken four years earlier recorded 1.2 billion people living on that planet. By now, most if not all of the population would be dead. Norristown, the capital city, would be covered with the four-year-old corpses of people who'd died fighting an enemy they could not possibly have understood.

Admiral Thorne believed the aliens had abandoned Terraneau long ago, but he did not understand them, either. He did not know about the mining operations and the shitload of toxic gas the aliens left behind. He didn't know that the Avatari used suns to finish their work, baking planets after they finished excavating them and filling them with gas. Over the next hundred thousand years, Terraneau's sun would expand and die.

The Avatari did not capture planets to annex them into an intergalactic empire; they destroyed planets in order to use them for mining purposes.

"I have a fix on the target zone," the pilot said.

"Do you think that was what New Copenhagen looked like from outside, sir?" Thomer asked.

"I've never thought about it," I lied.

"Captain, what do we do if the aliens are still down there?" the pilot asked.

"They're gone," I said, hoping I sounded more confident than I felt. "They don't have time for sightseeing, not with an entire galaxy to destroy."

As long as the ion curtain remained in place, the Avatari could return. The curtain might even work like a burglar alarm, sending a signal to the Avatari every time we poked a hole into the atmosphere. We would certainly set off alarms when we fired off our big bomb, but it would be too late for them to do anything once that happened. At least I hoped it would.

"Do you have the torpedo ready?" I asked.

"Ready to go, sir," the pilot said.

"Do you think this will work?" Thomer asked me.

"It doesn't matter what I think," I said. "We'll know one way or the other in about five seconds." I sent Thomer back to ride with the men in the kettle, then gave the pilot the order to fire the torpedo.

Back on the *Kamehameha*, engineers had built a toggle-switch trigger into the navigation console above the pilot's head. The pilot acknowledged my order, then flipped the switch.

The weapon fired. Staring out the front of the ship, I caught the quickest glimpse of the torpedo as it sped off from under the ship—just a flash of dull white and orange against the luminous backdrop of Terraneau, then the torpedo vanished into the glare of the planet.

We hovered nearly a thousand miles above the spot where the torpedo exploded. From this distance, the flash was bright but not blinding, just a small speck of white light that flared and vanished, leaving a hole in the shining sphere of the ion curtain. The hole was small and dark, with shimmering edges where the radioactive particles from the torpedo faded into the tachyons of the ion curtain.

I put on my helmet and opened an interLink frequency that would reach every man on all five transports. "Hold on tight; we're going in."

We shifted direction and picked up speed. Ahead of us, the hole looked like a dark speck on a glaring lightbulb. Two opposing gravitational forces fought for me—the artificial force created by the transport's gravity generator held me to the deck while the genuine gravity, created by our acceleration, tugged me toward the rear hatch. Feeling like I was falling upward, I became dizzy and dragged myself into the copilot's chair.

The planet filled the windshield. In the middle of the glowing horizon, the hole that we had created with our puny torpedo looked like a mere pinprick.

"I hope the corridor holds," the pilot mumbled to himself.

I looked over at him to consider what he had just said. When I looked up again, the hole in the ion curtain filled my view. It might have been a half mile wide. Compared to the shining border around it, the hole looked dark and deep; I could not see the end of it.

"Here we go," the pilot said. His words barely had time to register before we bored into the atmosphere with the force of a bullet slamming into a wooden plank. The transport shook violently, nearly throwing me out of my seat. A moment later, the shaking ended. We had taken a hard knock when we slammed into the atmosphere, but we tore through.

I had always imagined the ion curtain as a skin—a thin layer of glowing particles no deeper than a storm cloud. It wasn't like that at all. It must have been a full hundred miles thick. I felt like I was speeding through an endless tunnel.

The meters and lights around the cockpit flickered, and I realized that the door we had opened with our torpedo was shrinking. "It's closing in on us," I told the pilot.

"I see that, sir," he snapped.

The lights in the cockpit winked on and off again. The outage lasted less than a second, but it felt longer.

"If it closes in on us . . ." I started.

"We're dead either way," the pilot interrupted. He was right. Only a lunatic would take a transport balls-out on a vertical drop. With its stubby wings, this bird was anything but aerodynamic. If we dropped too quickly, we would never pull out.

I glanced down at the instruments and saw the altitude and speed meters flashing nonsense. The radar screen turned dark. Then, just as suddenly as we entered the ion layer, we plummeted into open air, and the systems went normal. The sky above us glowed like a sun, and the world below us was green and blue. In the forest below us, I saw a reminder that we had entered Avatari-held space—a line of glowing spheres.

"What are those?" the pilot asked, partially standing to get a better look.

"Can you leave a beacon on this spot?" I asked, ignoring his question.

"Yes, sir," he said. He sat back, flipped a switch on the communications console, then craned his neck to get one last look back at the spheres. Once the beacon was set, he repeated his question, "Captain, what were those things."

Against my better judgment, I told him the truth. "It's an intergalactic transportation system."

"Like the Broadcast Network?" he asked.

"Something like that." In truth the spheres were nothing like the Broadcast Network, but I didn't want to talk about it. I had other things on my mind.

I radioed Thomer in the kettle. "How's the breakage back there?" I asked.

"Minimal, sir," he said.

Next, I radioed Herrington. He flew in the second transport. "Your men okay?" I asked.

"I've had smoother rides," Herrington said.

"And your men?" I repeated.

"One dumb shit asked if we could do it again," Herrington said.

I contacted Sergeant Philo Hollingsworth in the third transport. He said, "A few bruises; they'll get over it."

I got no response from the fourth and fifth transports. The pilot checked the radar and confirmed that both ships were gone.

CHAPTER
SEVENTEEN

Seen from the inside, the shine from the ion curtain made my eyes hurt, but it did not leave me blind. Given another few hours, my eyes would adjust. The same thing had happened on New Copenhagen; we wore sunglasses much of the time, but we learned to live with the glare.

We entered the airspace over Norristown. The wreckage that had once been a capital city reminded me of ancient ruins. The skeletons of a few tall buildings poked out of the debris below us like plants growing out of a rocky field. A three-story-tall water tower pointed up at us like an accusing finger. Norristown, once a showcase city, had become an entropic mess, with heaps of rubble, broken streets, and the occasional straight edge of a wall or walkway.

We passed over a suburb in which pockets of homes and parks remained untouched by the destruction around them. A church with twin steeples rose out of a ground like a giant gravestone. Past the church, the deep blue depths of the Norris River cut across town. I spotted the remains of a suspension bridge. Half of it lay visible under the water like a sunken ship; the other half looked solid enough to cross.

A line of riverside apartments still stood. We would need to search those buildings for survivors.

"How does it look?" Thomer called up from the kettle.

"Familiar," I said. A veteran of New Copenhagen, Thomer knew what I meant.

"I've located the airfield up ahead," the pilot said. "It looks clean. Do you want to go in for a landing or do a flyby?"

I could see the field as well. It had been an Army air base— nothing more than a few corrugated steel hangars, a two-story temporary tower, and a long, open tarmac.

"Go on in," I said, my thoughts more centered on what to do once we landed.

The pilot signaled the other transports to land, and we touched down. As he had said, the area was clean. Taking a quick look through the windshield, I might have gone so far as to call it deserted. I saw no wreckage, no choppers, and no bodies. The buildings looked untouched.

Thomer led a team of men to sweep and secure the area. When he gave us the all clear, Herrington and Hollingsworth shouted their platoons out of the transports. The sergeants had their men off-load our gear and the jeeps. With its open grounds and hangars, the field might work for landings and rendezvous, but it would never serve as a base.

As my men unloaded the gear, I eavesdropped on a few of their conversations over the interLink. They sounded nervous.

. . . could be anywhere.

Maybe they left the planet? I heard they left.

I don't know about you, but I'm shitting ice cubes. I specking hate this place.

It's better than being stuck on the ship.

How the specking hell is this better than the ship? The sky is a specking lightbulb, the buildings are blown to shit. How in the hell is this better than being aboard a ship?

I hear there's plenty of scrub on this planet.

Scrub? That changes things.

"Scrub," was Marine-speak for women and one-night stands. Hearing them talk about scrub, I thought for a moment about Ava. There was something about her . . . Maybe it was her eyes, or maybe it was the brassy way she talked about Ted Mooreland and Al Smith; something about her stayed with me.

As I swept through the open frequencies, I heard a Marine singing "Amazing Grace," and I had to laugh. *Don't waste your breath,* I thought. *The god they wrote that for doesn't know you exist.* Hymns were meant to be sung by men with souls and heard by the god that created them, leaving us clones out of the loop.

We weren't created by God, we were devised by scientists; mortal men who borrowed parts from God's creation and used them in a scientific process that every major religion condemned. Those same religions said we were created without souls.

"Gods too decompose," I said to myself. It was a quote from Nietzsche. "Friedrich, old pal, I gave up on you too quickly."

Once we finished this invasion, I would give Nietzsche another try.

After we pulled the gear from our three remaining transports, I divided the men up. Thomer and I would take two platoons into town. Hollingsworth would guard the landing field with the third platoon. Herrington had the important job: he and a pilot would take a transport and locate the Avatari mining site.

Back on New Copenhagen, we had found the mines by tracking seismic activity. Herrington would have it a little easier. He had a device that detected the toxic gas that the Avatari placed in their excavations.

Our jeeps could transport eight men, but you wouldn't want to pack more than five men into them during combat situations.

Having lost two transports we were down to six jeeps, meaning we could drive forty-eight men into town.

Nine years of war had hardened me. As a new recruit, I would have grieved for the men in the transports we lost on the way through the atmosphere; now I worried more about losing manpower, not men. Instead of blaming myself for casualties, I concerned myself with completing the mission.

As we left the airfield, I saw Herrington's transports go wheels up. All short wings and stout metal walls, the bird lumbered off the ground unsteadily, righted itself, then shot away, disappearing against the glare of the ion curtain. I watched it depart, all the while calculating the odds of our success.

We traveled slowly into downtown Norristown. The first few miles took us along the overgrown streets of an industrial district. Weeds choked the ditches, and tall grass grew up along the fences. Except for cracked windows and an occasional collapsed façade, the one- and two-story buildings in this part of town had survived the war untouched. Dusty cars sat in parking lots and along the street. Most had flat tires. We saw no bodies—none at all.

"It looks like they just walked away," Thomer said on a direct frequency.

"I wonder how far they got," I said. After that, we both went silent. I listened in on my men and found very little chatter. They were alert, which was good, but I could feel the tension among them. The Marine handling the machine gun on my jeep flitted the barrel back and forth, scouring the street for any sign of movement; he was a man who would shoot first and ask questions later. The men in the seats behind me had their M27s ready. Obviously, these men had not fought on New Copenhagen or they would have known that M27s were useless against the Avatari.

M27s might not do much to an alien, but they were hell on Earth when it came to crowd control. I had a feeling that any survivors we found around this wreckage would be scared and dangerous. Speaking on an open frequency, I told my men, "Think before you shoot. We're looking for survivors, not aliens, and we want to keep them alive. You got that?"

It was a rare rhetorical question, but it still netted me a few *aye, aye*s. The boys were nervous.

"Sir, how will we identify the aliens?" one man asked. The Pentagon never released the images of the Avatari to the public. Only the veterans of New Copenhagen would have seen the aliens in action.

Thomer fielded the question. "Shoot at anything eight feet tall or taller."

"Eight feet?"

"And made of stone," Thomer added.

Silence followed as the inexperienced Marines tried to decide if Thomer was joking.

"There are spiders, too," I said.

"Oh yeah, the spiders," Thomer said. "If you see a spider the size of a jeep, it's probably not friendly."

"Don't listen to them, you dumb speck. They're just playing with you," Sergeant Hollingsworth said. I heard laughter in his voice. Hollingsworth had not been with us on New Copenhagen. He didn't know. He thought we were hazing the kid.

"I assure you, Sergeant, this is no joke," I said on a platoonwide frequency. Then, opening a direct channel between me and Hollingsworth, I added, "Thomer is going easy on you, Sergeant. He hasn't told you about their guns."

"Yes, sir," said Hollingsworth.

Two hours after leaving the airfield, we passed a billboard for a shopping mall. All of the buildings in this part of town had been demolished. Wind whistled through the pipes, bricks, and fragments of walls that rose like spines out of the grounds. We passed the remains of a fence here and the jagged remains of a warehouse there; but nothing over ten feet tall remained standing in this part of town. In the distance, three tall skyscrapers towered over the road, but that was a few miles ahead.

We drove over patches of road when they appeared between mounds of debris and rubble. Glass and plaster crunched under our tires. We passed a park in which a row of barren flagpoles stood out of the ground like giant needles. The clang of the wind smacking the tackle against the shafts of the flagpoles echoed like gunfire in the empty streets.

The Army airfield was on the east side of town. We drove west toward the heart of the city. The destruction was so complete in some parts of Norristown that the landscape looked like a painted desert. We passed an area in which a ten-foot knoll the color of red brick lined the road to our left and a thirty-foot hill of gray concrete and rusted steel lined the road to our right. The dusty shards of black glass along the top of the hill reflected the light from the sky.

"This can't be Norristown, sir," my driver said.

"This is it, Corporal," I said. "That hill over there probably stood thirty stories tall when the aliens arrived."

The driver slowed the jeep and studied the panorama around us. Perhaps he was trying to reconstruct the city in his mind, or he might have been watching out for an ambush.

A large river ran through the center of Norristown. As we approached it, we saw the arches and towers of a large suspension bridge spanning the water. I recognized the architecture from the flight in; it was the bridge that had collapsed on one side. "We're not going to be able to cross here," I said, as we mounted a rise and the entire bridge became visible.

"No, sir," my driver said.

The closer half of the bridge—a brick-and-metal structure with grand arches, thick rails, and a spider work of cables—looked solid enough. One of the arches from the far side of the bridge poked out of the water like the elbow of a swimming giant. The rest of the bridge had vanished beneath the river.

Surfing channels on the interLink, I heard men groaning. We could very well have a big fight coming up, so I could not afford for these men to become discouraged.

We passed a row of small apartment buildings overlooking the river. Following the mostly clear road that ran along the waterfront, we searched for another bridge. A couple of miles up the road, we found an old concrete arch bridge that seemed untouched by the war.

It wasn't until we crossed the bridge that we started seeing bodies. After four years out in the open, they were no longer rotting corpses, just bones. Had I removed my helmet, I would not have smelled the scents of death and decay; they were long gone.

From what I could tell, the people on this planet had died in groups. We might drive for blocks and see nothing more than an occasional Army helmet or fatigue-clad skeleton, then we would turn a corner and enter a boneyard in which the ground seemed paved with skulls and femurs. I understood this, of course. The concentrated areas were places where battalions made a stand; the scattered remains were soldiers who died in retreat.

The Marines who fought on Terraneau did not fight alongside the soldiers in these battles. We passed avenues that looked as if they had been paved with skeletons draped in dirty camos—places in which the Army made a stand. A few blocks later, Marine battle armor lay strewn along the street.

"Harris, why do I feel like I'm back in Valhalla?" Thomer asked.

Valhalla was the capital of New Copenhagen.

I did not respond, but I was thinking the same thing.

As we drove through one particularly corpse-sown battlefield, I saw a battery of rocket launchers leaning across the top of the wall of a two-story building like a drunk leaning to keep from falling to the ground. There were so many bones scattered along this stretch of road that it would have taken an army of archaeologists and psychics to reconstruct the skeletons. My driver steered the jeep right through the center of the mess. He had no choice but to drive over the dead, the wreckage lay everywhere. Our tires ground bones into the cement. Camos tore. Helmets popped and flattened or shot out from beneath us.

As we pushed deeper into the downtown area, the rubble of buildings that had once lined the roadway now covered it. Crossing a dune made of walnut-sized pieces of debris, our jeeps left cat tails of dust in their wake.

The Avatari seldom left buildings in their wake. When they calibrated their weapons to destroy skyscrapers, the buildings dropped like a man shot through the heart. Some broke off at their base, leaving straight edges poking up through the ground; but most caved in on themselves.

"Captain Harris, we're picking up traces of shit gas in the air," Herrington said. He was out of interLink range but the communications gear in his transport had a long-distance communicator that could reach my commandLink. Driving through the ruins of Norristown, I had almost forgotten that Herrington was out looking for the mines.

"Have you found the opening?" I asked.

"Not yet, but we've got to be close. You don't get this much shit in the air unless there's an asshole nearby."

"Keep me advised," I said, and signed off.

We drove into the downtown financial district, an area mostly reduced to dust. Less than a mile ahead of us, the three remaining high-rise towers rose out of the ground like giant pillars. They were straight-edged versions of Jack's beanstalk, and they seemed to reach all the way up into the shining white-gold sky.

Two of the buildings had black glass exteriors, the third had a silver metallic finish. These might have been the tallest buildings on Terraneau. Had they fallen, their rubble would have flooded three blocks in every direction.

The black marble walls of the first building were pocked with holes and scrapes from large-caliber bullets. Some of the street-level windows were shattered, and others were cracked. If people had died here, the bodies had been cleared out. The driveway into the parking lot looked like it had been swept clean.

If I had to guess, I would have said that the battle had wound down by the time it reached this part of town. Had soldiers entered these buildings, the Avatari would have demolished them. Apparently nobody did.

I had my driver park our jeep, and the other jeeps stopped behind us. A few of the men hopped out of their rides, while others stood on the vehicles. Everyone scanned the area.

"Listen up," I called over an open channel, drowning out unauthorized conversations between my men. "We're going to split up.

"Thomer, you take three jeeps and head out to Fort Sebastian. I want to know about weapons, power, and survivors." Fort Sebastian was the local Army base. The force defending Terraneau used it as their hub.

"Aye, aye, sir," Thomer said. Fallzoud haze or straight, Thomer would locate the fort and expedite. I could depend on him. He gave the command, and the last three jeeps in our convoy split off from the rest. I watched them leave, then I addressed the men who remained with me.

"We came here looking for survivors. I don't give a shit

about dead bodies, so don't waste my specking air-space gabbing about them. Got that?"

They got it.

"We'll search the whole damn city if we need to, but we're going to start here, with these buildings. Now fall out."

These men knew the drill. They broke into platoons and fire teams. As they headed toward the buildings, I reminded them about their priorities.

"Listen up, Leathernecks, we are not here to act like the specking police. We did not come here to specking serve and protect. If you see survivors, do not expect them to be rational human beings.

"If you see survivors, assume that they are armed. You may have noticed there are a lot more dead bodies than weapons on the streets. If the bodies are there, and the weapons are gone, you bet your ass that whoever took those weapons is alive and scared and dangerous as hell."

"Sir . . ." one of my Marines began.

"What is it?" I snapped.

"Begging the captain's pardon, sir, but this Marine saw lots of human bodies."

"We're racing against the clock," I said, cutting the man off. "Spit it out, man."

"Sir, this Marine did not see dead aliens, sir."

"Yeah, they evaporate when they die," I said.

"Can we kill them, sir?" the Marine persisted.

"Damn straight we can kill them," I said, which was not entirely true, but it was not entirely untrue, either. We could break them, and they would stay broken for a couple of days. They would evaporate, then the particles would re-form, and they would spawn again. The key to beating the bastards was finding their mining site and setting off our nuke. God, I hoped Herrington found the mines.

"You have your orders," I said. "Call me if you find survivors."

I hopped out of my jeep and entered the building, stepping over a shattered glass panel. Shards of glass sank and shuffled under my boots. Inside, the lobby was as silent and still as death itself.

CHAPTER
EIGHTEEN

"Herrington, you found anything yet?" I called from just inside the lobby of the skyscraper. I looked around as I waited for his response, studying the security desk and the large glass panel that listed the offices on each floor. The desk looked forlorn and abandoned intact. The safety glass over the directory was still in its frame and thick with dust.

I walked down the hall that led to two rows of five elevators. All of the doors to the elevators stood open; they looked like closets.

"I think we found it," Herrington finally replied from his transport. "Do you want me to go down for a closer look?"

"Not a chance, Sergeant," I said. At that moment, it seemed like the mission might go according to plan. Herrington had already found the mines, and there was no sign of the aliens, all we needed to do was to deliver our nuke and look for survivors. "Leave a beacon over the entrance and get back here as quickly as possible."

"Yes, sir."

I contacted Hollingsworth back at the airstrip and told him to queue up the transport with the nuke. I hoped to have Herrington swap birds and send him back with most of my men.

For now, I turned my attention to finding survivors.

Besides me, seven other Marines entered this building. We would search the building in two fire teams. Fire teams consisted of a rifleman, an automatic rifleman, a team leader, and a grenadier. I played leader in absentia for one of those teams, sending my men to explore the lobby.

"Captain Harris," my rifleman radioed in. He was on point.

"What is it?" I asked in a testy voice. Officers need to act officious, or their subordinates become insubordinate.

"I see a large mess at the back of the lobby. Should we search it?"

"This whole place is a mess."

The man laughed. "A mess *hall*, sir . . . a cafeteria."

"See any survivors?" I asked.

"No, but it looks like somebody is still using the facilities. I'm knee deep in empty cans and boxes."

"Get this—somebody is using the oven for a fireplace," my grenadier added.

"But you haven't spotted anybody with a pulse?" I asked.

"No, sir."

I told the team to "stay alert" and signed off.

Past the open doors of the elevators, I found a stairwell. Someone had removed the door from its hinges and left it leaning against the wall. I searched the stairwell using my heat-vision lenses to make sure no one was waiting for me around the corner. The area was clear.

Inside the stairwell, flights of stairs formed a helix leading to the top of the building. I did not think I would need to climb to the top. The building was over a hundred stories tall; without the elevators and air-conditioning, any survivors living in this tower would confine themselves to the lower floors.

The light from the ion curtain filled the lobby, but it trailed off as I started up the stairs. My visor switched to night-for-day lenses in the darkness. I climbed a couple of flights, scanned the area for heat signatures, and kept my M27 ready.

When I reached the second-floor landing, I found an open doorway leading to a mezzanine. Looted shops with smashed windows lined the halls past the doorway. A flood of trash, papers, and broken furniture covered the black marble floor.

After wasting a few minutes sifting my way through the wreckage, I headed back to the stairs and climbed three more flights to the next floor. The door to this floor was closed.

"Has anyone found anything?" I asked on a company-wide frequency. Everyone but Thomer replied with a negative. He had something to report.

"We found Fort Sebastian," he said.

Switching frequencies to a direct line with Thomer, I asked, "How does it look?"

"We're outside the fort right now, sir," Thomer said. "It's pretty banged up."

"How banged up?" I asked.

"Remember the shielded bunker the Army used on New Copenhagen? They set one up just like it over here."

Shielded bunkers were supposedly sturdy enough to survive a nuclear blast. Soldiers stationed in the bunker would be cooked and irradiated by the time the blast dissipated, but the bunker would survive. Unfortunately, shielding and bunkers meant nothing to the Avatari—the bolts from their guns bored through their walls.

"How did it hold up?" I asked.

"It looks like the Avatari used it for target practice," Thomer said.

"Any signs of life?" I asked.

"It's full of bones," Thomer said. "I found a rat's nest."

"How about MREs, clean blankets, screaming children, or shit that hasn't dried to powder?"

"Nothing," Thomer said.

"Find any guns or grenades?"

"Someone cleaned the place out."

"It would seem so," I agreed.

"Want me to search the rest of the bunker?" Thomer asked.

"Don't waste your time," I said. "You might as well move on to the fort. Keep an eye out for working generators. They needed juice to talk to the fleet. If you find the generators, you'll probably find the survivors."

"Aye, sir," Thomer said before he signed off.

Thomer's search was not going to be easy. In the grand tradition of all things Army, the layout of Fort Sebastian defied reason. According to our maps, the base was as big as a farming town.

Trusting Thomer to follow orders, I returned to my own search.

I opened the door to the next floor slowly. Using the external speaker on my helmet, I called out: "This is Captain Wayson Harris of the Unified Authority Marines. I repeat, I am a Unified Authority Marine. Is there anyone in this building?"

The announcement was greeted with silence. The door swung open, revealing another gloomy hallway.

I stepped out of the stairwell and into that hall. The equipment in my visor picked up sounds easily missed by the human ear. Someone far to my right was trying to ease away from me. The person must have thought he could hide by clinging to the shadows. Using night-for-day vision, I saw it was only a kid. He had to be in his teens. He crawled along the wall until he reached a door, then he looked back toward me and turned the knob. Light leaked into the hall as he opened the door. The boy slithered through the opening and closed the door behind him.

"I found a survivor," I said over the open frequency.

"Where are you, sir?" Hollingsworth asked.

"Was he friendly?" asked Herrington.

I answered Herrington first. "He wasn't armed."

"That's good news," said Hollingsworth.

"Where are you, sir?" It was the automatic rifleman from the fire team I had abandoned.

"Third floor."

"We're on our way, sir."

I was not foolish enough to follow that kid into a blind situation without backup. As I waited, I tried identifying myself again. "This is Captain Wayson Harris of the Unified Authority Marines," I repeated, with my voice so amplified that anyone on that floor of the building could hear me.

Scanning the wall using the heat-vision lens in my visor, I located several people hidden beyond the wall. Judging by the way they crouched along the floor, they seemed to be frightened of me.

I toyed with the idea of yelling, "Come out with your hands up," or possibly, "I know you're in there." They might have mistaken me for an alien. Hell, by the standards of whatever society had formed on this planet since the invasion, these guys could be criminals on the lam.

My fire team joined me. "Where are the survivors, sir?" the automatic rifleman asked.

"Hiding behind the door," I said. As I pulled out a grenade and set it for the lowest yield possible, my backup instinctively backed off. I called to the people hidden on the other side of the wall: "Stand away from the wall."

"Sir, I found the mines." It was Herrington.

I wanted to hear his report, but I had other priorities at the moment. "Not now, Herrington," I said as I tossed my grenade toward the wall and took cover.

"Aye, aye, sir, but do you want me to reconnoiter the spheres on my way back?"

"Herrington, I'm a bit busy at the moment," I snapped.

"Yes, sir," he said.

The first explosion, the one from my grenade, had enough force to blow a ten-foot section out of the wall. The second explosion, the one caused by whatever explosives the friendly natives had rigged, sent a rush of flames across the hall.

"What the hell was that?" my rifleman asked.

"That, Corporal, is why you stay under cover when there is fire in the hole."

"I don't think they were happy to see you, sir," the grenadier said.

"That's just 'cause they don't know him," said the rifleman.

We searched the first five floors of the building. The place had been occupied recently, but now stood abandoned. Reviewing the confrontation, I decided that throwing a grenade might not have made a good first impression, and time was running out.

CHAPTER
NINETEEN

"Captain Harris, we've located survivors. Do you want us to make contact?" The call came from the fire team I had sent into the metal-skinned skyscraper. The Marine on the line, Corporal Hunter Ritz, sounded too helpful.

"Negative, Corporal. The natives are not friendly," I said.

"The natives in this building may be hostile, but they don't look dangerous, sir," Ritz said. "It's like a cathouse in here."

"A cathouse?" I repeated.

"Yes, sir. A brothel, sir."

"As in hookers and whores?" I asked, suddenly understanding his motivation to volunteer.

"Maybe not hookers and whores, but they are all of the female variety, sir," Ritz said. "It's pretty much paradise as far as I can tell. We've checked several floors; there are no men."

"Keep your armor on," I said.

"We're going to need to make contact sooner or later, sir, and they don't appear to be hostile. Maybe we could just ask them for directions."

"Keep away from them, Ritz. That is an order. Do not start up a conversation. Do not deliver your best pickup line. You and your men will observe the targets, but do not engage."

"Yes, sir."

"And try to stay alert, asshole. There's no point keeping the hens in a henhouse unless you have a watchdog to guard it."

"Yes, sir."

I had left the *Kamehameha* with 250 men, 100 of whom I lost entering the atmosphere. We did not have enough men to take this city by force, not from the survivors and certainly not from the aliens. If I lost anyone else, I would not even have enough bodies to deliver the big bomb to the mines, and I did not want to be stuck on this planet for the rest of my life.

Unfortunately, Ritz had contacted me on an open frequency to report his discovery.

As I scanned through other frequencies, I heard Marines offering to help guard the place they had already dubbed "the Norristown brothel and home for wayward girls." I had to admit, I was just as curious as everyone else. Was the building a harem? A brothel? Maybe a boot camp for Amazons? In a broken society, there was no telling what a building filled with women could mean.

"Sir, we have a problem?" one of my men reported. "The locals have arrived."

Using the commandLink, I looked at the situation through the other man's visor. He must have been standing at a window staring down at the street. Below him, the residents of Norristown had arrived en masse.

There were hundreds of men in the street, standing silently, prepared to fight but not yet rioting. In the center of this mob, my three jeeps looked like tiny islands. No one had overturned our vehicles, but the tide closed around them.

I sent my next message out on a company-wide frequency that even Hollingsworth and Herrington would hear. "Boys, we have a street full of survivors."

"How did you find them?" Thomer asked.

"They found us," I said.

"Do you want me to bring my men?" Thomer asked.

"Stay put, they're behaving themselves so far," I said as I headed down the stairs toward the lobby. As I stepped on to the floor, I could see men just outside the lobby staring in. Without taking my eyes off the street, I backed into the stairwell and trotted back up the stairs to the mezzanine, where I could have a closer look at the street below.

I loped over the debris left behind by looters and stole up to the window, my nerves tense. A large mob of men had formed on the street, but they showed no interest in entering the building. They milled around like an army of vagrants. Many carried M27s or handguns. A few of them had rocket launchers. Every weapon I saw was standard military issue, probably gleaned from the streets.

As I surveyed the scene, I noticed Corporal Ritz peering around the shattered glass of a fifth-floor window. My visor read his virtual tags. He looked in my direction, probably spotting me through the window with his telescopic lens.

"Do you think they know we're up here?" Ritz asked.

"Can you think of any other reason for them to be here?" I asked.

"Look at those bastards. There must be a thousand of them."

I estimated them at five hundred or six hundred, but kept it to myself.

"Are they armed?" Thomer asked.

"Every last mother-specking one of them," I said. "I think we know where all the guns disappeared to."

The mob filled the streets and sidewalks in a single, unorganized mass. At any moment, I expected some leader to climb onto one of our jeeps and rally his troops with a speech, but it did not happen.

"Ritz, what's happening in the brothel?"

"Not much, sir," Ritz said. "I don't think the ladies know we're in here."

"So we have a standoff," I said. "They don't want to come in, and we don't want to step out."

"Maybe they don't know who we are, sir," Ritz said. "Maybe they don't know we're Marines."

"Maybe they don't care," I said. Who knew what kind of anarchy had taken hold in Norristown. These people probably knew no authority higher than a gun.

I decided it was time to introduce myself. Pulling both a grenade and a rocket launcher from my belt, I took twelve paces back from the window. I set the grenade for a relatively low-yield explosion, and tossed it toward the window, then hid in a doorway. The explosion sprayed shattered glass onto the street. Bright light poured in through the shattered glass wall.

"What are you doing?" Ritz asked.

"I'm introducing myself," I said.

The men in the street scattered as glass showered down on them. Not giving them a moment to regroup, I bolted for the window and fired my rocket at one of the jeeps. I hated sacrificing a perfectly good ride, but explosions and burning metal made a strong impression.

The rocket hit the rear of the jeep just above the fuel tank, touching off a second explosion. The jeep did an anemic flip through the air, crashing onto its front bumper, then landing upside down. Greasy black smoke rose from the chassis along with a bloom of orange-and-red flames.

Down below, all of the men on the street turned their guns in my direction, but nobody fired. Finally, a man stepped out of the crowd and climbed onto the nearest jeep. He wore Army fatigues and a Marine Corps combat helmet. He spoke to me over an open channel on the interLink, his voice sounding so damn familiar we might have been old friends.

He said, "I understand your need to intrude upon our privacy, Captain, but why in God's name are you shooting at us?"

CHAPTER
TWENTY

Hoping that the mob would overestimate our numbers, I had my Marines trail me as I left the building.

The locals made way for me as I entered the street, allowing me and my Marines to pass through unchallenged. I worked my way toward the flaming wreckage of the jeep and the man in the combat helmet who stood beside it. As I came closer, he removed his helmet, revealing shoulder-length hair and a flowing beard. I hardly recognized him.

I came within a few feet of the man and removed my helmet as well.

"What are you doing here, Captain Harris?" asked the Right Reverend Colonel Ellery Doctorow in a voice that held both hostility and restraint. This was the man who had told the fleet to go away. He sounded like he was about to do it again. Gone was the slightest trace that this man had ever been an Army chaplain.

"We came to liberate Terraneau," I said.

Doctorow laughed. "You hear that? He came to rescue us," he called out to his men. Those close enough to hear him laughed. Then turning to me, he said, "The aliens left here long ago, Captain."

Somehow, Doctorow seemed to have gone from highest-ranking shaman in the U.A. Army to some sort of acting governor of Norristown. Hell, for all I knew, he might have set himself up as the lord high emperor of all Terraneau. Whatever his domain, these men clearly followed him.

Doctorow was not as tall as he looked in his picture. He stood over six feet tall, but I still had an inch or two on him. He had aged over the last four years and had become less military in his bearing. The photo that came with my orders showed Doctorow still in his fifties; now he looked more like a well-preserved sixty-five-year-old. He stood erect, but he was too thin. He had let his coal-colored flattop grow into a shaggy mane that reached down to his shoulders, and his thick salt-and-pepper beard had strayed over to the salt side of the equation.

I did not know whether to call the man by his military rank or religious title. Since he was out of uniform, I decided to go the religious route. "Reverend Doctorow," I began.

"I prefer 'Colonel,'" he corrected.

"Colonel, you see that bright stuff up there in the sky?" I asked.

"Hard to miss," Doctorow said.

"They call that the 'ion curtain,'" I said.

"I'm familiar with the term. The scientist who coined it was stationed at Fort Sebastian."

"Was he a dwarf?" I asked.

Doctorow smiled. "It sounds as if we have a common acquaintance."

"Dr. William Sweetwater," I said.

Undoubtedly remembering dark days past, Doctorow said, "They tried to lift him off the planet as the invasion began. Sounds like he made it."

"I met him on New Copenhagen," I said.

"New Copenhagen? The aliens made it all the way to New Copenhagen?"

"Yes, sir," I said. There was nothing more to say.

We stood in the road, in the junction between the three skyscrapers. Doctorow's horde surrounded us, but they also gave us a lot of space. The seven men who had come down with me had worked their way to one of the jeeps. The tone of our meeting was neither friendly nor hostile. "They would have finished us off on New Copenhagen if it were not for Sweetwater," I said. "The little bastard saved us."

"Saved you from what?" Doctorow asked. "The aliens don't do much once they capture your planet. They leave their ion curtain in the sky; they knock down buildings. But they're not all that bad.

"They killed off our army, but they left us alone once we stopped trying to fight them." He wore a reassuring expression, the smile of a parent explaining the difference between right and wrong to an ignorant kid.

"They haven't left," I said.

"We haven't seen them for years."

"You do know that there's a line of glowing spheres no more than twenty miles from here?" I asked. "The aliens use those to spawn. You know that, right?"

Doctorow placed a hand on my shoulder. It was a condescending gesture, and it made me angry. He leaned toward me and spoke in a whisper so that no one would hear what he said. "That, Captain Harris, is why we asked your fleet to go away."

I did not go into detail, but I told Doctorow about New Copenhagen. I described how the Avatari had hollowed mountains and filled them with gas so toxic the fumes slowly melted your skin. I told him how the aliens would expand the nearest sun and use it to bake Terraneau until it was cinder and gas.

"Is that a fact?" Doctorow asked, already acting a lot less sure of himself. "That changes things. How long do we have?"

"It will be a few thousand years before the sun goes on broil, but we've already located the gas," I said. "It's nasty shit."

"There's no need for vulgarity," Doctorow said; but I had the feeling that he said it out of reflex instead of conviction, the same way he might say "God bless you" to a man who sneezed. As a former Army man, he knew the score. Among military men, swearing isn't a vice, it's a specking art form. Once he finished considering what I said, he added, "I don't suppose you have any proof?"

"Excuse me," I told Doctorow. I replaced my helmet and tried to reach Herrington. He did not answer, so I called Thomer instead.

I wanted to send Doctorow to the mines with Herrington, but I could not raise his transport. Somehow, he had flown out of range.

I contacted Hollingsworth and told him to get a transport ready, then I told Thomer to return to the airfield. With Herrington gone, Thomer would need to take his place. He would take Doctorow to see the Avatari mines, and he would lead a team into the mines to detonate the bomb.

As one of the only three men in the Unified Authority to enter an alien dig site and survive, Thomer had the right résumé for offering guided tours around Avatari mines; but I still worried. The Right Reverend would undoubtedly notice Thomer's Fallzoud-induced lethargy. Thomer was more alert than he had been back on the ship, but he still reacted to questions a fraction of a second too slow.

Thomer arrived at the airfield first. He loaded seventy-five Marines onto the transport, then waited for Doctorow to show. Once the Right Reverend rolled onto the field, Thomer led him onto the transport, and they took off for the mines. They did not leave empty-handed. I hoped Doctorow would not notice the large crate in the cargo hold or ask why seventy-five Marines had come along for the ride.

So far, nothing on this mission had gone according to plan.

"Captain Harris, sir?" Hollingsworth called from the airfield just moments after Thomer and Doctorow took to the air.

"What do you have?"

"I'm still not getting through to Sergeant Herrington."

"Maybe something is wrong with his equipment," I said.

"I understand, sir, but I haven't had any luck locating his transport with our radar." Hollingsworth was using the equipment on our third transport. Powerful equipment.

I wondered how long it had been since I spoke with Herrington. A couple of hours had passed. He said he had located the mines. He had said something else, but I was distracted. I'd missed what he said.

Then I remembered what he had said. "Oh shit," I groaned. "Speck."

"What is it, sir?" Hollingsworth asked.

"Herrington said he was going to fly by the Avatari spheres," I said. "He said he was going to swing by the spheres on the way back to the airfield."

"I don't understand." Hollingsworth sounded confused. Not having served on New Copenhagen, he could not fit the pieces together.

"Sergeant, you'd better have your pilot patch me through to Thomer's transport," I said. "We have a hell of a problem."

I looked around the street. Mixing what was left of my men and the local militia, there might have been a thousand of us. We mostly had M27s and machine guns. My men would have some rocket launchers and grenades. We were cooked.

"Captain Harris, I have them," Hollingsworth said.

"Thomer."

"Yes, sir."

"Doctorow, you there, too?"

"I'm here," Doctorow said.

"Herrington is dead," I said. "The Avatari are on their way."

CHAPTER
TWENTY-ONE

Herrington's transport simply vanished. That meant it went down quickly, so quickly that the pilot never even had time to send a distress signal. They could have had an equipment failure, but I knew damn well that they hadn't. They were shot down. They reached the spheres and ran into the Avatari with their specking light rifles.

I remembered that the last thing I told Herrington was that I was too busy to talk; then I snuffed out that guilty memory. There would be time for recriminations later.

The beacon Herrington left by the mines was just over eight thousand miles away. Flying at 2,250 miles per hour, it would have taken him nearly four hours to get from the mines to the spheres. That meant he went down about an hour ago.

The spheres were approximately twenty miles from town. An army with light armor could close that gap in under an hour, but the Avatari moved slowly. Once they emerged from the spheres, it would take them hours to make the long march into Norristown.

Using interLink communications, I went over my calculations with Doctorow and Thomer and Hollingsworth. "Are you sure about this?" Doctorow asked. "For all you know, Herrington's radio might be on the blink."

I reminded him that the radar no longer showed Herrington's transport.

"So what do we do?" Doctorow asked.

"We're going to have to fight," I said.

"Then you're on your own, Captain. This is your fight; they came here looking for you." Doctorow sounded angry, like a man who suspects his friends are trying to con him.

I wanted to tell Doctorow to go speck himself. I wanted to tell him we could all die together if he preferred it that way. I kept my mouth shut, partially because I needed his help and partially because I knew he was right.

"What if we lit up the nuke?" Thomer asked. "We're closing in on the mines."

"It's too late for that," I said. "We're going to have to fight them. One way or another, we're going to need to fight them."

The Avatari emerged from their spheres as energy, then created their bodies by attracting tachyons out of the ion curtain. Exploding a nuclear device in the mines would draw loose tachyons out of the atmosphere, eradicating the ion curtain. It would not pull in tachyons that had already attached themselves to an avatar.

"Do you want me to scout the area?" Hollingsworth volunteered. "I could take a transport and be back in no time."

It sounded like an unnecessary risk, but I allowed him to persuade me. "I wouldn't mind having an ETA on the bastards," I agreed. "Just don't get shot down."

Hollingsworth said he would be careful and signed off.

Perhaps hearing Hollingsworth throw himself into the fire reminded Doctorow of his days in the Army. Maybe he'd just rethought things. Something made him change his mind, and he said, "If the mines are as bad as you say they are, we're all facing a death sentence. If it will help, Captain Harris, my militia will join you."

"A thousand men with M27s; I'm not sure what good that will do."

"My militia is five thousand men strong, and we have a lot more than machine guns. We have an exit strategy we've been saving in case of an emergency."

"We have an army of indestructible aliens marching into town. I think that qualifies as an emergency," I said.

"It sounds like an emergency to me," Doctorow agreed. As it turned out, the Right Reverend Colonel Ellery Doctorow had a very good exit strategy indeed.

CHAPTER
TWENTY-TWO

Norristown did not have enough electricity for everyday life, but the city's emergency generators produced more than enough juice to power the sirens. All around town, sirens blared, calling the militia to arms and warning everyone else to abandon the town. When it came to evacuation, I had little doubt that the general population of Norristown took their warning sirens seriously.

The sound of the sirens tore through the air as we crossed town, their moaning wail carried across the ruined landscape unobstructed by walls or towers.

I rode with the locals in a truck to go see the place that Ellery Doctorow described as "the darkest spot on Terraneau." On the way, we would stop by the Norristown Armory. According to Doctorow, the locals had collected enough guns and bombs to put up a fight.

"Captain Harris, I found Herrington's transport," Hollingsworth radioed in over the interLink.

"Any survivors?" I asked, already knowing the answer.

"I can't tell from here. Do you want me to go in for a closer look?"

"No," I said, seeing no reason for him to risk his life to confirm something we both already knew. With the ion curtain forcing us to fly low, our transports made easy targets for the aliens. "Do you see any sign of the aliens?"

"There's some kind of glow coming off some hills," Hollingsworth said. "Should I go have a look?"

"No!" My voice lurched as I yelled this, but I could not help myself. Hollingsworth had not been on New Copenhagen. He had no idea what he was dealing with. "That glow is the aliens. Mark the area on the map and get back to the airfield."

A moment later, the positions came in on the virtual map in my visor. Hollingsworth marked the spot where Herrington went down. It was twenty-three miles west of town. He also marked the aliens' position, approximately eighteen miles west of town. One thing about the Avatari, they moved at a glacial pace. I took off my helmet so I could speak with Kareem O'Doul, Doctorow's right-hand man.

"The aliens are eighteen miles west of us." I had to shout so that he could hear me over the blare of the sirens. "That gives us four or five hours." Now that I had my helmet off, cool wind blew hard against my face. It felt good.

O'Doul was a small, dark man with nearly black eyes and skin the color of walnut shells. His hair was brown but very close to black. "What about your missing transport?"

"They found that, too."

"Shot down?"

"Yes, they got it." I surveyed the landscape and listened to the sound of the sirens. "Do your people know what to do when they hear sirens?"

"They know," he answered. "We have a fleet of buses for evacuating town. When people see the buses, they climb on without asking questions.

"I'm more worried about giving them someplace to come home to."

"You and me both." I mumbled this far too quietly for him to hear me. We could not fight the Avatari. Even with the militia on our side, we could not engage them head-on. Instead of fighting like Marines, we would employ guerilla tactics, the old hit-and-run offense.

"How fast can your men rig the tunnels?" I asked.

"I've seen them do miracles. You're talking about blowing

a big area. If they had more time, they'd give you a real work of art."

He sounded like a veteran. "Sounds like you have some demolitions experience," I said.

"Army Special Forces," O'Doul said. "I'm not your demolitions man. We have a couple of ex–Navy SEALs rigging the bombs."

"SEALs?" I asked. About eight years back, the Navy phased out its natural-born SEALs, replacing them with a line of specially equipped clones. "Survivors from the alien invasion?"

"Retired," O'Doul said.

"Old guys?"

"And they aren't getting any younger. Good thing setting up charges is like riding a bike," O'Doul said. "These boys will be hobbled and senile before they forget how to set a charge."

"Good thing," I agreed. If his demolitions men were former SEALs, we were in good hands. The Army and Marines had talented demolitions experts, but the SEALs were in a class of their own.

O'Doul drove through the broken city desert and into a ghost town where two- and three-story buildings stood untouched and abandoned. The doors of all of these structures hung open, and a few had broken windows; but for the most part, the war had passed them by.

"Welcome to the new capital city of Terraneau," O'Doul said.

A network of squat five-story buildings spread out around the area like a maze. Sky bridges ran between the buildings, connecting them like a strand of spider's web. There was no mistaking these for anything but government buildings, they were too ugly to be anything else.

"You stashed your arsenal in a government complex?" I asked.

"Under the complex," O'Doul said. "We saw the aliens knocking buildings down and thought it might be safer underground."

We made the same mistake on New Copenhagen. We placed our arsenal in a parking lot under a large hotel. The strategy backfired when the Avatari destroyed the hotel.

As we drove down the ramp leading underground, I checked back with Thomer and Hollingsworth. Thomer had found Herrington's beacon and the mountain in which the aliens had dug their mines.

Having seen the enormous entrance carved into the granite face of the cliffs and read the meters showing the toxicity level of the air, Doctorow became as cooperative as a newly minted cadet. When I put him on the line with O'Doul, he gave the order to mobilize the militia.

When Hollingsworth's transport touched down, the militia sent trucks out to the airfield to bring him and the rest of my men into town.

Holding on to the unreasonable hope that he might respond, I tried to reach Herrington as well. I could not adjust to the idea that I no longer had Sergeant Lewis Herrington watching my back.

Four men with M27s stood at the entrance to the parking lot. They opened the iron gate, allowing us to enter the first level of the garage. The sound of industrial generators echoed through the structure.

We drove down one level and parked outside a fenced enclosure. Looking through the chain link, I saw that Doctorow had indeed stockpiled enough weapons to start a galactic war. From outside the fence, I saw shelves covered with M27s and rocket launchers. Pallets with crates of ammunition lined a wall. Behind the shelves and pallets stood three rows of Jackals—fast-moving jeeps with overpowered engines, rear turrets, and light armor.

A dozen armed guards stood inside the fence. When they saw O'Doul approach, they unlocked the gate. I followed, entering the organized madness of an armory made by the kind of men who submit to an alien occupation.

The armory had stacks of combat armor, more likely salvage than surplus. A fleet of tanks sat in one corner of the garage. They had both gas-spewing Rumsfelds and powerful LGs. These vehicles would be worse than useless against the aliens, their slow speeds would make them easy targets, and their armor would offer no protection against Avatari light rifles.

Taking a cursory look around, I saw rocket launchers, grenade launchers, rifles, pistols, cannons, landmines, and robot defense units called trackers. "We're going to need particle-beam cannons and handheld rocket launchers," I said.

"We have enough rockets to send your men out with a thousand launchers each," O'Doul said.

"And all of yours, too?" I asked. "I'm going to need men and vehicles."

"I'm not sending my men out there," O'Doul said. Sending men to rig tunnels was one thing; sending men into battle was another.

"Doctorow told you to give me whatever support I need," I said. "I need vehicles, I need drivers, and I need men to fight on the line."

O'Doul did not like it, and I got the feeling he did not like me, but he knew I was right. He ordered his men to load trucks with particle-beam cannons and handheld rocket launchers, and the men went to work.

Hollingsworth arrived a few minutes later. Looking at the stacks of weapons, he gave a low whistle, and said, "Man, you have enough shit here to overthrow an empire."

I hoped he was right.

The underground garage/armory had seven levels, but at this point in the mission, the back of the third level was what interested me.

The rear wall of the third level opened to an underground train station. There were no lights in the station, just a platform that disappeared into utter darkness.

"Welcome to the blackest spot on Terraneau," O'Doul said. "I've seen assholes more brightly lit than this place." I noticed that as he relaxed around me and my Marines, he became more and more profane.

"Where's it go?" I asked.

"It's the Norristown subway system. Where do you think it goes?" He stepped onto the platform and shined a torch out toward the tracks. The light was not especially bright. It dissolved into the blackness a few feet in. The area in the beam was a gleaming, polished, magnetic railway system hidden under a blanket of darkness so dense I felt like I could breathe it.

"Hit the lights," O'Doul yelled to the guards.

A string of bulbs lit up along the ceiling. Instead of illuminating the tunnel, they produced a series of dim bubbles that vanished in the distance.

I put on my helmet and stepped through the opening. Even with night-for-day lenses, I could not see very far. I saw the plasticized world around me clearly enough—twenty-foot-wide platforms on either side of the tunnel; six magnetic tracks laid out like stripes that rolled out as far as the eye could see; and dead monitors, which had not displayed train schedules for years. Without juice running through them, the magnetic tracks were simply four-foot-deep grooves.

"You're going to use these tunnels to rig your charges?" I asked.

"Unless you have a better idea," O'Doul said.

"How solid are the tunnels?" I asked. "Are you going to be able to get to the zone?"

"We've mapped every inch of these speckers, Harris. I know my way around these bitches better than the guys who ran the trains. You just deliver the aliens to the right place at the right time, and I'll cream their asses."

"How are we planning to get the bombs in place?" Hollingsworth asked. Like me, he had his helmet on. "There is no way in the world that these guys are going to power a big system like this with a couple of emergency generators."

"You let me worry about that," O'Doul said. "The bombs are my problem; the aliens are yours."

"Begging your pardon, sir, the bombs are my problem, too," Hollingsworth said. "My orders are to coordinate efforts between your militia and our Marines. I'm staying with you."

"Speck. What the speck!" said O'Doul. Judging by his language arts, he had become totally at ease around us.

O'Doul, Hollingsworth, and a small army of drivers would shuttle the charges to the target area on the west side of town. They could probably have loaded all of the explosives into a single commuter train had the trains been running. Instead, they loaded the explosives onto the gas-powered sleds that the transit authority had used for tunnel maintenance.

Their job was to set the trap; my job was to kick the hornet's nest. I was taking 73 of my 148 remaining Marines along with 200 men from the local militia to meet the Avatari. All we had to do was lead the specking aliens into O'Doul's blast zone, then get the hell out of there before the bombs went off. We would definitely take casualties on this one. We were dealing with the Avatari, and the one thing you could count on with those bastards was death and destruction. But if we ran a hit-and-run offense, I thought we might limit the breakage.

I had my men stock up on rocket launchers and grenades. If we were forced into a close-range fight, we would use particle-beam weapons. That would be the last resort. When O'Doul asked me what weapons I thought his drivers should take, I gave it to him straight, "All they will need are body bags and Jackals."

Then we loaded up and left the armory.

As we drove west through town, I looked back at my convoy. We had thirty-five jeeps and thirty-six Jackals, all borrowed from the armory and piloted by militiamen. Those Jackals were our best bet. They had rocket arrays set up on their front fenders, machine guns with armor-piercing bullets in their rear turrets, and hundreds of horses under their hoods.

We headed south, then west across Norristown, entering areas as desolate as the Martian desert, in which I did not see so much as a living plant. The streets were buried under slag and debris. The parks were nothing more than burned-over lots with the occasional stream running through them. Using the Geiger counter in my visor, I took radiation readings and found more than a few hot spots. The first Norristown defenders must have resorted to nuclear-tipped ordinance as the war wound down.

After leaving the downtown area, we entered a storm-torn suburb in which the occasional tree, or house, or chapel stood as a reminder of how life should have been. As the invasion began, the troops defending Norristown would have sacrificed this area the way doctors amputate a cancerous limb. They would have let the aliens in, then bombarded the place with everything they had. The pockmarked remains of expended minefields covered much of the area.

My men traveled in jeeps; the militia rode in Jackals. Jeeps were smaller and a lot more vulnerable, but you could hop in and out of them as fast as you liked. With their armored walls, Jackals were not so easy to enter. I rode in a Jackal, but it was only as a show of confidence. The guy doing the driving was a high-ranking member of the Norristown militia. O'Doul had designated him Jackal squad leader. I could see why—the son of a bitch showed no fear at all.

The Jackal leader flipped some switches on his dash, and said, "I have the aliens on radar." He swung the screen over so I could have a look. The Avatari were still a couple of miles ahead of us. Their ranks showed up as a solid white block against the glowing green background of the screen.

"Do you know that part of town?" I asked.

He laughed, "I used to live there . . . had a nice house with a swing set in the back. They had good schools in this part of town."

"I bet the schools aren't much of a selling point anymore," I said.

"But the house prices have dropped," he said. The guy had a sense of humor. We were driving through the wreckage of his old neighborhood, but he could still tell jokes. I liked that.

"Know anyplace between us and them that might give us a high-ground advantage?" I asked.

He slowed the Jackal and pulled the radar screen over for a closer look. "There's Hyde Park," he said. "It's not exactly mountainous, but the bluffs might work out."

"Let's go," I said.

He used his radio to relay my orders to the other Jackals, and I sent my Marines the info over the interLink: "We're headed to a park where we should have a slight elevation advantage."

It took about three minutes to find Hyde Park, a long, ter-raced pasture with slopes overlooking the western edge of Norristown. The charred remains of a two-story community center stood in the middle of the park like a large chapel over-looking a cemetery.

The jeeps led the way, skidding to a stop at the edge of a ridge so my Marines could climb out. The Jackal leader pulled up near my men and stopped. I asked him if I could use his radio to speak to his men. He nodded.

Taking the microphone, I said, "You boys driving the Jackals, you remember your job is to harass, not to fight." Then I thanked the Jackal leader for the ride and wished him luck. From here on out, I would ride in a jeep.

I took my spot on the hill, pulled out my first rocket launcher, and prepared for the battle.

CHAPTER
TWENTY-THREE

Every last one of us on those hills was a Marine. We were the ones with the combat armor, the training, and the frontline experience. I listened in on my men when they spoke. I heard them breathe when they were silent. The only thing I could not hear was their thoughts.

You see them out there? Where the specking hell are those speckers?

They'll be here soon enough. You in a rush to see them?

The iron-gray-colored horde appeared in the ruins below us. They were far away, small and indistinct. I did not think they had spotted us yet when I gave my final instructions.

"The objective at this stop is not—I repeat, not—to kill aliens," I said over an open frequency. "I'm not handing out medals for kills. Got it? Fire off a rocket, and back away. The name of the game here is catching their attention, not holding on to real estate. Anybody who falls behind gets left behind, so do us all a favor and save the heroics."

As I finished my piece, a trio of Jackals rushed in. They sped across the grassy shelf like a formation of fighter jets, speeding over the battered landscape firing shots, then rushing away. One of the Jackals bounced over a crater left by an explosion, lurched over the lip, and flew through the air. It landed as smoothly as a cat jumping from a ledge.

The militia made its first strafing run while the aliens were still three-quarters of a mile away. Their light-armor Jackals looked like toys from that distance, and the Avatari looked no bigger or more distinct than the bristles on a toothbrush. Zooming in for a closer look with the telescopic lenses in my visor, I watched as the lead vehicle fired three rockets into the horde, then made a skidding swipe, the gunner in its turret swinging around so that he could fire large-caliber bullets into the aliens' ranks the entire time. Those bullets could drill a brick wall to dust. They would cut a man in half, but it took three shots to bring one of the aliens down.

The Jackals made their run, then sped to safety. The aliens might have fired after them, but two more formations rocketed onto the ridge from different directions, fired, retreated.

Looking over the battlefield, I decided that the Avatari had not come with their standard fifty thousand troops, maybe not even with a quarter of that number. Not that it mattered. They had more than enough soldiers to win a fair fight. If our Jackals stumbled, they would swat them like bugs.

One of the Jackals in the third formation rolled as it skidded around to escape. It might have hit loose gravel, or one of its bulletproof tires might have popped, or the turn might have simply been too tight. The Jackal canted onto two wheels, then rolled onto its side, spinning out of control. Jackals were made to roll and right themselves; but as soon as this one landed on its wheels, a hailstorm of light bolts seared through it. The Jackal exploded in flames.

Doctorow's militia had done its job. I contacted the Jackal leader and told him to pull his men back. I did not have to tell him twice.

The Avatari continued toward us. "Two shots. Two shots, then make for the jeeps," I called over an open frequency. I wanted the drivers and grenadiers to hear me.

Down below us, the Avatari continued their march, slow-moving, unflinching, unafraid. Using telescopic lenses, I could see them clearly now—bodies the color of stone; eyes, lips, and ears all made of the same rocklike material as their skin.

Their eyes stared straight ahead, like the eyes of a crudely sculpted statue. Their faces never twitched.

The Avatari stood eight feet tall. Their rifles were four-foot tubes made of gleaming chrome. They fired yard-long bolts of light that traveled as fast as the eye could see and burned through shields, armor, buildings, and men—and then kept going.

They marched toward us. "Steady . . . steady," I called to my men. I remembered Nietzsche as I looked down at the alien army: *When you stare into the abyss, the abyss stares back at you.*

Using the equipment in my helmet, I measured the distance between us and the enemy. Six hundred feet. In another kind of fight, this would have been the moment to fire or to retreat. We could not hit them with HURL rockets at that range. They could hit us, though. A few of them fired in our direction, the bolts flying wild into the sky.

I yelled for my men to drop, but a couple of morons remained on their feet. "Get down!" I repeated, as the Avatari picked them off. Natural selection works among military clones nearly the same way it does in nature. Sadly, the rest of us were every bit as sterile as the idiots whom the Avatari had just shot dead.

Perched on my knees, I measured the range again. The aliens were 575 feet away. An Avatari bolt struck a Marine a few feet to my right. A lucky shot. It bored through the ground at the front of the slope, then through ten feet of earth and into the Marine before sailing off through the air. Tiny flames burned around the three-inch hole in his helmet. I knew without looking that the armor around the hole would melt and dribble into the wound.

The man was lucky that the bolt hit him in the head, he died instantly. It did not matter if these bolts hit you in the head or the foot; they killed you either way. A shot through the head was more merciful because it killed you instantly. Anyone shot in the leg, hand, or arm went into shock and died in a fit of convulsions.

To this point, not a one of my Marines had fired a shot. They waited for the order to shoot. With the Avatari 480 feet away, I gave the order to return fire.

"Two shots and retreat. Two shots and withdraw!" I bellowed. Over the interLink, I could hear my squad leaders repeating the command. You hear things without thinking about them during battle. Once the shooting begins, all the loose talk becomes chatter, something no more distinct than static.

I pulled a handheld rocket, aimed, and fired at the first phalanx of aliens as it reached the bottom of the slope. Handheld rocket launchers were a foot long and about the same diameter as the handle of a mop. You pointed the launcher like a flashlight to fire it, then threw away the empty tube. The Avatari spotted me and returned fire. I fell back as dozens of bolts came soaring toward me.

"Head for the jeeps," I yelled, my voice so loud in my helmet that it caused a ringing in my ears. Three stray bolts shot up through the dirt near my feet. More flew through the air above me.

I had made a mistake telling my men to fire two shots, even a single shot was dicey. A living enemy would have run for cover or charged our position, these bastards kept marching forward, returning fire as they went. They were avatars, not living beings. They had nothing to fear.

I turned to run and stumbled. In the brief moment I was down on my ass, I saw three of my men die. Looking up and down the slope, I saw that I had lost eleven men in all. I repeated the order to fall back, then pulled out a second rocket launcher, sprang to my feet, and fired.

Dropping low as light bolts flew through the air and ground around me, I turned and sprinted to the jeeps, no more than twenty feet behind the last of my men. It was early in the fight, but we'd already lost eleven men and one Jackal, a bad omen.

"Want me to risk a drive-by?" the Jackal leader asked.

"Hit them when they reach the top of the hill," I said. "One pass and get the hell out. Don't push your luck, you saw what happens."

"Pushing your luck—you mean, like staying to fire a second rocket after telling your men to retreat?"

"Get specked," I said. He was right, though. I shouldn't have piped off that second rocket. This was combat, the first action I had seen in two years, and I was having a combat reflex.

It was part of my Liberator architecture. When the battle got hot, the glands that made me a Liberator pumped testosterone and adrenaline into my veins.

"You coming, Captain?" the Marine driving the last jeep asked.

"Yeah, on my way," I said. I took one last look back in time to see a lone Jackal slice its way across the hill. The gunner swayed back and forth, and the muzzle of his machine gun flashed nonstop.

I sprinted to the jeep and jumped in. We bounced and jostled over the deeply scarred ground, easily outpacing the aliens. Once we were far enough away, I ordered the drivers to slow down. We needed the Avatari to follow us.

"How are you doing with the explosives?" I asked Hollingsworth on a direct Link.

"O'Doul is a prick," he said.

"Is that opinion professional or personal?"

"Personal," Hollingsworth said. "My professional opinion is that the bastard knows his way around a charge."

"How long before the area is ready for visitors?" I asked.

"He's got several teams working. The team I'm with is just putting on the finishing touches. We're about to evacuate the area.

"I'd hate to be around when this place goes up, not with all the shit they have wired. These boys aren't taking any chances.

"How's it going on the front?"

"Peachy, Sergeant, just peachy."

The Avatari behaved more like security men than soldiers, but they were not stupid. If they saw us driving at fifteen miles an hour, they would know we were baiting them. We had to make them believe that we thought we could win this thing. We'd take casualties, but everyone who signed up for this show knew the score.

I had my driver step on the gas so we could get to the head of our all-jeep convoy. The target zone was ten miles southeast of us. We could stick to a fairly clean road if we veered north, but that would have taken us in the wrong direction.

The area around us was little more than dunes of rubble and the burned-out skeletons of small buildings. It looked like a fire had swept through. I saw nothing that would give us a strategic advantage, so I called in a Jackal strike. "Make it look like you mean it," I told the Jackal leader.

"Like I mean it?" he asked.

"Make it look like you came to fight, not to lead them into a trap."

"We'll take casualties," the Jackal leader warned.

I sighed, and said, "Understood."

When I looked back, I saw groups of Jackals heading toward the Avatari from two different directions. More waves might have moved in from other directions as well.

I had hoped for hills or at least a stretch of buildings, but the best I could find was a small neighborhood seven miles south. Everything else was beaten so flat that the small ring of houses stood out like an island in a sea of debris. "Pull in there," I said, pointing to the burb.

"We lost three more vehicles on that last strike," the Jackal leader radioed in. "I'm down to twenty-eight cars."

"Should I send some jeeps to pick up survivors?" I asked.

"No," he said, his voice devoid of emotion. "Like you said back at the armory, 'Jackals and body bags.'"

"I found a spot where my men can make another stand, but we'll need time to set up. Can you buy me another minute or two?" I asked.

"I can do that."

"And, Jackal leader, kick in the shins, not the balls," I said. "Just slow them down, don't even think about trying to win this."

"No problem," he said.

We drove over a slight rise, and I glimpsed two squads of Jackals heading back toward the aliens. Moments later, I heard the chatter of distant machine guns.

We entered the remains of what must have once been an upscale bedroom community. We had maybe a mile lead on the aliens, giving us a ten-minute head start.

"Pull over," I told my driver.

The other jeeps followed.

I gave the order for my riflemen and grenadiers to fall out, and they leaped from the jeeps, rocket launchers ready. "Here's the drill, stay out of the houses. Do not get yourselves trapped in a yard or a building. The name of the game is shoot and run . . . shoot and run. You got that? Shoot and run. If you get a chance to fire off a second HURL, you do it; but the drill here is to fire off a shot and head for the jeeps."

The yards around the houses were four years overgrown. The grass reached my knees, and flower beds had gone to seed. The houses were large, surrounded by tiny lawns and tall fences. I leaped over a tangled hedge and pulled my first launcher. In a normal gunfight, I would never hide behind bushes, they cannot protect you from anything more powerful than a slingshot; but fighting the Avatari and their blasted light rifles, concealment was the only protection. Nothing, not even the yard-thick walls of a shielded bunker, could protect me from those bolts.

Looking up and down the street, I saw men hiding behind fences, peering around houses, and ducking behind abandoned cars; all better barriers than my hedge but utterly useless in this situation.

"Harris, they're headed your way," the Jackal leader warned me. Even as he said that, a line of Jackals came tearing down the street. One had large holes where light bolts had fused through its turret. A dead gunner hung slumped over the machine gun, his lolling head twisting as the jeep banked around a curve.

"Jackal leader, what is the status of your squad?" I asked.

"We're hauling our asses out of here," he said.

"How bad are your casualties?"

"Three and a half down," he said. "We lost three more Jackals and one is running without a gunner."

"Send that one back to the armory," I said.

"I can't do that," the Jackal leader said. "It's my ride."

"What do you expect to accomplish driving with a dead gunner?" I asked.

"I am not leaving my men."

The Avatari approached us, walking across the ruins that had once been the outskirts of the community. They were several hundred yards away, their first ranks advancing over cement slabs and weed-infested lawns, trampling grounds in which toys and dreams had been lost.

The Avatari slowed their advance. In the past, the bastards had fought with mindless intensity. This time, they surprised me. They performed an actual military maneuver: They spread their ranks. I smiled, thinking they might reenact Pickett's Charge, but then the ends of their formation broke off. The specking sons of bitches wanted to flank us.

"Shit!" I said. Then to my squad leaders, I said, "Break off the attack. Head for the jeeps."

The Avatari opened fire.

There were so many bolts in the air, it looked like a specking blizzard. They could not have seen us, but the bastards figured out our hiding places. Three bolts struck a car, forcing the men hiding behind it to run for better cover. A bolt hit the first man in the head the moment he jumped out from behind the car, leaving a smoking hole through his head and helmet. The man collapsed to the street.

The second man did not make it much farther, but for just a moment, I thought the third might reach safety. Bolts flying over his head and shoulders, he ran crouched toward a garden gate. As he started to leap the gate, a bolt struck him between his shoulders. He fell like a bird shot in flight, slamming into the gate. Half-hidden by the tall grass, he lay quivering until he died.

If I could have, I would have put him out of his misery, but three bolts flared through the hedge just a few feet from me. The dried branches near me caught on fire. Without looking for a target, I raised a hand and fired off a rocket, tossed the launcher, then fired another.

"Head for the jeeps!" I yelled. "Get moving! Get out of here!"

Strange as it might sound, I was glad to be in this fight. There must have been a fifty-fifty mix of blood and hormone running through my veins. My skin prickled the way it did when I took a hot shower on a cold night.

A half block ahead of me, a bolt struck the windshield of an abandoned car, melting its way through. The bolt did not shatter the dirty glass, it simply bored a hole through it. I saw another bolt pass through a tree with a trunk as wide as a water barrel. In the yards and on the street, the dead, my dead lay scattered like leaves blown from a tree—men in dark green combat armor, some dead and some convulsing as the shock snuffed out their lives.

I ran as fast as I could, not along the street, like most of the men who had died, but through yards and behind houses. If the aliens saw me, they could shoot me no matter what I used for cover.

My driver radioed. "Captain, where are you? They're closing in around us."

No more than thirty yards ahead of me, three aliens stepped out from around the corner of a house. They were tall, their heads almost reaching the eaves of the roof. They looked like earthen statues made by primitive sculptors who had not quite mastered the human form. They held their rifles muzzles up. Somehow these bastards had flanked me without even knowing I was there.

Ducking behind a tree, I watched them fan out.

"Captain Harris?" My driver's voice came over the interLink.

"Get out!" I shouted.

"But . . ."

"Out! That's a specking order."

I had a particle-beam pistol, an M27, and three rocket launchers. I wasn't going to win a war armed like that, but I might keep myself safe for a while.

"Sir . . ."

"Are you on the road?"

"Just pulling out"

I dived through a hedge and landed in the overgrown remains of what may once have been a nice backyard. I saw a small fountain in one corner of the yard and a pile of lawn furniture in another.

"Captain Harris?"

"What is it?" I asked in a voice meant to scare the driver off.

I could hear the heavy footsteps of two-thousand-pound soldiers behind me. They might have been after me, but I thought it more likely they were just searching for targets. In my experience, the Avatari worried about armies, not individual men. They did not distinguish between officers and enlisted men; our command structure meant nothing to them.

"Let me come back for you," the driver said. He was a good Marine, he did not want to leave a man behind.

"You made it out?" I asked.

"Yes, sir."

"What was the damage to my men?" I asked.

"Heavy casualties, sir."

Hearing half-ton footfalls as the Avatari tromped through yards, I ran to the back of the house and kicked my way through a glass door. Stealing a quick glance over my shoulder, I saw a burly, stone-colored leg step through the bushes as I slipped into the house.

"Do not come back, Corporal. I repeat, do not return here. That is an order."

"But, sir . . ."

"Stow it, Marine, I'm busy here."

I entered the house through the kitchen and continued through to the living room, where a knee-high gate blocked off a corner filled with blocks and stuffed animals. Having spent my youth in a military orphanage, I had no experience with the classic family home; but I got the feeling the last family to occupy this residence had had kids. Pinched between bookshelves and some long-extinct potted plants, a holographic television stood as a mute witness that life had once existed in this home.

Beyond the plants, I found a door.

"Captain Harris, what are you going to do?" At first I thought it was my driver carrying his concern to the point of insubordination. When I checked the label on my visor, I saw that it was Sergeant Hollingsworth.

"I found myself a basement. I can hide down here," I said, looking down the stairs and into the darkness. "I'll just dig in and let the bastards pass me by."

"You might not want to do that, sir," Hollingsworth said.

"Why the hell not?" I asked.

"You're on the edge of the blast zone."

"What?" I asked.

"The train system passes right under you."

"Shit," I said, hoping that I sounded more distracted than scared. But it wasn't the intel about the blast zone that set me off, it was the sounds of breaking glass and heavy footsteps. The Avatari had found my hiding place.

CHAPTER
TWENTY-FOUR

Hearing an alien enter the house, I quietly closed the door behind me and hurried down the stairs. When my visor switched to night-for-day lenses, I saw a line of dusty pictures showing a happy family—two parents, three children, the oldest might have been ten years old. I wondered if they survived the invasion, or had I found myself in the company of ghosts?

"You can't wait them out in the blast zone, sir." Hollingsworth sounded exasperated.

"I have company," I said.

"Aliens?"

"No, it's Ava Gardner coming to say she can't live without me," I said. I regretted saying that the moment the words left my lips.

Above my head, the ceiling groaned under the weight of the alien . . . or aliens. Looking around for somewhere to hide, I found mostly mouse shit and cobwebs. The skeleton of a dead dog lay on one corner of the floor, locked into its pen by a wire fence. In life, it had been one of those rodent dogs, just a few inches tall and full of attitude. A few scabs of fluffy white fur still remained on its skull and legs; the rest had been picked clean by rats, mice, or maggots. There were no eyes in its skull.

Hearing heavy footsteps above me, I began feeling frantic. "Hollingsworth, you said this was the edge of the zone? How close to the edge? Any chance this house could survive the blast?"

The explosion would take place thirty feet down, I might be safe if I was far enough from ground zero. Even if the house collapsed, I might survive. I had armor to protect me.

"I don't like your chances, sir," Hollingsworth said.

I heard the sound of wood smashing, and light poured down the stairway. The light cast a long shadow along the wall. I had done the very thing I told my men not to do—I had gotten myself cornered. I had come down to a dead end. There were plenty of places to hide down here, but the only way out was up the stairs.

"Harris, where are you?" the Jackal leader asked.

I watched the wooden stairs that led back up to the house and wondered if they could handle a full ton of alien bulk. My pulse was up. I had already put away my rocket launchers and switched to my particle-beam pistol. This was close combat, far closer than I wanted to get. With the joules of energy inside their tachyon shells, the Avatari could fry the circuits in my armor just by touching it.

I imagined the stairs collapsing, leaving me and a two-thousand-pound alien trapped together as the bombs went off. The house might come down on top of us, or the ground could open under our feet.

"Captain Harris, where are you?" the Jackal leader repeated.

"Still in the last drop zone," I whispered, though I knew it was unlikely the avatar could hear me.

An avatar stepped onto the top step. I heard the footstep, then the groan of straining wood. My heart pounding so hard I could feel it in my ears and neck, I held my pistol up and ready to fire.

The alien took another step, and I could see its foot, a simple rectangle with no ornamentation representing shoes or toes. The wooden stair bowed beneath the weight, but did not break. I could have shot the bastard at point-blank range at that second. I could have shot its foot out from under it, then shot it a second time in the head once it fell. I waited.

"You wouldn't happen to know what I'll run into when I get out of this house?" I asked on a frequency that both Hollingsworth and the Jackal leader would pick up.

"The last I saw, the area around you was lousy with those alien speckers," the Jackal leader said. "Maybe hundreds of 'em."

"Harris, you need to get out of there," Hollingsworth said.

"Yeah, that's what I hear," I said. "Jackal leader, think you could do me a favor?"

The alien continued down the stairs in slow motion, taking two steps at a time. It poked the barrel of its rifle down and surveyed the base of the stairway. I wondered how well the Avatari could see in the dark.

"What?" the Jackal leader asked.

"Give these bastards a swift kick to the nuts," I said. "See if you can move them deeper into the blast zone."

There was a moment of silence. When the Jackal leader spoke again, he sounded nervous. "I'm down to eleven cars," he said. The man who had just run a sortie with a dead gunner hanging from his turret sounded sheepish.

"Eleven cars?" We were almost out of cars, but things had come down to the wire. Resolved that I would probably die in that basement, I no longer cared about my safety. We needed to lure the aliens closer to ground zero.

"It's too late to back out now," I said.

"This isn't just about getting your ass out of there?" the Jackal leader asked. He already knew the answer, but he wanted reassurance before he would send men out to die.

"I'm guessing my ass is fried no matter what happens," I said. The alien came down two more steps, pointing the muzzle of its rifle back and forth across the basement as it went.

If the aliens gave off a heat signature, I could have counted their numbers through the floor with the heat-vision lenses in my visor; but the Avatari gave off no heat. If this one was alone, I could cap it. But if it had come with friends . . .

"We're on our way," the Jackal leader said. I heard a car door shut in the background and knew without asking that he had just sent his navigator to man the turret in the back of his Jackal. "I hope you make it out of there, Harris."

I would never hear him speak again.

Standing eight feet tall, the alien had to duck its head before it could reach the bottom of the stairs. When the bastard lowered its head, I shot it in the back. Hit by a particle beam, a human target would have exploded. This son of a bitch simply quivered and fell.

A second avatar started down the stairs. I hoped there were only two of them; if these bastards called for backup, I was specked.

The stairs creaked as the second avatar started down. I

found a hiding place behind a table, not far from Fido's bones. I aimed my pistol and waited in the darkness, but the alien stopped halfway down the stairs. Moments passed, and then it went back the way it came from.

I tried to contact the Jackal leader, but the connection was gone.

"Hollingsworth, what's happening out there?" I asked.

"The enemy is almost in position, maybe a quarter of a mile off," Hollingsworth said.

I walked to the bottom of the stairs and stepped over the broken alien. It lay facedown, as still and as stiff as a fallen tree.

"How much longer?" I asked Hollingsworth.

"They're almost in place. Any minute now."

"Okay," I said. There was a shift in the shadows along the wall. I paused and looked up the stairs, but the area was clear. With my connection to the Jackal leader down, I had no way to tell the Jackals to break off their attack. Like me, they needed to get to safety before the bombs went off.

The Jackals might not make it to safety. I had lost many of my men. I was about to ride out the explosion at the edge of ground zero. It looked like we might win the battle, but everything had still gone wrong.

"Okay, light the fuse," I told Hollingsworth.

"What about you?" Hollingsworth asked.

"I'm going to make a break for it," I said. I had already started up the stairs. "Tell you what, Sergeant, if you get the men together when we get back to the ship, I'll slip you all into the officers' club for a brew."

"We can buy you a few more minutes if we send in . . ." Hollingsworth began.

"You have your orders, Hollingsworth."

"Yes, sir." I heard neither pity nor regret in his voice, only resignation.

I struggled to come up with some way to radio the Jackals, but they were militia, the interLink did not reach them. Only the Jackal leader had an interLink connection; and without him acting as middleman, communications with the Jackals had gone dark.

CHAPTER
TWENTY-FIVE

Knowing that I might only have a minute to get out of the blast zone, I did not stop at the top of the stairs. I stepped through the splintered doorway into the living room. An alien stood in the middle of the floor, its massive silhouette forming a dark cameo against the beige curtains, which glowed against the ion light.

The alien had its rifle ready, but not pointed in my direction. Its body little more than an animated statue, the avatar might or might not have been able to hear the world around it. When our scientists dissected the bastards, they found that their ears and eyes were little more than ornamental grooves.

This alien sensed something. It spun and aimed its rifle in my direction, but I fired first. The sparkling green particle beam hit the side of the alien's head.

The bastard did not fall right away. Even as its head split open, it stood motionless, as if trying to decide whether to collapse or shoot me. Not waiting to see if I had sufficiently broken the alien, I fired again, then sprinted toward the kitchen. I stopped suddenly. Through the shattered glass of the back door, I saw three more Avatari circling the yard just outside.

Only a few seconds had passed since I had ordered Hollingsworth to set off the bombs, but the seconds hung like minutes in my mind. I ran back through the house and crashed through a front window, landing on a tree-lined avenue that ran the length of the neighborhood. The grass on the lawns had so overgrown that it spilled on to the sidewalks, but the street still looked like something out of a picture book.

I saw three avatars hunting along the street and there might have been more in the brush. At the end of the block, I could see a Jackal stopped beside a tree. At first glance, it looked parked and abandoned; but when I used telescopic lenses, I saw burns on the hood, a blackened windshield, and holes in the doors. From where I crouched, I could not see the turret in the back; but there would surely be a dead gunner hanging out of it.

Hollingsworth's voice came over the interLink on a frequency that every Marine would hear. "The aliens are in place, evacuate the blast zone. I repeat, evacuate the blast zone."

Several responses of "aye" and "copy that" came back over the same frequency.

Only a hundred yards, and three Avatari stood between me and that Jackal. If I crossed those yards without getting shot, and the engine still ran, I thought I might make it out of the blast zone alive.

As I prepared to make my move, the sound of breaking glass came from the back of the house. I did not look back. I held my particle pistol in my left hand, where it would be all but useless, and readied a rocket launcher in my right.

The first bolt missed my head by inches. I did not wait to see where it had come from. Instinctively, I spun and returned fire, shooting off a valuable rocket. Tossing the empty tube, I pulled another rocket and fired it at the closest alien between me and the Jackal. The rocket struck the alien in the chest, slinging its arms, head, and chest in different directions.

"Last call to evacuate the blast zone," Hollingsworth called out over the interLink. "One minute till detonation. One minute."

I ran in a zigzag pattern, snaking my way across the street, somersaulting over the hood of an old car, and sliding ass first to the ground. Light bolts slammed through the hood, the windshield, and the front tires. The car exploded in an eruption of orange and yellow and black, the force of the explosion slamming me to the ground.

That explosion must have thrown me ten feet, enough to save my life. When I looked back, I saw dozens of bolts shoot through the flames.

A few yards ahead of me, one of the aliens stepped around a hedge. I fired my last rocket, a worthless shot that went wild, hitting nothing.

Switching to my M27, I raced toward the corner. I must

have hit that damn alien a hundred times before the bastard finally fell.

As I rounded the corner, I saw broken avatars all along the street, dozens of them, along with the hulls of demolished Jackals. There had been a bloody showdown. Some of the Jackals lay on their sides instead of their wheels. One had crashed into a house.

Avatari soldiers moved along the street to my left and to my right. I fired my M27 at them, and they fired bolts at me. If they'd so much as nicked me, I would have died; but I did not have time to worry about light bolts and painful death. I tossed my M27 aside, pumped my legs as hard as I could, and kept my eyes on the door of the Jackal ahead. I focused on the holes in the driver's-side door because they riveted my attention.

The Avatari had fired several bolts into the windshield of the vehicle to bring it down. Some of the armored glass had melted, and the rest of the smoke-stained glass was nearly opaque. The door on the driver's side hung limp from a single hinge. Running as fast as I could, I took in details without analyzing them.

A bolt flew past me, spearing the turret in the rear of the Jackal. The wall of the turret fell off, revealing the head and shoulders of the dead gunner inside. His body hung from the back of the big gun.

Avatari milled around the far end of the street, beyond the Jackal, but they had not yet noticed me. Even if I'd had the rockets, I could not have fired at them. The clock was ticking.

The Jackal's engine was still running, I heard its heavy purr. The driver's door tumbled to the ground when I pulled it. Inside, the decapitated body of the driver sat belted in behind the wheel. His head was missing from the jawbone up, an unusual wound. The heat from a bolt must have boiled the fluid inside the dead man's skull, causing it to explode.

There was no time for manners, not with the Avatari on the street and the bombs about to explode. I unbuckled the dead man's harness and shoved him aside. When I slipped the Jackal into gear, the vehicle lurched forward, causing the dead man to roll toward me. I felt something hit against my armor, looked down, and found myself staring into the open tray of the dead man's mouth, his lolling tongue, the curve of teeth and molars, and the bone and muscle hinges that once connected the jawbone to a skull.

I vomited inside my helmet. God, I was like a kid fresh out of camp. Scared out of my wits, so excited I wanted to scream, sick to my stomach, and choking on the acrid fumes of my bile, I tore off my helmet and wiped my mouth. It felt good to breathe fresh air.

A bolt sheared through the passenger's side of the cab, passing through the empty seat and into the gun nest behind it. Two bolts struck the cab of the Jackal and more flashed across the hood. I could not dodge their fire. All I could do was drive and hope I would have more luck than the dead man beside me.

Leaning forward over the wheel so I could see through the melted windshield, I headed straight down the street, skidding around one corner, then another, picking up speed as I went. I dodged cars and Avatari, smacked into a curb, then pounded through a hedge before reaching the edge of the little row of houses that had survived the war. Ahead of me, the west side of Norristown stretched out like a barren wasteland.

Driving three-quarters blind, I headed west and hoped for the best. Then came the explosion. It sounded as if all of Terraneau had erupted, as if God had cupped his hands and clapped them around the planet.

A shock wave rolled across the open plain, carrying with it a wall of smoke and dust as tall as a mountain. I did not see it coming. One moment the path ahead of me was clear, the next, a shock wave struck my Jackal from behind, lifting it onto its front wheels, then dropping the rear wheels back to the ground. The road buckled and bowed, but the ground did not cave in.

Trying to land on solid ground, I gunned the engine. The Jackal shot up the side of a tall dune and took to the air over the crest. When I landed, the jolt knocked my dead copilot free from the seat, and he toppled to the floor.

Looking at the hideous remains, I felt no guilt at all. I had come to liberate a planet. In order to accomplish my objective, I had needed civilian assistance. They had a militia. Yes, this man had died, but we had defeated the Avatari with a couple hundred men and a handful of vehicles.

"You did well, Harris," I told myself. But looking at the dead man beside me, something told me I had not done as well as I had hoped.

CHAPTER
TWENTY-SIX

I was not the first Marine to vomit in his helmet, and I doubted I would be the last, but I still derided myself for doing it. I would need to turn in the helmet for cleaning before I could wear the damn thing again; and even after the cleaning, the ghost of my bile would linger for another month.

Then I remembered my new rank. As the commander of the Scutum-Crux Fleet, I could requisition new equipment anytime I specking well pleased. As I headed back to the armory, I tossed my helmet, pleased with myself for hiding the evidence of my weakness.

I had one of those moments of clarity in which the future looked so bright. We had defeated the Avatari with a tiny army, and now Thomer could set off the nuke, and we would have the planet to ourselves. No one would know about my helmet. The fleet was mine, and Ava was waiting for me back on the ship.

I found my way to the government complex, the great fortress that had once symbolized the strength of the Unified Authority in this part of the galaxy. This complex had been the seat of government in the Scutum-Crux Arm, and it would be again.

I drove down the ramp into the underground garage, convinced of my invincibility. My revelry ended the moment I stepped out of the Jackal.

"You made it out?" O'Doul broke off from a different conversation and turned his attention on me. I saw the ex–Special Forces commando in his swagger. The man was about six-three, and for the first time I realized he was not just some skinny old man, he had muscles made of scrap wire.

"You sound surprised," I said, still believing in my own immortality.

"You were in a house surrounded by aliens in the middle of a blast zone." He looked over at the Jackal. "And you fought your way out in that?"

Shrugging my shoulders, I said, "It took some damage."

Other men came to investigate the commotion. Philo Hollingsworth must have sneaked up on me. One moment there was no one beside me; but when I looked to my right a moment later, there Hollingsworth stood.

"You specking son of a bitch asshole!" O'Doul screamed, looking at the Jackal instead of me. "I told you not to go. I specking told you not to go!" Anger and anguish resonated in his voice.

He looked at me and said, "Mu took five Jackals with him. What about the others?" then looked in the cab of the battered Jackal. "Oh, no! No! No! No!"

I came over to ask what he'd seen, but O'Doul rounded on me. His dark eyes looked rabid. He grimaced, and said, "They should have left you."

Glancing over O'Doul's shoulder, I saw that the body of the dead driver still lay on the floor of the vehicle. Only then did I recognize the dead man's bloody clothing. It was the Jackal leader.

"Twelve men went to rescue you," O'Doul snarled.

"I didn't know," I whispered.

"You didn't know," O'Doul said, shaking his head. "Doctorow, Mu . . . How many people trusted you and died today?"

"Doctorow? Doctorow is dead?" I asked, remembering that he had gone off with Thomer.

"We lost contact with Thomer's transport," Hollingsworth said.

My legs went weak. I felt dizzy, almost ready to collapse. Thomer disappeared? First Herrington, now Thomer.

Then I remembered the mission. Without that bomb, we

would not be able to destroy the curtain. At most, the battle we had just fought would buy us three days without that bomb. I felt puny and impotent.

For a moment, I thought O'Doul would attack me. We stood there, all of his militiamen forming a ring around us, his eyes boring into mine. His breathing was loud. Instead of attacking me, he did something worse. He turned his back on me. He pulled the body out of the Jackal and carried it the way a man carries a child or a bride. He said, "This man was my brother, Muhammad." And then he walked away.

All the thoughts of victory and invincibility vanished from my head. The words of Nietzsche abandoned me as well. I thought about Ava waiting for me in my quarters; but this time, instead of fantasizing about sex, I thought about holding her. I wondered when and if I would ever see her again.

"When did we lose contact with Thomer?" I asked. The words came slowly. I was a man ready to fall over and looking for balance wherever I could find it. "Give me an update."

The militiamen slowly peeled away from us. I no longer mattered to them.

"Fifteen minutes ago," Hollingsworth said.

"Before or after you set off the bombs?"

"After, right after," Hollingsworth said.

"That might not be a problem," I said, seeing a ray of hope. "It might even be good. It means they're in the mines. They're placing the nuke."

"Wouldn't they have called in first?"

I shook my head. "I told him to wait for the bombs to go off, then to head in." I gave that order back when Doctorow first floated his idea about blowing up the subway tracks.

"We're still down to eighty-one men," Hollingsworth said.

When he first said this, I thought it sounded pretty good because I did not calculate Thomer and the seventy-five Marines he took into the mines in the equation. For one bright moment, I thought Hollingsworth meant that we had eighty-one men plus the seventy-six Marines placing the nuke in the mines. When I did the math, it didn't add up, and I realized he meant that only five of my men had survived our brush with the aliens.

We started the mission a few hours earlier with 250 men, and at that moment I could only confirm that six were alive. Herrington, the old leatherneck son of a bitch had survived more than thirty years of service, and now he was gone.

"How about the militia?" I asked. "How many Jackals made it back home?"

Hollingsworth shook his head. "You drove the only one that made it back."

I took a step back. We were alone now, Hollingsworth and I. We stood in a giant underground garage with the entire level to ourselves. Looking over Hollingsworth's shoulder, I saw the torn-up, broken carcass of the Jackal I had driven in, the dead gunner still peering from the turret in the back. A thin trickle of oil leaked from the seals around the Jackal's chassis, and three of its tires were flat.

I groaned.

If we did not bury our dead quickly, dogs, rats, and insects would find the men in those Jackals. They would gnaw at their flesh and pick at their bones. O'Doul was right about me. I had been the death of the men who trusted me.

Nietzsche was right as well. *When you stare into the abyss, the abyss stares back at you.* Those men had died trying to save me. I owed them a debt I could not repay.

"Just what I need, more ghosts," I muttered to myself.

"Ghosts?" Hollingsworth asked. He looked confused.

"Ghosts," I said. "If there is one thing Marines have, it's ghosts. We take them everywhere we go."

"I don't understand," Hollingsworth said.

"No, but you will," I said. As a relatively new Marine who had ridden out the Avatari invasion on a battleship, Hollingsworth had little if any combat experience. He had not lost many friends.

We saw the results of the blast before we heard from the transport. I was at the airfield helping stow gear on what was likely the last of our transports. We did not need to load the transport. If Thomer succeeded in setting off his bomb, we would leave the gear on Terraneau. If he failed, we'd be stuck on the planet, gear and all. Either way, the only reason to repack was to distract ourselves.

Paying little attention to the darkness around me, I looked out of the kettle and saw my men staring into the night sky. I trotted down the ramp and stared into the beautiful blackness with its ribbons of clouds. Above the clouds, stars sparkled like diamond shards.

"They made it," Hollingsworth said. He laughed. "God-damn, they made it."

My pilot had already picked up their radio signal by the time I reached the cockpit. "I've got them, sir," he said. A moment later, Thomer's voice came over the speaker.

"Thomer, report," I said, my hands trembling around the microphone.

"We set off the nuke."

"There's a night sky above Norristown," I said. "Did you take casualties?"

"No sir. We did not see any opposition."

"That's good news, Thomer," I said. "That's really good news." I clung to the words "no opposition" as if they were a lifeline in a stormy sea.

"I'm not sure what kind of damage we did to the planet," Thomer said. "We did a flyby, several mountains caved in after the explosion. Those mines ran several miles deeper than the ones on New Copenhagen. We never reached the bottom."

I should have expected the mines on Terraneau to be bigger than the ones on New Copenhagen. Those mines only ran a few hundred feet deep, but the Avatari had only worked on them for a couple of weeks. Who knew how long the aliens had been burrowing on Terraneau.

"Well done, Sergeant," I said. And then I told him about our defense of Norristown. Considering what we had accomplished, I did not paint a very glorious picture.

"They outnumbered you, sir," Thomer said. It helped a little. I thanked him and told him we needed to report back to the *Kamehameha* as soon as possible.

Thomer congratulated me, then he signed off.

It only took me a minute to reach Admiral Thorne. Having seen the ion curtain disappear from the atmosphere, he had expected the call.

"Congratulations, Captain."

"Thank you, sir," I said. "How does the planet look from topside?"

"The radiation readings around the Dansforth Mountain Range are off the charts. People will be avoiding that site for the next few thousand years." Thorne gave a perfunctory laugh.

Looking through the windshield of the transport, I watched Hollingsworth lead what was left of my men. Five Marines stood where 150 Marines had recently landed.

"What's the damage look like?" Thorne asked.

"I lost sixty percent of my men."

"A small price to pay to rescue a planet, Captain, but I wasn't asking about casualties. What does Norristown look like? Are there many survivors? If you know who is in charge, tell him I want to tour the city."

"The city is almost gone. I can't say what the rest of the planet looks like, but Norristown is just about a bust."

"What about Colonel Doctorow? Did you find him?"

"Yes, sir, we found Doctorow. You want the leader of Norristown . . . he's your man."

"You'll give him my message?" Thorne asked.

"Yes, sir. If it's all right with you, sir, I'd like to stay here this evening to debrief him. He should be landing shortly. I can . . ."

"As you wish, Captain. I will need to speak with him separately."

"Yes, sir," I said, my curiosity turning to paranoia. What did I know about Thorne? I still trusted him, but I wondered what he wanted to tell Doctorow.

CHAPTER
TWENTY-SEVEN

The people of Norristown might not have welcomed our visit, but they were glad to be freed. The party they threw lit the horizon.

Most of my men headed into town to join in the celebration, but I stayed back to deal with my regrets and my ghosts. I wanted some time to myself.

I spent the night in a transport, sitting in the pilot's seat. The cockpit faced east. Beyond the gates of the airfield, I saw the outskirts of Norristown. A myriad of lights marked the part of town where the locals held their celebration. I stared on past the lights to the mountains just visible on the other side of town. Beyond the mountains, the sun had already begun to rise. The sky looked like it was carved from the skin of a very ripe peach.

Romanticizing sunsets and starry skies did not fit in my nature; but after the ion curtain, I welcomed the brindle sky.

Thomer came into the cockpit and sat with me.

"What are you doing here?" I asked.

"I didn't feel like having a good time, so I came to see you."

"Thanks," I said.

"It was either that, or I could have shot up some Fallzoud."

Three or four minutes passed before we spoke again, then Thomer asked, "Do you think they're gone for good?"

I started to answer, then took a moment to consider the question again. The sun had begun to rise. Glare shone through the windshield.

"Those sons of bitches must have a million million planets under their thumb. I think they can afford to let one or two slip away," I said.

Thomer nodded. "A million million planets," he repeated. "What is that, a trillion planets? You really think that many planets exist?"

"Damn it, Thomer, I'm a Marine, not an astronomer," I said. "How the hell should I know?"

"Yeah, good point."

After that, neither of us spoke. We sat there, staring out the windshield, glad to see a sunrise.

"Captain Harris, are you in there?" The voice came from the rear of the transport.

I walked to the door and called back, "We're up in the cockpit." Without waiting for an answer, I returned to the pilot's chair and sat down.

I recognized the voice; the Right Reverend Colonel Ellery Doctorow had come to invade my privacy. Would he congratulate me for liberating his planet or berate me for killing so many of his men? I didn't care either way.

The metal soles of his boots clanged against the floor of the kettle. I heard only one set of footfalls. At least Doctorow had come alone.

He struggled up the ladder, then he said, "Permission to come aboard." There was irony in his voice, but the attempt at observing protocol seemed sincere just the same.

"Come on in," I said.

"Want me to leave?" Thomer asked.

"Don't leave on my account," Doctorow said.

Thomer did not leave, but he abandoned the copilot's chair so that Doctorow could sit. The Right Reverend looked out of place in that seat with his long hair and beard. He had not come empty-handed. He had brought a basket with a dozen bottles of Earth-brewed beer. Under different circumstances, he might have been able to sell those bottles for a hundred dollars apiece

"Are you thirsty, Sergeant?" he asked, offering Thomer the first beer. He offered me a bottle, then opened one for himself.

"Have I come at a good time?" Doctorow asked.

"It's fine," I said in a quiet voice.

"You know, Captain Harris, you had me scared when you first arrived. I thought fleet intervention would only make things worse. I was wrong." He held out his beer in a gesture of salute.

"I spoke with Fleet Command an hour ago," I said. "The last atmospheric readings came up completely clean. From what they can tell, the aliens are gone."

"Yes. Admiral Thorne gave me the same report," Doctorow said, a warm smile showing from under his beard. "A toast then, to a free planet, with afternoon skies and stars at night."

"Afternoon skies and starry nights," I repeated. We traded nods instead of tapping bottles, then we drank. Somehow he had chilled the beer. It tasted cold and fresh.

Thomer sipped his beer, enjoying the flavor. Doctorow downed most of his bottle in one long drink. I drank more like Thomer, enjoying the feel of the alcohol on my tongue.

"It almost doesn't seem real," Doctorow said. "After all those years, you chased the aliens away in a single day. Who would have known?"

"It did not go as well as I hoped," I said. "Have you spoken to O'Doul?"

"Oh yes, Kareem," Doctorow said. "He's a man who understands sacrifice. You did what you had to do. He knows that."

"Does he believe it?" I asked.

"Down deep, yes. He'll never come out and say it; but, yes, I think that is precisely what he believes."

"So what's next for you, Captain Harris?"

"Now we rebuild Terraneau," I said. "We have enough engineers and equipment to have Norristown lit and self-sustaining by the end of the month. We're all going to go hungry if we don't start building some food stores soon."

"A farming planet? Excellent," Doctorow said. "Where do you intend to set up your base?" Doctorow asked.

"Fort Sebastian," I said.

Doctorow seemed to expect that answer and shook his head. "I am not sure that will be an acceptable arrangement, Captain."

"It's not as if we have other options," I said.

He put up a hand to stop me. "Admiral Thorne told me about your situation."

"Yeah, well, I never planned on retiring in Scrotum-Crotch," I said, forgetting myself and using the Marine-speak name for the galactic arm.

"There's no need for vulgarity, Captain," Doctorow said. Our eyes locked for a second, and I saw good humor and maybe a little embarrassment in his expression. "Sorry," he said. "Force of habit from my days as a chaplain."

I apologized as well.

"I am sure we can find a more suitable arrangement. Terraneau is a large planet, surely we can find locations other than Norristown for you to use as a military base."

"I don't get it. Why can't we use Fort Sebastian?" Thomer asked.

Doctorow fixed him with a plastic smile. "It's not the base that I would object to. It's what happens to the town around it."

"So you're worried we won't behave ourselves," I said. "What is this, your own personal theocracy?"

When Doctorow answered that he was trying to foster a community, not a theocracy, I asked the question I had wanted to ask since we first met. "How did you become the king of Norristown anyway?"

Thomer shifted nervously as I asked this. On Fallzoud or off, he had a deep respect for authority.

"The bard of Norristown might be a better description," Doctorow said. He pulled his third beer out of the basket and drained it. "Anyone else for another?" He had come with twelve beers. After we each took one more, only three remained.

Outside, a new day had begun.

"Will you look at that—there's a sun in the sky over Norristown," Doctorow said. "Do you know how long it's been since I've seen one? It may not mean much to you . . ."

"It means a lot to me," I said, giving Thomer a commiserating glance. "How about you, Sergeant? Does it mean anything to you?"

Thomer nodded. "Like swimming underwater and suddenly getting your first breath of air."

"Yeah, right, like getting your first breath of air," I said, impressed with Thomer's analogy. It was too good an analogy. I would not have expected it from a Fallzoud jockey.

"Colonel Doctorow, what did you mean by the bard of Norristown?" Thomer asked.

"In a figurative sense, I am in charge because I am a singer of epic verses," Doctorow said.

"Is that what you do?" asked Thomer. He felt comfortable around Doctorow. Clearly they had bonded during their mission to the mines.

"You seem to be the man in charge," I said.

Doctorow told me the history that I had missed. He talked about the fall of Norristown and the deaths of over a million soldiers. After the aliens spread their ion curtain around the planet, the Army had managed to hold out for a month. During that entire time, Doctorow remained on active duty, delivering sermons to men who he believed had no souls and blessing the mass graves of men who he believed had no hope.

"It came to nothing," Doctorow said. "Prayers, works, faith . . . nothing."

"Sounds like you lost your faith," I said. I did not tell him about my misplaced faith. I did not think it mattered.

"Lost my faith?" Doctorow echoed. He shook his head. "I still believe there is a God, if that is what you mean by faith. But if He is anything like I picture him, He's not much of a shepherd."

"If not a shepherd, then what?" I asked.

"Just a voyeur. Just a cosmic witness. A bystander who probably thinks it's strange that we still call to Him for help when He hasn't done anything to help any of us for thousands of years. He probably hears us calling and laughs."

" 'For with the old Gods things came to an end long ago,' " I said, still spouting Nietzsche. " 'One day they laughed themselves to death.' "

"What was that?" Doctorow asked.

"It's something an old philosopher said," I said. "He said the Gods laughed themselves to death."

"Well, now there's some blasphemous bullshit," Doctorow said.

"There's no need for vulgarity, Colonel," I said, purposely trying to make my voice like Doctorow's when he had corrected me. We all laughed.

"'Gods laughed themselves to death . . .' You have to admit, it does sound pretty stupid," Thomer said.

I did not say anything. Until that moment, I had always thought it sounded mystical and wise.

Doctorow changed the subject. "Thomer says you're a Liberator clone. Is that right? He says you know you're a clone."

"That's right," I said.

"He says he knows he's a clone, too," Doctorow added.

"We do live in an age of miracles," I said. "So, you were explaining to us how you became the poet of Norristown?"

"Not so much a poet, maybe a historian," Doctorow said. "I recorded the defense of Norristown, one funeral at a time. I was like a New-Age version of Homer recalling the siege of Troy. Now you've come along and changed the ending of the story." He paused, pulled out his fourth beer, and chugged it.

"How did you end up in charge?" Thomer asked.

"Most of the line officers died. Some took their own lives. That left me the highest-ranking man on base.

"When the fighting died down, the people came to Fort Sebastian looking for protection; and I . . . I gave them the best advice of all. I told them not to fight. At the time, I told them to trust in God because God would protect them.

"As it turned out, we didn't need God to protect us. Once we stopped taking up arms, the aliens went away."

"Maybe that was how God protected them," Thomer said. We both stared at him. This was his night for deep thoughts.

"You're defending God?" I asked.

"It just seems like that's how God works," Thomer said, sounding defensive.

"That was how I rose from a chaplain to leader. Funny, it happened so gradually that I never stopped to think about it."

"So are you governor of Norristown or the whole planet?" I asked.

"I don't know," Doctorow said, thinking the question over. "I've never been outside of Norristown. We lost contact with the rest of the planet."

"Why did you put all those girls in that building?" Thomer asked.

"They're orphans," Doctorow said. "We put them there so we could keep them safe."

"Safe from whom?" I asked.

"Just safe," Doctorow said.

"The building I was in, was that a dorm for orphan boys? Were they just trying to keep themselves safe when they rigged the walls with explosives?" I asked. "They almost killed me."

"They weren't trying to hurt you, Captain Harris. They barricaded the door with a propane canister from their kitchen. It was the heaviest thing they could find. Fortunately for all of us, they were already running for the fire escape when you tossed your grenade at the door." He chuckled. "That kind of behavior is another reason why we would prefer for you to build your base away from Norristown."

PART III

THE RISE OF THE SCUTUM-CRUX FLEET

CHAPTER
TWENTY-EIGHT

Usually I rode in the cockpit, but on the ride back from Terraneau, I chose to ride in the kettle with what was left of my men. We had two transports and eighty-three men—counting pilots. The whole lot of us would have fit comfortably on one transport; divided between two birds, the gaps were conspicuous.

I sat near the rear in an especially dark corner of the cabin, sneaking glances around the kettle and browbeating myself for our losses.

"Captain Harris, do think you can find your way to the enlisted man's bar?" Private Roark asked me. I'd noticed Roark on the way down to Terraneau, he was one of those life-of-the-party types.

I heard what he said, but it sounded like he had spoken in a foreign language. Go have a drink with the men, always a good move for morale . . . assuming they want to have a drink with you. Why would they want to drink with me? I was the man who sent them out to die.

Just a day earlier, I'd told Hollingsworth I would smuggle these men into the officers' club. Now I wondered if he took that as a reward or a punishment.

I looked up at the kid but did not speak. This shook his confidence. He waited several seconds, then added, "We're going to celebrate, sir."

The *Kamehameha*'s two thousand enlisted Marines shared a single bar, a drinking hole I knew well. These men had fought hard, now it was my turn to make a show of strength. "Are we talking a one-shot deal, or are you boys planning to pull an all-nighter?"

"I can't speak for anybody else, but I'm staying till I'm too drunk to find my rack," Roark said.

"I may be late," I said. Now that I thought about it, I liked the idea of downing a few beers with the boys, but the drinks would have to wait. My priorities might have been all wrong, but they were all mine.

Roark nodded and went back to join his friends.

I heard the sigh of the boosters and knew that we had entered the docking bay. My heart thumped in my chest. Adrenaline coursed through my veins. So did testosterone, I suppose; but the reflex I was experiencing had nothing to do with combat. The landing gear clanked and groaned as we landed, and I sprang to my feet.

"Thomer, see that the gear is unloaded," I said, as we taxied through the locks.

"Yes, sir."

"If anybody asks for me, tell them I will handle debriefings tomorrow."

"Aye, aye."

The miserable doors of the kettle ground open so slowly. I did not wait until they slid all the way apart. As soon as I could squeeze through the gap, I trotted down the ramp and out the docking bay. My men probably thought I needed to get to a bathroom.

And, in a way, I did.

Men saluted me as I rushed down the hall. I returned their salutes and hurried on. I was a Marine on a mission. I reached my quarters and opened the door to find an empty room with a neatly made bed. The door closed behind me.

"Ava," I called in a soft voice.

Nothing.

For a moment, and just a moment, I worried that something had gone wrong. That thought passed quickly. I opened the bathroom door and switched on the light. Hearing a faint gasp, a sound so soft I could easily have missed it, I turned toward the shower.

The bedroom appeared clean and completely untouched, but the bathroom looked lived in. A bouquet of empty MRE pouches filled the wastebasket, a set of utensils lay in the sink, and a shadow moved behind the glass of my shower stall door.

"If you don't come out of there, I'm going to have to come in," I said.

I heard a soft giggle, and the water in the shower began to run.

"So that's how it's going to be," I said. I pulled the shower door open, and there she was, dressed in a tank top and panties, allowing the warm water to splash her hair and back. She looked at my combat armor, and said, "Honey, I was hoping you would be hard, but this is ridiculous."

We showered together, and we made love. Afterward, we lay in bed. I stroked her wet hair and kissed her. Dreading her reaction, I told her I needed to go to the bar for drinks with my men, but she just cocked an eyebrow and smiled.

"You're not upset?" I asked.

"I will be if you come back empty-handed."

I drank with my boys and grabbed a few beers before leaving the bar. On my way back, I stopped by the mess hall and picked up food for two. By the time I made it back to my quarters, I had a small salad, sandwiches, fruit cocktails, cheesecake, and four beers.

Always cautious, Ava remained hidden in the bathroom when I entered. Instead of calling out to her, I spread our meal across my desk.

I called out, "I hope you're hungry," and out she came.

She looked at the food, then looked at me with her "this is better than sex" smile, and I knew that I had graduated from benefactor/lover to friend.

Ava and I ate together and talked. She wanted to know everything that happened on Terraneau. I told her about Herrington first, then about the rest of my men. She squeezed my hand and stopped eating, but said nothing.

I thought that was the perfect response. If she had tried to empathize with me, she would have driven me away. I had been through something she could not possibly comprehend.

When I asked what it was like hiding out in my quarters, she said, "I talked to myself. I hid in the bathroom talking to myself, and I never ran out of things to say. It beat living with Teddy. At least I had somebody to talk to."

"What did you talk about?"

"With Teddy?"

"When I was gone," I said.

"I talked about you," she said. "I talked to myself about every man I have ever been with, and I compared them to you."

By this time we were in bed, both of us naked. I had my arms around her. She felt warm. "How did I do?"

"Uhm?" she purred.

"How did I do?" I asked.

"Now, what kind of question is that?" she asked.

"An honest one," I said.

"Harris, I never thought of you as the insecure type."

"I have my moments," I said. I pulled her in even tighter than before, so that everything from our shoulders to our thighs pressed together.

"Ouch," she cooed.

"Are you going to answer me?" I asked.

"I don't know why I would," she said. "If I say you are better than any of them, you won't believe me. If I say some of them were better than you, you'll get jealous. I think I'll just plead the First."

"The right to free speech?" I asked.

"The right to tell you to shut the speck up, Harris."

"Oh," I said. We lay there in each other's arms. I wondered how I matched up with Ted Mooreland. When I began to feel insecure, I thought about how I compared to General Smith. As my thoughts drifted, I started to fall asleep.

"I wasn't telling you to let me go," Ava complained. I had not actually let her go, but I had loosened my grip around her. "What is it like down there?"

I told Ava about the building with the orphan girls. I told her how my men found it and how Doctorow had tried to protect it. When I finished, she laughed, and said, "It sounds terrible, like a monastery."

When I did not respond, she said, "Oh God, you're not thinking about . . ."

"You'll be safe there," I said.

"With the latter-day vestal virgins?" she asked. "That's not safekeeping, Honey, that's solitary confinement."

"You wouldn't need to stay there long, just until we get the planet sorted out. It can't be any worse than hiding in the shower and talking to yourself."

She started to say something and stopped. She shifted on the pillow until our faces were only three inches apart, then she reached up and stroked my eyebrow with a finger. "How did you get this scar over your eye?"

"Are you trying to change the subject?" I asked.

"No," she said in a childlike, flirtatious way. "How did you get that scar?"

"I got it in a fight," I said.

"But Marines wear helmets. Wouldn't your helmet protect you?"

"It was a fight, not a battle."

"Like in a bar?"

"Not in a bar, in a ring,"

"Oh?" She reached around my back, where four parallel scars ran across my ribs. "How about these scars."

"Same fight," I said.

"These must have hurt," she said.

"They did," I said.

"How many men were you fighting?"

"Just one," I said.

"I hope you hurt him, back."

"I did."

"As bad as he hurt you?"

"He died."

Silence. I made a mental note not to tell Ava about killing people right after making love.

"You've killed a lot of people, haven't you, Harris?" she asked.

I did not want to talk about it. Stealing a page from her playbook, I tried to change the subject. "When you make movies, what's it like doing a love scene?"

"It depends on the actor," Ava said, the flirtatious tones drained from her voice. I had hit a nerve; but, on the bright side, I had successfully changed the subject.

I named a few actors and Ava told me she despised all of them. According to the gossip, she'd had off-screen romances with every last one of them.

I thought about her undressing in love scenes with actors she didn't like. Maybe it was like killing, maybe you just got used to it. Maybe she'd just gotten used to me, too. I did not want to think about that.

As I finally started to fall asleep, a parade of ghosts invaded my thoughts. I saw Herrington, white-haired and good-humored Herrington. I thought about transports falling through the atmosphere. And I thought about ghosts from other wars, too.

I brought in a large breakfast of eggs, toast, and bacon the next morning and told Ava my plans while we ate. I would meet with Admiral Thorne in a few hours, and I hoped to tour the ship with Master Chief Warshaw; but first, I had a staff meeting.

After breakfast, I went to the conference room, where I met Thomer and Hollingsworth. We all arrived on time, then we sat and we waited, and waited. The sailors arrived at the meeting thirty minutes late.

"Where is Warshaw?" I asked, as I surveyed the table.

"He couldn't get away," said Senior Chief Petty Officer Lilburn Franks.

"Couldn't get away?" I asked. "This is a staff meeting." Under normal circumstances, I would have sent an aide to collect Warshaw. Attendance at staff meetings was never optional. "Do you know what he is doing?" I asked Franks.

He shrugged in a casual, offhand way.

I could already feel my blood pressure rising. Part of me wanted to go Machiavellian—to crush the insubordination at the start and make an example of Warshaw. I decided to take the "making friends and influencing people" route instead, against my better judgment.

"I hear you and your boys saw action. What did you come back with, about one-third of your men?" That quip came from Senior Chief Petty Officer Perry Fahey. He stared in my direction, his heavily made-up eyes locked on mine, daring me to react.

Sitting beside me, Thomer took this in but said nothing. I had the feeling he had recently dropped a load of Fallzoud.

When the drug wore off, though, I thought Thomer might have a thing or two to say.

"Perhaps you see some humor in battlefield losses, Senior Chief," I said.

"Humor?" he asked.

"Is there something funny about the deaths of 170 Marines?"

"Um, well, no." Fahey looked up and down the table, hoping for support from the other sailors. They all looked away. Senior Chief Franks looked at his computer. The guy next to him straightened his cuffs. Another stared down into his lap.

"I lost a close friend in that action, Senior Chief, Sergeant Lewis Herrington. Do you remember Herrington? He attended our last staff meeting."

"I remember the sergeant."

"He died liberating Terraneau." When I used the term "liberate," it sent a shock through the room. Coming from someone with my background, the word carried an implicit threat. "Is there a joke I am missing here, Senior Chief? If there is, I would sure as speck love to be in on it."

"No, sir," Fahey said.

"Herrington died scouting for the enemy. Is that funny, asshole?"

This was Hollingsworth's first staff meeting. He had come to fill Herrington's seat. Hearing this verbal mugging, Hollingsworth looked nervous.

"No, sir. I am sure Sergeant Herrington was a good man," Fahey said, but he still had a slight smile at the corners of his mouth. He should have been smiling; he had just accomplished his private mission without my suspecting a thing. He had distracted me. Gary Warshaw was now the furthest thing from my mind.

Officers in the Marines do not think like their counterparts in the Navy. The intrigues of Fleet Command were entirely new to me.

Still trying to calm myself down, I introduced the new addition to our council. "This is Master Sergeant Philo Hollingsworth. Sergeant Hollingsworth will take over Herrington's responsibilities."

I got the feeling that a few of the officers knew Hollings-worth. Nobody congratulated him, however. We all sat mute.

"Let's get started," I said. "With Warshaw gone, that puts you on the hot seat, Senior Chief Fahey. What's your schedule for Terraneau?"

"My staff is overseeing that project," Senior Chief Petty Officer Jim Milton offered. "I landed a team of engineers in Norristown at 0600.

"Their preliminary reports are optimistic. After surveying the damage around Norristown, they say they can restore the power grid by the end of the week."

"For all of Norristown?" I asked, remembering that most of the city was little more than rubble.

"The north, east, and central sectors, where most of the people live."

"How soon can they get the juice going citywide?"

"The prospects look good, sir. The power plants were outside the city, in an area that the aliens never attacked. From what we've seen so far, the underground power lines are still in place, except in one area just west of town. Apparently an underground train system collapsed in that part of town."

Hollingsworth and I exchanged glances. We knew all about that particular disaster.

"What about Fort Sebastian?" I asked.

"Same thing, sir. We'll have it ready for your Marines in the next week."

"Captain Harris, I heard you were going to restrict the use of that base," said Franks, the ranking NCO on the battleship *Washington*.

"That is correct," I said.

Even before I finished speaking, Franks said, "You can't be serious about that. These men have not had shore leave for four years."

"The locals are nervous about having us around. I don't want to do anything to upset them."

"It sounds to me like somebody else is calling the shots around here," sneered Fahey.

"Colonel Doctorow said . . ." I started.

"He's got you licking his boots does he?" With this statement, Fahey graduated from contempt to outright insubordination. Once again believing he had the other NCOs watching his back, he became downright fearless.

"We need Doctorow's cooperation," I said, hating myself for trying to justify my decision.

Fahey looked up one side of the table, then the other, and said, "Doctorow is no big deal. Show him who's in charge. Haul his ass up to the *Washington*, and we'll straighten him out. We're calling the shots in this corner of the galaxy.

"I mean, speck, according to his records, the bastard is absent without leave. If he's a specking criminal, throw him in the brig."

In the moment of silence that followed, Fahey made a show of rolling his eyes. Franks, sitting beside him, chuckled. The two of them exchanged some private joke, speaking so quietly that no one else could hear them.

All of this positioning ran counter to my Liberator genetics and my Marine training. I wanted to kick the chair out from under Fahey's ass. If Franks joined in to help him, so much the better. I even felt the beginnings of the combat reflex, testosterone and adrenaline entering my bloodstream at a very unwelcome time.

Fahey went on. "I'll let you in on a secret, Harris. If you plan on running this Arm, you need my crew a hell of a lot more than you need Doctorow." He was baiting me. He was trying to get me to threaten him. He leaned back in his chair, batted his heavily made-up eyes at me, and drummed his fingers on the table.

I knew that I could gain nothing by playing his game. So there we sat, nobody speaking, a verbal standoff in an undeclared mutiny. The standoff lasted for nearly a minute, no one wanting to be the first one to speak. The first officer to do so would lose face.

I was the one who ended it. "Where do we stand on the blockade?"

"What blockade?" asked Franks.

"I issued orders for a blockade around Terraneau," I said. "I sent those orders to Master Chief Warshaw. Do you know if he received them?"

"He did," Fahey interrupted, offering no more information.

"And do you know if he has drawn up plans for the blockade?"

"Yes."

"Yes? Yes, he drew up plans?"

"Yes, I know if he drew up the plans," answered Fahey, a smug grin forming on his lips.

Taking a deep breath, fighting the urge to rip the man's throat out, I asked, "Okay, so has he drawn up plans, Senior Chief?"

"Nope."

"Do you know why he has not carried out my orders?"

"He was busy, so he passed the orders to me." Fahey raised a hand to stop me, the way a senior officer might raise a hand to quiet a subordinate. But I was not a subordinate. I was the senior officer in the meeting. "I have not drawn up the plans. There's no point to establishing a blockade around a planet in an arm that we have all to ourselves.

"We're the only ones here, sir. Haven't you figured that out?"

If Herrington had been here, he might well have pulled his gun and shot Fahey on the spot. Old-school Marines like Herrington had no time for this kind of shit. God I missed Herrington.

This time, however, Fahey had given me all the ammunition I would need. "Okay, Senior Chief, so you have taken it upon yourself to countermand Master Chief Warshaw's orders. Is that correct? Before I have you arrested, would you like to explain why you have ignored a direct order from Master Chief Warshaw?"

It had not occurred to Fahey that he had unintentionally attached Warshaw to the orders. The self-satisfied grin suddenly melted. "Captain, I guess I do not see why Terraneau would need a protective blockade."

"You don't?" I asked.

Now he was in full retreat. "No, sir. We have no enemies in this Arm, the Broadcast Network is down, and the aliens do not use ships. Having a blockade won't make a bit of difference if they return."

"And you only comply with orders you agree with? Is that correct, Senior Chief?" I asked.

"No, sir," he said.

"Fahey, are you unable to obey orders or simply selective about which orders you follow?" I snapped out each syllable of each word, speaking slowly. "Should I charge you with dereliction of duty or mutiny?"

"Mutiny?"

"Okay, mutiny it is," I said.

"No, no, I was asking you, are you charging me with mutiny?"

"Master Chief Warshaw gave you an order, and you chose to ignore it. He did give you the order to draw up a blockade? Is that correct?"

"Yes, sir."

"And you decided against it?"

"I can draw up the plans and have them to you within the hour," Fahey said.

"That would be acceptable, Senior Chief," I said.

I turned to the other men in the room, and asked, "Do any of the rest of you have concerns that I need to know about?" When none of them said anything, I ended the meeting.

Watching the various NCOs file out of the room, I took stock of my situation. My fleet was stranded in space, my first lieutenant was openly mutinous, and the captain of my Marines had a Fallzoud habit. The only planet my fleet could reach wanted nothing to do with us, and I wanted to start a war with the nation that had created me. I wondered if things could get any worse.

I soon discovered that they could.

CHAPTER
TWENTY-NINE

"You need to bust that prick down," Thomer said, once the sailors left the room. "Slam his gay ass in the brig."

"He isn't gay," said Hollingsworth.

"What do you mean he isn't gay?" Thomer asked. "The son of a bitch comes to staff meetings wearing makeup."

"Why do you think he wants to get to Norristown so bad?" Hollingsworth shouted the question. "Thomer, you don't know how good you had it."

As always, Thomer received that last comment with a certain lethargy. In an unnaturally subdued voice, he said, "We were massacred by aliens and locked in relocation camps."

"That's not what I meant. I know they ran you through the wringer." Thomer's slow demeanor had a calming effect on Hollingsworth. He lowered his voice.

"The enlisted men on this ship have not seen a woman for four years. Until you guys came with plans to retake Terraneau, we had no reason to think any of us would ever see one again. Do you know what that does to a man?

"They're clones, Thomer, not eunuchs. If anything, their gonads are too active.

"Given a choice between a few months in a prison camp and a life sentence on a ship with nothing but men, which way would you go?"

"What about the makeup?" I asked.

Hollingsworth shrugged his shoulders and said, "Most clones would much rather give than receive. Men who are a little more, er, uh, flexible wear makeup to identify themselves."

"You thought you would never see a woman again?" Thomer asked. Sympathy showed in his eyes, but the downturn at the corners of his mouth made it clear he found the whole thing revolting.

"Wait, now . . . You and Fahey didn't . . . you know?" I asked.

"No," Hollingsworth said. "We weren't even on the same ship."

"Did you . . . you know?"

"Thomer, I didn't think I'd ever see any scrub again."

"Yeah, I guess so," Thomer said, sounding unconvinced.

It was time to put my cards on the table.

I looked over at Thomer and said, "Sergeant, I need to have a private chat with Sergeant Hollingsworth." He left without saying a word.

I could not trust Fahey and probably not Warshaw. Lilburn Franks seemed more interested in running the fleet than politics, but he was the only one. Because of the normally adversarial relationship between swabbies and sea soldiers, I thought I could count on Hollingsworth and the other Marines who came with the fleet. I hoped I could.

Now that it was just me and Hollingsworth in the room, I turned to him, and said, "Do you know what happens if you kill all the rattlesnakes? You get silent snakes instead.

"The only reason I didn't bust Fahey on the spot was because I always know where he stands. He's an asshole, but he telegraphs his punches, and that makes him useful. Warshaw's a different story."

"Warshaw's all right," Hollingsworth said. Nervous that I had asked Thomer to leave, Hollingsworth went into full-fledged fight-or-flight mode. He paced the floor, rapped his knuckles on the table, and spoke in an unnecessarily loud voice. "I know Warshaw much better than I know Fahey, we've been on the same ship for six years. He's all right."

"You thought Fahey was cool, too," I pointed out.

"I still do," Hollingsworth said. "He's a good sailor. He just . . ."

"He practically declared a mutiny," I yelled. "He's trying to pick a fight with me. Do you know what would happen if I let him goad me into a specking war? Which way do you think his sailors will go?"

Hollingsworth sat down. He leaned back in his chair and considered the question but did not answer.

"Right or wrong, every sailor in Scrotum-Crotch is going

to side with Fahey if I bust him," I said. "Think about that . . . and while you mull it over, I have another question for you. Where are your loyalties?" I fixed Hollingsworth with an angry glare.

He met my eyes and did not look away. "You know where I stand. I'm a Marine."

"Good," I said.

"So if it comes down to a fight between me and Warshaw, I have you at my back?"

"Yes, sir," Hollingsworth said.

"What if they accuse me of going against regulations?"

"Then I guess we both go to the brig."

"How about Unified Authority law?" I asked.

This time Hollingsworth took longer to answer. "What are you talking about?"

Now I spoke slowly and very clearly, making sure he caught the significance of every word. "Hollingsworth, if you have any questions about where your loyalties lie, you need to speak up. You are either all in or you're out."

"I'm in," he said. "I'm all in."

I took a deep breath, then I said what I had been hiding. "I want to declare war on the Unified Authority."

A heavy silence hung over the room like a storm cloud waiting to burst. I was not joking, and he knew it. "Does Thomer know what you have in mind?"

"He does," I said. On the flight back from Terraneau, I'd told Thomer exactly what I wanted to do.

"What kind of war? They're a trillion miles away," Hollingsworth said. "Don't waste your breath if you're planning to declare independence; they won't care. You'll just give Warshaw more ammunition to shoot you down."

"What if we can take the fight to Earth?" I asked.

"Attack Earth?" Hollingsworth mostly mouthed the words.

"Attack Earth," I said.

"Take my word on this one, Captain Harris, you can't hit them without a self-broadcasting fleet. Every man on this ship has spent the last four years of his life trying to figure out a way to get out of here. There is no way out."

"Would you come along for the ride if there was a way out?"

"You're serious about this?" Hollingsworth asked. "You're really serious about this?"

"Sergeant, you know why we are out here. How do you feel about being abandoned on the outer edge of known space?"

"Have you discussed any of this with Warshaw? Sooner or later he's going to need to hear about this," Hollingsworth pointed out.

"Yeah, I know."

"So how do we get back to Earth?" Hollingsworth asked.

I told Hollingsworth something that I had told to only one other person—Thomer. I told him about a self-broadcasting fleet that was even larger than the Earth Fleet. The only problem was that all of its ships had been destroyed.

CHAPTER
THIRTY

Three days after we returned from Terraneau, I called Hollingsworth over the ship intercommunications system. "Sergeant, I hear you know how to fly a transport."

"I haven't logged many hours, but I had the training," he said. "There's not much to it."

"I have an errand I need to run on Terraneau," I said. "Think you can take me?"

"Yes, sir," he said.

"It's a private matter, Sergeant. Do you think you can keep a lid on it?"

"Yes, sir, I won't discuss it with anyone, sir," he said.

"Meet me in the docking bay, in thirty minutes. I already have a transport signed out."

Ava seemed excited to leave. I took this personally, of course. In my mind, she wasn't leaving the ship behind, she was leaving me. When I asked her why she was so excited to go, she talked about "solitary confinement" in my quarters and days spent hiding in the shower.

I watched her dress in her combat armor. She stepped into boots that made her three inches taller. Then she strapped on the various plates, rigid scales that camouflaged her sensuous curves and contours.

"Are you going to miss me?" I asked.

"Of course I will miss you," she said, examining herself in the mirror. I sounded needy and hated myself for it. She sounded unaware of me, and I hated her even more.

"Are you nervous?" I asked.

"Not at all." She combed her hair with her fingers, spreading the silky strands out, then twisted it into a knot so that it did not fall below the base of her helmet.

"I'll talk to Doctorow. I'll explain everything."

"Of course you will," she said.

"He'll take care of you."

"I'm sure he will, darling." She fitted the helmet down over her head. I had hoped she would kiss me before she sealed herself in her helmet, but I suppose it did not occur to her. She turned to me, and asked, "How do I look?"

"Like a Marine," I said.

"We should get going," she said, as she started for the door. Then she stopped. I hoped she would take the helmet off and kiss me. Who knew what might have happened if she did, we could afford to be a few minutes late. But she looked back, and said, "Maybe you should go first, Harris. You know, just in case someone's in the hall."

I stepped out the hatch, looked up and down the corridor, then brought her out.

The docking bays were on the same deck as the Marine compound. It only took a few short minutes to walk to the bay. Hollingsworth had the transport open, and we walked in.

He met us in the kettle. Hollingsworth and I wore our Charlie service uniforms. Ava, of course, had needed to keep her armor on. She looked out of place, like a man in a suit and tie on a beach.

"Sergeant Hollingsworth, this is Corporal Rooney," I said.

Ava knew enough about Marines etiquette to pass. Trained

actress that she was, she used body language to convey a lack of interest in Hollingsworth. She walked up the ramp, leaving Hollingsworth and me in the bay.

As Ava moved away, Hollingsworth asked me. "Why is he dressed in armor? Is he on some kind of field mission?"

"Don't ask," I said. "Everything dealing with Corporal Rooney is on a need-to-know basis."

A grim expression crossed Hollingsworth's face, and he acknowledged this with a nod. "Yes, sir," he said. "I'll take us out."

It only took fifteen minutes to fly the three thousand miles from the *Kamehameha* to the airfield. Ava and I spent the time in the dark and silence of the kettle, sitting side by side on the wooden bench that ran along the walls. She kept her helmet on in case Hollingsworth came down. We did not hold hands, and we spoke very little. I did not want to risk Hollingsworth's overhearing us. How could I explain hiding a woman aboard the ship to a man who had not seen a woman in years?

Moments after the transport touched down, and the kettle doors opened, Hollingsworth slid down the ladder and asked me if he should "keep the meter running?" I told him that I needed to drive Corporal Rooney into town and asked him to inspect the engineers' progress around the airfield while I was gone.

"Is Rooney coming back to the *Kamehameha* with us?" he asked.

"I don't see how that is any of your specking business, Sergeant," I said. He saluted and left to inspect the airfield.

Ava and I drove a jeep into town. When we'd planned this errand, I had told her that she should keep her helmet on for the short ride. I now regretted the decision. It's hard to speak to people in combat armor. They can hear you, and you can hear them, but the conversation passes through electronic filters.

Driving through the eastern outskirts of Norristown, I asked Ava, "Are you excited?"

"Honey, are you joking? I haven't changed my clothes for three months now."

"You had the tank tops," I pointed out.

"Marine tank tops and boxers don't count. They're not *clothes*, they're *gear*."

"Are you looking forward to anything besides a new dress?" I asked.

"Yes," she said. "I want to go for long walks in new clothes. And I want to talk with people."

"We talked," I said. In truth, I had spoken more with her than with just about anyone ever.

"No offense, dear, but I mean other girls. Talking to Marines is nice, but it's not girl talk. You're sweet, but you're all guy. Take my word on this one, there are a lot of things that guys do not understand." These words and the feminine voice coming from the combat helmet played nasty tricks with my mind.

After that, I felt tongue-tied.

"Are you going to be okay, Harris?" she asked.

"Yeah, of course," I said.

"You know, you're pretty silly," she said. "You're never going to be very far away. I mean, how far can you get? You're stuck here just like the rest of us." She laughed.

We entered the city center, or what was left of it, and Ava became silent. She looked around, taking in the devastation. The way she gripped the side of the jeep, her armor-gloved hands curled like claws, she reminded me of a nervous new Marine riding a truck into a battle.

I could not hear what was happening inside Ava's helmet, but I imagined her terror at seeing the broken world. She might be fighting to breathe.

"It's okay, Ava," I said, stroking her back and realizing she would not feel my hand. "They're gone. The aliens are gone. They're gone for good. You'll be safe here."

"Wayson, maybe I should go back to the ship," she said.

I pulled the jeep over and cut off the engine. Placing my hands on her shoulders, I turned Ava so that she faced me. I wanted to remove the helmet so I could be sure her eyes stayed on mine. "They are gone. You will be safe on this planet."

"But what if they come back?" she asked.

"They won't," I said, though I had no way of knowing

whether that was true. I would protect her if they did, though. I knew that much.

"I didn't know it would look like this," she said. "I don't know if I can ever feel safe here."

"You'll be safe enough. Besides, you know what they have here that we don't have on the ship?"

She shook her head. The movement was barely perceptible with the helmet over her head.

"They have dress shops."

"But what if . . ."

"And shoe stores."

"Can you protect . . ."

"And jewelry stores."

"Damn it, Harris, you are such a specking guy."

"Thank you," I said.

"It's not a compliment." She laughed. Her laugh sounded like a metallic shutter coming through the audio equipment in her helmet. She took off her helmet, shook out her hair, and said, "If the women on this planet are anything like they were back in Hollywood, all the good stores will have been looted."

I was sorry to see her go. When Ava turned brassy and sarcastic, that was when I liked her best. I wondered how quickly she would forget me.

As we approached the three buildings the locals used for dorms, Ava's confidence dried up. She looked around at all the flat land and the rubble dunes. "This was a city?" she asked. She had to know what it had been.

"The aliens that hit this place four years ago, they're all gone now. We chased them away," I said.

"But how can you be sure?" she asked.

"They haven't returned to New Copenhagen," I said. "It's been two and a half years now."

I could hear her breathing. Her nervousness seemed to carry on the wind. "Maybe this isn't a good idea."

"You'll be safe," I said. I repeated myself, then I told her to put on her helmet. I did not want anyone to spot her until she was safely with Doctorow. I gave her a moment to adjust to her new surroundings and drove the rest of the way to the dorms.

Per my request, Doctorow met us at the dorms. Also per my request, he came alone. He had plenty of opportunity to hide observers or even snipers around the area, but I did not think that was his style.

He came wearing Army fatigues with the blouse unbuttoned and a T-shirt beneath.

"I did not expect you back so soon, Captain," Doctorow said, as I climbed out of my jeep.

"I have something to discuss in private," I said.

Looking past me and toward my jeep, Doctorow said, "We're still not alone."

"Actually, that's the reason I came."

He leaned into me and spoke in an angry tone. "Captain Harris, I hope you don't expect me to let this man anywhere near my dorm building. That is simply out of the question. Only a fool permits a weasel to enter his chicken coop."

As Doctorow spoke, I nodded to Ava, and she removed her helmet.

"How about an additional hen?" I asked.

Her hair now hung in a disheveled knot and her "queer gear" makeup was not the right shade for her eyes, but her skin was pale as a cloud and just as luminous.

"Good God," Doctorow said.

Ava smiled, and said in her softest, most flirtatious voice, "There's no need for profanity." Hoping she would make an optimal first impression, I had prepped Ava to say this the first time anybody made an off-color comment. I had planned on slipping the word "speck" into something I said. This was better.

"Ava, this is Colonel Ellery Doctorow," I said.

"Hello, Colonel Doctorow, I'm Ava Gardner," she said in a low husky voice that left men helpless.

"I see that," Doctorow said mechanically, his eyes transfixed.

She climbed out of the jeep, shook out her hair, and let it fall around her shoulders. She looked like a child wearing an adult's armor.

"I heard rumors that she was, I mean that you were, there are all kinds of stories about you being . . ."

". . . a clone?" she asked, finishing the sentence.

I felt a momentary jolt of pity for Doctorow. The gaze Ava gave him had always stripped away my confidence. When she turned on the charm, she left me feeling like an inferior species, like a caveman watching a ballerina.

Pity gave way to envy when Ava's gaze did not shift back toward me. I wondered if perhaps Ava had gotten what she needed out of me, and envy turned into embarrassment. I remembered the things Ava had told me about Ted Mooreland and General Smith and wondered what she might say about me.

"What brings you to Norristown?" Doctorow asked.

"She needs a place to stay," I said, pointing to the building for girls.

"Would that be okay with you, Colonel?" Ava asked, her eyes still holding him captive.

"No offense, ma'am, but you're a bit old to room with these girls," he said.

"Who takes care of them? They must need tutors and nannies. I can cook or clean." She sounded downright domesticated, the perfect little housewife/sex goddess.

"I think she will be a lot safer here than on a ship," I said.

"I see what you mean," Doctorow conceded, though he seemed to have his doubts. He thought for a moment. "Of course she can stay. Of course."

"Well, I guess my business is done here," I said as I turned to leave, knowing that the empty pain I felt at the moment would turn into bitterness soon enough.

Both Ava and Doctorow stood rooted in place. I wondered if they even noticed, then she yelled, "Harris!"

I turned, and saw her running toward me. She crashed into me, which might have been a pleasant experience if she hadn't been wearing hardened combat armor. When she threw her armor-plated arms around me, her custom-made exoskeleton dug into my shoulders. She pressed her mouth against mine.

"What kind of a good-bye was that?" she asked.

"I thought you were done with me," I said.

"I swear, Harris, you are such a guy." She smiled as she

said this, her face just a few inches from mine. "I'll be waiting for you." She rubbed her armored shell against me, and added, "Come back soon."

"As soon as I can," I said.

"Sooner," she said.

"Sooner," I said.

THIRTY-ONE

Feeling like my life had headed in a good direction, I rode with Hollingsworth in the cockpit on the way back to the *Kamehameha*. He reported on the progress our engineers had made erecting hangars along the airfield. I didn't really care what the engineers had or had not accomplished. I had Ava on my mind.

Maybe I was in love, maybe I was just more deeply in lust than I had ever been. I liked her strength. Sure, she'd panicked while we drove through Norristown, but so had some of my Marines.

As we took off, I searched the skies for traces of the ion curtain and came up dry. We cut across a clear blue sky, which faded white, then darkened into blackness as we climbed. Hollingsworth suggested ways to build rapport between the Marines and sailors under my command, and I pretended to listen. Off in the distance, I saw a giant disc floating in the darkness and realized that it was a broadcast station. The network was made up of mile-wide satellites.

I still had Ava on my mind, but I did what I could to hide my excitement from Hollingsworth and from myself. As we approached the fleet, I stared at the various ships, their triangular outlines reminding me of moths and wedges. Hollingsworth located the *Kamehameha* in the logjam and got us clearance to land.

He was a good pilot. He brought us in smooth and fast, and touched us down gently. I still missed Herrington, the old veteran with whom I had fought some major battles, but Philo Hollingsworth was a good Marine.

The sled brought us through the locks and into the docking bay. With the docking bay in control of his transport, Hollingsworth powered down the engines and switched off the cockpit controls. Once he finished, we headed down into the kettle.

"You know, Captain Harris, I was thinking about Fahey. He's okay. I mean he popped off pretty bad in that meeting, but do you blame him? I mean, he's got to be desperate to find some scrub." Hollingsworth dispensed this advice as the kettle doors opened.

"I hope you're right, Sergeant, because I'm going to flatten the specker next time he crosses me," I said. I wished Hollingsworth had not brought up Fahey. The mere thought of him made my stomach tense.

"Okay, well, what I really want to say, sir, is give Warshaw a fair break. He's not like Fahey. He's a stand-up officer. We've been on the same boat for four years now, and I can tell you, he's not the kind of guy that shoots you in the back."

"Speak of the devil," I muttered.

Across the deck, Master Chief Petty Officer Gary Warshaw stood shouting orders to a pack of sailors. When he saw us, he worked up a smile and came bounding in our direction. I noted the spring in his step and decided it did not bode well. No matter what Hollingsworth said, this man was no friend.

In his right hand, Warshaw carried a folder with the seal of the Office of the Navy. Parking himself at the base of the ramp, the master chief looked up at me and saluted. "Captain Harris, may I have a private word with you, sir?"

Hollingsworth excused himself, shooting me an I-told-you-so self-satisfied smirk. He must have thought Warshaw had come to shake hands and ask to be my buddy. I made a mental note: reliable or not, Hollingsworth was a piss-poor judge of character.

"What can I do for you, Master Chief?" I asked, trying to smother the voice in my head. I got the same feeling in my gut dealing with sailors that I got pulling the pins from live grenades.

"I hope you don't mind, sir, but I asked Admiral Thorne if he would join us," Warshaw said, looking slightly apologetic.

"Not a problem," I said, ignoring the tightening knot in my stomach. I really wanted to kill this man. I could feel the beginnings of a combat reflex. My nervous system did not differentiate between war and infighting.

Warshaw led me out of the landing area without any further explanation, and I followed without asking.

"I'm sorry I missed your staff meeting the other day. I hear you and Fahey had some friction."

"You might say that," I agreed. "Fahey seems to think he can ignore my orders."

"I'll have a word with him about that," Warshaw said, sounding a little embarrassed. I took that as a good sign.

After that, the conversation trailed off. Trying to restart the collegial patter, Warshaw said, "Congratulations on liberating Terraneau. That's quite an accomplishment."

"I lost most of my men," I said. "I'm not entirely sure that congratulations are in order."

"You rescued a planet with a handful of Marines; congratulations are in order," Warshaw said. He was all muscles and smiles, a man trying too hard to be my friend. "I haven't seen the official report, but I understand the fighting was fierce."

There was no official report; I had not written it yet. I did not point this out, though. If Warshaw wanted to be my buddy, I would go along for the ride. Maybe he would reveal a few of his cards.

He didn't. He chatted me up as we walked most of the length of the ship, finally ending up in a conference room near the bridge. Thorne had already arrived. The normally passive admiral sat at the table looking irritable, his thin lips pursed and his eyes not quite meeting ours as we entered the room.

As a man holding the rank of master chief petty officer, Warshaw did not have the authority to call commissioned officers to meetings. He did not seem to care. Paying no attention to the look on Admiral Thorne's face, he slid into the conference room and took a seat.

"What is this about?" Thorne asked as I sat down. Apparently he thought this meeting was my idea.

I shrugged.

"Actually, Admiral, I called this meeting, sir," Warshaw said. "Well, maybe not me. I suppose you would say that Admiral Brocius is calling the shots."

"Admiral Brocius?" Thorne repeated. "He's back in Washington."

"Yes, sir," Warshaw said.

An embarrassed smile wormed its way across Warshaw's mouth, and he said, "I took the liberty of traveling to Earth."

"You what?" asked Admiral Thorne, his voice hard but low.

"I caught a ride back to Earth on the last transfer ship," Warshaw said.

"Unless one of my senior officers approved that trip, you were absent without leave, Master Chief," Thorne said.

"You'll need to take that up with Admiral Brocius, Admiral. He approved my leave . . . retroactively." Warshaw placed the folder with the Office of the Navy seal on the table and pulled two envelopes from it.

He slid Admiral Thorne an envelope with his name on it, then he handed me one with my name as well. A small triangle of foil sealed the back of the envelope—an automated security seal. When I pressed my thumb against the foil, it read my thumbprint and curled open.

As I removed the sheet of paper inside, Warshaw said, "Sorry, Harris, it's nothing personal."

I pretended not to hear him. My combat reflex was full-bore at that moment. In another minute, I might not be able to stop myself.

Beside me, Admiral Thorne silently read the contents of Admiral Brocius's memo, his face an impassive mask. I did the same. I read and realized that Warshaw had not the slightest clue of what was written in these orders, the poor bastard.

When I looked up, I met Warshaw's gaze. He had the petulant expression of a little boy caught breaking rules he does not like.

Thorne reread his letter, then folded it and slipped it back into its envelope. I placed mine face down on the table.

"So it's official, Harris, once Admiral Thorne is gone, I will assume command of the fleet."

"I see," I said. The orders I had just read mentioned more than a change in command.

"You will retain the rank of general and assume command of the Marines," Warshaw said.

Thorne started to say something, but Warshaw interrupted him. "I'm sorry to have gone around you, Admiral, but it had to be done. I could not allow them to leave the Scutum-Crux Fleet in the hands of a Marine."

"I understand," said Thorne.

"Do you have any questions, Captain Harris?" Warshaw asked. He sounded as if he were already a commanding officer, not a noncom speaking to an officer.

I shook my head.

"Admiral Thorne?"

"You took this directly to Admiral Brocius?"

"I served under him for twelve years in the Sagittarius Central Fleet," Warshaw said. "Any other questions?" He paused, then said, "If neither of you have anything else to discuss, I think I'll get back to work." With that, he left the room.

"I never did care for that son of a bitch," Thorne said, as soon as the door closed behind Warshaw.

"Which son of a bitch?" I asked. "Brocius or Warshaw?"

"Either of them. Both of them," Thorne said.

I passed Thorne my orders.

Wayson Harris,
Captain,
UAMC, Scutum-Crux Fleet

Captain Harris, it has been brought to my attention that there are questions about the transfer of power in the Scutum-Crux Fleet. Master Chief Petty Officer Gary Warshaw has lodged a formal complaint about a Marine taking control of the fleet.

As the ranking Naval NCO, the master chief believes he should assume command of the fleet. I have considered his petition and agree.

You shall remain Commandant of the Marines.

*Further, per Master Chief Warshaw's suggestion, we
shall rely upon the survivors of Terraneau to elect
their own planet administrator.*

*Harris, it is vital that this transfer of command be
carried out without incident. Once Admiral Thorne
and his officers have transferred out, you are authorized to deal with Warshaw as you see fit.*

> *Admiral Alden Brocius,*
> *Office of the Navy*

" 'Deal with Warshaw as you see fit'?" Thorne said as he
finished reading. "Am I misreading this, or did Admiral Brocius just authorize you to kill that poor bastard?"

"Let's just say he is not going to limit my options," I said.

"Can you make heads or tails of this?" Thorne asked as he
slid the envelope to me. I pulled out the orders. The page was
blank except for three names: *Grayson, Moffat, Ravenwood.*

"Does that mean anything to you?" Thorne asked. "I assume this message was meant for you as well."

"Yes, sir."

"What's Grayson?"

"Not 'what.' 'Who.' Colonel Aldus Grayson. He was my
commanding officer for a short while."

"What happened to him?" Thorne asked.

"Somebody shot him."

"People get shot all the time during war," Thorne pointed
out.

"There were no enemies in the vicinity," I said. "A lot of
people think I shot him."

"Did you?"

"That's the rumor," I said.

"And Moffat?"

"Another CO."

"Did you kill him, too?"

"Yeah. There were witnesses that time."

"Was he the guy on New Copenhagen? I heard about
him."

"There were two inquests, I was cleared of all charges both
times," I said.

"What about Ravenwood? Another dead officer?"

"It's a planet."

"You killed a planet?" Thorne asked.

"The Marines had an outpost on Ravenwood."

"Ravenwood Outpost . . . shit, I know about that," Thorne said, recognizing the name. Ravenwood was the Scutum-Crux Arm's answer to Roanoke. Every platoon the Marines sent to Ravenwood Outpost vanished. According to the official report, no one ever made it off the planet alive. That was a whitewash. In truth, no one ever lasted his first night on that planet.

"Do you know what happened on Ravenwood?" Thorne asked.

"I know exactly what happened," I said. "Admiral Huang used it as a training ground for a new breed of SEAL clones. He used the Marines as live bait. They came, they tried to defend themselves, and they died. Huang's killer SEALs polished them off quick."

"But what does that have to do with you and Warshaw?" Thorne was no fool. Watching his face, I could tell that he had the riddle partially solved.

"If I had to guess, I'd say he brought up Grayson and Moffat to let me know that a little friendly fire might be in order."

"Yeah, I figured that out. What about Ravenwood?"

"War games," I said.

"They're not just sending you away; they're going to use you for target practice," Thorne said in astonishment.

"That's my guess," I said.

THIRTY-TWO

The military philosopher Michael Khumalo said, "Your most dangerous enemy is the one you mistake for a friend." Advice to live by.

Besides Thomer and Hollingsworth, I shared my plans with no one. Admiral Thorne had his suspicions; but he was a bright guy and knew better than to ask.

My plans fell into place in the weeks after we liberated Terraneau. Convinced that everyone was playing according to Hoyle, the brass began using battleships to ferry clones to our fleet. They started with one; but after another week, they upped the ante by sending three. With three big ships, they could ship six thousand clones at a time. Given another week, they might well have completed the transfers.

I played possum as the first big shipment arrived. When I heard that the battleships were coming again, I opened the books to an ally I was not sure I could trust. I found Warshaw's billet and tapped the CALL button on the intercom.

"Yeah?" the voice barked.

"It's Harris," I said.

"What do you want?" he asked.

"I'm about to declare a war. Since you command the fleet, I thought I'd let you in on my plans," I said.

"I don't have time for jokes, Captain," Warshaw said.

"I'm not joking."

The master chief's door slid open.

Warshaw had just come back from the gym. He wore baggy sweatpants and a loose Navy tank top. His clothes bulged over his chest, shoulders, arms, and legs and hung loose over his gut and hips. Quarter-inch veins formed patterns on his shoulders and biceps. Veins showed along his bald head as well.

"You better not be specking with me," he said. He stood in the doorway, blocking me from entering his quarters.

"Did Admiral Brocius show you the orders he sent me?" I asked, as I held up the envelope.

"He told me what was in them," Warshaw said.

"I don't think so." I handed him the envelope.

Warshaw pulled the letter out, his eyes focused on mine. He made no effort to hide his mistrust. Leaning against the doorjamb, he unfolded the paper and read. When he got to the end, he froze. " 'Deal with . . . as you see fit'? What the speck is that supposed to mean?"

"Here's what he told Thorne," I said as I handed him the second envelope.

"I don't get it," he said. " 'Grayson, Moffat, Ravenwood.' What is that supposed to mean?"

"Grayson and Moffat were officers I killed," I said. "Ravenwood was a frontier outpost where they used Marines as live targets for training Navy SEALs. It doesn't sound like your buddy Brocius has your best interests in mind."

Warshaw shook his head, and hissed, "That son of a bitch." Then he rethought it, and said, "No way. No way, Harris, I don't specking buy it." Then he carefully refolded the letters and placed them back in the envelopes.

"Yes you do," I said. He had to know that I hadn't forged the letters, they were printed on Office of the Navy letterhead.

He sighed. "Brocius gave me everything I wanted. He told me I was right about everything and thanked me for helping him avoid a 'colossal mistake.' That was what he called it, a 'colossal mistake.' "

Watching reality hit Warshaw, I almost felt sorry for the boot-licking son of a bitch. Almost.

"So this letter gives you permission to what . . . shoot me? Throw me in the brig?"

"Or both," I said, hoping to drive home the differences between Marines and sailors.

"But what does Ravenwood have to do with this?" Warshaw asked.

"That's Brocius tipping his hand. It's his way of telling me why he handed over the fleet in the first place."

"And you think he gave us the fleet to use us for training exercises? Is that right?"

"That is exactly what I think."

"Even if it is true, I don't see how this changes anything. We're stuck here, Harris. They can't hit us, and we can't hit them."

"They can hit us."

"How are they going to hit us? With the specking Earth Fleet? They have thirty self-broadcasting ships. We'd rip them a new asshole if they came out here."

"We'd rip them a new asshole if they came out here in the fleet we know about," I said.

"You think they have a new fleet?"

"They have something we don't know about," I said. "You served with Brocius."

"Damn right I did, twelve years' worth," Warshaw said.

"Did you ever hear about his casino?" I asked.

"I heard about it," Warshaw said.

"The man does not gamble, but he has an entire casino in his house," I said.

"He gambles," Warshaw said. "He puts his money up."

"He plays as the house, which buys him slightly better odds. That's how Brocius likes to play, with the odds stacked in his direction."

"Yeah . . . yeah, that's his MO. He stacks the deck."

"Before he sends a fleet into harm's way . . ."

Warshaw nodded, and said, "You think it's new ships."

"That's my guess," I said. "And you can bet they're bigger, faster, and more powerful than what we have out here."

"So what do you have in mind, Harris?"

"We don't want to play his game if he's giving himself house odds," I said.

Warshaw laughed. "Good luck attacking Earth without a self-broadcasting fleet."

"Three self-broadcasting battleships are about to arrive on our doorstep," I pointed out.

"Touching those ships would be an act of war," Warshaw said.

I tapped the envelopes. "They've already declared the war, I'm angling to get off the first shot."

Warshaw walked over to his desk and sat down to think things over. He pumped his left fist so he could watch the muscles in his forearm bulge and relax, bulge and relax. "Three battleships aren't going to do us much good. The first time we tried to take them into Earth space, Brocius would nail us."

"So we don't enter Earth space. We take them someplace else, someplace they're not expecting us to appear. We start up a salvage operation in the Galactic Eye."

Warshaw stared at me, a quizzical look in his eyes. "The Mogat world? I thought it was destroyed."

"Not the planet, the space around it. The Mogats had four hundred self-broadcasting ships in their fleet," I said.

"The way I heard it, there's not much left of those ships," Warshaw said.

I did not need a history lesson on the destruction of the Mogat Fleet, I was there. I took a step toward Warshaw, and said, "That doesn't mean we destroyed the equipment inside those ships. There are four hundred ships with broadcast engines and broadcast generators circling that planet. What do you want to bet that some of those generators and engines are still in working condition?"

Warshaw smiled. "You know, General Harris, I always wanted to command my own self-broadcasting fleet."

CHAPTER
THIRTY-THREE

The next week passed slowly as I orchestrated one set of missions and submitted fabricated reports for another. Officially, my Marines had begun the reclamation of Norristown. The Corps of Engineers sent thousand-man teams to clear debris, fix roads, restore power, build farms, and bury the dead. They also refurbished Fort Sebastian. The project went quickly.

Behind the scenes, my Marines scouted Terraneau for a new base, food stores, and a place to build a prison. We found most of the cities in the same condition as Norristown—destroyed and populated by scared civilians. The Avatari had laid most cities bare and left others entirely untouched.

We found no rhyme or reason to the destruction. The aliens never even entered Carlton, the tenth largest city on Terraneau. The people had power, sewage, even running water. The only part of the city hurt during the invasion was the spaceport, and the residents destroyed it themselves, thinking that having a working spaceport might attract the Avatari.

We found several small towns untouched but empty. The aliens might or might not have killed all of the people, but we found no corpses. The houses and stores simply sat empty, as if the people had just packed up and left. One of those abandoned burgs was Zebulon, a town with a population of five thousand that had mysteriously whittled down to zero without leaving a suicide note.

Not an organization to let things go to waste, the Corps of Engineers converted Zebulon into a relocation camp and renamed the place, "Outer Bliss," in honor of the Texas relocation camp outside Fort Bliss. The Corps surrounded the town with electrified razor-wire fences and guard towers, then invited me to inspect its work. Thomer and I flew down for a look.

The landing field and barracks were on the outside of the fence—a sturdy flattop with a Quonset-hut hangar. Outer Bliss sat on a plateau in the high desert. My men would be hot during the day and cold at night until the Corps could add heating and ventilation.

The prison area was a lot nicer than the Texas facility from which it took its name. Instead of living in sheds, the inmates would occupy houses and a small hotel. They would have pools, two movie theaters, school facilities for meetings, and a gymnasium for sports. Thomer and I walked the empty streets, the dry desert wind whistling as it whipped around houses and lampposts.

"This beats the hell out of Clonetown," I said. "Maybe

they made it too nice." Yes, I was bitter. The inmates in this camp would spend their incarceration in relative comfort. In all fairness, we were moving fifteen thousand men into a town with living facilities for five thousand people, but they would not be forced to take communal showers or sleep in sheds made out of corrugated metal.

We had reached a somewhat shady lane lined with dead trees and brick homes. Sitting on a small rise a few blocks ahead of us, an empty elementary school presided over a neighborhood that had not seen children in several years.

Thomer looked around, and said, "I used to dream about growing up in a town like this. I bet kids used to ride bicycles down this street."

Suburban as a shopping mall, Outer Bliss did not compare to the horror of Clonetown. Then I reminded myself that the men who would soon populate this prison were, themselves, innocent victims. Natural-born or not, they were not politicians. But they would all be natural-borns . . .

"It's too specking nice," I said. "It's like we're sending the bastards on a specking vacation."

Thomer continued walking. He did not even look over at me. He simply said, "It's a prison, Harris. They aren't going to like it."

The grass in the yards had died and withered. There were no dogs or cats in the town. The Corps had hunted down anything larger than a squirrel, then fumigated the houses to kill the rats and mice. It also hauled out the cars, the trucks, the tractors, anything that could be used to crash the gates.

We entered a grocery store and discovered that the people had left food behind. We explored a bank and found the safe-deposit boxes intact. We toured a two-story motel. The beds were made but the blankets were dusty. I wondered if the Corps had dressed the beds or if this was the last job of maids who had vanished four years ago. We saw no signs of death or violence, nothing to suggest that the inhabitants had been forced to move.

Back on the *Kamehameha*, I tapped the intercom button outside Admiral Thorne's quarters and asked him if he had a moment.

"What is it, Harris?" He did not sound unfriendly, just a busy man with a lot on his mind.

"It's about transfers," I said.

"Very well," he said, and the door opened. Thorne was no fool. When he saw the two MPs I brought with me, he knew the score. He stood and stared past me, into the hall, watching the MPs.

"You're making your move," he said. The old man stood motionless beside his desk, a pen in his hands. His wispy, white hair a mess, his blue eyes slightly red from days with very little sleep, his skin pale from years spent away from the sun, he did not put up a fight. "Am I under arrest?" he asked as the door closed behind me.

His words felt like a splash of cold water. "We're not arresting anybody."

He braced and asked, "You're not going to kill . . ."

"I had the Corps of Engineers convert a small town into a relocation camp. It's a damn sight better than what they put us in back on Earth," I said.

"Is that what this is about? Is this revenge or revolution?" Thorne asked, the calm never leaving his voice.

I thought about the question for a moment. We were not sticking Thorne and his crew in our camp for revenge. We were doing it because we had no other choice. If we didn't relocate them, they would try to stop us, and lives would be lost. We were putting them in our prison to protect them, I was sure of that much.

"Both," I said.

"I see," Thorne said. He stood still, staring into my eyes, clearly trying to decide whether he should say what he wanted to say next. He might have a pistol someplace in his room. He certainly had a panic button that would sound Klaxons on every ship in the fleet. I hoped he would not do anything foolish.

When he spoke, the words gushed like water breaking through a dam. "I can help you, you know. There's nothing for me back on Earth. I have more ties here than I do on Earth."

"Help me what?" I asked.

"I can help you run the fleet. I can help you fight your war.

You found some way to get back to Earth, didn't you? You wouldn't do this if you didn't know what you were doing. I can help."

"Why would you do that?" I asked. Thorne struck me as an honest man, a fair man, the least aristocratic officer I had ever known; not the type of man who trades sides to stay in power.

He placed the papers on the desk. "Harris, they transferred me to the Scutum-Crux Fleet thirty-seven years ago. I've spent more of my life on these ships than on Earth. The fleet is my home.

"My parents died while I was still at the Naval Academy. I can't think of anyone I care about on Earth."

If the rumors were true, Thorne had more ties to this corner of space than he wanted to admit. Scuttlebutt had it that he had a common-law wife on Terraneau. I had never asked him about it, but the rumor went a long way toward explaining why he had never put in for a transfer.

"You are an officer of the Unified Authority Navy," I pointed out. "I'd be crazy to trust you." But I did trust him.

"I can help you. I have command experience." He tapped his knuckle on the top of his desk, and asked, "Can we speak, man-to-man? Can we at least discuss my offer before you arrest me, General?"

Suddenly he was calling me "General." He was right. Once we made our move, our field ranks would come into play.

I nodded. As I sat, I said, "I'm not arresting you."

"But you are placing twenty thousand men in a prison camp."

"I prefer the term, 'relocation camp.' And as of the last transfer, you're down to about fifteen thousand natural-borns."

"Let's be honest with each other, General," Thorne said. "Who is going to run your fleet? Gary Warshaw, the man Brocius appointed? He's a good sailor, but he's an engineer. There's a reason why the Navy never promotes engineers to the rank of Admiral. They don't have the background to command a ship. They fix things, they don't run them. How do you think Warshaw is going to do in battle?"

"There's always Franks," I said.

"Lilburn Franks," Thorne said. He leaned back in his chair and smiled. "He'd be better than Warshaw; at least he's spent time on a bridge. He's smart, too; but he's loyal to Warshaw through and through. He'll never be loyal to you. Give him a chance, and Franks will stick a knife in your back."

I was pretty sure I believed the other things Thorne had said, but that last bit about Franks stabbing me in the back I accepted without question.

"Admiral, you have a transport waiting on you, sir," I said, as I rose to my feet. I hated sticking Thorne in the relocation camp. The truth was, I hated the idea of placing anyone in that town-turned-prison-camp. By the end of the day, every natural-born sailor with the bad luck to have remained in the Scutum-Crux Fleet would find himself a guest of Outer Bliss.

"At least think about what I said?" Thorne asked, both looking and sounding a bit desperate.

"I'll take it under advisement," I said. I wanted to take him up on his offer, but I had other concerns at the moment. My next act would be a declaration of war on the Unified Authority. With Warshaw fighting me for control of the fleet, Admiral Thorne's offer did not figure very prominently on my list of priorities.

CHAPTER
THIRTY-FOUR

Other than Warshaw, only Thomer and Hollingsworth knew my agenda. My lieutenants deserved to know who they were fighting and why. I decided to keep my plans hidden from everyone else. I was, after all, plotting a revolution.

Six transports sat in the starboard docking bay of U.A.N. *Washington*, a big Perseus-class fighter carrier. Six more sat in the port-side docking bay. In all, the transports had enough space to ferry twelve hundred men to the self-broadcasting battleships moored just outside our fleet. The plan was to load the transports with twelve hundred natural-born officers, but we were about to stray from the script. We would load the birds with Marines in combat armor.

The U.A.N. *Washington* had been one of the first ships in my fleet to go all-clone. The ship had also become a de facto transfer terminal. The self-broadcasting battleships sent transports filled with clones transferring to the Scutum-Crux Fleet to the *Washington* and received transports filled with natural-borns returning to Earth from that ship.

The ritual was about to end.

First, we needed to remove the Earth Fleet pilots from their transports before they could set off any alarms. We sent two-man teams to seize the transports—men with commando training who knew how to work quietly and would not hesitate to commit murder. If a pilot managed to do so much as tap his microphone, we would find ourselves stuck in the Scutum-Crux Arm forever.

The sergeant on my team would receive a field promotion to major once we became the Enlisted Man's Marine Corps. He had been in the Corps for twenty years.

I stole up to the rear of the transport, held my gun ready, and peered inside. For this op, I used an S9 stealth pistol, a sidearm developed specifically for covert operations. The S9 used magnetic actuation to fire fléchettes with iron shafts and depleted-uranium tips. The guns were light, lethal, and silent.

Had I spotted anyone in the cabin or cargo hold, I would have shot him; but the kettle was empty. "Clear," I whispered into my mike, and the sergeant slipped ahead of me and up the ramp. He crouched beside the cargo netting, his gun trained ahead. "Clear," he said.

I shuffled up the ramp, barely lifting my feet so my boots would not make noise against the steel deck. I kept my pistol raised and ready, aimed on the door of the cockpit, my finger tight across the trigger. S9s were rated accurate to twenty-five yards—not exactly the sniper's weapon of choice.

Hiding behind one of the girder ribs of the ship, I signaled the sergeant to catch up and checked in with my other teams.

All twelve teams had managed to board the transports without incident.

Even with the ambient sound sensitivity in my helmet switched to maximum, the sergeant's soft footsteps sounded no louder than somebody sweeping the floor with a wire brush. The man clearly had stealth-op experience.

"I'm going up," I said.

The sergeant glided into a shadowy niche from which he had a clear line of sight to the cockpit, and said, "I've got your back." He knelt and aimed his pistol, his armor blending into the darkness.

I crept up to the ladder, my pistol now stowed in its holster. My armored gloves made a soft clicking noise as I wrapped my fingers around the posts. At this point, the pilot would not be able to see me without leaving the cockpit, but he might hear something.

Transport 3 is secured, Thomer said over the interLink. He had captured his bird.

There was an eight-foot climb from the floor of the kettle to the narrow catwalk that led to the cockpit door.

"Captain, I can see him in there," the sergeant said.

"Is he coming out?" I froze.

"Standing in the doorway."

"Think he heard me?"

"I can't tell." The sergeant paused, then said, "Okay, he's moving back in."

Transport 5 is secure.

I've got 6.

Seven is secure.

I climbed to the top of the ladder, walked to the door of the cockpit, and swung in, lowering my pistol into place. The pilot started to reach for his communications set, then stopped.

"Don't be stupid," I said.

He looked at me, nervousness and indecision showing in his expression. Despite my warning, he reached for the microphone, and I fired three shots. The first dart pierced the top of his skull, just above the temple. The second hit him in the ear. The third hit him in the base of the neck. Had they been bullets, any one of the shots would have blown his head apart.

S9s had a nice soft touch. Instead of passing through the

pilot and destroying equipment, the fléchettes lodged deep in the pilot's brain and throat. He died instantly, thin streams of blood pouring out of his wounds.

Transport 2 is secure.

I waited until I had heard from all eleven of my teams, then I added that we had captured the lead transport. I also sent the message to Warshaw. That was his signal to radio the battleships that their transports were en route.

I dragged the dead pilot out of the cockpit and tossed him into the kettle. The steady stream of blood leaking from the holes in his head reminded me of motor oil oozing from an engine.

The sergeant knelt beside the body and examined the wounds. He looked up, and said, "Nice work."

Once we captured the transports, it only took fifteen minutes to load our Marines. We would not use stealth pistols for the next part of the mission, we would use M27s loaded with standard rounds. Each of the battleships carried a five-thousand-man crew. We'd be outnumbered ten-to-one. Long odds.

With the natural-born pilots dead or captured, we used our newly trained Marine pilots to fly the transports. Our pilots sealed the kettle doors and started toward the atmospheric locks. Once again, I found myself standing in the crush of a hundred Marines crammed into a kettle, willing myself calm as I stared into the future.

The floor shook as the sleds pulled us through the locks.

"Listen up, Marines," I said. "This little chat is the only briefing you will get on this op. The objective of this exercise is to commandeer ourselves a trio of battleships. I don't know what kind of resistance we will run into, but we are dealing with sailors here; I don't expect them to put up too big a fight.

"Are you with me so far?"

Every man answered. In the Marines, officers do not ask rhetorical questions.

"Any questions?"

"Sir, who is the enemy?" asked one of my sergeants.

"The new Navy," I said, opting for total honesty.

"New Navy, sir?" several men asked.

"The brass at Navy Headquarters wants to train their new all-natural-born navy by testing it against us." This was true, though I had made the unauthorized decision to accelerate the process.

"Are we packing blank rounds and dummy grenades?" another man asked.

"Good guess, but dead wrong. We're using live rounds, boys," I said. "Tag 'em and bag 'em."

"We can't use live ammo on U.A. sailors." Dozens of men said that or something like it all at once.

"This is a full-contact exercise. We use live rounds on maneuvers. Today it is man against man. In another month, they will bring their new ships out here, and we'll get to see how nicely they play the game.

"Now listen up, drill or no drill, we are going to lose men. This is military Darwinism, boys—one side lives, and one side dies. Let's show them what a clone force can do, hoorah."

"I don't belong here! I'm natural-born!" The clone who said this sounded absolutely terrified. More than a thousand other clones responded by laughing, each of them believing that he was the only natural-born enlisted man in the fleet.

We only had a minute before we would reach the battleship, and I had one more order to give. "I'm looking for the smallest body count that gets the job done," I said. "If they surrender, take 'em alive. Otherwise, just remember, we're doing this for the good of the Unified Authority."

I heard a twelve-thousand-man *Aye aye, sir!*

We were sending four companies to board each of the three battleships. All of my company commanders and platoon leaders had their assignments. Maps of the ships and virtual beacons had been programmed into every man's visor. If we struck quickly, we would have the element of surprise on our side. With every passing moment, the sailors on those ships would have more time to arm and defend.

Normally, as I headed into battle, I would listen in on the conversations around the kettle. This time, however, I spent the remainder of our short trip lost in thought. I wondered what the security structure would be like on the battleships. Sailors did not carry sidearms. The armory might issue pistols or M27s to sailors pulling MP duty; but for the most part, the only weapons they packed were their wits. Needless to say, that left most sailors empty-handed.

The capital ships in the U.A. Navy carried a detachment of Marines who handled ship security. As far as I knew, the Unified Authority no longer trained new Marines. That meant these ships would either have sailors carrying guns or soldiers doing the work of Marines. Neither option impressed me. As long as they let us dock . . .

"Captain Harris, we're cleared to land." My pilot had just given me the thirty-second warning.

"Okay, we're coming in for a landing," I said, using an open interLink frequency that all my men would hear. "The watchword on this op is speed. Hit hard, hit fast."

We landed. Boosters hissed. Runners clanked and groaned. I moved to the rear of the ship. My Marines lined up behind me, pressing against my back. I did not need to look back to know they had their guns out and ready. I would lead the way into this battle. As the first man off the first transport, I would set the pace.

We stood in the dim light of the kettle, waiting for the heavy doors to open. Scanning the interLink, I did not find a single conversation. The motors in the kettle walls whined, and the heavy iron doors began to slide apart. Staring down the ramp, I saw technicians servicing the engines and deck-hands running errands, all unarmed and unsuspecting. They paid no attention to me as I clambered down the ramp. The men working on the engine were natural-borns. One had blond hair, two had brown. My instincts told me to shoot them, but I did not listen. I stormed down the ramp and ran past them. They did not look up at me.

"Asshole!" "Coward!" "Failure!" I muttered curses at myself as I ran across the docking bay, hating myself for not having pulled the trigger.

A couple of techs stood near the door. I wondered if I had what it took to kill anyone anymore. When had I become so timid? Why had I let those men live? If one of them so much as touched an intercom, we would all be stuck in Scrotum-Crotch forever. I hated myself.

The spatter of automatic gunfire echoed across the deck. Someone had cleaned up after my mess. I did not need to look back to know that the mechanics working on the engine were dead. My self-loathing turned to shame.

Hearing the commotion, the techs near the door finally looked up, only curiosity showing on their faces. Then they saw the parade of armor-clad Marines and reacted. One ran for the communications panel on a nearby wall, the other ran for the door. I shot them both—the man reaching for the panel first, then the sprinter. The guy heading for the door threw his arms wide when my bullets drilled into his back and neck, his head lolling back while his chest and shoulders thrust forward. He looked like a runner making a final burst to cross the finish line.

When I reached the door, I pressed my boot against the dead man's shoulder and slid his bloody body out of the way. I felt no remorse; I would not have shot him had he not turned to run. "Soldiers have an army, sailors have a navy, the Marines have a corpse," my old drill instructor used to say.

The corridor outside the docking bay was nearly empty, empty enough that I did not worry that anyone heard the shots. Even if someone had been nearby, the doors were thick, and we had suppressors on our M27s. The gunfire sounded no louder than the sound of a racquet striking a tennis ball. Any sailors happening to pass by the door would not even stop to think about what they had heard.

With a hundred men following behind me, I headed toward the bridge. Another hundred headed aft, toward the engine room. That left two hundred men to locate the armory and neutralize whatever resistance the sailors offered. In the past, battleships carried a complement of a thousand Marines. It occurred to me that even if this ship carried a regiment of "new" Marines, my four hundred could still win the day. My men were veterans of a more-established service. If the Unified Authority had an all-natural-born-Marines corps, the men in that corps would be untried men in an untried service.

The hall from the docking bay to the center of the ship was long and straight, wide enough for ten men to walk abreast. The way was bright and surprisingly empty.

We slipped through the halls quickly, making only a half-hearted effort to keep ourselves concealed. We stopped at junctions, peered around corners for targets, then moved on.

A door opened and a sailor started to step out, saw us, and ran back inside. Two of my men followed him. I heard the soft chatter of suppressed gunfire and knew our secret was safe.

"Check every door," I told my men.

"It's like a ghost town," one of my sergeants radioed in.

"Beta Team report?" I snapped.

Upon leaving the docking bay, we had split into four squads. Beta was the team I sent to capture Engineering. Alpha, my squad, would take the bridge. Gamma would look for the armory, assuming the ship had one. Delta would watch the halls and squish anything that looked dangerous.

"We're approaching the engine room." A moment later, he radioed in again. "It's like they're taking a lunch break or something, there's only a couple of techs here."

"Secure the area and report," I said. "Gamma?"

"We have the armory." Gamma had the shortest route to cover. The armory was on the same deck as the docking bay.

"Any problems?"

"Just a dumb-ass janitor who tried to run. I had to cap him."

"Anyone else there?"

"The place is empty, Captain."

"Delta?" I asked.

"Still deploying."

"Okay, Delta leader. Fast and quiet. If they don't stop and drop, waste 'em."

It occurred to me that I had not heard the screech of the Klaxons. Apparently no one had spotted us yet.

Swinging around a doorway, I saw five sailors lazing around a coffee dispenser. I signaled caution to the Marines behind me. When we went in to take them, one of the sailors threw his hands in the air to show he wasn't armed. My Marines shot the other four. Blood, meat, and coffee splattered the wall. Bodies fell.

"What do I do with him?" a private asked. He pointed to the scared shell of a man kneeling on the floor with his hands laced behind his head. The man hung his head till his chin pressed against his neck. He just knelt there, whimpering.

"Guard him," I said.

"What about . . ."

I looked at the quailing sailor, and said, "We either guard him or kill him. Your choice." Then I went to an open frequency, and said, "Listen up, Alpha, this break room is now our official holding pen. If you take a prisoner, you bring him here. You got that?"

They said they did.

The private cracked his M27 against the back of the sailor's head, and said, "Stay down there, asshole." He forgot to broadcast externally. Alpha Team heard him, the captured sailor did not.

The corridor funneled into a wide berth near the center of the ship. As we reached this area, we finally ran into resistance. Somebody fired a shot. The bullet struck the wall about five feet ahead of me, leaving a scrape. Two more shots followed.

I ducked against a wall, peered around the corner. The shooter hid behind a bulkhead.

"You three, flank him, take him," I ordered the men standing behind me. As I fired a few shots, they scampered back down the hall and took an alternate route.

Moments later, the alarms finally sounded. The Klaxons were so loud that they made my helmet vibrate. The audio filters in my helmet dampened the noise, but it must have been excruciating for the sailors.

Somebody fired three hopeless shots in my direction even though I was completely hidden behind the corner. The shots came spaced a few seconds apart. I returned fire in three-shot bursts. My job was not to kill the enemy, just to keep them pinned. A moment later, automatic fire rang out, and my Marines let me know that the coast was clear.

Before leaving, I went to have a look at the fallen resistance. There were two of them, sailors on MP duty with sidearms and armbands. They lay facedown, their blood spreading into puddles.

I noticed my heartbeat as I ran up the stairs leading to the next deck. It was normal. Running down the corridors of this battleship, facing only token resistance, I had not built up enough of a sweat to start a combat reflex. I might just as well have been playing Ping-Pong or herding a flock of sheep.

"Beta, report?"

"We have control of Engineering, sir."

"That's it?" I asked.

"We killed a guy."

"Any prisoners?" I asked.

"Yeah, sixty-three of 'em. There was a guy who took a swing at me with a wrench, but everyone else gave up without a fight."

Sixty-three men in Engineering? I didn't know you could operate a battleship with so small a crew.

"Captain, we have secured the lower decks." It was the Delta Team leader.

"Any problems at the Marine compound?" I asked. The Marines would be stowed on the bottom deck.

"The deck was empty, sir."

"There are no Marines in the compound?" I asked.

"It's an empty space, sir. The whole compound is empty. There aren't even any racks in the barracks."

I considered this as we reached the bridge. The captain of the ship could have sealed off the bridge, but he didn't. The hatch stood wide open, revealing a huge floor that looked like an office complex. There were desks and dividers and computers. You did not fly a ship like this with a flight stick or yoke; even the combat maneuvers were programmed into a computer.

We had not seen any real resistance. On the bridge, the captain of the ship made his stand as best he could. He met us at the entrance, flanked by six men carrying M27s. He and the two armed men beside him wore the khaki uniforms of officers—a one-star admiral with a captain and a commander by his side. The four men behind them were simple seamen.

"What is the meaning of this, clone?" The old man spat out the words as he approached us. Annoyance showed in his eyes. Fear showed in the eyes of the men around him.

Seeing this angry old man's composure, I felt my nerve slip just a bit. "I am commandeering your ship."

"Clone, this is treason." He used the word "clone" twice, and I suspected he would use it again. He wanted to trigger a death reflex, the bastard.

"I'm not going to have a death reflex," I said, "but if I hear you say that word one more time, I will shoot you on the spot."

"You son of a bitch," the old man said. "You're behind this, aren't you? You're that Liberator clone." I got the feeling that last use of "clone" had just slipped out and did not shoot.

Trying to sound more confident than I felt, I said, "Tell your men to lay down their arms."

"And then what? You've already committed treason, how about murder? How many of my men have you already killed?"

"Admiral, I am running out of patience."

The admiral told his men to drop their weapons with no more than a nod. Then he said, "You do know they will come for you? You can't possibly get away with this."

"They were always going to come for us," I said. "We were sent here for combat exercises."

When the admiral heard this, his raised his eyes to my face and took a half step backward. That was the only sign of fear I ever saw from the man. "You're damn right you were, and you will get everything you have coming to you."

The admiral surrendered the bridge, and we captured three battleships without taking a single casualty. In the back of my mind, though, I asked myself, *What have I done?*

CHAPTER
THIRTY-FIVE

Senior Chief Petty Officer Perry Fahey, now wearing full face makeup that included lipstick, rouge, and false eyelashes along with mascara, opened the next staff meeting with, "Captain Harris, I hear congratulations are in order. You managed to hijack three ships filled with unarmed sailors on

a peaceful mission without losing a single man. That's quite
an accomplishment. What's next on your agenda, blowing up
a school for girls?"

I wanted to kick the bastard's chair out from under him,
but that was what he wanted as well. He wanted to provoke me
into a fight, then claim I was not ready to command. Instead, I
smiled, and said, "You said that entire line without stuttering
or wetting your pants, Senior Chief. Well done."

"I, I don't stutter," Fahey said.

"Really? You stuttered up a storm at our last meeting," I
said.

It was a childish display on both our parts, but I got what I
wanted. I stopped myself from lashing out with my fists.

Warshaw and Franks sat impassive, watching to see
what Fahey would do next. I remained silent, waiting for
the same.

What Fahey said next let me know that I was not the only
person worrying about whether it had been a mistake to start
this war. "You got us in a specking war." He looked at Warshaw and Franks for support, then added, "What are you
going to do next, bomb Terraneau?"

Franks laughed.

Maybe they had rehearsed the whole thing. Fahey's out-
burst gave Warshaw the opportunity to position himself as an
officer-statesmen. Neither laughing nor smiling, he said, "You
did assure me that those ships had come to fight."

"No, Master Chief, I never said any such thing. I said
that the Unified Authority plans to use our fleet to practice
maneuvers."

"There weren't even any Marines on board those ships. It
seems clear to me that they did not come to fight," Warshaw
said. He spoke slowly, showing restraint.

Fahey didn't bother with things like restraint. "They won't
make that mistake again, now, will they?"

I turned to Fahey, and said, "The Earth Fleet has thirty-
two battle . . . excuse me, as of two days ago the fleet has
twenty-nine self-broadcasting battleships. It has twenty-five
self-broadcasting destroyers, and a few self-broadcasting
cruisers. How many battleships do we have?"

Warshaw and his crew sat mute.

Hollingsworth leaned forward, and said, "I believe we have ninety battleships, sir."

"Ninety, you say?" I asked. "Ninety?" I pretended to fumble with a complex mathematical equation. "Why, ninety, that's more than thirty!"

Thomer chipped in. "I believe it is three times more, sir."

"Three times, you say?" Then, dropping my momentary befuddlement, I turned to Warshaw, and said, "I don't expect they'll make too much of a fuss over those ships."

"So which is it, Harris? You don't get it both ways. Are we so much stronger than them that they're afraid to come after us, or are they planning to use us for target practice?" Franks asked that question. If the son of a bitch analyzed and responded this effectively in battle, he'd make a hell of a captain.

"They're not ready to attack us just yet," I said.

"This is why the Navy always commands." Warshaw pronounced his edict with a regal attitude. He leaned back in his seat and rubbed a hand across his chin. "I suppose we're both guilty on this one. I should have known better than to listen to you."

With the Broadcast Network down, the Navy would not be able to verify the fate of those battleships without sending ships out to investigate. In a few hours, the brass would realize that their three battleships were not coming back. They would suspend any flights pending an investigation. Once Intelligence determined that we had commandeered their ships, they would abort the transfer entirely.

For all intents and purposes, I had received my field promotion to general. Warshaw was now an acting admiral, and though our ranks were similar, our authority was not. He commanded the ships. I commanded the Marines, a body of fighting men that he and his sailors considered just another form of cargo.

Warshaw would do whatever he thought he needed to preserve his command. The next time I left the ship, for instance, I might not be allowed back.

I left the conference room and headed for the Marine compound, Thomer and Hollingsworth in tow.

"Okay, Sergeant Hollingsworth, why in hell was Fahey in full drag? The bitch was wearing everything but a dress and wig," I said.

"Why are you asking me?" Hollingsworth protested.

"You said you knew him. You said he's a good man."

"That doesn't specking make me his fashion consultant."

"Okay, fine. Why do you think he came to the meeting like that?" I asked.

"It seems pretty obvious."

"It does?" I asked.

"You confiscated makeup from the bitches on this ship. He came in kabuki face to show that he isn't scared of you. It seems pretty obvious."

"Yeah, I should have known it was something like that," I admitted. Now that he pointed it out, it did seem obvious.

"Do you want to go get drunk?" Thomer asked.

"Not today," I said. I needed to stay sober and think about my next move.

"How about you?" Thomer asked Hollingsworth.

"Sounds good," Hollingsworth said.

"You don't mind if we get drunk?" Hollingsworth asked me.

I laughed and told them to enjoy their last minutes as enlisted men. By the time they returned from the bar, they would be a brigadier general and a full-bird colonel.

So I returned to my billet to relax. I took off my shoes and stripped out of my uniform. An hour-long nap sounded good, then maybe a meal. First things first, though; I needed rest. After turning off the lights, I climbed into my rack, then groped along the table beside my bed until I found the pair of mediaLink shades that I had checked out from the commissary. The shades let me tap into the ship's media center. Since returning from Terraneau, I had been reading the collected works of Friedrich Nietzsche.

I beseech you, my brothers, remain faithful to the earth, and do not believe those who speak to you of otherworldly hopes! Poison-mixers are they, whether they know it or not.

Poison-mixers? "That shows what you know," I muttered to the Nietzsche in my head.

The soft ring of my communications console broke into

my thoughts. When I answered, Warshaw asked me to come
to the bridge.

"What is it?" I asked.

"You're either a prophet, Harris, or you've gotten us all
killed," he said.

"More U.A. ships?" I asked as I climbed out of bed.

"A lot of them."

"How many is a lot?" I asked.

"Twenty battleships."

I had my blouse buttoned and my pants up. Stepping into
my shoes, I said, "That's half their fleet."

"There's no backing out now, Harris," Warshaw said. "I
hope you were right about everything."

It took me five minutes to get from my billet to the bridge.
Warshaw and one of his top NCOs, Senior Chief Hank Bishop,
met me at the lift when I arrived. Well, he had been a senior
chief. Now that we had broken relations with Washington,
Bishop was the captain of the *Kamehameha*.

Warshaw had not yet ordered the call to quarters, but
the bridge was on full alert. Technicians ran system checks
and radar sweeps. Amber lights flashed on several computer
consoles.

Warshaw led me to a large table in the center of the bridge.
On the table, a holographic display showed our fleet and the
intruders as quarter-inch three-dimensional models on a
green-and-black grid. Our ships filled the center of the grid.
The U.A. ships moved along the edge of the display.

"Why haven't you sounded the alarms?" I asked.

"If we sound general quarters, they'll hear it," Bishop said.
"The fleetCom system notifies all U.A. ships in the area when
one ship sounds general quarters."

"What's so bad about that?" I asked.

"That's not how we do things in the Navy," Warshaw said.
"We don't go off half-cocked."

I wanted to tell Warshaw to get specked, but I controlled
myself. "I don't see what's wrong with telling them we're ready
for a fight. They came here looking for a fight; we should let
them know that we're willing to give it to them."

"They will take it as a sign of guilt . . . like we have something to hide," Warshaw said. He turned and faced me, fury

flashing in his eyes. "Why the hell do I bother even trying to explain these things to a Marine?"

"Because you need me as much as I need you."

"For now," Warshaw said, calming slightly. "Here is the situation, Harris. They sent two unarmed research vessels to look for their ships. The only contact we have had was with those first ships. They asked us if we knew what happened to their battleships. We told them that we haven't seen them.

"Apparently they don't believe us," Warshaw said pointing to the display.

I shook my head. "Twenty self-broadcasting ships. If we could take them . . ."

"We can't," Warshaw said. "If we make a move, they'll broadcast out."

I expected a show of force. As the staff meeting ended, I had said as much, but I had not expected twenty ships. That was half their fleet. Even with twenty ships, they would not have any leverage. Not on our turf. They might make some hollow demands, but we would say, "No," and their self-broadcasting fleet would return to Earth with its tail between its legs . . . figuratively speaking. Sending so many ships had been a mistake, it made them look weak.

On the holographic display, the ships meandered around empty space. They could have been looking for debris or maybe the radioactive signature of a broadcast engine.

"What would you do if you were in their shoes?" Bishop asked me. "What if an enemy stole three of your tanks?"

"They don't have a hound's breath of a chance against us, not with only twenty battleships," I pointed out.

"Obviously. That is why they haven't engaged us," Warshaw said. He pointed to the display. "They're staying well out of firing range."

"But they are in an offensive formation," Bishop added.

Warshaw shook his head. "It's aggressive, but not offensive," he said. "They're still far enough apart to break and run if we attack."

Bishop looked more closely, thought it over, and agreed.

"Where are the ships we commandeered?" I asked.

"Over here." Warshaw sounded distracted as he pointed to the center of the display. He'd parked the commandeered ships in the center of the fleet. As he showed me the location, something struck me. Normally testy, the master chief was now showing a surprising amount of patience.

"There's something else, isn't there?" I asked.

Warshaw and Bishop traded a silent glance, then Warshaw gave me an embarrassed grin. "You were right about the Navy building a new class of ships. Our engineers found these." He pressed a button, and the holographic image of a ship replaced the tactical map on the table.

"Is this a battleship?" I asked quietly as I inspected the design. The three-dimensional image showed a long and slender hull. For the last hundred years, U.A. capital ships had been moth-shaped wedges. This boat was shaped like a knife.

"We found plans for an entire fleet," Warshaw said.

As Warshaw said this, a sailor came and saluted.

"What is it, Brown?" Bishop asked.

"Sir, the battleships have changed course. They're coming toward us, sir."

"Sound general quarters," Warshaw shouted.

Bishop struck a button on the table and Klaxons began. Warning lights were already flashing when I came onto the bridge; now the ambient lighting faded, and the glow of blinking amber flashed across the bridge.

Bishop fiddled with a dial on the table, and the tactical view of the ships reappeared, only more magnified.

"Scramble the fighters," Warshaw ordered.

Bishop repeated the order.

"Scrambling fighters, aye," an officer yelled.

"Send out all three carrier groups," Warshaw yelled.

I might have only been a lowly Marine, but I recognized overkill when I heard it. Warshaw was sending thirty-five fighter carriers to intercept twenty battleships.

"How many ships are incoming?" the fleetCom asked.

Across the bridge, communications officers relayed orders as loudly as they could against the distant blare of the Klaxons.

"Keep your fighters in close," Warshaw told Bishop.

Watching Warshaw, I thought he looked like a schoolboy spouting information he had memorized but did not understand. He'd spent his career as a deckhand, never expecting that he might one day become an officer. There was no strategy in his attack; he was simply throwing every ship in his fleet at the enemy.

But strategy would not make a difference in this near battle. Bright flashes appeared on the 3-D display. The enemy battleships broadcast to safety before coming close enough for us to shoot at them.

CHAPTER
THIRTY-SIX

Earthdate: December 12, A.D. 2516
Location: Golan Dry Docks
Galactic Position: Norma Arm

We needed the three U.A. battleships for several reasons. We needed ships with broadcast engines if we ever wanted to travel beyond Terraneau. Commandeering Pershing's self-broadcasting cruiser would have given us broadcast-travel capabilities, but it was a runt of a ship, and we needed cargo space for what I had in mind.

We also needed ships with the location of the Mogat home world stored on their broadcast computers because none of us had the slightest specking idea how to find the place. The Unified Authority Navy sent all of its self-broadcasting battleships to fight in the final battle against the Morgan Atkins Believers. Before a ship can self-broadcast to any location, coordinates must be programmed into its broadcast computer.

The computers on the battleships we captured yielded unexpected treasures. Along with the location of the Mogat home world, we found external diagrams of the new ships and a tentative launch schedule. Over the next three years, the Unified Authority planned to swap out its old fleet for an all-new one. From what we could tell, the new ships would be slightly smaller than earlier models. Our engineers were unable to decipher the weapons.

Hoping to glean a little more information about the new fleet, we decided to take a detour as we flew out to the Mogat home world.

Lilburn Franks—formerly a senior chief petty officer in the U.A. Navy but now an upper-half rear admiral in the Enlisted Man's Fleet—suggested we swing by the Golan Dry Docks on our way to the Mogat Fleet.

The dry docks sat in an otherwise-unpopulated corner of Norma, the smallest and innermost of the galactic arms. Long noted as the Unified Authority's most advanced shipyard, the Golan facility measured eight miles from top to bottom and included hundreds of cubic miles of construction space. If the Navy had new ships under construction, the Golan Dry Docks was where it would build them.

We broadcasted our newly confiscated three-ship fleet out to that remote corner of Norma. There were no planets within a light-year of the dry docks, just acres of star-riddled darkness.

I sat in an observatory just off the bridge with Warshaw and Franks—a high-powered conclave. With our field ranks in effect, I now had the rank of lieutenant general. Thanks to his visit with Brocius, Warshaw was an admiral. Franks was a rear admiral. We wore uniforms befitting our new status. Franks and I fit our uniforms perfectly. Warshaw's blouse strained around the bulging contours of his chest, shoulders, neck, and arms.

Warshaw sat ramrod straight in his chair, looking massive and muscular. When he was sure Warshaw was not around, the late Sergeant Herrington sometimes referred to him as the "Careless Hairless" because he shaved his head, eyebrows and all.

Beside him sat Franks, a man with an aggressive streak. Franks leaned forward in his chair, excitedly scanning the scene through the panoramic viewport. We had broadcasted in thirty-five million miles from the dry docks, far enough away that their sensors would not spot the anomaly of our entrance—far enough away to give our broadcast generator time to recharge in case the U.A. had ships patrolling the area. The enormous generator that built up the energy for us to broadcast required eight minutes to recharge.

Warshaw and I chatted about the overall mission. Franks listened in while keeping one eye on the viewport and the other on a telemetry readout. If another ship approached, Franks would notice it before anyone else.

"Doesn't matter where you go, it always looks the same out here," I said.

Franks disagreed. "Spoken like a Marine," he said.

This took Warshaw and me by surprise. "Not all the same?" he asked.

"Of course not," said Franks. "We're in the Norma Arm, the stars are more closely clustered here."

Warshaw laughed, and said, "It doesn't look any different."

"No, it wouldn't to you," said Franks.

"What is that supposed to mean?" Warshaw asked.

"You're an engineer. You spend your time in the belly of the ship taking equipment apart and making sure it works right. What do stars matter to an engineer. You're too busy with your seals and readouts to care about space."

"Get specked."

I turned to the viewport and looked over at the other battleships flying beside us. Their bulbous forms showed in full silhouette against the bright backdrop of stars. In most situations, ships of this make vanished into the darkness of space, their charcoal-colored hulls offering nearly perfect camouflage. Against the Norma stars, however, the ships stood out like crows flying across a morning sky.

"What makes you think the dry docks are still in use?" Warshaw asked.

"Where would you go if you were going to build a fleet?" Franks answered the question with a question.

"It's a long way from Earth . . . hard to protect," Warshaw said.

"Who are they protecting it from, the aliens? The aliens go after planets, not satellites," Franks said. Then he looked down at his holographic display, and added, "Gentlemen, and in your case, Harris, I use the term loosely, we have arrived."

I looked out through the viewport and saw nothing other than open space.

"Have you ever been to the dry docks?" I asked Warshaw.

"No, have you?" He sounded confident that I had not.

"I've been there," I said. I would have said more, but something about the way Franks knelt over his display distracted me. He brought up a floating holographic display of the dry docks.

"I'm getting a reading from the dry docks facility," Franks said. "There's some kind of activity going on around it." He flipped a switch that brought up a shoebox-sized virtual representation of the bridge.

"Sound general quarters," Franks told his virtual bridge, sounding calm, like a clone who was bred for command.

"Have they spotted us?" asked Warshaw. He walked over to get a closer look.

"Look at this. Look, here, and here," he said, pointing at the display. "See these three ships here, they're moored outside the dry docks," Franks said. "That means they are operational. At the very least, they have been out for a test flight."

He turned back to his virtual bridge, and said, "Bring all weapons systems online. Relay all orders to B2 and B3." For lack of better names, we currently referred to the captured battleships as B1, B2, and B3.

"Do we even know if they are capital ships?" Warshaw leaned over the monitor. "Maybe they're just cargo."

I once thought all sailors were alike, the same way Warshaw or Franks probably believed all Marines were alike. Watching these two clones operate, I now saw vast differences.

Franks, who had spent his career in navigation and weapons, had an intuitive understanding of tactics and situations. Warshaw, the more decorated and experienced of the two, had worked his way up in Engineering. He could keep a ship running; but when it came to commanding a ship, he was out of his depth.

I half expected Warshaw to argue or try to take control of

the situation, but he didn't. "Do you think they pose a threat?" he asked.

"Better safe than sorry," Franks answered, without looking up from the display. "If they are building the new fleet out here, then those are going to be ships from that fleet."

"They could have come from the Norma Central Fleet," Warshaw suggested.

Franks shook his head. "The Norma Central Fleet is a thousand light-years away."

I started to say something but stopped myself as I realized that I no longer had a part in the conversation.

"How far to the dry docks?" Warshaw asked.

"We're still about 1.5 million miles out."

"Think they know we sounded general quarters?"

I wanted to ask if they even knew we were here.

"They know. They went on high alert, too," Franks said. "This is our chance to get a closer look at those ships. Who knows when we will get another shot like this."

I didn't like the odds. We had three ships, and so did they, but our ships were sixty years old. They had brand-new equipment. I pointed this out.

Warshaw took up the cause. "We can't risk a fight. Until we pick up more equipment, these ships are all we have."

"Now they're sounding general quarters," Franks added. He seemed more fascinated by this turn of events than bothered by it.

"That's enough, Franks. Get us out of here," Warshaw repeated.

"We're safe. Hell, for all we know, they might not have crews on those ships," Franks said. Then, to the helm, he added, "Set speed to fifty thousand." At fifty-thousand miles per hour, it would take us thirty hours to reach the dry docks.

This seemed to calm Warshaw slightly. He asked, "What if they do have men aboard?"

"Doesn't seem likely," Franks argued.

"Who would have sounded general quarters?" Warshaw asked.

"Dry-docks security could have triggered the alarms."

"Why sound general quarters on empty ships?" Warshaw asked.

"It could be a bluff," Franks said. "They might be bluffing to make us think their ships have gone online. We don't even know if their specking weapons systems are operational. For all we know, those ships are empty shells."

He looked down at his display and muttered something I could not make out. At that moment, the bridge let us know that two of the three moored ships had launched in our direction.

"What's their speed?" Franks asked the bridge.

The answer, "Five hundred, sir," came from the virtual bridge.

"Franks, get us out of here," Warshaw commanded.

"We might not get another opportunity like this. They're only sending two ships out, that's three of us against two of them."

"They'll be in firing range in two minutes," Warshaw said. "Looks to me like they are spoiling for a fight."

"Here is a chance to see the new class in action. Do you really want to run?" Franks argued. He was right. It was our one chance to gather intelligence by watching those ships in action, but I thought it might be fatal intelligence.

"Take us out of here," Warshaw growled.

Franks sighed as he gave the order to his virtual bridge. "Contact the other ships. Tell them to broadcast to Mogat space."

The viewport darkened, the lightning danced, and we traded one space panorama for another.

THIRTY-SEVEN

Earthdate: December 12, A.D. 2516
Location: Mogat Home Planet
Galactic Position: Norma Arm

We broadcasted in a hundred thousand miles above the Mogat home world, roughly half the distance between the Earth and its moon. Before hearing Franks's little lecture about differences in space, I never paid attention to the textures of the stars. Out there in the Galactic Eye, space looked like black velvet walls studded with millions of Christmas lights. The only direction in which I saw undisturbed darkness was toward the planet below us.

What the Avatari had hoped to do to New Copenhagen and Terraneau, they had already accomplished on this planet. They had captured the planet, saturated it with toxic gas, then baked it by expanding the nearby sun. The extinct sun loomed like a shadow orbited by a cinder of a planet.

. . . *And when he invented hell for himself, behold, that was his very heaven,* I thought, another little gem from Nietzsche.

"Scan the area," Franks ordered his virtual bridge.

My eyes adjusted before my mind could accept what they saw. We drifted slowly toward the graveyard, a floating reef of dead ships and debris left in the wake of the U.A. Navy attack on the Mogat Fleet. As my eyes took in the starry surroundings, I began seeing shadows of inert shapes. I saw hulls and wings, whole ships and partial ships outlined in light, floating in place, as sharp and as dead as fish in a jar of formaldehyde.

A voice came from Franks's console. "The area is clear, sir. It doesn't look like anyone has been out here in years, sir."

"Well, General Harris, we have twelve crews and four hundred ships to explore," Warshaw said as he rose to his feet. "Did you plan to join us?"

"I do," I said, more aware than ever that I had come on this operation as an observer. This was a job for engineers and technicians. Having a leatherneck along would add nothing to the equation.

"Have you ever been on a wreck before?" I asked Warshaw as we left the observation deck and cut our way across the bridge.

"No. I hear it can get ugly," he answered.

"It's pretty grim," I said, remembering a mission in which I had explored a wreck. There were bodies floating weightless, frozen in the null heat. Once the hull of a ship gets pierced, the air, heat, and pressure flush out of the hole, and the inside of the ship becomes as sterile as the space around it.

"Maybe you know the answer to this. I always wondered, what happens first when your ship gets smashed? Do you freeze, suffocate, or explode?"

"It's that bad?" Warshaw asked.

He must have thought I was joking or trying to make a point. I wasn't. That question had remained on my mind since the first time I boarded a Mogat wreck.

"Admiral," I said, "this tour will haunt you for the rest of your life."

CHAPTER
THIRTY-EIGHT

In my experience, sailors and officers waged wars like gods. They sat on high, out of the line of fire, sending more expendable souls to bleed and die on the battlefields.

But both the officers and the sailors came along for the ride this time. I wondered if Warshaw or Franks had ever seen the aftermath of a space battle. The flash-frozen bodies on these ships would look exactly as they had the moment after the battle. Without oxygen or heat, they did not decay.

We piled into transports, cramming the kettles beyond capacity with 120 men each, plus equipment. Unlike Marines, human crustaceans in their hardened combat armor, engineers wore soft-shells—rubberized suits that were flame-, chemical-, and radiation-retardant, but little else. Far from bulletproof, engineering armor wouldn't even protect them from an assailant with a mechanical pencil. As little more than an observer on this mission, I was issued soft-shell armor. By the time the transport doors closed, I already knew I hated engineering armor.

Crushed against the back wall of the kettle, I felt a bolt digging into my side. When another man stepped on my foot, I felt it. It didn't hurt, but I didn't expect to feel anything.

The visors on the soft-shelled armor showed the names and ranks of the men around me. Instead of night-for-day lenses, these suits had cheery little torches along their visors. They had a good reason for this backward step in technology. Night-for-day vision wreaked havoc with depth perception and showed the world in monochrome. Working with color-coded wires, circuits, and diodes, these engineers needed to know red from green. Hell, even their armor was color-coded. Weapons techs wore red armor, electronic and computer systems specialists wore yellow, and engineers wore blue.

I'd brought contraband on this mission. As the only Marine in a flock of sailors, I felt duty-bound to bring a weapon— a particle-beam pistol. If Warshaw ever came on a mission with me, I'd allow him to bring a wrench . . . in the spirit of fairness.

The sailors around me had to have been chatting on the interLink, but I was deaf to them. Reminding me that this was a naval mission, Warshaw refused to give me a commandLink, the bastard. He alone could listen in on every conversation and speak on private frequencies with whomever he liked.

That left me in isolation. I stood in the tightly packed kettle alone with my thoughts.

The audio equipment in my armor was not as sensitive

to ambient sound as the equipment in combat armor. I knew when we lifted off because I felt it, but I could not hear the boosters. Instead of telescopic lenses, my engineering visor had a magnification lens. Engineers don't snipe, they inspect circuits.

"They're away," Warshaw said. On the off chance that the U.A. sent a patrol through Mogat space, we sent our ships back to Terraneau.

"The battleships?" I asked. I knew the answer before I asked, but I wanted to talk. I was lonely. Goddamn.

"Yes, the battleships. Harris, you said you entered one of these ships once. Is that really true or were you just slinging shit?"

"The Mogats scuttled a ship in the Perseus Arm, I went out to explore it."

"How did you get in?" Warshaw asked.

We sure as hell didn't ride in on a gigantic specking transport, I thought. "There was a gash on bottom of the ship. We flew a ten-man sled in through one of the holes."

"Did you try opening the docking-bay doors?"

"Nope."

"Did you have engineers with you?"

"Nope, SEALs."

Warshaw sort of snorted, and said, "SEALs."

"They knew their stuff," I said.

"Yeah, I'm sure they did," Warshaw said. "Look, Harris, you mind going out with A Team? It sounds like you have more experience finding your way around a wreck."

"No problem," I said.

A moment later, Warshaw's voice came over an open channel as he addressed every man on the transport. "We're opening the rear hatch. A Team prepare to launch."

The pilot maintained the gravity field within the kettle, keeping us rooted to the ground, even as he purged the air from the kettle so that we would not be flushed out when he opened the doors. Once the atmosphere turned into a vacuum, the doors slid apart, revealing an open field of space and stars.

One of the men at the top of the ramp panicked. He screamed for help over an open frequency and tried to fight his way to the back of the kettle. Warshaw addressed the kid over an open frequency. "Westerfield, get out there."

"I, I can't. I can't."

"That is an order," Warshaw said, but the softness in his voice made it more of a request than an order.

"I can't do it."

Warshaw ordered the other sailors to let the kid through, and then asked, "Is anyone else too specking scared?"

I reminded myself that these were sailors, not Marines. They had grown accustomed to having an atmosphere and walls around them.

"No other takers?" Warshaw asked. "Okay, A Team, move out."

That was my call. There were about twenty of us on the team. We walked down the ramp, the gravity becoming weaker the farther we got. Halfway down, I could have kicked off hard and flown into space. When the first man reached the bottom of the ramp, he held his motivator over his head and lifted off.

Engineers used handheld motivators instead of attaching jetpacks to their armor. The device looked like a pair of binoculars with handlebars instead of a strap. Their thrust technology used noncombustible gas emissions instead of flames. When I switched on its power, my motivator lifted me from the ramp and into open space.

Following the sailor before me, I banked around the stern of the transport. As we flew along the transport, the pilot switched on the runner lights along the hull, lighting the rust-colored skids and smooth steel underbelly of the sturdy bird. Each motivator had a row of knuckle-sized safety lights blinking a ruby red signal along their top.

Our team leader hit some button, and a headlight appeared at the front of his motivator. He only flew about fifty feet ahead of me; but I could not see him, just the cone of his headlight. The men ahead of me lit lights on their motivators as well.

We circled the wreck of a massive battleship like a swarm of flies approaching a beached whale. The holes along the belly of the ship were large enough for us to fly through, but the bottom deck of the ship had imploded.

"General Harris, sir?" My visor identified the man on the line as our team leader contacting me on an open line.

"What is it, Ensign?"

"Sir, do you know what kinds of weapons they used on this ship? I've never seen such extensive damage."

Having spent the last six years of their lives trapped in the Scutum-Crux Arm, none of these boys had ever seen combat up close. "This is what happens when you get hit with your shields down," I said. What I did not add was that this ship had gotten off lightly.

"Their shields were down?" the team leader asked. "Why would they lower their shields in battle?"

"We lowered the shields for them," I said. "The Mogats used a centralized shielding technology that they broadcast to their fleet. Once our SEALs shut down the central shield generator, the ships were unprotected."

"You were in on the Mogat invasion, sir?" The team leader did not ask that question; it came from another member of our little team. I heard a tone of awe in the boy's voice.

"Yeah, I was there," I said, trying to keep the darkness of my thoughts out of my voice. "A lot of good men died. We lost a lot more men than we should have."

We flew across the battered underbelly of the battleship and up the port side. My interLink connection remained fairly quiet as men fanned out and inspected holes and burns along the face of the ship. Three decks up, one of the men found our doorway.

"The outer lock of the docking bay is open," the man reported.

Knowing that the end had come, some Mogats had piled into a transport to abandon ship. They almost made it to safety. The broken nose of the transport poked out of the docking-bay hatch like a missile launching from a silo. The outer hatch of the docking bay had come down on the transport like a giant cleaver, slicing halfway through the kettle and crushing the rest into a bow-shaped heap.

The transport had made it through all three atmospheric locks when the first torpedo or laser pierced the hull of the battleship. Once the hull integrity failed, all of the outer hatches would have automatically sealed to protect the ship against the vacuum of space. In theory, sealing hatches creates pockets of oxygen in which sailors can survive for days. I'd been on enough wrecks to know that air pockets preserve fires, not lives. Rescuers never arrive in time. Scavengers may come looking for treasure, but the hope of rescue is the last resort of fools.

We flew in around the crushed transport. The eight-inch-thick hatch had slid down like a blade on a guillotine with enough force to flatten the nearly impregnable walls of a kettle.

Small diodes embedded in my visor sent out a fifteen-foot shaft of light. Beyond that beam of light, blackness shrouded everything not illuminated by the beams from another man's helmet.

As I worked my way in along the side of the transport, three men floated in place, staring into a spot where the hatch had sliced through the kettle wall. Seeing the wreckage of the transport gave these boys a good introduction to what they would find inside the ship.

"Move along," the team leader said. "We have a job to do. Perryman, Miller, Ferris, see if you can open the locks. Goldberg, Lewis, figure out a way to sweep this place out. I need the runway clear." By "sweep" he meant for them to purge the transport.

"Aye, aye, sir."

Until we found a way to open the inner doors of the atmospheric locks, we would not be able to enter the ship. A trio of beams played along the wall until they all centered on the same panel. Using small torches, three engineers cut away the panel and discarded it. Behind the panel, they found a small lever, which one of them pumped up and down as if using a socket wrench. After four or five twists, the door pinning down the transport lifted toward the ceiling, rocking the injured transport as the hatch rose from the kettle.

"How can it still have power?" I asked the team leader.

"Emergency hydraulics."

Three engineers placed charges along the rear of the transport. There was a flash, a small explosion, and the wreck rolled into space.

"That was easy," the team leader said over an open channel.

Getting rid of that transport was the only thing that came easily. The other emergency controls were all on the inner sides of each hatch, meaning our engineers needed to cut through each of the locks, then open the way for the rest of us.

It took Warshaw's engineers most of an hour to untangle the first lock, but they learned as they went. The next lock only took ten minutes. After they opened it, we entered the enormous, blackened cavern of the landing bay. Up to that point, the sailors only knew there would be bodies aboard the ship. Now they saw some.

Men in overalls hung suspended just off the ground, their limbs so stiff and brittle they might have been made of glass. I spotted a man whose face hung from his head like a flap of skin on a badly stubbed toe. The exposed parts of his skin had the blue-white color of an evening cloud. The skinned remains of his head sparkled like coal. His blood hung above him in a tangle of beaded icicles.

The team leader started to say something and vomited. I felt bad for the man, I did. Once the transport came, he could clean his equipment; but without steam cleaning, the air in that armor would never be sweet again.

"Good God," the team leader bawled.

"Get used to it, Ensign. Everybody on this ship is going to look like that," I said.

Nobody said anything after that, at least they did not say anything to me. For all I knew, the rest of the team was playing twenty questions. I doubted it, though. Most of the men stood in a huddle staring at the body, the lights from their visors shining on a loose flap of skin that had once been a face.

Trying to get the mission back on track, I asked the team leader, "Ensign, are you planning on bringing our transport inside to dock?"

"Yes, sir," he said, his voice so mechanical that I could not tell if he understood what I'd said.

CHAPTER THIRTY-NINE

In the blackness of the runway, the transport's runner lights showed crystal white, bleaching everything they shone on. With the ship destroyed and no power for the runway sleds, our pilot had to fly the transport all the way in, a slow and testing process.

Negotiating past one of the locks, the transport shined its lights directly over me, and I learned the hard way that engineering armor did not have automatic tint shields. Unaware that my visor would not protect my eyes from the glare, I watched the transport's lights as it taxied up the runway. Then the lights hit me. Even after I looked away, orange and yellow ghosts blurred my vision.

The transport touched down and Admiral Gary Warshaw congratulated A Team for opening the docking bay. He followed up with, "Okay, men, you have your assignments. Let's get this ship finished quickly, we have three hundred more to go."

The rear of the kettle opened, and a swarm of technicians slid out, carrying toolboxes and meters and equipment I could not have identified.

As Alpha Team made its way into the ship, four of its members had to return to the transport. Poor bastards—they were the ones who threw up inside their armor. Their teammates would give them grief once the mission ended.

"Harris, you still dry inside your armor or do you need to visit the head?" Warshaw asked.

"Marines don't lose their lunch when they see breakage," I said, hoping to hell that he had not somehow heard about my little vomiting fit on Terraneau. He hadn't.

"Get specked, Harris," he said.

I spotted Warshaw gliding down the ramp. He moved

with the ease of a man who has logged time in zero-gravity situations.

Looking around the bay, I decided that we had come to the right place if we wanted outdated transports or other obsolete equipment. A row of salvageable transports lined the far wall of the landing area. Tools, bodies, and furniture lay in an avalanche blocking our way to the ship. A couple of engineers pushed their way through the debris and jimmied the door open.

This battleship was a long-dead twin of the one we flew in on. They had the exact same floor plan. The halls of this ship were dark and silent, but they had the same turns and passages.

I did not use my motivator to fly through the halls. I kicked off surfaces and redirected my momentum by pushing off the walls. I passed through a mess hall so large it could have substituted for an aircraft hangar. The tables, which were bolted to the floor, had not moved, but a pile of bodies lay stacked against one wall. Strands of blood formed a web over the jumble of corpses. I had to break that web to reach the hatch on the far side of the mess.

Warshaw and his men had tasks to accomplish on this ship. For now, I was little more than a tourist come to see the grisly sights. I traveled through officer country across a rec room and finally down toward the lower decks. When I reached the Engineering sections, I spotted Warshaw and his men gathering around the broadcast generator—a group of eighteen bullet-shaped cylinders that stood thirty feet tall.

"Looks like it's in solid condition," I said, noting that none of the brass cylinders had so much as a dent.

"Nah, this one's a complete bust," said Warshaw.

"The cylinders look fine," I said.

"Yeah, well, they would look perfectly sound to a Marine, they're big, unbreakable, and made of metal. It's the rigging on top that takes all the damage." He sounded confident, but I wondered just how much time and training Warshaw had when it came to broadcast technology.

"How about the broadcast computer?" I asked.

Warshaw did not answer for several seconds, but I knew better than to repeat the question. I waited. He put a finger

over the part of his helmet that covered his ears, and I realized
he wasn't ignoring me, he was receiving a message. Finally,
he said, "Harris, the team on the bridge has spotted incoming
battleships."

"Franks must be in a hurry, he's not due back for . . ."

"U.A. battleships, the ones we spotted by the dry docks,"
Warshaw said.

"Shit," I said.

There was no way those could have tracked us here. There
was no way to track where ships broadcasted themselves.
"Maybe it's some kind of routine patrol," I said.

Warshaw ignored that idea, and said, "Who knows what
they have on those ships. They probably read the data off our
computers before we broadcasted out." He was guessing, but
it sounded like a reasonable guess.

Warshaw and I headed to the bridge together, flying
through the dark corridors as quickly as we could. By sticking to inner corridors, we managed to skirt around most of the
damage, but we passed a lot of bodies. The sailors in the outer
halls would have been sucked out into space. In the heart of
the ship, though, the dead remained, floating forever in their
cryogenic sepulcher.

Flying up an elevator shaft, we made our way to the bridge.
In a working ship, it would have taken ten minutes to sprint
from Engineering to the bridge. Floating weightless in this
ghost ship, we made the trip in less than five.

"Have all of the transports docked?" I asked.

"You shitting me?" Warshaw asked. "Three of 'em are
socked away. The other nine are playing possum."

In a graveyard like this, with four hundred capital ships,
turning off your engines and letting your transport float would
leave you all but invisible.

Two men dressed in the red armor of weapons techs met
us at the command area. They spoke on a direct frequency. I
could not hear anyone with my Link unless I called them or
they called me. Warshaw was well within his rights when he
labeled this a "naval operation," but he'd stuck it to me when
he assigned me standard communications equipment instead
of a commandLink. Bastard.

Without a word of explanation, Warshaw headed toward

one of the off-bridge conference rooms. I had no idea whether I should follow him or not. I trailed after him, feeling more isolated by the minute.

The oblong room had a table and a viewport with a panoramic view of utter blackness. I went to the viewport and stared into the void outside, the light from my visor forming bright spots on the glass.

"Harris, kill the light on your visor," Warshaw said. He sounded angry.

Now I was embarrassed and angry at myself. He was right. It was less significant than a needle, but a passing ship might spot the light from my helmet.

Though I could not see it through the viewport, a vast outer-space battlefield lay on display outside this ship. Without outside illumination, I could not see the broken ships or the desolate planet beyond them. And then, off in the distance, I saw the first trace of light.

"I see one," I said to Warshaw.

I could not see the ship itself, just a gold-tinted luminescence that slowly hovered in our direction. As it glided toward us, I recognized the knife-blade shape of the hull. A general glow poured out of it, shining on the derelicts and debris as the battleship pushed past them.

Warshaw and two of his men came for a look. I wondered what they said to each other, and was reminded how much I hated Warshaw for sticking me with a standard Link.

The ship ambled closer, the glow from its hull lighting up everything it passed. The battleship floated by a defunct Mogat ship. In the gold glow, I saw scars along the dead ship's sides. The hole in the bridge was so large, a skilled pilot could have steered a transport through it.

I noticed something about the glow around that battleship as it approached. It was like a skin.

"Admiral," I said. By this time, he had left the viewport and stood talking with his techs. "Warshaw," I repeated.

"Not now, Harris," he said.

This was a new technology. The ships I had served on had projected shields that formed an invisible box around the ship. I chanced a quick glance back at Warshaw and saw that he had spread some kind of chart across the conference table. He and four of his men stood huddled together over the table, Warshaw pointing to a spot above the chart. As a ranking officer, I belonged in their conference. I looked back at the oncoming battleship, then went over to the table.

At first, I thought it must be a joke. The map or chart Warshaw had spread was blank, just a square of plasticized cloth with no marks at all. It took me a moment to understand. The cloth projected a virtual display that Warshaw and his techs saw through their visors. That function had not been activated on my visor. Paraphrasing Warshaw's mantra in my head, I mumbled, "specking naval operations." I returned to the viewport and saw a second battleship cruising toward us.

"Warshaw, there is a second battleship out there," I said.

"I'm aware of that," Warshaw said, his voice sounding testy. "I'm also tracking a third ship coming in at about five o'clock. Now, if you don't mind, Harris, I'm busy at the moment."

I did mind.

The first battleship came closer, cutting through the empty space with the confidence of a shark gliding through open waters. I studied the way its shields adhered around it like a second skin, as if the ship had been dipped and coated in glowing plastic. Sparks flashed in the shield when anything struck the ship—tiny explosions that flared and faded in the silent darkness.

I looked back toward Warshaw and saw him pointing at invisible details above that mat. Was it a map? A schematic? I should have been in on the planning. Yes, I was a lowly Marine, but I was also the highest-ranking officer in the fleet, damn it. Except, of course, Brocius had given Warshaw a third star. We had the same specking rank, even if this was a naval operation.

"General, would you like to join us?" Warshaw asked. It was not a friendly invitation. He was not asking me to help with the planning. He wanted to give me an obligatory briefing, the same kind of briefing company commanders give their platoon sergeants before throwing them into a battle.

Outside the viewport, the first battleship pulled even with us, then flashed past. I stared out into the darkness for another second, unable to tell whether the light to my left was the second battleship or a visual echo burned into my irises from the first ship.

"Harris, care to join us?" Warshaw repeated, a note of annoyance in his voice.

"They have new technology in their shields," I said, as I turned to join the planning.

"Yes, I suspect they do," Warshaw agreed.

"It looks like it's based on Avatari technology," I said.

"What kind of technology?" A perfunctory question.

"The technology the aliens used," I said.

"I wasn't aware that the aliens used ships," Warshaw said. I could hear other people on the Link as well. I had been invited into a conference.

"They didn't, but they lent the technology to the Mogats," I said.

"The Mogats used alien technology in their shields? That explains a lot," Warshaw said. I heard notes of agreement in the background. "We found disabled shield generators on almost every ship we've boarded. A few of the ships didn't have any shield systems at all."

"That's because they used a central generator that the aliens gave them," I said.

"Do you think the aliens might have given a similar generator to the Unified Authority?"

Of course not, you pompous, preening son of a bitch, I thought. "I think the Navy may have deciphered their technology. Lord knows, they've had enough scientists trying to work it out.

"If they do have it worked out, we're screwed," I added.

"We're going to find out," Warshaw said. "In fifteen minutes, we're going to open fire on those ships."

CHAPTER
FORTY

A three-dimensional map of the area appeared in the air above the table. The hulls of twelve ships appeared in red, surrounded by the hulls of another three hundred ships in green.

"The red ships are the ones we've boarded," Warshaw said.

I wanted to congratulate him for his ability to state the obvious, but I knew better. If he reverted into "naval operation" mode, he would leave me in the dark until we either died or returned to the fleet. "I thought we had more teams out," I said.

"Some of the teams have not been able to break into their ships," Warshaw said. *Poor them.* That meant those teams would spend the battle playing possum in their transports.

"Judging by the way they are patrolling, the U.A. ships know we are here, but they have no idea where we are hiding. One of them bumped into a transport without scanning it."

"How is the transport?" I asked.

"The pilot is shook-up, but . . ."

"No, how is the transport itself?"

One of the techs said, "The pilot did not report any problems."

"What are you getting at, Harris?" Warshaw asked.

"Just curious," I said.

The shields the Mogats used absorbed energy. If a Mogat ship bumped a transport, its shields would have drained the transport's batteries. I decided to file the information away rather than share it.

"My teams have found functional weapons systems on seven of the ships," Warshaw said. As he said this, the display darkened as five of the red ships turned a swampy blue. The seven remaining red ships formed a misshapen ring.

I pictured the landscape in my head. If I had it right, the ships the U.A. sent to chase us down had passed right through that ring. Assuming Warshaw's men could get those weapons systems up and running, they could incinerate those ships the next time they passed through. It sounded too good to be true. In fact, it sounded downright impossible.

"How can these wrecks have working weapons systems?" I asked. These derelicts had been floating in space for years. I did not understand how they could have working systems.

"Functional, not working," Warshaw said. "We've isolated the weapons systems from the rest of the ship and supplied our own power."

"What about shields?" I asked. "Can you get them working?"

Warshaw laughed. "It sounds like those U.A. battleships make you nervous."

That summed up my feelings accurately. On the battlefield, I had some control over the environment. Out here, all I could do was sit back and watch. If the ship went down, I would go down with it.

"What do you have, lasers and torpedoes?" I asked. Having seen all of the damage along the hull of this ship, I wondered how reliable the torpedo tubes might be.

"Just lasers," Warshaw said. He sounded distracted, as if he was holding a conversation with someone else at the same time that he answered my questions. He had the command-Link, he could do that . . . the bastard.

"No torpedoes. What if you can't get through their shields?" I asked.

In the sixty years since the construction of the ships in this derelict fleet, the Unified Authority had stopped building lasers into battleships and switched to a more effective particle-beam technology; but even particle beams did not cause the trauma of a torpedo.

"Then we're dead," Warshaw answered in a voice that sounded like a verbal shrug of the shoulders. "We're as good as dead if we don't find a way to get rid of those ships before Franks comes back."

He had a point.

* * *

I never claimed to understand the naval approach to combat. For some reason that defied all logic, Warshaw insisted on pulling the trigger from the bridge. On a working ship with operational systems, that would have made sense. On this derelict, he sat in a pitch-black chamber filled with lifeless computers, broken systems, and an audience of stiffs.

I remained on the off-bridge observation deck, watching the battlefield through the viewport. In the distance, I caught brief glimpses of light, nothing more than a streak here and there. Perhaps we had hidden too well the first time the battleships patrolled our little corner at the edge of the graveyard.

Fighting this battle no more aggressively than a spider tending a web, we could not hit those U.A. battleships until they entered our trap. Franks would return in another thirty-two minutes. We either had to clear the enemy ships out of the area or they would catch our self-broadcasting fleet off guard. Time was running out.

Staring out the viewport and seeing nothing but darkness, I gave up on the Warshaw Plan. We were in a life-and-death battle, and he wanted to fight it like a specking engineer—relying on antiquated weapons and enemies blundering into his trap. Granted, booting up the weapons systems on a bunch of derelict ships was a brilliant piece of speckery; he had ginned up a fighting chance in a lost situation. But we would not win unless we took the reins.

Five minutes ticked by before any of the battleships appeared again. I waited alone in that blasted conference room, in the stark gloom. The light of one battleship appeared in the extreme corner of the viewport. The big ship was so far away that its light might have been the signature of a firefly.

What were they doing out there? If they had the ability to track us this far, they should have known that Franks had taken our self-broadcasters back to Terraneau. They had to know.

The spark of light that looked no bigger than a firefly cut a twisted path in the distance. No longer swimming in straight strokes, the battleship conducted a more methodical search, dodging this way and that as it came closer. It circled completely around one wreck.

A second battleship appeared, loosely shadowing the first.

The third one would have to be nearby, guarding their flank. Another eight minutes passed as the battleships slowly meandered into range.

"What if only two of them come in range, are you going to take the shot?" I asked Warshaw.

"Take the shot? Is that Marine lingo?" he asked.

Engage, shoot the specker, give them a laser enema, a dozen responses ran through my mind, some positive, some not. I said nothing.

"There are three U.A. ships out there. We won't accomplish our objective by only sinking two of them," Warshaw said.

"Franks is going to broadcast into the area in less than thirty minutes. This may be the last time any of those ships stumbles into your shooting gallery," I said.

"Stay out of this, Harris," Warshaw repeated. "This is not a friendly game of bullets and grenades. Battlefield tactics don't work here."

"Taking out one of those birds may just even the odds for Franks," I said.

"Bullshit, Harris. If Franks comes in unprepared, they'll use him for target practice." Warshaw signed off as one of the U.A. ships swished past my viewport. I checked the time—21:49, just eleven minutes and Franks would fly in to rendezvous.

Warshaw had driven one point home above all else, that we were as good as dead unless we destroyed all three enemy ships. Without announcing my intentions, I slipped out of the observation area and headed back to the docking bay.

I dropped down two decks, skirted a badly damaged corridor along the outer edge of the ship, and found an inner corridor leading toward the rear of the ship. Lights flickered inside one of the hatches as I passed. I peered in and saw some of Warshaw's men removing a panel from a wall. They ran cables from a jeep-sized crate into the circuits they had uncovered.

I did not have time to worry about weapons systems, though I would die in the next few minutes if Warshaw's men could not get the weapons systems working.

My plan hinged on my finding a pilot for the transport. I

entered the docking bay, not sure whether the man piloting our transport had remained in his bird. Someone had pivoted the transport around so that its nose pointed out toward space. The rear doors sat wide open, revealing an empty kettle, the gravity off. I launched myself up the ramp, paused just long enough to seal the rear hatch, then kicked off the floor to the cockpit, not bothering with the ladder.

For one cold moment, I thought that the cockpit was empty, but then a man in pilot gear hovered over to meet me.

"What are you doing here?" he asked.

Staring into the pilot's face, I switched on the edge lighting around my visor, hoping to blind him. Then, bracing my knee under a bolted-down chair so that I had some purchase, I grabbed the man and slung him across the cockpit. He landed in his pilot's chair and said, "Hey!"

"Hey"? I thought. What an asshole.

I whipped out my particle-beam pistol, a tiny, unimpressive-looking weapon with a great capacity for doing damage, and I tapped it against the pilot's visor. "I want to go for a ride," I said. When he did not respond right away, I added, "Call for help, and I'll fry you on the spot."

I was already too late.

"Harris, what are you doing?" It was Warshaw.

The asshole must have started calling for help while I was slinging him into his chair. "You miserable little prick," I said to the pilot, tapping my pistol against his visor as I spoke each word.

"Please, just . . ."

"Harris, get your ass up here." Warshaw barked the command at me as if he were speaking to a buck private.

"Do you want to die now, or take your chances?" I asked the pilot.

"Harris, I said get up here. Now!"

The pilot must have thought my question was rhetorical. He did not answer.

I needed to keep the guy scared. No matter what else happened, I needed him so scared of me that he did not consider consequences. Still leveraging myself with my legs, I leaned forward and slammed my fist into his gut.

If he'd been dressed in stiff combat armor, I would have

broken my fingers and wrist long before he felt a thing, but he felt this blow. The poor son of a bitch doubled over right there in his seat, burying his visor in his knees. His soft-shelled armor might not have offered him much protection, but it let him double over better than combat armor would have.

Judging by the way Warshaw shouted, "Harris, what the speck do you think you are doing?" I decided the pilot must have been pleading for help when I hit him.

"This is a Marine operation, Admiral," I said. Then I turned my attention to the pilot. "Next time I use this, asshole," I said, pressing my pistol to his visor once more. "Now, get us out of here."

"We'll settle up, Harris. When this is over, you and I are going to settle up," Warshaw yelled. He might have said more, but he had more important things on his mind than my mutiny.

Warshaw's hands were tied. His engineers had opened the locks but never brought them online. He could not shut the doors on me, and I was the only man on the ship with a gun. He had no way to stop the transport from leaving, and the terrified pilot was not going to put up a fight.

"Where are we going?" the pilot asked. He sounded as if he was still fighting for breath.

I cuffed the man across the side of his head with my pistol. I did not enjoy terrorizing the boy, but I needed him scared and obedient. "Just take us out, fast."

"There are battleships out there!"

"I know, I saw them," I said.

"They're going to see us," the pilot said. "They'll shoot us down."

"If they want us, they're going to have to come and get us," I said, trying to remember the layout of Warshaw's map. I tapped my pistol on the pilot's visor, and he lifted us off the deck and started down the runway. Our transport lumbered through the tunnel at such a slow rate that I might have been able to outrun it on foot.

21:53:36

At 2200, Franks would arrive. That gave us six minutes until he broadcast with his shields down and his guns asleep. I pistol-whipped the pilot, and growled, "Faster, asshole."

The pilot did not say anything, but the transport picked up speed.

21:54:00

We slipped through the locks, one after another. As we broke into open space, the pilot flipped a switch to shut off the runner lights.

"Leave 'em on," I said.

"Are you out of your . . ."

I swatted his soft-shell helmet with my pistol again. I did not hit him hard, nothing that would give him a concussion; but I certainly hit him with enough force to make a lasting impression.

Looking out into space, I tried to figure out our position in relationship to Warshaw's map. "Does this bird have any more lights?"

"No, sir," the pilot said. He sounded suitably scared.

I could see the shapes of the wrecks against the stars, but they meant nothing to me. With no other choice, I called Warshaw over the interLink, not entirely sure he would read me now that I had left the ship.

After seconds of silence, he answered. "Harris. What the hell are you doing?" he asked, his voice filled with curiosity and disdain. He did not like me, but he did not think I was running away. "If you give away our position, I will . . ."

"I'm not giving away your position, dipshit, I am giving away my position," I said.

"You won't be able to outrun those ships if they spot you," Warshaw said.

"I don't want to outrun them.

"Harris, you don't have any guns."

"But you do," I said.

"I did not authorize . . ."

"Yeah, can we discuss that later?" I asked.

21:54:51

"Where do you want the damn ships?" Franks was going to return in another five minutes and nine seconds, and Warshaw wanted to talk about who did or did not authorize my flight. What an ass.

"You're thirty-five miles out of position," Warshaw said. Things went quiet. At first I thought he had abandoned me, then I realized he was explaining the lay of the land to my pilot.

As I waited for him to come back, the glowing figure of a battleship came around a hull and filled our windshield. Suddenly, I felt like a very small fish in a very large pond.

"Shit," my pilot said.

I started to tell him to get us out of there, but he figured it out on his own. He swung the transport into a forty-five-degree rotation that pointed us toward a narrow passage between two wrecks and hit the boosters. Had I been floating beside the copilot's seat, I would have been thrown back against the rear of the cockpit. I grabbed the seat in time to save myself.

"You probably should strap in, sir," the pilot said. I heard something unexpected in his voice: concern. As I struggled to pull myself into the chair, the pilot did me another kindness—he switched on the gravity generator. That shifted the center of gravity from the rear of the ship to the bottom. Gs still pulled at my back, but I was able to sit down and buckle myself in.

For a moment, the only thing I could see through the windshield was the hulls of destroyed ships, but then a trace of golden glow appeared along the top edge of the windshield.

"Watch out," I said, pointing toward the ship.

"There's another one behind us," the pilot said.

The beam of a searchlight rolled along the alley ahead of us, questing to touch us, lighting the dark hulls of the ships wrecked long ago. Fortunately for us, radar would do no good in this floating junkyard. They would need to spot us to shoot us.

"Hold on, sir."

The nose of the transport dropped, and the entire ship seemed to somersault over itself. Suddenly, we were rocketing in a completely new direction. Had I been standing, I would have been slammed into the windshield, then rolled around the cabin.

For a moment I saw nothing but stars, but then a glowing hull slid into view. The pilot cut a sharp right and took us behind another wreck.

Not realizing anyone was listening in, I said, "What I'd give for a torpedo."

"You wouldn't want to do that, sir. Some of these wrecks are unstable," the pilot answered.

"How unstable?"

"That's why they haven't fired at us yet, they don't want to trigger a chain reaction."

Fuel, uranium reactors, oxygen, unexploded torpedoes . . . all of a sudden, I realized my own naïveté. I had boarded these death traps with the nonchalance of a Marine in a china shop.

"Warshaw?" I called, and got no answer. Specking great. I was out here in an unarmed transport with three uber-ships hunting me down, and I lost contact with Warshaw.

"Warshaw, goddamnit, where are you?"

There was no answer.

"Where do we go, sir?" the pilot asked.

"I don't know," I admitted. "Warshaw set up a trap, but I have no idea where it is."

The pilot did not answer me. Maybe he had given up, too. Seconds ticked by. Then, with an abrupt change of direction, we headed into a narrow gap between two ships. The pilot must have reached somebody.

"Are we headed toward the trap?" I asked.

"It's the other way, but we don't have any choice. They cut us off."

21:55:28

If Franks came back in on time, he would arrive in less than five minutes. He might be late, that would be a reprieve. He could also arrive early, while we were still playing cat and mouse with the battleships. Maybe he would save us, or maybe he would die trying, and I would spend the rest of my life trapped in a floating graveyard orbiting the planet on which so many Marines had died.

"You better get us there quick," I said.

"They've got us hemmed in on every side, sir," the pilot said. Then, with desperation in his voice, he added, "Don't hit me with that gun. For God's sake, please don't hit me again!"

"Just get us there," I yelled.

"As long as we stay close to the big wrecks, they aren't going to shoot," the pilot chanted. "They aren't going to shoot." He made a sharp turn, then darted under the bulbous bow of a derelict battleship. I caught a glimpse of the jagged edges of a torn hull.

"They won't shoot," the pilot repeated. He had to make the transport twist and drop to avoid an outcropping where two of the wrecks had drifted into each other. Transports were not designed for maneuverability. Behind us, the walls of the kettle groaned with every turn.

As we snaked our way between the demolished wreckage of the Mogat Fleet, a U.A. battleship closed in beside us. For a brief moment it was no more than a thousand yards away, and it kept its distance, like a cat waiting for a mouse to leave its hole.

"We have to get across there." The pilot pointed in the direction of the ship.

I looked at the empty stretch ahead, knowing that we would be an easy target the moment we entered it. We could not continue straight ahead, a ship blocked our way. "Cut your engines," I said.

"What?" asked the pilot.

"Cut your engines and put up your shields."

The wing of a dead capital ship stretched out, just at the edge of my vision.

"We'll hit that ship," the pilot said.

"Yeah, it's called the element of surprise," I said.

"Plowing into that wreck shield first could set off an explosion," he reminded me.

"You see any other options?" I asked.

"Hold on tight."

The transport did not slow when the pilot cut its thrusters, it slid forward at that same speed. I braced myself in my seat, helpless, as we drifted toward the wreck. We came in at an angle, skimming off the giant wing like a stone skipping water, the blue-white pane of our front shields shimmering like lightning in the darkness and once again becoming invisible.

The momentum would have bucked me out of my chair if not for the straps holding me in my seat. There were no fires or explosions inside our ship, transports were made to take worse beatings than this.

The collision did not rebound us in the direction we wanted

to go, but at least the ricochet sent us in a different direction than the big battleship. Leaning into the windshield, I watched the glowing, shielded hull of the battleship as it drifted away.

Fast and large and flying in a frictionless field, the U.A. ship was unable to turn sharply and follow us. Instead, it fired its particle-beam cannons at us. One of the green beams missed us entirely. The other glanced off the shields around the cockpit.

"Do you know where we need to go?" I asked the pilot.

"Yes, sir," the pilot said, as he started to double back into a shoal of ruined ships.

"So get us there!" I yelled.

"There's no cover in that direction!"

Something solid, probably a torpedo, struck us hard along our back. The shot sent us skittering into a spin. Had our engines been damaged, we might have gone cartwheeling into space, but our tough little transport adapted. The pilot hit the engines, using one set of boosters to stop our spin and another to launch us in what I hoped was the right direction. The yaw from his sudden turn wrenched me to one side.

"Is that where we want to go?" I asked.

"Not quite there," the pilot admitted. As he saw me reach for my pistol, he added, "I know what I'm doing. Don't hit me!"

21:56:42

I needed to forget about the specking clock.

The debris around us was just as large as our transport. We battered our way through chunks of ship, unrecognizable trash, furniture, and an occasional corpse. We flew past a familiar shape: another transport, one of ours, playing possum. A second or two later, we slid into a tight alley between the busted hull of a destroyer and the ruins of an even bigger ship.

Two glowing U.A. battleships circled us at a leisurely pace, like vultures waiting for their meal. They had all the time in world. We were small, slow, and unarmed.

21:57:10

"Please tell me we are headed in the right direction?" I asked the pilot.

Warshaw answered the question. The first laser flared

out like a spear, striking the battleship head-on. The steady stream of silvery red laser fire lashed at the U.A. ship's bow, striking just below the top deck.

The second of the Unified Authority battleships charged in, heading toward the source of the attack. As it did, another ship fired its lasers. The shields around both U.A. ships flashed brighter and brighter as the second battleship tried to return fire. When the third battleship entered the shooting gallery, Warshaw ordered all of his ships to let loose.

The light from the shields grew brighter and brighter. From where I sat, it looked as if the scene were happening in daylight instead of deep space. Listless derelicts floating like clouds, their laser beams straight as the spokes of a wheel, fired lasers into the glowing shields of the U.A. ships.

The shields around one of the U.A. ships began to fail, allowing our lasers to strike the unprotected hull. The ship took damage. Bubbles appeared along its bow. The bubbles punctured the outer walls of the ship, and flames appeared. Where there are flames, there must be oxygen—air was leaking from the outer wall of the ship. Death.

We must have drifted within interLink range. Warshaw had created an open channel so that his men could hear what was happening. I heard men cheering and shouting. Warshaw shouted, "One down!"

The guns on the second ship fell silent as its shield failed. The side of the ship bubbled, then burst, spewing flames, men, and debris into space. Fires danced and died inside the hull, and the ship went dark. The space around it went dark as well, except for the silver-red threads of laser drilling into the third ship.

My pilot went wild. He cheered with the sailors manning the lasers. He pumped his fists in the air. Listening in to the chatter on the open channel, I heard one man crying and another saying a prayer.

The shield around the third ship changed color from honey gold to a sickly green, and suddenly the ship seemed impervious to our lasers. Pinpricks of light appeared around the hull, tiny little flashes as if someone had lit up little electrodes in sequence.

"What is . . ." I started to ask the question out loud without meaning to.

Someone said, "They're firing torpedoes," over the inter-Link. It might have been Warshaw.

The crew of that final Unified Authority battleship did not need to aim, they just trained their torpedoes along the laser beams. The derelicts were massive, but brittle and unprotected. One moment, we had seven ships spinning a laser web around the last U.A. battleship, then there were only three. Two of the old derelicts simply went dark when the torpedoes hit them. The other two lit up like skyrockets.

The U.A. battleship fired off a second fusillade of torpedoes, then it exploded. Particle beams and torpedoes slammed into it from three different directions, nearly shearing the ship in half. The green shield evaporated as the hull cracked open and twisted. An enormous fireball flashed and vanished, leaving behind a pitch-black carcass.

Franks had arrived. His three battleships flew in tight formation, cutting across the graveyard like eagles coming in for the kill, but there was nothing left to kill.

"I thought you came here to collect equipment, not fight a war," Franks said over an open frequency.

The clock in my visor said the time was *21:59:57.*

CHAPTER
FORTY-ONE

Brigadier General Kelly Thomer sat slumped in his chair, his arms dangling over the sides, his breakfast barely touched. He had potatoes, eggs, toast, bacon, and orange juice—a meal for a man with an appetite. As I looked at his hollowed cheeks and sunken eyes, I did not think that the man matched the meal. The fluffy yellow kernels of scrambled eggs sat in an untouched pile on his plate. All of the Marines I knew painted their eggs with ketchup.

"Are you planning on eating those eggs or hatching them?" I asked.

He woke from his trance, and said, "Oh yeah," then splashed ketchup on everything but his toast.

More than anything else, Thomer looked bored. When I asked him about his last dose of Fallzoud, he said he had not taken it for days. Fallzoud was a serotonin inhibitor. I got the feeling that Thomer's serotonin had been inhibited past the point of no return.

"How'd it go with the Mogat Fleet?" He asked the question, but he did not strike me as interested in hearing the answer.

"We ran into U.A. battleships," I said.

"That's good," he said.

"No, that's bad," I said. "Live ships. They chased us into the Mogat graveyard."

"Oh," Thomer said. "You know when you found out you were a clone, did it bother you that you never had a family? I mean, I'm kind of grieving my parents, like they died or something." He stared at me and through me, his brown eyes unblinking. He looked halfway down the road to catatonic.

"Why in God's name are you grieving for people who never existed?" I asked.

"Yeah, but I didn't know that they didn't exist, and now I do. It's kind of like they died a second time. See what I mean?"

There was a certain logic to what he said, twisted as it was.

The conversation left me incredulous. I told Thomer, "Well, I'm sure they would have been really excellent parents, had they ever existed and had they not died," and went to work on my eggs.

Thomer just sat there, staring over his ketchup-covered tray, his body gaunt, his arms nearly limp, his fork hanging off his plate. He had the kind of slack expression I would expect to find on a person who had died in his sleep.

Deciding to change my tactics, I asked, "Did I ever tell you about my friend, Vince Lee?"

Thomer shook his head but said nothing.

"I served with him on this very ship. He was one of the Little Man Seven, one of the seven Marines who survived the battle on Little Man." I normally did not need to explain who the Little Man Seven were, but Thomer looked like he might have moss growing under his brain.

When Thomer said nothing, I went on. "Yeah, well, Vince came back from Little Man a hero. They promoted him from corporal to lieutenant and transferred him to the *Grant*.

"I lost touch with him for a couple of years after that. The next time I saw him, I was back on Little Man with Ray Freeman." Ray Freeman had been my partner when I was technically absent for the Corps without leave. He was a mercenary, a mountain of a man who could kill enemies with a knife, a bomb, or his bare hands, but he preferred using a sniper rifle. Thomer knew Freeman, he'd contracted out to fight in both the Mogat and New Copenhagen campaigns.

"So Vince turned up on Little Man, only he wasn't himself anymore. He'd gotten himself hooked on Fallzoud and figured out he was a clone, kind of like you.

"Things went from bad to worse after that. He started calling himself the 'King of Clones,' and the next thing you know, he got all of the other clones on his ship hooked. Once he got everyone all good and luded, he told the whole crew they were clones, and nobody died from it.

"And that's where things hit rock bottom. Vince and his buddies killed all of the natural-borns on the *Grant* and declared independence."

"What became of him?" Thomer asked.

"I killed him," I said, offering no explanation.

Thomer reacted no more strongly to this bit of information than he might have reacted to my telling him that temperatures were cold in space. He sat slumped in his seat, eyes vacant, muscles relaxed. I wondered if he even noticed the implicit threat in my story.

"Thomer, you need to get off Fallzoud," I said.

"Why?"

"You're turning into a specking zombie. You say that you haven't shot up for a while, but you're acting like you just dosed."

"Maybe I did take it this morning," he said.

What could I do? When his head was clear, Thomer was the most dependable man I had, a battle-tested Marine with an analytical mind and a reliable temperament. I did not want to write him off as a burnout, but I could not afford to keep this husk of a man as my first in command.

"We have a staff meeting," I said.

Thomer tried a bite of toast, then drank his juice. We tossed our trays down the cleaning line and left the mess. Walking in silence, we headed up to the fleet deck.

Only six officers attended the meeting: Gary Warshaw, Lilburn Franks, Perry Fahey, Kelly Thomer, Philo Hollingsworth, and me. We had ten stars among us, even if they were only "field" stars.

Warshaw had already let me know that he planned to conduct the briefing. As he pointed out, until I got around to killing him, he was in command.

The six of us sat in a room with enough space for thirty officers, huddled tight around a table and speaking so loudly our voices echoed.

"So, Harris, I hear you got to command your own ship." Fahey sounded almost gleeful. He batted his shadow-dusted eyes at me. Fortunately, the lipstick and rouge had gone away. "Commanding a specking transport with a one-man crew, was that a lifelong ambition?"

Sitting beside Fahey, Warshaw looked at the ground and fidgeted. The battle between Fahey and me had taken on a life of its own, independent of Warshaw. He no longer had any control over it.

Franks stared at Fahey, true annoyance showing on his face.

But Fahey went on. "What did you call your cruise? 'A Marine operation'? Slick, Harris."

"You got a point you're trying to make?" I asked, hoping to get the meeting back on track. We did not have time to waste with all of this infighting. Now that the Golan engineers had branched out into broadcast engines, they could have established some kind of permanent broadcast Link with Earth. The entire Unified Authority might know about our trip to Mogat home world.

"You killed off the Marines you took to Terraneau. You killed off half the sailors you took to the Mogat Fleet. What's next, Harris?" Fahey screamed this last jab, spit flying from his lips. I wondered if maybe he had lost a lover on the Mogat mission. He half stood in his chair, looking ready to leap across the table.

I killed half the sailors I took to the Mogat Fleet? I did not know what he meant at first, but I figured it out quickly. There had to have been men manning the lasers on those derelict ships. Of course there had been men, engineers and technicians, and they died when the Unified Authority battleships fired back at them. But their deaths were not my fault . . . they couldn't be.

"I told you, it wasn't like that," Warshaw said in a subdued voice.

"The speck it wasn't!" Fahey yelled. "I can't believe you're defending this asshole. Who's next, Harris? Are you going to keep killing us off till you have the fleet to yourself?"

"I was in charge, Fahey," Warshaw said.

"You weren't in charge of that specking transport. That was General Harris's show, his 'Marine Operation.' We lost five hundred qualified techs because of this bastard. That's what happens when you treat a Marine clone . . ."

"One more word, Fahey, and I will slam your ass in the brig so hard you'll be shitting cots and bars," I said.

Warshaw put up a hand to stop me. He spoke the words quietly and forcefully as he said, "Stow it, Fahey. One more word out of you, and I'll throw you in the brig myself."

Fahey turned to look at him. The two clones looked like distortions of each other. They were cut from the same helix, but little about them matched. Fahey was young and thin, his makeup making his brown eyes look large and doelike. Warshaw was in his forties, a mighty man with huge muscles and a shaved head.

Their faces were identical, but their expressions could not have been more different. Warshaw looked calm, maybe a little sad. Fahey looked out of control, as wild as a dog pulled from a fight. Whites showed all the way around his eyes, and beads of sweat formed on his forehead.

"What are you going to do, Gary, take away my command? Is that what you want? Are you out of your specking mind?" Fahey's mouth worked into a sneer that showed most of his teeth.

Warshaw did not look crazy. He looked tired and focused, like a man finishing a twelve-hour work shift, as he said, "Senior Chief, you are relieved of command."

Fahey fell back into his seat. "Gary," he said. "What are you doing? You're taking his side?" At that moment it struck me that there was nothing feminine about Perry Fahey other than his makeup. He did not speak in a falsetto or behave like a woman.

"I am relieving you of command and stripping you of your field rank," Warshaw said. He turned to me, and said, "General Harris, would you have one of your Marines escort this man to the brig?"

"Aye," I said. I turned to Hollingsworth and issued the order.

Hollingsworth rose from his seat and walked over to Fahey. "Senior Chief, I have orders to deliver you to the brig. Please come with me," he said, in a flat voice.

The two men had once been friends, it showed in both their expressions. Fahey stared at Hollingsworth, anger and amazement showing in his eyes. Hollingsworth looked stiff, like a man gearing up for an unpleasant task.

"Idiots. You're all idiots," Fahey muttered, as he rose to his feet. He allowed Hollingsworth to lead him out of the room without speaking another word. Watching them leave, I wondered if I should have had Thomer escort Fahey instead. Hollingsworth and Fahey had served together, and I still had questions about his loyalties.

"It's about time somebody put him away," Thomer said, shattering the tense silence in the room.

"I apologize, General Harris. I do not know how Fahey came up with that shit. When I told him about what had happened, it never occurred to me that he would twist it like that," Warshaw said.

"I never liked that asshole," said Franks.

Listening to them, I knew we needed to change our chain of command. Warshaw was right, I could not run this fleet. Ships and the strategies of open-space combat were not my forte. Unfortunately, Warshaw, the veteran engineer, was not much more qualified than I was. He knew how to fix ships, not how to run them.

I took a deep breath, flashed a weary smile, and said, "Let's move on."

The other officers nodded. Thomer, who seemed to have woken from his funk, shuffled in his chair and sat upright.

"I'll start," Warshaw said. He stood and stretched, his massive shoulders and neck bulging. "We have several teams working round the clock on the G.C. Fleet. We have identified 328 ships that look like they might have salvageable broadcast equipment. The other ships are so banged up, we've written them off."

"Is that wise? I mean, we're going to need all the gear we can get," Franks interrupted.

"First, we go for the low-hanging fruit," Warshaw said. "We don't know how much time we have before the U.A. sends more ships to guard the area."

"How is the work going?" I asked.

"We've landed teams on 125 ships."

Finding himself in his natural element, reporting on an engineering operation, Warshaw cut an impressive figure. I wondered how he would react when I suggested placing someone else in charge. The hit to his ego might blind him to the realities.

"We tested the shield systems on one of the ships, but it was a complete wash," Warshaw said. "Harris, you said the signal for the shields came from the planet. Is there any chance we could reestablish it?"

"The planet is filled with shit gas," Thomer said.

"Excuse me, did you say 'shit gas'?" Franks asked, sounding more than amused.

"Bad stuff," I said. "Take my word for it, there's no point sending anyone down there. Even if the shield equipment didn't break, we'd never be able to get to it."

"Okay, but what is shit gas?" Warshaw asked.

"Is that a scientific term or something you Marines came up with?" Franks asked.

"I didn't name the stuff," Thomer said. He had become defensive.

Of the two field admirals, Warshaw conducted himself more like an officer. He moved to regain control of the meeting. "Okay, it was just a thought. Without those shields, everyone we send out to the G.C. Fleet will be vulnerable if the Unifieds return." Now the U.A. were the "Unifieds." In the military, enemies must have a derogatory nickname to be taken seriously.

"Can you retrofit the G.C. Fleet broadcast equipment onto our ships?" Franks asked.

"That's the big question, isn't it?" Warshaw sighed. "I don't see why not."

"Have you landed crews on the U.A. battleships we shot down?" Franks asked. "We need to have a look at their technology."

"That's probably a Marine operation," Warshaw said.

"A Marine operation?" I asked.

"We've surveyed those ships from the outside," Warshaw said. "The systems are out, but that doesn't mean everyone aboard them is dead."

CHAPTER
FORTY-TWO

Once our official business ended, Thomer returned to his quarters to rest, and our conclave dwindled to three: Warshaw, Franks, and me. As soon as the door closed behind Thomer, the dynamics of the meeting changed. Instead of two admirals and a general, our psychology seemed to revert to enlisted-man status. Differences in branch and pay grade no longer mattered, we were Gary, Lil, and Wayson—three guys serving on the Scrotum-Crotch Fleet.

Warshaw had an aide bring in some bottles, and the booze poured freely.

"What is going on with Thomer?" Franks asked. "I can't figure the guy out. One moment he's spaced out, the next moment he's the only guy in the room with a clue what to do." He poured himself a tall glass of vodka.

We each had our personal poison of choice. Franks, who apparently preferred flame to flavor, had his bottle of vodka. Warshaw drank whiskey in small shots. I drank beer. They might get drunk, but I wouldn't. I could have set up a drip line and taken an entire keg intravenously without getting inebriated.

I did not want Warshaw or Franks to get smashed, but a little lubrication would take the edge off our conversation. Removing the sharp edges would be good.

"He's on Fallzoud," I said.

Warshaw made a low, whistling noise that sounded like a bomb falling out of the sky. "Fallzoud? That's some serious shit. Why do you keep him around?"

"After New Copenhagen, he needed it," I said, as if it answered the question.

"I heard New Copenhagen was brutal," Franks said.

"You have about thirty thousand New Copenhagen survivors in your fleet," I said. "Almost all of the clones who transferred in with me fought there."

"Are they all on Fallzoud?" Warshaw asked. It was a fair question—a lot of them were.

"Not all of them, but a bunch. They handed it out like candy in Clonetown. It made us easier to control," I said.

"Clonetown? What the hell is Clonetown?" asked Franks.

Warshaw knew. He said, "That's what they called the relocation camp."

"You had thousands of clones living in a relocation camp called 'Clonetown'? Why didn't they all have a death reflex and die? I mean, shit, what does it take to make those speckers realize they're clones?" Franks, of course, was one of "those speckers"; but he seemed not even to suspect it. Now on his third glass of vodka, he was in no shape to suspect much of anything.

Warshaw had not touched his drink yet. I needed him to drink before Franks became too drunk to think. Hoping to encourage Warshaw to drink, I uncapped two beers and downed them in quick order.

Warshaw answered, "It's just like the orphanages, Franks. Think about it. All those clones packed together, each of them believing they are the only natural-born. It's the same god-damn thing."

I finished another beer. "Thomer knows," I said.

Warshaw flicked his thumb across the top of the bottle with so much force that the seal broke, and the cap spun off. I would have brought Warshaw a stein for his whiskey if I thought he'd use it, but he used a specking shot glass, not even a tumbler. He filled the glass and tossed it down, refilled, but waited to drink. The veins and muscles in his neck flexed when he downed his drink.

"Thomer knows what?" Franks asked. If he lost any more of his edge, we'd have to tuck him in for the night.

"He knows he's a clone, asshole," Warshaw said. He downed another shot.

I downed another beer.

"He can't know that, or he'd be dead," Franks said.

"I heard that could happen," Warshaw said. "I heard there were drugs that would block the reflex. Fallzoud must be one of 'em."

"He had a pretty good idea where he came from before he got hooked," I said. "I've known Thomer a long time. He always had his suspicions."

"Speck! That's hard shit. I mean, God, who'd want to be a clone?" Franks said.

Warshaw stared at him. Even if he'd wanted to inform Franks that he, too, was a clone, Warshaw's neural programming would not permit him to do it.

"I'm trying to get him off the Fallzoud," I said.

"What happens to him if he quits?" Warshaw asked. "Can he still have the reflex?"

"Probably not," I said. "If he were going to have a reflex, he'd probably have had it when he dried out between ludings."

"Poor bastard," Franks said. He drained his glass but made no move to pour a refill.

"Harris, are you nervous about sweeping those battleships tomorrow?" Warshaw asked. He drained another shot, reloaded, and drained it again.

"Not really. There aren't going to be any survivors. You

guys blew the hell out of those ships, no one could have survived that." I thought about the frozen dead I'd seen on other wrecks and tipped my beer in salute.

Seeing me drink seemed to relax Warshaw. He tossed another shot.

"If they sealed off some parts of the ship, those areas might have air and pressure," Warshaw pointed out.

"What are they going to do about the specking cold?" I asked.

"What about reinforcements?" Warshaw asked. "What if they sent for help?"

"How would they call for reinforcements, they'd need a broadcast network."

"The Mogats sent messages," Franks said. "I heard they set up spy stations in every arm."

"They did, but they had to build them around their own private broadcast network. They had mini broadcast engines that sent and received messages."

"Maybe these ships have mini broadcast engines, too," Franks said. He slurred his words as he spoke. "You don't specking know if they have mini broadcast engines on their ships."

"Maybe," I admitted. "But why would they have come in alone if they could have called for help?" I asked. "They would have called for backup."

Franks started to reach for his bottle, and paused. "They had newer, better ships," he said. "Those cocky pricks probably thought they could take us easy."

"They probably did," I agreed.

Franks nodded. Warshaw tossed back yet another shot of whiskey. If he wasn't properly lubricated by now, he never would be.

Deciding to make my move, I said, "You know, you and I are both in the shits," to Warshaw. "My second-in-command is a Fallzoud sinker, and yours is in the brig."

"Fahey? Don't you worry about his ass. I'll take care of him," Warshaw said.

I heard sharpness in his voice. My bringing up Fahey burned through the whiskey haze. "You told me that no Marine was fit to command a fleet," I said. "Do you remember that?"

"Something like that, yeah," Warshaw agreed.

"Engineering officers don't cut it either," I said. "When was the last time you heard about an engineer making admiral?"

"You son of a . . ." He jumped to his feet, his fists tight and his arms flexed.

I put up a hand. "I'm not trying to take over. I don't believe either one of us is fit for command."

Warshaw calmed slightly. His fists opened, and his shoulders relaxed, but he did not sit down. "What are you saying, Harris?"

"I'm saying we both need to step down," I said.

"And get passed over for command?"

"You think Marines aren't fit for command because they don't understand naval operations."

"Damn specking right they don't," Warshaw said. He dropped back into his seat.

"You're right. We don't. The problem is, engineers don't know shit about operations, either. What this fleet needs is a bridge officer, not a wrench jockey."

"You mean him?" Warshaw asked, his mouth working into a sardonic smile. He nodded toward Franks, who sat passed out in his chair, his back slumped, his face flush against the conference table, saliva forming a pool in front of his opened mouth. He snored softly.

"You're joking, right?" Warshaw asked.

Feeling embarrassed, I said, "He's next in line."

Warshaw laughed.

"Bullshit. I'm next in line, Harris. Admiral Brocius gave me this command."

That was how we left it. Warshaw running the fleet, me commanding the Marines, and Franks passed out in his seat.

CHAPTER
FORTY-THREE

Technically, I should have brought Hollingsworth on this mission, but I'd already sent him to run Fort Sebastian instead. I should have left Thomer as a liaison with fleet operations, but I thought some action would do him good. I needed to know if I could count on him in battle, and this seemed like a safe testing ground. All we had to do was explore a derelict ship, locate and capture any survivors who wanted rescue, and offer a fatal helping hand to any survivors who wanted to go down with their ship.

I sat in the cockpit with the pilot as he flew my team out. It was the same clone pilot I had hijacked the last time I came out to the Mogat home world. Back then he was a sailor. Now he'd put in a transfer to become a Marine—as my staff pilot no less. Apparently we'd bonded while dodging U.A. battleships in our unarmed transport.

The newly destroyed U.A. battleships did not resemble the wrecks around them. It wasn't just the difference in their shape and color. The Mogat ships were not just sunk, they were annihilated. Some had imploded hulls. Several decks had been entirely sheared away from one Mogat destroyer. The U.A. ships had gone dark, but they looked like they could be repaired.

"I like the look of this ship a lot better now that it's dead," the pilot said as we approached one of the wrecks. He and I had played a serious game of tag with this ship not all that long ago.

"Let's just hope it stays dead," I said.

Light still shone through cracks in the battleship's hull. The batteries backing their emergency lighting might hold out for months. Flames, fed by oxygen leaking out of improperly sealed cabins, flickered deep in the recesses of the ships. Their unsteady glow reminded me of candles.

"I feel like I'm sneaking up on a sleeping bear," the pilot joked.

"A dead bear," I said. I hoped it was dead.

"You better hope it's dead, sir," the pilot said. He acted like we were old friends. I didn't mind. More than anything else, I felt embarrassed for what I had done to the guy. I had done what I felt I had to do, but I still felt bad about pistol-whipping him.

Without its shields, the battleship had the same beige and gray colors as the ships in the Scutum-Crux Fleet. Its skin had laser burns and trenches along its outer hull, the scars of war. The white glare of sparks flashed in some of the crevices. Most of the ship was dark. The sparks and flames added up to little more than a scattering of bright scales.

We moved in slowly, our runner lights blazing on the hull. Toward the bow of the ship, about a hundred yards back, we found the hatch to the docking bay and sent a team of technicians armed with laser torches.

The process went slowly. The pilot opened the kettle doors. A couple of minutes later five techs drifted into view. They spent fifteen minutes evaluating the situation, then finally got to work. The laser-resistant outer wall of the ship cut slowly, but it did cut.

"Do we have our shields up?" I asked the pilot.

"Do we need them up?"

"Luck specks the unprepared," I said.

Outside, our techs stripped away the outer skin of the hatch, revealing a panel filled with rods and hydraulics. Once the shield covering was gone, the work went quickly. A few more cuts, and the outer hatch fell away from the ship.

"Looks like we're in, sir."

The techs went ahead of us to clear the atmospheric locks. A few minutes later, we entered the runway at a crawl. Our runner lights revealed the signs of battle. The deck was cracked. Sixty feet ahead of us, the doors of the next lock hung askew. Beyond the broken hatch, a lightning-colored bouquet flashed over the top of a shorted-out electrical panel.

"Looks like you're on your own from here, sir," the pilot said.

"Looks that way," I agreed.

"Okay, Thomer, lead them out," I said over the interLink.

"Everybody out. Hit the deck and fall in!" Thomer yelled. The men obeyed. As I left the cockpit, I saw the last of the men floating down the ramp. Off-loading and forming ranks took longer in zero gravity.

Not showing any traces of Fallzoud confusion, Thomer took charge. He sounded more like a sergeant than a general. That was good. In my experience, generals did not bring much to the battlefield.

I looked over the ranks. The hundred armor-wearing Marines were a sight for sore eyes. They did not wear jetpacks. Unlike the motivators used by Navy techs, our jetpacks gave off flames. In the wrong environment, those flames could trigger an explosion.

"Listen up," I said. "The fleet sent us here to look for survivors. It's probably a waste of time, but that is why we are here. Search each deck for heat signatures. If you find something, report back before going in to investigate. I repeat, if you find somebody with a pulse and a face, call for backup."

I should have given them a more detailed briefing, but I did not think it would be necessary. Instead, I said my short piece and let Thomer divide up the company. I sent them out in fire teams, four-man units that made a lot more sense in other situations. Fire teams were supposed to include a rifleman, an automatic rifleman, a grenadier, and a team leader. In this situation, everyone carried a particle-beam pistol.

This particular ship was the second of the U.A. battleships to stumble into Warshaw's shooting gallery. It had taken the least damage. With the third battleship fighting its way out of our trap, Warshaw's techs had shifted their fire over to that ship the moment this one went dark. What had looked like a quiet death from the outside, however, didn't seem so gentle now that I had entered the ship.

We threaded through the broken, second lock and found the third lock fully open. By the time we reached that final lock, we were walking along the deck. I had already noticed this when Thomer hailed me to say, "General, the gravity generator is still online."

Wondering what other equipment might still be up and running, I answered, "Tell your men to stay alert." If the grav-

ity generator had survived the fight, the environmental systems might have also survived; and if there was heat and air,
there might well be survivors.

Listening in on the commandLink, I heard one Marine
say, "We had a battle simulation just like this back at the
orphanage."

"Damn, I remember that sim," a second man said. "That's
the one where you have to defend the ship or blow the sucker
up."

"Keep it quiet," Thomer ordered.

I knew that simulation as well. The holographic simulation
took place on a disabled freighter. One team played as sailors
and the other as pirates. The pirates were the aggressors, sent
to capture the ship; and they had every possible advantage.
They had better guns. They did not have to worry about laws
or regulations. They even had more men on their team. The
simulation was set up so that they outnumbered the sailors
three to one.

But the sailors always won.

Since blowing up the freighter kept it out of enemy hands,
all the sailors had to do was set the reactor to overload. It
wasn't fair, but it was realistic. I thought this and realized that
from the U.A. point of view, this operation had the same zero-
sum solution. If the U.A. Navy found itself unable to salvage
this ship, they would demolish it before allowing us to capture it.

"Thomer, tell the men to look for anything that looks like
it could explode."

"Like on the *Corvair*?" Thomer asked.

Corvair? I thought. The name sounded so damn familiar.
It only took a moment for me to place it. *Corvair* was the
name of the ship in the simulation. "That is precisely what I
am talking about."

Thomer issued the order, then spoke to me again. "I hated
that simulation. I always ended up a pirate. We never won."

Because of the darkness, our combat visors defaulted to
night-for-day lenses, but we would also need to use heat vision in order to search for survivors. It would not be hard to
locate heat on this busted scow, the ambient temperature had
dropped to absolute zero.

I switched to heat vision and saw that the men in front of me radiated red with an orange halo against the cobalt world around them. Normally men in combat armor did not give off a heat signature. They did in space.

The fire teams spread out quickly. Eight teams headed toward the lower decks, where we would have found Engineering and the Marines on other ships. Who knew what they would find with this new design.

I commandeered a team, telling them to follow me as I headed toward the bow of the ship. I entered a hall and quickly located a stairwell that would take us to any deck. The stairs were wide enough for five men to climb abreast.

Two flights up, I paused to check the lay of the land, switching to heat vision as I looked down a hallway lined with sealed hatches. Four of the hatches showed dark orange. There was heat behind those doors. A fifth hatch had not been sealed. Blades of yellow and red danced outside that doorway. I switched to my tactical lens and watched the flames. Whether it was oxygen or some other gas, something leaking from that room was fueling the fire.

I marked the rooms with a virtual beacon, which I sent to Thomer. "I have some interesting prospects up here," I said.

"I'll send a team by," Thomer said.

The correct response would have been, "I'll send a team by, sir," but I overlooked it. Worrying about being addressed as "sir" may sound petty, but it isn't. The Marine Corps was built on discipline. Without that discipline, we were just another gang of soldiers.

I wished there was some surefire way to dry Thomer out without killing him.

I led my fire team up two more flights and surveyed the next deck. It looked exactly like the same scene one deck down, sans the flames. Almost all of the doors radiated heat, but the hall itself was as cold as space.

A man had died in this hall. He lay on the floor. Seen through night-for-day lenses, the dead sailor's hands were the color of snow. Coin-sized speckles of blood had formed on the ground around his head. Frozen blood showed in the gash along the back of his head. If I'd stomped a boot down hard enough on the man, he would have shattered like a porcelain figurine. His bones were the least rigid part of his body, now that the veins and capillaries had frozen solid.

None of the hatches on the sixth deck radiated heat, and we found no bodies. What we did locate was the wound that had killed the ship—where the first lasers hit once the shields had given way. I remembered seeing a narrow beam hit the ship on the bow, just below the bridge. Once the lasers pierced the hull, the cabin pressure must have flushed all of the bodies into space.

The seventh deck looked like a battlefield. We passed the frozen bodies of dozens of dead sailors right off the stairwell. I had to kick one out of the way just to enter the hall. The man must have fallen to his knees as he died—at least his body had frozen in that position. The palm of his hand had frozen to the floor. It snapped off just above the wrist when I kicked his body out of the way.

I listened in on my fire team.

Man, this place is a specking morgue.

I hate specking space battles.

At least these guys died fast. I saw a guy take five days to die after he got hit in the gut.

I knew a guy that got burned. The poor bastard hung on for six months.

The way to the bridge was an obstacle course, and we found at least a hundred frozen dead in the various stations around the bridge. Fifteen crewmen lay in a huddle around the weapons section. I found the captain of the ship sprawled out on the floor near the front of the bridge. His skin was a glacier blue, and his eyes were open and frozen.

"Did you see that, sir?" my fire team leader asked me.

I had. It was just a fleeting glimpse, but I had seen a man in soft-shell armor slip through a doorway.

"Thomer, I've got a contact. Seventh deck, just off the bridge, I repeat, we have a live one!" I switched to an open frequency. "There's been a change of plans, boys. There is life aboard this ship, and that means there may be traps. I want everyone to stay where you are until you receive further instructions. Do not engage. I will personally snap every finger off the first sorry speck who fires his gun on this ship."

I had not gotten a good look at the man. He had flittered

across the hall outside the bridge. With my peripheral vision hampered by my helmet, I might not have seen him at all, had he not stumbled over a frozen body and flailed before ducking out of sight.

"What did you see?" Thomer asked on a direct frequency.

"One contact," I said. "He's dressed in soft-shell." All of my men were dressed in combat armor.

In the simulation, the defending team only needed one member to prevent the pirates from capturing the *Corvair*. If the ship was rigged, it would not matter if the Unified Authority had one man on this ship or a million, we would not be able to take it.

"I hope this isn't like the specking *Corvair*," I told Thomer.

"It isn't," he said. "You don't really die when you pull the pin in a simulation. If they pull the pin on us, they die, too."

I thought about that. Thomer had a point. Any survivors on this ship were as likely to be engineers from the dry docks as sailors. They might not be willing to go down with their ship.

Looking around the deck, I noted that the bridge looked like something from a nightmare. The computers, the chairs, the stations, all remained in perfect order except for the dead men surrounding them. Death had come in a frozen flash to this part of the ship.

"Have your men reached the Marine compound?" I asked Thomer.

"It's empty."

"How empty?" I asked, wanting to make sure we were dealing with a sailor or an engineer, and not a Marine.

"No beds, no racks, no equipment."

"No Marines," I said in a hollow voice, a reaction meant more for my ears than Thomer's. "Got anybody down in Engineering?"

"A couple of teams," Thomer said.

"Good. Tell them to shut down anything that looks like it still works. Don't smash things, just break them a little."

"The gravity generator?" Thomer asked.

"Gravity generators, life-support systems . . . I don't want power going to any systems."

"You said he was wearing armor," Thomer said.

"I think so."

"So he's got heat, light, and air," Thomer pointed out.

"That's not going to save him next time he needs to take a dump," I said. "He'll freeze his ass off." I thought of a disturbing image—the remains of an engineer who froze to death during the act of defecating.

There might only have been one survivor left on this ship, or there might have been hundreds. It didn't matter. Confronted with a shoot-out, they would be more likely to pull the proverbial pin than they would be if left alone and facing a slow death in space. People do heroic things in the face of fire; but when the end comes gradually and their bodies betray them and their only enemy is their own natural needs, heroism gives way to the instinct for survival.

When we returned twenty-four hours later, boarding the derelict battleships was no longer a Marine operation. All we needed were some engineers and a chaplain.

CHAPTER
FORTY-FOUR

"Harris, you son of a bitch, I demand you return my ships," the captain said. Natural-borns had become as interchangeable in my mind as clones. It didn't matter whether it was Admiral Brocius or General Smith or Captain Pershing, or this guy, Rear Admiral Lower-Half Hugo George, the man from whom I had commandeered our self-broadcasting fleet, they all sang the same angry song.

"Sure, Admiral, I'll just give you back your three battleships, and we'll call it even," I said.

That set him off. "You specking pissant clone!" George, a young admiral at forty-five, rose to his feet. Fire showed in his eyes, which were the exact same mud brown as mine. A vein ran down the center of his forehead. As he shouted, the muscles along the sides of his neck flexed.

Just the two of us sat in the little interrogation room. I did not need guards though I had a couple waiting outside. On his feet and snarling, George stood an inch taller than me, but years in a command chair had left him softened. He had a gut, not a big one, but a gut, nonetheless.

Before coming to the Outer Bliss penal colony, I'd looked up George's record. He'd distinguished himself as a ship's captain fighting Mogats. His battleship destroyed more defenseless Mogat battleships than any other ship in the fleet, once we disabled their shields. Apparently, he knew when to attack and when to wait.

"Sit down, Admiral, you're embarrassing yourself," I said. I leaned my chair against the wall behind me, bracing my knees against the table, which was bolted to the floor. To get to me, the admiral would either need to jump over the table or run around it. Considering his size and conditioning, I ruled the element of surprise out of the equation.

He stood there fuming, leaning over the table, his hands in fists. Seconds passed, and he said nothing. Finally, he sat down.

What I knew, what he did not know, was that over the last three weeks, Warshaw's engineers had attempted to install salvaged broadcast engines on several of our battleships. We flat-out lost one ship when we tested it. God knows where it went. Two ships exploded. One ship survived the broadcast, but the electricity from the anomaly fried every wire, switch, and computer on the vessel. The electricity hadn't done the crew any favors, either.

We also had one mostly successful test. It did not go off without some flaws. The ship's shields and weapons systems shorted out. One of the engineers monitoring the broadcast engine died when an arc formed between the wrench in his right hand and one of the cylinders.

Minor hiccups on the road to success.

"Release me and my men," George demanded, in a quiet voice that betrayed the ragged edges of his self-control.

"You mean you haven't enjoyed your vacation in Outer Bliss?" I asked.

He did not answer.

"I have no interest in holding you here any longer than I need to."

"Then return my ships," he demanded.

"Nope."

"Stealing my ships was an act of war, Harris."

"Yeah, well, what are you going to do about it?" I asked, still reclining in my chair. "The Navy sent half its self-broadcasting fleet to threaten us. We have three times as many battleships as they do, and our ships are Perseus-class design. The only boats they have that can reach us are G.C. Fleet vintage, sixty-year-old ships. You don't really think they are going to attack us, do you?"

George took a moment to compose himself, then said, "The pendulum swings both ways. You've got the advantage now . . ."

"I'm glad you brought that up," I said. "When we do finally let you out of here, I was hoping you could deliver a message for me."

"A message?"

"You know those next-generation battleships they're building at the Golan Dry Docks? We destroyed three of them."

"You what?" George asked.

"Read 'em and weep," I said. "Three of those new battleships against three G.C. Fleet antiques manned by all-clone crews, and we made a clean sweep of it. What do they call those new ships anyway? Around here we call them Asshole-class ships, but I figure you probably have a better name for them."

"You're lying. You're specking lying to me," George said.

"You know that I am not lying," I said, though, of course, I was certainly withholding information. I was not about to mention Warshaw's hot-wiring derelicts. I wanted to see if I could shake old Hugo's confidence.

Admiral George greeted my comment with silence. Finally, I stood up, and said, "Well, it looks like there's nothing more to say." This was my third debriefing of the day, and I wanted it to end as quickly as possible. I had more interesting business to conduct back in Norristown.

I knocked on the door, and the guards opened it.

"Take him away," I said.

Admiral George left without a word. I think he was as glad to get away from me as I was to see him leave.

Once I shut the door, Warshaw said, "Wayson Harris, you evil sack of pus! You lied to that pathetic asshole. You let him think we took those ships head-on. Now, why would you do that?"

Warshaw's disembodied voice came from the *Kamehameha*. He was monitoring my interrogations using the two-way communications gear that the Corps of Engineers had built into the ceiling.

"We're going to send him home sooner or later. If we convince him the ships are no good, he might scare Brocius and Smith into giving us more time. You know Brocius and his fetish for house odds. If he thinks we beat his ships in a fair fight, he's going to scrap his plans until he's sure he's got the upper hand."

"I don't imagine we'll be sending Admiral George home anytime soon," Warshaw said.

"Maybe not," I agreed.

"Think he bit?"

"Maybe. It shut him up," I said.

"He's a prick. I'm glad he's in the brig," Warshaw said. "Who do you have next?"

"Fahey," I said, trying to hide my distaste.

"You and Perry face-to-face? I'd pay big money to see that one," Warshaw said. He could not be here. Every bit as much the engineer as I was the Marine, Warshaw "needed" to oversee every facet of the work with the broadcast equipment. He had not spent much time on the *Kamehameha* once the broadcast equipment started rolling in.

"I have a case of Earth-brewed that says that one of you will not leave the room alive." How the hell Warshaw had found a case of Earth-brewed beer was beyond me.

"You're not sure which one of us?" I asked.

"I can hope, can't I?" He could also watch. Along with the audio equipment, there was a tiny camera in the ceiling. If Fahey and I got physical, the bastard would show the feed to every officer in the fleet . . . especially in the unlikely event that I lost.

"Save your beer, there isn't going to be a fight," I said.

"No, Harris, I want the bet. Tell you what, I'll give you odds. You put up a twenty against the whole case. What's that, five-to-one? Ten-to-one? What do you say?"

"Just don't try to back out," I warned him.

There was a knock on the door. I barked out an order, "Enter."

The door opened and in came Perry Fahey, recently demoted back to senior chief petty officer; only now he was more of a "pretty" officer than a petty officer. He had on the customary eye shadow, mascara, lipstick, rouge, and false eyelashes. He had let his hair grow beyond regulation. It was only touching his ears, but that was long by Navy standards.

Watching the polite way the guards led Fahey into the room, I knew I had to arrange for my men to R & R someplace with women and soon. The MP who led Fahey into the room held the door and smiled at him. The MP bringing up the rear patted Fahey on the back. He did not shove him through the door, he did not give him a warning blow to the kidneys to show him what would happen if he misbehaved, he reached out and gave him a supportive pat on the shoulder. I watched this and knew whose side they would be on if Fahey and I came to blows.

I pointed to the chair on the other side of the table, and they led him to it.

"Why don't you guys stay here for this one?" I said.

Maybe it was just my imagination, but I could have sworn I heard the word "speck" hiss out of the ceiling.

I had a good reason for having them stay. With them standing over Fahey, I could see if they reached for their pistols. If I sent them outside, they might well come into the room with their pistols drawn.

"Hello, Senior Chief. It looks like you are making the most of your stay here," I began.

"Get specked, Harris," Fahey said.

"Well, it certainly looks as if you have done just that," I said, looking from Fahey to the two sailors/MPs guarding him. They both looked away from me.

"I'm trying to decide what to do with you," I said. "I suppose I could leave you here till you rot, but I'm leaning toward other options—send your ass back to Earth or have you shot."

"Put me back on active duty," Fahey said. He could not possibly have expected me to put him back on active duty. He had to be pumping me for information. I decided to play along and see where he took me. "Do you expect to come back as a senior chief petty officer?" I asked.

"As an admiral," he said. He sat there motionless, his eyes fixed on mine. He did not blink, did not look from side to side. His eyes were narrow and angry, and the smile on his face was angry and derisive.

"I don't think so," I said.

"Think about it, Harris. Who do you have that can run a fighter carrier. Who do you have commanding the *Washington*?"

"Tom Hampton comes to mind. He's a good man."

Hampton was Fahey's second-in-command. In truth, I did not trust him any more than I trusted Fahey.

"Hampton? You have got to be kidding me! Hampton can't fly a ship. The guy doesn't know his ass end from his hockey stick."

"I don't suppose you have personal experience on that matter?" I asked.

"Get specked, asshole," Fahey growled.

"I thought you and Hampton were buddies."

"Oh, I have a lot of friends, Harris. Believe me, I have friends."

"I believe you. In fact, that is precisely why I came today. I've been looking over your record, Senior Chief. It says that you're only twenty-six years old. Is that right?"

"What about it?"

"That's awfully young to have made senior chief. You're five years younger than any other senior chief in the fleet. Did you know that?"

Fahey smiled and shook his head.

"Impressive," I said.

"Like I said, I have friends," Fahey said.

"Whom do you mean? Who are your friends? What about Warshaw? Are you and Warshaw friends?" I asked.

"Sure we are," he said.

"You were only promoted to senior chief just three weeks before I arrived. That makes you the least senior man of your pay grade in the fleet."

"So?" Fahey sneered. "I'm good at what I do."

I shot a glance at a guard, and said, "I bet you are."

The guard flushed, but he did not reach for his pistol.

"Once you were promoted to senior chief, who placed you on my command staff? Who placed you so high in the chain of command? Was it Warshaw?" I asked.

"Forget it, Harris. You don't know what you are talking about," Fahey said.

"Maybe not," I said. "So I suppose we're done here." We weren't done, but I wanted to see how Fahey would react.

"I can help you," Fahey said, showing me a downright friendly smile.

"How can you help me?" I asked.

He leaned across the table and spoke quietly, as if confiding a secret to me in a crowded room. "Warshaw promoted me."

"Were you lovers?" I asked.

"Lovers?" Fahey asked. "What we did had nothing to do with love. I touched my toes for him, if that's what you mean."

"You piece of shit!" The nearly animal scream echoed from the ceiling, changing the mood in the room from tense to explosive.

"Warshaw?" Fahey sat up, searching around the room for the big man.

"You lying piece of shit! Harris, shoot that specking liar. No, don't shoot him! I want to come down there and kill him myself!"

A mischievous grin spread across Fahey's lips. "Sorry, Gary, I kept it quiet as long as I could."

Until that moment, I had planned on executing Fahey; but now I felt sympathy for the bastard. I said, "That's a very serious accusation, Senior Chief."

"Harris, you can't possibly believe that bullshit," Warshaw said.

If the guards had ever planned on making a move, they

no longer would, not now that they knew the room was under observation. I looked at them, and said, "Take Senior Chief Fahey back to his cell."

They hesitated for a moment, and I rose from my chair. If they made a move, I wanted to be ready. But one of them helped Fahey to his feet, and the other walked around the table and opened the door. As he left the room, Fahey turned to me and spat out the words, "Specking son of a bitch Liberator clone."

I met Fahey's eyes and grinned. And then he was gone, and I was alone in the room with the disinterred voice of Warshaw.

"You let that backstabbing, son of a bitch walk out alive!" Warshaw said.

"I wanted my beer," I said. "We had a bet."

The room went silent. After a moment, Warshaw told me, "Don't believe a word he said, Harris."

"The stuff about Hampton?" I asked.

"About me," Warshaw roared. "It's all bullshit."

"I'm not an expert in these areas; but as I understand it, there's generally a big, strong protector for every lipstick-wearing queen; and you do take your weightlifting—"

"Harris, I never—" he interrupted.

And I interrupted him back. "Warshaw, you were still a master chief petty officer when he was promoted. You might have recommended him for the promotion, but you couldn't have approved it."

"Yeah . . . yeah, you're right." Warshaw sounded relieved. He could see me, but I could not see him. There was a camera in the ceiling, but no monitor for showing images. Being in this room was like being on the reflective side of a one-way mirror. And that was too bad. I would have liked to have seen the sweat rolling down Warshaw's bald pate.

"There's only one man who could have approved Fahey's promotion," I said.

"It wasn't Thorne," Warshaw said. "He had a woman on Terraneau."

"And when was the last time he got to see her?" I asked.

"That horny old bastard." Now there was admiration in Warshaw's voice.

There were still pieces missing from the puzzle. Fahey knew more than he was letting on. I did not mention this to Warshaw, however. Instead, I looked into the camera, and said, "Just remember, you owe me a case of Earth-brewed."

CHAPTER
FORTY-FIVE

I had one more debriefing to conduct; but it could wait, so I called it a day.

The two-hour plane ride from Outer Bliss to Norristown would give me time to think about the future. I piloted my own Johnston R-27, a little twelve-seater commuter capable of both space travel and atmospheric travel. I did not know how to fly anything as big as a transport, but I had no trouble with this little bird. I'd once owned a little Johnston Starliner myself.

Before taking off, I scanned the Zebulon plateau. The runway stretched along the outside of the relocation camp. Three rows of electrified razor-wire fence separated the right side of the runway from the prison. A line of portable barracks sat off to the left of the runway.

Outer Bliss was a naval facility with MPs for guards. I would have preferred to post Marines, but Warshaw said his men needed the shore leave.

I took off into an early sunset with clouds the size of mountain ranges, painted orange and peach by the last dregs of sunlight. As I took off, I searched the sky for hints of silver—not the literary device used to denote a brighter future but the first traces of the Avatari ion curtain. Nothing. Below me, Terraneau looked like an artist's rendition of the ideal planet. In the ebbing light, the cobalt sea had turned to steel. A few, small islands shone against the horizon. Beyond that, the clouds parted, revealing black-satin skies filled with twinkling stars. Somewhere up there, a broadcast station orbited the planet. It orbited so low that on clear nights, people could spot it without a telescope when it passed before the moon.

By the time I reached Norristown, the sun had set and lights sparkled all across the landscape. With the Corps of Engineers' help, Doctorow and his people had repaired the power lines. Most of the city still lay in ruins, but streetlights now shone along the avenues. Lights blazed in the three skyscrapers/dormitories.

Before I could call it a night, I would have dinner with Ellery Doctorow, a formality I could not afford to ignore. The peace between Doctorow and the fleet remained tenuous. After seeing Fahey and the guards, I was more convinced than ever that my men needed a place where they could go for entirely immoral rest and recreation. We had found other cities, but only Norristown had the facilities and the population to accommodate us.

But Doctorow did not trust the military, and maybe he had it right. We did hide things from him. We didn't tell him we had built a relocation camp, and we did not tell him we had filled it up with prisoners. He found out about it on his own. Until he did, we had him convinced that the reconstruction of Norristown was the only thing we had going on Terraneau.

The real reason I had come was to see Ava, of course. We had not spoken for weeks. I worried that she might have moved on. Hearing that she had taken up with some local would not kill me, but I would feel it. Sometimes my jealousy got the better of me, and I fantasized about hiding her in my quarters again. My insecurities got the better of me, and I thought it would be a relief when she finally moved on.

As I came into the airstrip for a landing, I saw a car waiting just outside the gate—a white sedan, a civilian vehicle, Doctorow's car. He left his headlights on, shining twin shafts of light through the fence.

I touched down, rolled the R-27 in toward the tower, and parked it. I climbed out and pulled my rucksack from the back.

As I walked toward the gate, I heard a voice I recognized. "Harris, over here." Ellery Doctorow stepped into the beams, his silhouette nearly swallowed in the glare. He waved a hand to catch my attention. "Harris!"

I slung my rucksack to my left hand and waved with my right just as the loud crack rang through the air.

At first, I had no idea what happened. I was waving, walking toward the gate, then I was on the ground. The force of whatever hit me had picked me up and thrown me on my ass. I felt the bruising on my back first, and then my chest began to burn, and I realized the front of my blouse was wet.

Doctorow came running through the gate. In the glare of the headlights, I saw Ava's outline, too. She came running after him. I recognized her hair . . . her beautiful hair. I touched my chest and saw that my hand was covered with blood. I felt dizzy and winded, but not weak.

It didn't make sense. I could not have been shot.

PART IV

AND THEN THERE WAS WAR

CHAPTER
FORTY-SIX

Doctorow yelled, "Harris, don't move!" as he ran over and knelt by my side.

"Wayson!" Ava screamed. She was already crying.

"I'm not hurt," I said, propping myself up on my elbows. In an act of bald stupidity, I had not brought a gun, not even a pistol to defend myself. I had not a prayer of defending myself if the sniper decided to finish the job.

"You have to stay down, Harris," Doctorow said as he pushed on my shoulders.

"I'm not hurt," I complained.

"Captain, you are covered with blood," Doctorow said, now forcing me back down.

Ava fell on her knees and reached for me, but I pushed her hand away. I did not want to get the blood on her.

"Wayson . . . Oh damn! Oh damn! Wayson," Ava said. She looked at me and cried.

"I'm not hurt," I repeated. I tried to sit up again, but Doctorow pushed me back down. I had an urge to slug him.

Then my former partner, Ray Freeman, strode in through the gate, as silent and as mysterious as a shadow. He carried a sniper rifle with a smart scope in his left hand.

Ava turned and saw Freeman's gigantic outline against the headlights. She screamed even louder than she had when she saw me get shot.

"Admiral Brocius says you broke the rules. He wanted me to give you his regards," Freeman said in a low, slow voice that reminded me of cannon fire echoing in a valley.

Seeing Freeman, Doctorow forgot all about me. He turned and stared, finally allowing me to sit up. I made it to a sitting position, and said, "You shot me, you specking son of a bitch."

"I assassinated you," said Freeman, his voice little more than a whisper. He turned and started to walk away.

I sprang to my feet and followed.

"Wayson, what . . . are you . . . what?" Ava did not know what to say.

"What in God's name is going on?" Doctorow asked.

I ignored them and chased after Freeman. "You're delivering messages for Brocius now?"

Just as I caught up to him, Freeman turned to look at me. The light from the headlights caught half his face, and I saw nothing but ice in his expression. "They're coming for you." He said this so quietly that neither Doctorow nor Ava could hear him.

"How much time do I have?" I asked.

Freeman did not answer. He might or might not have known, but he would not say which. The man stood seven feet tall and weighed in at over three hundred pounds. He had no fear.

"So that's it?" I called after him. "Brocius sent you all the way to Terraneau just to hit me with a specking simmy?"

Freeman stopped again. He looked back at me, and said, "Next time, it will be a bullet." And then he walked around a hangar. I heard a car start and saw taillights pull away.

"Friendly fellow. Who exactly was he?" Doctorow asked, as I climbed into the backseat of the car with Ava. As the acting administrator of Norristown, he had a nice car, with lots of leather and chrome, but he did not merit a chauffeur. He did have a radio, however, which he used to report my "assassination."

Freeman had hit me with "simunition," a kind of round specifically designed for faking assassinations. Instead of a slug, his cartridge housed a capsule designed to burst on contact and shower me with blood.

Unfortunately, Freeman always used a high-velocity rifle. Simunition or live round, any projectile coming at that speed would knock a strong man flat on his back. The round hit me hard enough to rip my blouse, and I was not anxious to see what else it had done.

I unbuttoned the remains of my shirt and found that the fake blood had soaked through my undershirt. I pulled that off as well and used it to wipe the blood off my chest. Not all of the blood was fake. A welt the size of an egg had formed just above my left nipple. The skin at the top of that welt had broken open, forming a crater on my chest

Freeman's aim was as good as ever. If he had used a real bullet, it would have passed right through my heart.

Ava gasped and reached slowly to touch my chest. She cared. I felt encouraged.

She looked like an angel as she watched me, even more beautiful than the first time I had seen her. She wore a yellow dress with a low-cut neck and stringy, little straps that hung over her shoulders. Her dress was bright and happy and clean. It reminded me of daisies. I wanted to grab her, hold her, and press her body against mine, but I had to keep my mind on business.

"His name is Ray Freeman," I said.

"You know him?"

"We used to be partners," I said.

Peering through the rearview mirror, Doctorow saw me bunch the remains of my blouse into a ball, and said, "Partners eh? I'm betting you did not run a dry-cleaning service."

"You're hurt," Ava whispered. She touched her fingertips to the wound as gently as a butterfly lands on a leaf. Tears ran down her cheeks.

"No, not a dry-cleaning service," I agreed. "We did pretty much the same thing he's doing now."

"Shooting people with blood bullets?" Doctorow asked. "Sounds like a fairly specialized niche. Did you get much business?" Clearly, he did not think highly of mercenaries.

Realizing that I was sitting on a powder keg, I did not answer.

By that time, we had driven across the long stretch of destruction that separated the airstrip from the suburbs. The glow of streetlights replaced the starry sky. We drove past a school and a fire station. Light shone from the windows of both buildings. The familiar low glow from the streetlights helped me relax. It represented electricity, civilization, humanity.

We drove into a neighborhood with stores and schools and trees.

"That friend of yours . . . was he a black man, or was I just seeing things?" Doctorow asked.

Race had been abolished by fiat when the Unified Authority moved into space. As they spread humanity across their 180-planet republic, the founding fathers mixed people from every race on every planet. Heritage was discouraged and ethnicity all but banned as Earth's continents and countries became a distant memory. Freeman, a living anomaly who grew up in a religious colony founded by African-American Baptists, had to live with a new kind of prejudice from people who thought he should be extinct.

Ava ran her fingers along my chest so softly that she did not disturb the deep purple welt that had formed around the wound. She caressed my chest. She stared into my eyes. My body responded to her touch, and we kissed. For a moment, I thought we might make love right there in the backseat of Doctorow's car.

"There are three of us in this car, you know," Doctorow said.

Ava blushed.

I laughed, and said, "Feel free to pull over and go for a walk."

Ava hit me in the arm. Her punch did not hurt, but I turned to protect myself. The movement stung, but not much.

"Were you and Freeman friends?" Ava asked.

"Friends?" I asked. "I'm not sure Ray Freeman has ever considered anybody a friend. He doesn't have friends, only people he trusts and people he does not trust."

"Which are you?" Doctorow asked.

I unzipped my ruck and pulled out a clean blouse. I'd only brought one change of uniform for the trip. Assuming nobody else shot me, and that Ava and I did not wrinkle the fabric later, I would be fine.

"He trusts me."

"That's how he treats the people he trusts?" Doctorow asked.

"I'm still breathing," I said.

A fine sheen of blood continued to ooze out of the wound on my chest. I wiped it away. I knew that I needed to call this in. Franks needed to know that an enemy ship had run the blockade, and Warshaw needed to know that we'd been served fair warning. Freeman had said they were coming, but he did not say when. Maybe Brocius was bluffing, trying to get me to play by his rules. He would not come until he had a big enough force to settle the odds in his favor, I was almost sure of that.

"Maybe we should go to the hospital," Doctorow suggested.

"Why? Are you hurt?" I asked. I was a Marine, so I had to be stoic.

Doctorow laughed. Ava did not.

"Your friend scares me," she said.

"Me, too," I said, tearing a long strip from my undershirt to tie around my chest. "Can you tie this off for me?" I said, giving Ava one end, then pressing her hand against my chest. I leaned forward, looped the cloth around my back. Ava took both ends of the bandage and fixed them into a bow.

"What I don't get is why he's here in the first place. The government paid Freeman a lot of money to help liberate New Copenhagen. He doesn't need the money." I was also curious about how he got to the Scutum-Crux Arm and landed on Terraneau without being seen.

Now that I had finished with the wound, I looked out the window. I did not recognize the area. "Where are we?" I asked.

"We're almost there," Doctorow said. "My wife made dinner for us."

"Your wife? How did your wife end up on Terraneau?" I asked. He had transferred here just before the invasion, meaning he had either brought his wife to a war zone or married a local.

Doctorow laughed. "Not exactly. I have a widow on Earth. Sarah is my wife on Terraneau. We met after the alien attack."

"You mean you have two wives?" Ava asked.

"Well, it's always possible that Tina has died or remarried," Doctorow said. "It's been several years since I've seen her, but she was alive and married to me last time I checked.

"Technically, I suppose that makes me a polygamist," Doctorow said.

"Isn't polygamy a sin?" I asked.

"Only if God is watching and cares," Doctorow said.

I slipped on my spare blouse and fastened the buttons. Turning to Ava, I smiled and said, "See, good as new."

Ava brought up a finger, pointed at me, then poked it hard into my chest. When I winced, she asked, "How can you stand living like this?"

"He wasn't trying to kill me," I said. "If Freeman wanted to kill me . . ."

Doctorow finished the thought, "You'd already be dead. I had that feeling, as well. How do you know he won't come back to finish the job next time?" He thought for a moment, then added, "What did he mean when he said 'you broke the rules'?"

Doctorow did not know about my plans. Ava had some idea, but she did not know about our stealing three self-broadcasting battleships. This was not the time to tell them.

"It's a long story," I said. It was the best I could come up with. I was never any good at politics, words did not come naturally.

As he turned his car into the driveway of a two-story home, Doctorow said, "Ava, I'm afraid your boyfriend is keeping secrets from us."

Her boyfriend? I thought to myself. The evening was looking up.

CHAPTER
FORTY-SEVEN

Opening his front door, Doctorow said, "Whatever you do, Harris, don't tell Sarah about what happened at the airstrip. She's a bit on the delicate side, you wouldn't want to worry her." He winked as he said this, and Ava giggled, then Doctorow swung the door open, and bellowed, "We're home, dear."

A voice called out from deep in the house, "No need to

shout, El. I heard you coming up the driveway." "El" must have been short for Ellery.

"Sorry we're late, dear. Somebody assassinated Captain Harris as he came off his plane," Doctorow called.

"Should I remove his place from the table?" the woman called back. She came out of the kitchen, smiled at me, and said, "General Harris, you're looking well for a man who was just assassinated."

Sarah Doctorow was considerably wider along the bottom than she was across the top, giving her body a pyramid shape. Her bottom was so wide it looked like she'd stuffed bed pillows inside her pants. She was less heavy around the stomach, and her girth continued to taper as it reached her notably flat chest and sunken shoulders. She had a lovely round face with laugh lines around the eyes and a little girl's smile. Her face was a patchwork of colors, with spruce-colored eyes, ruby red lips that looked freshly painted, and cerulean makeup above her eyes. She wore her long, red hair in a simple ponytail.

I liked Sarah Doctorow the moment I saw her, but the romance did not last. She moved around the room like a human whirlwind, kissing her husband on the cheek, shaking my hand, then pecking Ava on the cheek and giving her a hug.

She turned to me, and said, "General Harris, you must be famished. I understand being shot takes a lot out of you." And then, without pausing to breathe, she turned to Ava, and said, "Ava darling, why don't you come help me in the kitchen? You can tell me all about that awful assassination." And just like that, Ava and Mrs. Doctorow vanished around the corner.

"Watch this," Doctorow whispered, then he cupped his hands like an actor pretending to yell, and called, "Can I help in the kitchen?"

The offer earned him a giggle from Ava and a belly laugh from Sarah. Ava said something about Doctorow being a good husband, to which Sarah replied, "Don't you believe it for a moment, sweetie."

"I had a word with Lieutenant Mars. He says a planetwide mediaLink will be up in the next week or two. We should be able to contact every city on Terraneau."

Mars was the top dog in the Corps of Engineers. He commanded the crews that built Outer Bliss and refurbished Fort

Sebastian. I was not aware of how far he had gotten with the mediaLink. I was not keen on the idea of Doctorow sending flights around the planet.

"Do you have working media stations?" I asked, making a mental note to contact Mars as soon as I got back to the fleet. I would tell him to slow it down on the media equipment.

"No, but we should be able to throw something together. Perhaps you have some broadcast equipment you could loan us," Doctorow said.

"I'm sure we can find something," I told Doctorow, knowing full well that we did have equipment we could give him and that I would not give it to him. Maybe I was cut out for politics after all.

"Would you like a drink?" Doctorow had a large wet bar stocked with enough bottles to run an officers' club for a night. He might have been a big drinker, but I had the feeling the booze was here for his political friends and rivals.

"Got any juice?" I asked.

"Powdered milk and powdered juice," Doctorow said. "Fresh food is still in short supply."

"I'll make it simple," I said. "Give me whatever you're drinking."

He poured me a tumbler, and I took it without looking to see what it was.

We went out to the patio and sat in the languid night air. Doctorow's house sat on a ridge overlooking Norristown. From the back porch, I could look out into the heart of the city, with its newly lit populated areas and its unlit badlands. In the center of everything, the three skyscrapers stood like sparkling columns.

"They have the elevators working in the dorms," Doctorow said, tracing the line of my sight.

"Does that mean people are living on the upper floors now?" I asked.

"Are you kidding? It's hotter than blazes up there. We haven't got the air-conditioning running yet."

I tried my drink. It was a liqueur, something that tasted a lot like coffee. I did not like it.

We sat on some metal furniture and stared out across town for several seconds. Finally, Doctorow broke the silence. "There's a nasty rumor going around these days that you are planning to start a war with the Unified Authority, General," he said. "Is that what Freeman meant by 'breaking the rules'?"

I thought about playing innocent or just plain denying everything, but there was too much to hide. "Something like that," I said, feeling uncomfortable. "Care to share how you heard about it?"

"It doesn't matter how I heard it."

"It may not matter to you," I said. "To me, it's a breach of security . . . a bad one."

"Do you plan on involving my planet in your war?"

"The war has already begun, but I didn't start it," I said. "The Unified Authority is phasing clones and obsolete fleets out of its military. They didn't send us here to free Terraneau, they sent us here for target practice."

Doctorow whistled. "Wow. I don't know what to say." He thought about what I had said, and finally asked, "What happened? I mean, clones . . . they were the heart of the military."

"A couple of generals blamed clones for all of the losses against the aliens."

"There was always deep-seated prejudice among the officers I knew. I won't say it made sense, but it was always there . . . always there," Doctorow said.

"Yeah, I know," I said.

"What did your friend mean when he said you broke the rules?"

"We captured three of their self-broadcasting ships."

"Were those ships attacking you?"

"The Navy was using them to bring clones in and ship natural-borns back to Earth."

"So, they came on a peaceful mission," Doctorow said.

"Yeah, I suppose so."

"You fired on those ships?" Doctorow asked.

"Hell, we had to do something, or we would all be trapped right now. We hijacked . . . commandeered three self-broadcasting battleships. Now, maybe we will be able to defend ourselves."

"Have they asked for their ships back?"

302 STEVEN L. KENT

I nodded.

"Are you going to return them?"

"I can't imagine why I would," I said.

"It sounds to me like you've started yourself a war."

"To us, it's a war. We're fighting for our survival. To them, it's a military exercise," I said.

"Just make sure you keep your war off my planet," Doctorow said, all of his former good humor missing from his voice.

"That's why we wanted the self-broadcasting ships. We want to take the fight to them."

"What do you think they'll call your war back on Earth? The Clone Rebellion? The Clone Uprising?" Doctorow finished his drink and placed the glass on the little table by his seat.

"I prefer the Enlisted Man's War," I said. "My men tend to keel over when they hear they're clones."

"I don't want you pulling my planet into your war," Doctorow said.

"We have a five-hundred-ship fleet orbiting this planet. The Earth Fleet is down to somewhere in the neighborhood of forty self-broadcasting ships."

"Forty ships that you know about," Doctorow corrected.

I went on as if I had not heard him. "We have a blockade around your planet. You and your people are safe."

Doctorow heard this and laughed. "Safe? Your friend with the rifle not only managed to run your blockade, he knew how to find you and put a bullet in your chest."

"Simunition," I said.

"What?"

"He used simunition, not a live round."

"You're missing my point, Harris. You weren't even able to protect yourself. You're in over your head. That's my point." Doctorow had raised his voice so that he nearly shouted the words.

Sarah came out to the patio. "How are you boys getting on?" she asked, pretending she had not heard us.

"It appears General Harris here has plunged us into another war," Doctorow snapped.

"Well, that's fine then," Sarah said, the smile never faltering from her face. I wondered if she even heard him. "Now, you boys come in before our dinner gets cold."

The Doctorows' dining room was a long and narrow rectangle with a small table surrounded by large empty spaces on either end. When I mentioned this to Ava, she laughed and said that the table could be extended to fill the room.

"The first time I came here, Sarah hosted a dinner party for twenty guests," Ava said. "We all sat at the same table." Ava sat to my right. Ellery sat across the table, glaring at me.

The Doctorows ate like people living in a war zone. Sarah had worked wonders with rice and beans and canned meats, but I got better food on the *Kamehameha*.

Ava and Sarah talked about movies. They chatted like sisters, Sarah asking questions about stars and Ava dishing up insider gossip that might well have been old news three years ago. Not that it mattered to Sarah—her planet had been cut off from movies and movie stars since the day the Mogats destroyed the Broadcast Network.

Doctorow and I traded a few questions, but we mostly listened in on the women. When we spoke, we talked about galactic wars; Ava and Sarah chatted about movie stars and gossip. Their conversation was more interesting than ours.

When Ava and Sarah finally hit a lull in their conversation, I commented that watching them converse, I would have guessed that they had known each other their entire lives, they might even have been sisters.

"We're new-old friends," Sarah explained. "We have Ava up to the house every weekend."

"Really?"

"Well, sure. You asked El to look after her," Sarah said.

"I appreciate it," I said, not sure what else to say.

"We've loved having her. I did not know what to expect when El first told me about Ava, her being a movie star and all," Sarah said. "A war hero and a movie star—my goodness, you two are going to be the life of the party wherever you go."

Ava smiled and gave my hand a squeeze.

We ate and chatted amiably, then Sarah changed the tenor of the evening. "You know, Wayson . . . Is it all right if I call you Wayson? General Harris just sounds so full of starch."

Ava chipped in, "I call him Harris."

"Wayson is fine," I said.

"You really are a hero. You saved the planet. I mean, I heard all about you chasing away the aliens with so very few men—absolutely amazing, like a miracle or something."

"Thank you," I said, feeling a little embarrassed.

She gushed on about my heroism, but then she said, "Who are you going to war with now?"

"He declared war on the Unified Authority," Doctorow said.

"But we are part of the Unified Authority," Sarah said, clearly confused.

"On Earth," Doctorow said.

"Oh, on Earth," Sarah said. She sounded impressed. "You better keep the fighting away from Terraneau."

"We'll keep you safe," I said, thinking that Doctorow must have rehearsed the entire night with his wife.

"See, now, Wayson, you're not listening to me. I have no doubt you will keep us safe, but that is not what I am telling you. What I am trying to say is that given a choice, the people on this planet are surely going to support Earth over a bunch of clones."

Sarah smiled and passed me the beans, apparently unaware that I might object to her antisynthetic comments.

"But Earth abandoned Terraneau," Ava said. "They had a fleet of ships circling your planet for four years without ever sending anyone to rescue you."

"We told them not to. El, didn't you tell them to leave us alone." She said this as a statement, not a question. "You told them not to come, isn't that right?"

"Yes, dear," Doctorow said. "I think we are all glad that General Harris decided not to listen."

"Well, of course we are," Sarah admitted, "but that does not mean we would pick clones over humans if it comes to a war. You understand that, don't you, Wayson?"

"Yes," I said. I understood her perfectly.

"God, I hate that woman," Ava said, as we walked through her front door. I had expected Doctorow to move her in with the girls in the dormitory, but that never happened. She never spent so much as a night in that building.

"I thought you two were old friends," I said.

"Honey, where I come from, she would not be allowed on the sidewalk without a leash and a muzzle!" Ava said. "I could never be friends with that two-faced, antisynthetic bitch. Do you know what she said behind my back? When she found out her husband wanted to put me in the girls' dorm, she told her friends they should set me up in a convenience store and call it a 'home for wayward clones.'"

"How about Doctorow?" I asked. "Is he any better?"

"I don't know how he puts up with her. They're completely different. He's a nice man, and he's honest, and . . ."

"She's honest, too," I said.

"Honestly antisynthetic. Was it always like this for you, Harris? Did people always treat you like that? I don't think anyone knew I was a clone when I first got here. They knew who I was, you know, they'd seen my movies, but then Sarah started telling everyone I was a clone. She's like a one-woman mediaLink. God, I hate her."

"Do you think she speaks for the rest of the planet?" I asked, knowing that in Ava's experience, Norristown was the rest of the planet. "Who's got more clout, Ellery or Sarah?"

"If it comes down to a fight between Sarah and Ellery, my money is on Ellery," Ava said. But I got the feeling she had told me whom she wanted to win, not who she thought would take the title.

I looked around the house. The living room was all done up in bright colors and glass tile. The home probably came furnished, just move in and put your name on the shingle, with a don't-ask-don't-tell policy when it came to the previous owners. There was a bright square above the fireplace where someone might once have hung a family portrait.

"Did Doctorow give you this house?" I asked.

"I pay the rent by teaching drama classes up at the dorms," Ava said, brightening up.

"Should I be worried about the other teachers?"

"Other guys? Wayson Harris is worried about other guys?" Ava laughed. She led me into the kitchen, where she picked out two mugs and made us coffee. "Ellery warned everyone about you. Between Sarah advertising that I am a clone and Ellery scaring the guys off, it gets pretty lonely around here.

"How about you?" she asked. "Any other women I need to know about?" She spoke more softly and came close. I put my hands on her waist and brought her toward me. We hugged, and I swung her gently back and forth. A few moments passed before we kissed. Somewhere in her breath, I tasted a trace of the imitation bacon Sarah Doctorow used to flavor her beans, but mostly Ava's breath just smelled like Ava. She kissed me, rubbed her body against mine, and giggled. "Wayson Harris worried about other guys." She laughed and pressed her face against my chest.

Somewhere in the back of my mind, I thought about Freeman and his warning, and I knew that I should call the incident in to Warshaw, but Ava wrapped her right leg around my left thigh, and she reached up and kissed my neck. She kissed me on the lips, and her taste lingered. I did not forget about Freeman, but the run-in just did not seem all that important at the moment. I would be back on the *Kamehameha* by lunch.

"You know what you said about my never forcing you?" I asked.

"You're not going to need to now," she said.

Sometimes things just work that way.

We went to bed and made love. When we were done, we held each other in the darkness. I felt cool fingers with skin as soft as flower petals probing the wound on my chest. Once she had finished examining my chest, Ava moved her hands to my face, where she ran her fingers along my eyebrow. This touched off a strange kind of search. She felt my thighs, my arms, and my neck. She finished by going over my back, stopping on a spot below the shoulder blade on my left side.

"Find anything interesting?" I asked.

"Yes," she whispered, in a voice as soft and sensuous as the feel of her skin against mine. "This is the worst one." She meant my worst scar. I had three inch-wide stripes across that part of my back.

"How did you get these?" she asked.

"Somebody scratched me," I said.

"Scratched you?" she asked, unable to hide her giggle. "Somebody scratched you? Poor baby."

I did not tell her he was a Navy SEAL clone genetically developed to have daggerlike fingers. Instead, I just said, "Yeah, poor me."

"Ted told me you were the toughest man in the Marines," Ava said.

"Nice of him," I said.

"Have you ever been shot?" she asked.

"Besides today?" I asked.

"Today doesn't count. You said he used blanks."

"He used simmies. They're not blanks. Blanks just make noise."

"I mean shot with bullets?"

"No, I have never been shot," I admitted.

"Really?" She seemed surprised. I wanted to tell her that being shot in real life was nothing like being shot in the movies. On the battlefield, you got it in the gut or the head and you died. Maybe you got shot in the arm or the leg, and the limb never worked right again. In the movies, heroes get shot and still manage to save the day. In real war, Marines get shot and never fully recover.

"Have you ever been stabbed?" she asked.

"I got scratched real bad," I said. The SEAL who put those scars on my back had dug so deep that he cut through muscle and damaged organs, but I felt no desire to tell her that. This conversation irritated me.

"You were in all of those big battles, and you never got shot? You know what, Harris? I think Ted was wrong about you," she said. She probably wanted to sound playful, this being an after-sex conversation. To me, though, she sounded childish. "I don't think you're the toughest man in the Marines. I think you're the luckiest."

There was just enough light in the room for me to see her hair, her face, her breasts. There was not a man in the Corps who would have disagreed with her about my luck at that moment, not even Ted Mooreland.

I fell asleep after that. I did not remember my dream when I woke up; but whatever I dreamed, it left me feeling small, worried . . . unlucky.

CHAPTER
FORTY-EIGHT

Knowing that I needed to report my run-in with Freeman as soon as possible, I woke up early the next morning and flew back to Outer Bliss. I had one final interrogation to conduct.

I went to the guardhouse and told the officer in charge whom I wanted to see. He had two of his men take me to the interrogation room, where I waited for fifteen minutes before there was a knock on the door.

"Enter," I said.

The guards led Admiral Thorne into the room, and I dismissed them. Thorne and I would be alone for this private conversation; not even Warshaw would listen in on this one.

Thorne came in, looking solemn and dignified. His time in the relocation camp had not treated him kindly. He had lost weight. His posture seemed stiff, which actually added to his air of dignity. I expected him to call me Captain Harris, but he surprised me.

"Good morning, General," he said as he entered, and he gave me a smart salute.

I returned the salute.

"So, what brings the commandant of the Scutum-Crux Marines to Bliss on the Plateau?" he asked.

"Bliss on the Plateau? Is that what they're calling it?"

"That's what the inmates are calling it."

"I have a few questions," I said. I motioned to the table, and we took our seats.

"Questions for me? I'm not sure what I can tell you, General. I am well aware of the war. Admiral George and Senior Chief Fahey aren't keeping confidences. I suppose you know that."

I nodded. "I'm beginning to figure that out." I could feel the tension building already. "How about you, Admiral? Do you keep confidences?"

"I am at this moment," Thorne said. "I have not told anyone but you about the harnesses I found on the carriers."

The harnesses—I had almost forgotten about them. Someone had booby-trapped the fighter carriers in the fleet to prevent them from leaving the space around Terraneau. Even if broadcast engines were installed on the carriers, we could not use them. The harnesses were designed to detect the electrical buildup needed to power a broadcast. They would make the engines explode. Admiral Thorne had showed me the harness on the *Kamehameha* the day I arrived.

I still had not told Warshaw about the harnesses. There was no need to mention them until we figured out how to install the broadcast engines on smaller ships.

"We need to talk about those," I said.

Showing me those harnesses had been an act of sedition on Thorne's part. As I considered it, he had indeed shown that his loyalty was to the fleet and not the Unified Authority. Someone was feeding information back to Earth, but I did not think it was Thorne.

"I was assassinated last night," I said. "Admiral Brocius sent me a message by way of a sniper and a round of simunition."

Thorne laughed. "Let you know that you were not untouchable, did he?"

"How did he do that?" I asked.

"Are you asking how he landed a sniper on Terraneau?" Thorne asked, leaning back in his chair, his fingers forming a church and steeple. "It sounds as if someone ran your blockade."

"He shouldn't have been able to get through," I said. "We have a fleet surrounding this planet."

"Blockades are for stopping fleets and convoys, General. Your ships weren't looking for a five- or ten-man spacecraft. If he came in a Johnston or Cessna, he might even slip past your ships."

"Without us spotting him on radar?"

"He would need to find a significant hole in your coverage," Thorne said. "Blocking off an entire planet isn't as easy as guarding a prison camp, not even with a fleet as big as yours."

"I figured that much out," I said. In truth, I had flown small craft through a few nets during the Mogat War. Using a small self-broadcasting ship, I had broadcasted in millions of miles away from well-guarded destinations so that no one would detect the anomaly from my ship, then flown in under the radar. I was not running active blockades, though, just entering guarded areas.

"How did the assassin know where to find me?" I asked. "The guy knew when and where I was."

Ray Freeman was a dangerous and resourceful man, more resourceful than any man I had ever known, but even he had his limits. He could not read minds or predict the future.

"Good question," Thorne agreed. He continued leaning back in his chair, flexing his fingers, the stiff expression on his face a mask hiding his emotion. I could not tell if he hated me or liked me, not that it mattered.

"You know you have a significant breach in your command structure. You do know that, don't you?" Thorne asked. "I knew you were coming to Bliss on the Plateau five days ago, Senior Chief Fahey told me."

"Fahey?" I asked. "How the speck does he know so much?" I could feel my frustration mounting.

"Sometimes you surprise me, Harris. He knows because he has friends on the *Washington* who keep him briefed."

I hit my boiling point. "Briefed? What do you mean 'briefed'? Are you telling me I have officers in my fleet who just ring him up and tell him our plans?" I knew the answer even as I asked. I let Hollingsworth take Fahey to the brig instead of Thomer. Hollingsworth was loyal to me, but he'd had sex with Fahey. He might well do small favors for Fahey if he thought they were harmless. He might, for instance, have let Fahey's friends know he'd been sent to Outer Bliss.

"Everything points back to Fahey," I said. He was the one who had set up the blockade around Terraneau. He might have built blind spots into it. He could even have sent that information back to Admiral Brocius. When natural-borns transferred back to Earth, they transferred out through the *Washington*—Fahey's ship. He could have sent messages with them or anyone else on the transports. Hell, he had plenty of opportunity to ride out to the U.A. ships himself.

"So was Fahey working for you?" I asked. "Was he your spy?"

"My spy? General, why would I spy on the fleet? I wanted to stay out here," Thorne said.

"But you promoted him to senior chief right before the transfers started. If he's been playing Mata Hari with my officers, you were the one who placed him where he could catch the right information."

"It wasn't me. That promotion came straight from Navy Headquarters . . . in the Pentagon. General Harris, I think you have your leak."

"Obviously," I said.

"No, hear me out. The guards practically let Fahey run this place. Half the men guarding this camp are sailors from the *Washington*, and they let him call his friends all the time. What if he used a predetermined frequency? What if he wanted you to put him here so he could get information out?"

I rolled that question around in my mind. If half the guards in the camp were from the *Washington*, Fahey might have picked them himself. The two guards who came in with Fahey were probably from the *Washington*. I got the feeling that Fahey and those men may have been joined at the hip a time or two.

I pounded my fist into the table. "Damn it!" I yelled. Fahey had outmaneuvered me again and again. He'd floated enough information for Ray Freeman, possibly the most dangerous man in the galaxy, to take a shot at me. "Damn it," I repeated more quietly.

"The Navy doesn't operate like the Marines. You're dealing with sailors now, and you can't make them act like Marines. Their world is a lot more sophisticated, and the parts don't fit together as neatly," Thorne said.

"Yeah, well, Gary Warshaw sure as hell agrees with you. He says I'm not fit to command a fleet."

"He's one to talk," Thorne said. "He's the other half of your problems."

"What do you think of Lilburn Franks?" I asked.

"He'd be a good choice for a second-in-command. At least he knows his way around a bridge, but he's a bit too aggressive. He understands naval strategy, but he hasn't seen what happens when things go wrong."

"Any other recommendations?" I asked. Thorne knew the SC Fleet better than any man alive.

Thorne sat up and went through the litany of NCOs I had available to me. I watched him closely as he spoke. The man looked old, but life still coursed through his veins. He didn't know it, but he was auditioning. Watching him speak, I decided that he still had a few good years in him. I could see it in his face.

"How about you? You still want to stay with the fleet?" I asked.

He looked me right in the eye and, giving me his best poker face, he slowly said, "Yes, you know I do."

"Why?" I asked.

"I told you, I've spent more than half my life out here. I . . ."

"Do you have a wife on Terraneau?" I asked.

"Not a wife, I never married her. Earth-born officers are supposed to wait for Earth-born wives. If it got back to Washington, it would have hurt my career."

"Children?" I asked.

"Three of them." He spoke evenly, slowly, a man trying to hide his excitement. He might have been in bed with the Unified Authority, or he might have been telling me the truth.

"And nobody ever knew about them?" I asked.

"Having illegitimate children is considered conduct unbecoming in certain circles. If word got back to Washington about the children, it would have ended my career."

"And that is why you want to stay in Scutum-Crux?" I asked. It explained a lot more than that. It explained why he'd continued flying around Terraneau, trying to break through the ion curtain for the last four years. It also explained his mystery visit to the planet the day the curtain went down.

"Why do you want to fight against the Unified Authority?" I asked.

Thorne leaned across the table, and said, "Why would I pick you over Earth? Why would I pick a bunch of clones over the Unified Authority?

"General Harris, I have been out here for more than half of my life. Those ships in your fleet, they are my home. Those men in your fleet, I've been flying with some of those men for thirty years now.

"I don't know what Alden Brocius has up his sleeve, but it's going to be powerful. Those ships I lived on and those men I served with, they're all going to die if I can't help them."

I took Thorne with me when I returned to the fleet.

FORTY-NINE

Thorne and I spent the short flight back to the *Kamehameha* in the kettle of the transport, discussing command structures and politics. We talked about possible scenarios and whom we could count on if Warshaw fought us for control of the fleet. As a Marine dealing with sailors, I would have few allies. As a natural-born and a relic of the old U.A. power structure, Thorne would have even fewer.

Leaving the atmosphere, the transport struggled for just a moment. Thorne looked around the dark cabin nervously. "I hate these things."

"It's nothing. You get a rattle whenever you leave the atmosphere," I said.

"Doesn't the shaking bother you?"

"You get used to it," I said. "I spent six weeks in a bird like this once."

"This is a short-range transport," Thorne said. He did not say anything more, but he did not need to. The lull in the conversation signaled his skepticism.

"They're supposed to have a range of two hundred thousand miles. I know all about it," I said. "We took ours closer to four billion miles."

"That would be suicidal," Thorne said.

"That's one way to look at it," I admitted.

There were two of us on that flight, Ray Freeman and I. We were escaping a Baptist farming colony, and the transport was the only way off the planet. We did what we had to do.

"General Harris, we're approaching the *Kamehameha*," the pilot called over the intercom. Three minutes later, we had touched down, and the doors at the rear of the kettle slid open.

Thorne and I exited the transport and headed up to Fleet Command without saying a word to anyone we passed.

Somebody must have alerted Warshaw as soon as we stepped off our transport. He and three of his lieutenants met us as we came off the lift.

"General Harris," he said, putting on a reasonable pretense of surprise.

"Admiral," I said.

He looked over at Admiral Thorne, and said, "Admiral Thorne, up for a visit?" Suspicion jingled in his voice.

This was not a discussion I planned to hold in a busy corridor, so I said, "Perhaps you and Admiral Franks could join us for a meeting in the conference room; we have a lot to discuss."

Maybe Warshaw had already put two and two together, or maybe he read my intentions by the stiff tone of my voice. Sounding more businesslike than usual, he told one of his lieutenants to send for Franks, then he turned and led the way to a conference room. We barely had time to find our seats before Franks joined us.

The cease-fire between me and Warshaw ended as soon as the meeting began. "What is it now, Harris?" he asked.

"I was shot last night," I said, opening my rucksack and pulling out the blouse. The blood was still tacky. The other men in the room all stared at it. They were mesmerized.

"Sweet shit," Warshaw said. He reached out and touched the stain, then looked at his fingers. The fake blood stained his fingertips.

I told them about Freeman and what he said.

"What does it mean?" asked Warshaw, temporarily forgetting about Admiral Thorne.

"It means a lot of things," I said. "It means at least one ship was able to run our blockade. It means we have a leak. Perry Fahey has been spying for the U.A. all along."

"You're sure it was Fahey?" Franks asked.

"Of course it was Fahey. That son of a bitch," Warshaw said.

After I rehearsed the evidence—Fahey setting up the blockade, the officers transferring back to Earth through the *Washington*, the way Fahey kept up with our movements from Outer Bliss—Franks seemed convinced as well.

"The assassin said they're coming for us? Did he say when?" asked Franks.

"Tomorrow, next week, your guess is as good as mine," I said. I did not regret waiting until I got back to the fleet to report the whole thing. The more I thought about it, the more convinced I became that Admiral Brocius would not move until he had an overwhelming force. We might still have a year to prepare.

No one asked for my interpretation of the comment about us breaking the rules. We all knew what it meant. I looked back at Thorne one last time to renew my confidence, then I said, "We're going to need an experienced officer at the helm."

"Good God, not that again," Warshaw moaned, rolling his eyes, his face so red he looked like he'd been boiled. As he often did when angered, he flexed his muscles and stared at me. His eyes bored into mine. The muscles in his neck, shoulders, and arms bulged. He squeezed his fists and relaxed his hands, squeezed and relaxed, pumping blood into his spade-shaped forearms.

How many officers had he silently intimidated with that little trick? How many rivals had he scared off? The big muscles might intimidate other sailors, but to me he looked like a mouse roughing its fur so it can look as big as a rat.

"What are you saying? I have been in the Navy for twenty-five years, you don't call that experience?" Warshaw practically whispered the question, the calm in his voice as precarious as a dagger wrapped in a silk scarf.

"You have no experience commanding a ship," I said.

"The hell with that," Warshaw said. "If you want to step down, Harris, go ahead. That's your choice. I earned my commission."

"I'm not asking you to resign your commission," I said, trying to sound reasonable.

Warshaw shook his head. He looked angry enough to launch himself at me. He looked crazed. "I run the ships! I run the specking fleet! You hear me, Harris? I am the goddamned commander of the Scutum-specking-Crux Fleet!"

"Harris, we've already been through this. Admiral Brocius put Warshaw in charge," Franks said. He might not have sounded so reasonable had he not gotten falling-down-drunk the night I recommended that he take over the fleet.

"I don't want to run the specking fleet, Franks. I want Admiral Thorne to run it," I said.

"Admiral Thorne?" Franks asked. "Why in God's name do you want a natural-born to run the Enlisted Man's Fleet? Why would you even trust him?"

I never got to state my case, however. That was when the Klaxons sounded.

CHAPTER
FIFTY

"We've detected two anomalies." The voice on the intercom belonged to Hank Bishop, captain of the *Kamehameha*. He was a good officer, a veteran sailor, but he sounded nervous.

"Have you identified the ships?" asked Admiral Thorne. We could not identify specific ships by their anomalies, but we could identify the class of the ships.

Bishop did not answer.

Warshaw glared at Thorne.

Franks jumped to his feet and bolted out the door. Having spent his career on the bridge of a capital ship, he had no trouble putting politics and power struggles out of his mind in an emergency. There was a call to quarters, and he needed to be at the helm.

I got on the intercom and raised Thomer. "This is not a

drill," I said. "Contact every ship; I want every last Marine suited up and ready to fight."

"Aye, aye," he said, then he followed up with an unexpected question, "Did you know this was coming?"

I did not have time to think about it at that moment. "Good question," I said. He and I could debate what I should have expected and what I could not have known over drinks once the alert was over. "Get a move on it, *Sergeant*," I said, temporarily forgetting Thomer's rank.

He responded, "Yes, sir," and signed off.

By the time Thorne and I left for the bridge, Warshaw and Franks were already there. The wail of the Klaxons thundered through the ship with its earsplitting decibels.

"When was the last time this fleet was in a battle?" I asked Thorne, as we boarded the lift from Fleet Command down to the bridge.

"We took on a couple of ships orbiting Little Man," Thorne said.

"Little Man," I repeated. I had been there for that fight. Was that six years ago? Seven? I could not remember.

It had not occurred to me before, but having spent his career in the outermost arm of the galaxy, Thorne did not exactly fit the bill of a battle-tested veteran. He was a graduate of the Naval Academy, but that graduation had happened nearly forty uneventful years ago.

We entered the bridge.

Fleet Command had been loud and relatively empty, the bridge was very different. The siren hummed low and steady in the background. Officers rushed from one station to the next. In the scramble, most of them ran around me, but a few pushed off me and continued without looking back.

Franks, Warshaw, and Bishop stood around the chart table in the center of the bridge, huddling together like chefs around a stove. As Thorne and I approached, Warshaw looked up, and asked, "What the speck is a U.A. officer doing on my bridge? Someone remove this man." He was not calling for bridge security to remove Thorne, he said it quietly, for my benefit.

"He's with me," I said.

Even before I finished saying this, Warshaw drowned

me out, yelling, "Great, I have a Marine *and* a spy on my bridge."

Franks pointed to something on the strategy table, and Warshaw seemed to forget about us.

The three-dimensional map on the chart table showed Terraneau, our fleet, and the area in which our telemetry detected the anomaly. It depicted open spaces as blue-black cubes. There were no stars in the three million miles between us and the anomaly, just open space.

Without looking up, Franks said, "They're headed toward us at one-fifth full." One-fifth full meant six million miles per hour, a cautious speed for closing long distances.

"Do we have a read on the anomaly?" Warshaw repeated Thorne's question as if he had come up with it himself.

"No information yet," Captain Bishop answered, as he edged around the table.

"Have we made contact?" Franks asked.

"No, sir. They're ignoring us," a communications officer called.

"Where are our self-broadcasting ships?" Warshaw asked. "They've got to be here for the ships."

Franks pointed them out. They were halfway between our fleet and the intruders, rocketing toward us as fast as they could.

I did not think Warshaw was correct in his assessment. We had captured three U.A. ships and destroyed three more. Until that moment, it had not occurred to me that we had captured or destroyed six of their ships. We didn't just beat them to the punch; we had declared an all-out war.

Seeing that our self-broadcasting fleet was safe for the time being, Warshaw seemed to relax. He leaned against a desk and took a deep breath. He started to say something, then stopped. On the table, seven new anomalies appeared almost on top of our fleeing ships.

Franks barked out orders like an experienced commander, or, I realized, a man who has spent his career watching experienced commanders. He sent orders across the fleet telling his captains to power up their shields, charge weapons systems, and put all fighter pilots on red alert.

Around the bridge, the various stations hummed with activity. Displays lit up, showing shield readiness and weapons status.

Looking at the chart table, I reckoned the second wave of U.A. ships were still a million miles away. They did not chase our ships. Apparently, they were satisfied with herding them into our fold. The more distant, first wave of ships continued toward us, but they were still two million miles away. It would take them at least twenty more minutes to reach our lines.

An ensign brought a coded message over to Warshaw, whose expression went from desperation to defeat. He read the message again and handed it to Franks.

"What is it?" I asked.

"It's from one of the engineers overseeing the work in the Galactic Eye. He says the Unifieds sent battleships to destroy the Mogat Fleet," Warshaw said.

"So much for harvesting broadcast engines," he said, planting his arms along the edges of the table to prop himself up.

Franks's face turned pale as he looked from Warshaw to me. "Maybe we should send our ships back . . ."

"Three ships," Warshaw said. "We have three self-broadcasting ships."

"Did we get all of our men out?" Thorne asked.

"No," answered Warshaw. He turned to me, and said, "We had eight thousand men out there."

On the chart table, another wave of anomalies appeared. Five ships broadcasted in this time, giving the U.A. a total of twelve ships in the area. They had twelve ships, we had five hundred. They would not attack.

"Just a few more days . . . all we needed was a few more days." Warshaw groaned in a soft voice, still leaning on the table for support. With his huge muscles and tired posture, he looked like a Hollywood hero resting after a long battle. "Not even another week. How the hell did they know?"

"The same way Freeman knew how to find me," I said.

"Fahey?" Warshaw asked. "I told you you should have shot that traitor bastard. He told them everything from the prison camp, didn't he?"

"Anything and everything he knew," I said. "He probably wanted us to arrest him."

"Wanted us to arrest him?" Franks asked.

"He's a lot safer down there than he would be up here with us," I said.

"Speck!" Warshaw slammed his fist on the chart table. Then we all went quiet as five more anomalies appeared. Now the U.A. Navy was up to seventeen ships. It didn't really matter if they sent their whole specking fleet, we had ten times as many ships as they did. They might have taken the Galactic Central Fleet from us, but they could not touch us here.

A small herd of officers had gathered around the chart table. Not only did Warshaw and Franks have aides, but it appeared that their aides had aides as well. It takes a lot of officers to control a fleet, and the Scutum-Crux Fleet was the largest fleet in the galaxy.

Six more anomalies appeared on the table, and suddenly it looked like the U.A. Navy might really attack. With twenty-three battleships gathered along one of our flanks, it no longer looked as if they had simply come to send a message. Most of those ships were still three million miles away, too great a distance for us to exchange shots; but it suddenly looked like they'd come for a fight.

We all shared the same thought—the Unified Authority could not possibly win a fight out here. They had fewer than forty self-broadcasting ships, and there were no fighter carriers in their self-broadcasting fleet. If it came to a fight, we could win just using our carriers. They had to know that. Brocius had to know that, and that was what scared me. If he had come to fight, he knew something we didn't know.

Ten more anomalies appeared. They had thirty-three ships in a single sector, the vast majority of their self-broadcasting fleet.

"What are they doing?" Warshaw asked. "That's almost everything they have."

Franks looked over at an aide, and snapped, "Get me analysis on those anomalies, now!"

Warshaw said what we all were hoping, "They're bluffing."

"No, they aren't," said Thorne.

Forgetting that he had threatened to have Thorne thrown off the bridge a few minutes earlier, Warshaw now tried to argue with him. "They're not going to send their fleet against us; we outnumber them ten-to-one. They'd be crazy."

But they were not trying to scare us, and they were not crazy. Fifteen more anomalies appeared on the chart table, giving them forty-eight ships, more self-broadcasting capital ships than they were supposed to have in their entire fleet.

An officer approached Franks with the first analysis of anomalies. He looked like he was choking on words, as he said, "We were not able to identify several of the anomalies, sir."

Twelve more anomalies bloomed on the chart table.

"Sixty ships," Franks whispered.

"They're sending in the new fleet," Warshaw said.

Ice-cold fingers seemed to have wrapped themselves around my vitals. Somewhere out there, in the dark clarity of space, some of those ships would have shining shields wrapped tightly around their hulls like a luminous skin. We had bested three of those ships in an ambush, but this time it would be a head-on collision.

On the chart table, the U.A. ships did not move. They seemed to have come all the way across the galaxy just to park.

"Those crazy speckers really came to fight," Franks announced. "They're massing a specking attack." Far from panicking, he sounded excited. This was an empirical experience for him; he was about to put his education to the test. Using signal officers to relay his orders around the fleet, Franks began reeling off a series of commands. I did not recognize much of what he said, but I watched the results on the chart table.

Our outlying ships slid into place. The loose configuration of the fleet tightened into a fist.

"He's circling the wagons," Thorne whispered to me.

"Sounds like a good call," I said.

"Not against a foe with superior firepower," Thorne said. "You want to spread out. We have more ships than they do. We should take a more aggressive stance and hit them from every angle."

"The way we fight this battle is not your concern, Admiral Thorne," Warshaw warned. "As far as I am concerned, you are still an officer of the Unified Authority."

Franks gave the order to scramble the fighters and sent

them to the front of the fleet. On the table, the simulation showed our self-broadcasting battleships approaching the fleet. The curtain of fighters split, allowing the battleships in, then closed in behind them.

"We better keep those babies tucked away," Warshaw said.

Franks looked up at Warshaw and nodded.

Fifteen more anomalies appeared. Three million miles away, the Unified Authority was preparing to attack.

"Seventy-five ships?" Franks sounded amazed. "How many ships do you have, Admiral Brocius?" he hummed. "How many are you willing to risk?"

Thorne stared down at the table, taking in every nuance and movement. He was like a blind man reading Braille. To me, the various blips and dots meant nothing. To him, they were ships with specific speeds and weapons capabilities.

Warshaw stepped between me and the chart table. I moved out from behind him; but as I stepped toward the table, he said, "Excuse me, General, this is a naval operation."

I shuffled back, aware that Warshaw really could have me removed from the bridge. Thorne wisely followed my lead. I floated over to him, and asked, "Where are our self-broadcasting ships?"

Thorne leaned forward slightly and pointed.

I would not have recognized them without his help. To me, they looked like little dashes in a field of dots and dashes.

As I looked at the symbols representing our self-broadcasting ships, I noticed they had stopped beside a small, red triangle. "Is that us?" I whispered to Thorne.

He nodded.

Looking at the tight formation on the chart table, I had a premonition and started edging my way off the bridge.

Ten more anomalies appeared. So the Unified Authority had eight-five ships. One of Franks's aides had a new round of analysis. "Sir, we can't be sure, but those ships appear to be fighter carriers."

"Fighter carriers? How the hell can they possibly have fighter carriers? It's not possible; there are no self-broadcasting fighter carriers." Franks coughed out the words as if they had barbs attached to them. He did not sound scared, but his confidence had dwindled.

Three more anomalies appeared about a hundred thousand miles away.

"What do they have now, a damn floating planet?" Warshaw asked.

"Explorers," the aide answered.

"Explorers? Why send explorers out here? What the hell do they want with explorers?" Franks asked.

We have three self-broadcasting ships, and they have three explorers, I thought to myself, and an evil memory came to mind. I remembered the sinking of the *Doctrinaire,* the most indestructible juggernaut of our time, and I ran from the bridge.

"Where the speck do you think you are going?" Warshaw yelled behind me.

I ignored him and ran to the observation deck.

CHAPTER
FIFTY-ONE

I looked out of the viewport and saw miles of space and ships. With so many ships hovering in such close proximity, the Scutum-Crux Fleet would appear as a single block on most navigation screens. The captains had lit the navigation lights along the hulls of their ships as visual beacons for fighter pilots to see.

From the observation deck, I could see hundreds of ships forming what looked like a mosaic of sparkling, monochrome tiles against the velvet backdrop of space. The glow of sunlight radiating from Terraneau shone up on the gray underbellies of our ships. With their wedge-shaped hulls, the ships of the SC Fleet lined up like the teeth on a saw.

Slowly pushing through the flotilla, our self-broadcasting battleships had diamond-shaped hulls and bloated bows. Their shape and charcoal gray hues bore no resemblance to the ships around them. They looked obsolete—military icons rescued from a different era as they hid themselves in a pod of naval ships. I did not see the self-broadcasters themselves, just the runner lights blinking along the lengths of their hulls.

From where I stood, I could see the massive bow of a nearby fighter carrier. The space ahead of us was filled with battleships. Beyond that, I caught a glimpse of several fighters, Phantoms, weaving in and out among the larger ships. The fighters looked like motes swirling in a dark wind.

"No! No! No!" I muttered, as I looked at the rows of ships standing as stationary as toys in a chest. It was just like Thorne said, only worse. Even Thorne could not possibly have realized what those self-broadcasting explorers would do in another moment.

I hit the intercom on the table and called down to the Marine compound. "Thomer, are your men loaded up?" I yelled.

"We're ready. How many do you want?" he asked.

"Every available man. Every available transport."

"Just the *Kamehameha*?"

"Fleet-wide," I said.

Knowing that Warshaw would never listen to me, I reluctantly went back to the bridge. As I entered, he glared up at me for a moment, and muttered, "What are you doing here?"

"You need to scramble your ships," I said.

Thinking I meant his fighters, Franks said, "We already launched." He did not understand, and I could not explain myself quickly enough. Time was slipping away. The Unified Authority did not need to cross the three-million-mile no-man's-zone to attack our self-broadcasting ships.

I fumbled for words, then blurted out, "Break formation. You can't give them a stationary target." Realizing too late that he would not understand, I added, "If the self-broadcasting ships stay in one place, Brocius will broadcast his ships into them."

"What are you talking about?" Warshaw sounded impatient. Standing off in a corner, even Admiral Thorne looked irritated by my babbling.

I took a deep breath to calm myself. "That was what happened to the *Doctrinaire*," I said. The Mogats had destroyed the *Doctrinaire* with a single shot by broadcasting a ship right into the center of it.

"He doesn't know what he's talking about," Warshaw said. "Get him off my bridge now."

I lost control and yelled, "Listen, asshole!"

"Warshaw." Admiral Thorne barely had to raise his voice to take control of the conversation; his voice was as cold and as bracing as a slap across the face. Franks, Warshaw, and I all turned to look at him, all of us giving in to native feelings of inferiority.

But Thorne was too late. The chart table displayed the event in miniature—tiny silver blooms appeared as one of the Unified Authority explorer ships broadcasted out. At that same moment, a bloom appeared in our ranks.

Explosions make no sound in space. We did not see or hear anything on the bridge of the *Kamehameha* as three battleships and thousands of lives died in a cataclysm as deadly as an atomic explosion.

A new set of alarms sounded throughout the ship, reporting the attack.

"What the speck?" Franks asked.

Warshaw, the consummate officer-engineer, turned to an aide, and yelled, "Damage report! I need a damage report!"

"They destroyed our self-broadcasting ships," I said, not even bothering to look at the chart table to be sure.

"But that's not . . ." Franks began.

"Admiral, thirty of their ships have broadcasted to the other side of Terraneau," one of the aides said.

"We lost three ships," another officer reported. He had not yet identified which ships were gone. Franks did not need the aide to tell him which ships—he already knew.

I could see it in Franks's face. He was beaten. He no longer wanted to fight now that his strategy had fallen apart. He looked at me, then he turned to Admiral Thorne. He needed someone to tell him what he should do next.

"Harris, you better get your Marines down to that planet," Admiral Thorne said. He had new color in his face. He had the energetic, excited eyes of a young officer preparing for a fight.

Warshaw watched the conversation, but remained silent. Maybe he finally realized he was not made to command a fleet. As damage reports filtered in, Warshaw left the bridge. I did not need to ask to know he was headed to Engineering.

Apparently seeing the same thing that Thorne saw, Franks turned to me, and asked, "Harris, how fast can you load up your Marines?"

"They're already on the transports," I said, speaking more to Thorne than Franks, but facing them both. We were ready, but we might already have been too late. By the time we launched, the U.A. ships would be on us.

"They're launching transports," an aide said.

"You better get going, Harris," Thorne said. He hunched over the chart table, reading details out of tiny points of light. "We'll give you whatever cover we can . . ." He did not finish the sentence, but I knew what he was trying to say. With all of those battleships out there, we were in for a bumpy ride.

CHAPTER
FIFTY-TWO

Amber-colored lights flashed along the walls, casting their orange glare along the ceilings. Klaxons clanged and bellowed. The hall outside the bridge was a quagmire, with sailors darting in different directions. I watched the crazed scene as I waited for a lift down to the docking bay, where Thomer and my men waited for me in their transports.

When the lift doors opened several decks down, I found the corridors leading to the docking bay all but deserted. The docking bay itself, however, was another matter.

We had two thousand Marines on the *Kamehameha*, including support troops who would remain on the ship until we had secured the planet. All two thousand men had crammed into the docking bays. Eight hundred of those men waited in the transports. The others waited on deck for the next flight.

As I made my way to the lead transport, I calculated how many Marines we could land on our first wave. With the exception of the Expansion-class *Kamehameha*, there would be twenty transports ferrying two thousand Marines from each of our thirty-five fighter carriers—seventy thousand troops. We had ninety battleships with sixteen transports each. That gave us another 144,000 Marines. And we had the men already stationed at Fort Sebastian. That would give us a massive first wave—more than 200,000 men. With a force like that, we could win the battle quickly.

"You do realize that generals don't lead the troops from the front line?" Thomer asked me, as I jogged up the ramp and into the kettle.

"It's a field rank," I said. "Field generals fight along with their troops."

Unfortunately, I was still wearing my Charlie service uniform and not dressed to lead troops into battle. Without the commandLink equipment in my helmet, I would be all but cut off from my men. I wanted to send someone to grab my armor, but we needed to launch immediately.

Remembering the isolation I felt when I went with Warshaw to the explore the Galactic Fleet, I watched the rear doors of the transport clap shut. The kettle was dark. Had I been wearing my armor, I would have had night-for-day vision available to me.

One hundred Marines had crammed into the kettle. They wore armor—one hundred identical men in one hundred identical suits. Without my armor, I could not tell them apart, which added to my frustration.

I pushed through the men and rushed up the ladder and into the cockpit. Thomer followed.

The pilot met me at the door of the cockpit. We traded salutes. He noted my Charlie service uniform, and said, "I guess I better keep the cabin pressurized."

"I'd appreciate that," I said. "Get us down there fast."

Sitting in the copilot's chair, counting every second, I looked out through the windshield as the sled dragged us through the atmospheric locks. The last door closed, and we went wheels up.

As we left the cover of the tube, the pilot asked, "What happened?" He sounded nervous.

Ahead of us, the remains of our self-broadcasting fleet looked like the burned-out remnants of an extinguished fire—three jagged, twisted hulls with sections that still glowed orange from fires within.

Standing beside me, Thomer looked hypnotized by the sight. His jaw hung slightly open, and his eyes remained fixed on the destruction. I took this as a good sign. Thomer was clean. With fresh Fallzoud running through his veins, he might not have noticed the destruction.

"What the speck hit them?" Thomer asked. He did not mean for me to answer the question, but I did.

"That, General Thomer, is what happens in a broadcast collision."

"A collision, sir?" the pilot asked.

"Those ships stayed in one place too long," I said. "The Mogats came up with the idea. You program an enemy ship's location into a broadcast computer, then broadcast a ship into it. The U.A. used unmanned explorers. The Mogats used manned ships. That was how they destroyed the *Doctrinaire*.

"You broadcast in past shields and defenses, and the electricity from the anomaly destroys the target."

"They broadcasted into the *Doctrinaire*?" asked the pilot.

"Shit," said Thomer, "that's brilliant." Looking at the wreckage of the three big ships, you could not help but be in awe, they were so thoroughly destroyed.

The attack began moments after we left the *Kamehameha*. A laser cannon hit us as we veered toward open space. The beam was a yard-wide stream of lustrous, silvery red fire that splashed across our shields but did not break through.

The pilot steered away from the beam. Moments later, a squadron of five Tomcats streaked past us. I did not see them until they shot over the windshield. The fighters turned in a tight formation and disappeared.

"Ours or theirs?" I asked, wondering if we would reach the planet.

"Those are ours," the pilot said.

"Those aren't," Thomer said, pointing to the line of battleships forming between us and the planet.

"How the speck do you like that? We're right back where we started, eh General?" the pilot asked. Only when he said this did I realize that he was the pilot I'd kidnapped for my joyride around the G.C. Fleet.

"What are those?" Thomer asked, pointing at three of the new U.A. battleships as they approached. The ships looked huge compared to the fighters around them.

"Battle group at three o'clock," I shouted.

"Hold on!" the pilot answered, moments before three torpedoes struck our transport. They hit in quick succession, one right after another. The transport never faltered, but I smelled the acrid tang of ozone coming from our engines.

"*Kamehameha*, we're hit. We're hit. We need protection," the pilot yelled into his microphone.

"How bad?" I asked.

"One more like that, and we're dead," he said.

A torpedo whizzed past us. I caught a glimpse of the flame from its tail, then it was gone.

A swarm of fighters flashed past us, closing the lane between us and the ships that had fired at us. They darted by us and closed in around one of the new battleships. In the brief moment that I watched the attack, several fighters burst into flames.

Then we broke through the atmosphere and the black of space gave way to light and color. Entering the atmosphere so hard and fast, the transport's walls rattled as if they would come apart. The sturdy bird did not come apart, however, and we found that we had entered the atmosphere only a few thousand miles from the Outer Bliss relocation camp.

"Signal all transports to head to Norristown," I told the pilot. I thought for a moment, and added, "And tell them to lay off the radio as much as possible, in case the Unifieds are listening in." They'd have no trouble eavesdropping on our transmission; the equipment in our transports was of U.A. design.

"Should we leave some men to help guard Outer Bliss?" Thomer asked.

"Tell the guards at Outer Bliss to surrender at the first sign of trouble," I said.

"Surrender?" Thomer asked.

"We may be guests there ourselves by this time tomorrow," I said.

"Do you think they know about Outer Bliss?" asked Thomer.

"Know about it? They've been in contact with Fahey all along. He's a U.A. spy," I said.

"That son of a bitch," Thomer muttered as he raised the guards at Outer Bliss and gave them my orders. They accepted the order without argument.

When he got off the radio, Thomer asked, "What about the people in Norristown? Will they help us?"

"I wouldn't count on them," I said, thinking about Sarah Doctorow and her warning that she and her friends would choose the Unified Authority if it came down to a fight. I did not doubt the bitch. "The best we can hope for is that they will stay out of it."

"Should I land at the airfield?" the pilot asked.

"No, head for the center of town." We had launched with nothing but our rifles, but I knew where we could upgrade our equipment.

"Contact Fort Sebastian," I told Thomer. "Tell Hollingsworth to mobilize his men and meet us at the armory."

Had I suited up, I could have made the calls and monitored the progress myself. Now, I had to depend on Thomer and hope he did not have some sort of Fallzoud-flashback.

The flight seemed interminable. I looked out the windshield and saw an endless sea that stretched to the horizon in every direction. The sun set behind us. I did not see other transports, but we'd had to scatter to make it through the U.A. blockade. We would regroup once we reached town.

"How do you know Fahey is a spy?" Thomer asked.

I told him everything. I told him about Fahey's affairs. I told him about Brocius appointing him to my chain of command and about Freeman. Thomer listened carefully. When I finished, he did not say a word; but I saw a new intensity in his eyes. The story had gotten through. For the first time since he began his Fallzoud addiction, I saw hate in Kelly Thomer's eyes.

"How long before we reach Norristown?" I asked the pilot.

"Two hours, maybe ninety minutes if we're lucky," said the pilot.

Forty-five minutes passed, and Thomer reported that the Unifieds had landed outside Outer Bliss.

"Remind them to surrender," I said.

."I don't think that's going to be a problem," Thomer said. "They've already handed over their weapons to their prisoners. The Unifieds are airlifting the natural-borns back to their fleet."

I checked the time. If we got lucky, we might reach Norristown in an hour, I told myself as I counted off the seconds in my head.

"General, I'm receiving a message for you from Fleet Command," the pilot said. He switched on the cockpit speaker.

"Harris?" Warshaw was on the other end of the line.

I leaned in toward the radio, and asked, "What's the situation up there?"

"I'll tell you what the specking situation is. We're getting our asses stomped, that's the situation. Harris, they're grinding us up. We've lost two carriers."

"We're on our way to Norristown," I said. "I'm not sure how many transports got through, but . . ."

"Seventeen transports broke through," Warshaw said.

"Seventeen?" I asked. I heard the number seventeen, but my mind didn't accept it. He must have meant the number of transports we had lost. "How many transports did they hit?"

Warshaw's long pause before answering me gave me a chill. "They shot down fifty-six transports before we were able to recall them. Their fighters got in the lane."

"Fifty-six transports?" I asked, not believing what I'd heard.

"They destroyed fifty-six transports."

The news splashed through me like a shot to the gut. I braced my arm on the panel above the radio and rested my forehead against the back of my forearm.

One moment everything seemed hopeless, then I remembered that our fleet still outnumbered theirs ten-to-one. Even with two fighter carriers down, we still had over thirty carriers. It was just a matter of time until our fleet overwhelmed theirs; the numbers were too far in our favor. "How long do we need to hold out until you can send more transports?"

"You're not listening, Harris. There aren't going to be any more transports. We're fighting for our specking lives up here, and we are losing."

Outside the cockpit, the sky had turned dark. Stars sparkled in the darkness, but there was no moon to break up the blackness around us. The ocean below us seemed to drop out and fade into a shadow.

CHAPTER
FIFTY-THREE

"No sign of them yet," Hollingsworth told Thomer for the fourth time. We would meet up with Hollingsworth at the garage under the government buildings—the one the local militia had converted into an armory. Hollingsworth and his men were already there. I had Thomer check in with him every fifteen minutes in case the Unifieds got there before we did.

Hollingsworth gave Thomer the same response every time: "No sign of them yet."

We also received constant reports from the fleet. They weren't pretty. The U.A. had a new class of fighters that outmaneuvered our Tomcats and Phantoms. We'd lost badly when our fighters engaged one of their squadrons; then Thorne wedged several frigates into the lanes and turned the fight around.

"We can't get past their specking shields," Warshaw said, when I called in.

I would have told Thorne to cut us loose and run, but he had nowhere to go. The new ships were quicker and self-broadcasting. They were killing us in a fair fight, and we had no chance of outrunning them.

It occurred to me that we were flying unprotected, too. The U.A. Fleet didn't need to send fighters into the atmosphere to destroy us. Their battleships could target us from space, but that did not seem to fit in with their plans.

Then the other shoe dropped. "Harris . . . ? Harris, do you read me?" It was Warshaw. He sounded frantic as he said five words I did not want to hear. "You are on your own."

Seconds later, we all saw the first flash. It was only a pin-prick of light, brighter but no larger than the stars in the night sky. It winked enough to catch my attention and vanished.

"Oh, shit," I whispered after the first flash. "Did you see that?"

Thomer had caught it. The pilot had missed it.

More flashes followed—a rapid series of second-long flashes all in the same spot. It looked like someone was flashing Morse code with a tiny light.

"What was that?" the pilot asked. I think he knew.

"Death," I said.

Unable to believe that a force as powerful as the Scutum-Crux Fleet could be defeated, the pilot tried to raise the *Kamehameha*. There was no response.

"Should we tell them?" Thomer asked, looking back toward the kettle.

"No," I said. Why discourage the men? They had a fight ahead of them either way. Better to send them in believing they have a chance.

The explosions continued for another thirty minutes. Watching the quick bursts of light and knowing each meant the deaths of hundreds of clones tortured me, then something worse happened. The explosions stopped, and I knew that the battle had ended. The peaceful sky meant that hundreds of thousands of clones were gone.

We did not speak to each other for the rest of the flight to Norristown. When he was not calling Hollingsworth, Thomer sat silently, staring out into the moonless night. We sat tensely—three men way out on a limb and waiting for the branch to break.

We would make our last stand in the ruins of Norristown, the city so many men had died to protect. As we flew over the southern edge of the city, we passed two- and three-story buildings that stuck out of the ground like giant grave markers in a cemetery gone to seed. Ground swellings below us marked the spots where buildings had collapsed. In my mind, each hill became a mass grave.

In the middle of this, the government building complex was a steel-and-glass anomaly. Its walls and walkways still intact, the government complex was a modern Camelot overlooking a decimated fiefdom. Hollingsworth had already mapped the grounds for tactical use. Following his instructions, we arranged our seventeen transports in strategic spots as we landed.

The transports weren't much to look at, but then the military had its own school of landscaping—FOCPIG. Military men love their acronyms. In this case, FOCPIG stood for Fire, Observed, Concealed, Protected, Integrated, non-Geometric; in short, it is the process of preparing a field for battle. In the FOCPIG school of landscaping, aesthetics mattered less than utility. Placed strategically, those transports would create nearly impenetrable obstacles that the Unifieds would need to run around.

Judging by the first wave of transports the Unifieds had sent, they'd come light. Until they sent a second wave, they would not have tanks or gunships, just men, guns, and a handful of light-armor vehicles. That would play into our preparations. According to the feng shui of FOCPIG, our job was to route them so that we could have every advantage. Using transports as barriers, we would steer the enemy between the outstretched arms of the government center—a natural gauntlet. Once they entered, we would have the high-ground advantage.

Thomer and Hollingsworth remained with me as I surveyed the grounds. Their underlings swapped in and out as they gave orders. After a few minutes, Hollingsworth went down to the garage for an inspection.

By now, I had armor of my own, brand-new equipment that Hollingsworth's men snagged out of the armory. The armor was stiff, and none of my preferences had been programmed into it, but it was better than isolation. When I got the chance, assuming I lived to get the chance, I would calibrate the ocular controls in the visor to read my particular eye movements. I could live with the glitches, the armor came with a commandLink, and that meant I could communicate with the men unassisted.

We walked along the roof of one of the wings of the building—"snipers' row." Hollingsworth and Thomer knew the drill. You placed snipers where they would have a good view of anyone passing by, then you waited. Often, you had to sit patiently letting viable targets march past in exchange for a clean shot at the men at the top of the food chain. Shoot the peons in the front, and you warn the bastards in the back that they're walking into a trap. Sniping is a game of patience.

Not that we were going to take anybody by surprise. There was only one way into the armory, and we marked that path by placing our transports along it. If they wanted us, the U.A. invaders would need to walk our gauntlet. I wondered what they would do once they entered it.

In the predawn hours of an otherwise calm summer night, we moved along the top of the building. Locked up in my combat armor, I did not worry about the breeze or rain. My bodysuit kept me cool and dry.

The grounds around the government center must have been beautiful at one time. I saw shattered concrete beds that must once have been a network of ponds. A border of waist-high grass grew around the complex. A soft breeze combed through the grass.

"They're coming, General," Hollingsworth called up from the garage. He must have had some kind of mobile radar set up.

"Do you have a count?" I looked out toward the horizon and saw only the wide, open expanse over the broken city. Off in the distance, the three remaining skyscrapers that Doctorow used for dormitories, glittered.

"Thirty ships coming in from the south," Hollingsworth said.

I had been looking east, but I now turned south, the direction from which we had just come. There were hills to the south. Even as I watched, dots appeared in the horizon. They looked no more significant than the sparks in the darkness.

"We've got company, boys. Get to your stations. Dig in. Get comfortable," I called over the interLink.

"Think they'll attack soon?" Hollingsworth asked.

"Not a chance. Not with only thirty transports in place. They'll want more than three thousand troops before they attack," I said. I assumed that, like our transports, their transports carried one hundred men.

I told Hollingsworth about the fleet, but we were not about to educate the rank and file until this conflict was over. He knew the Earth Fleet now controlled the skies, and he knew about the last message we'd heard from Warshaw. I did not tell him about the size of the enemy fleet. He did not need to know that the Unified Authority had defeated our 450-ship armada with a mere eighty ships.

"They'll probably land on the other side of town and build up their forces," I said. I knew how these operations worked. They would set up a camp and make us wait while their transports ferried in soldiers and equipment.

But I was wrong.

The transports did not stop at the southern edge of town. They flew over the suburbs. By the time they reached the ruins of downtown, the glow from their shields filled the sky. They were not the same antiquated design as the birds we flew in on, they had graceful wings and tapered shields. At about a half mile from our lines, the transports slowed and landed, lighting down like flies.

"Looks like they know we're here," Thomer said. He'd been so silent, I'd forgotten he was there.

Of course they know we're here, they use the same specking interLink frequencies we do. They're listening in on us, I thought to myself.

And they might not have even needed their damn technological advantage to find us because Sarah Doctorow and her pals would not think twice about ratting us out. And then there were the leaks—Perry Fahey and his friends in Outer Bliss would happily tell them everything they knew.

"Switch off your safeties, boys, we're going live," I said over an open frequency. The invaders probably heard me, as well. From here on out, I would keep my conversations short and switch frequencies between calls. I could not stop them from listening, but I didn't want to make things too easy for them.

I remained on the roof with the snipers, Hollingsworth joined the grenadiers in the wings, and Thomer went down to the underground garage. Between the troops we had manning the buildings and the Marines we positioned in the garage, we had nearly five thousand men. Based on the number of their transports, I estimated their strength at three thousand.

Time ticked away slowly, seconds seemed to stretch themselves into minutes. I wondered what they were doing. Were they off-loading equipment? Were they playing with us, making us wait, to consider our situation? I kept expecting more transports to arrive, but the skies remained clear.

"How's it hanging, Harris?" The message came over the commandLink, on a frequency reserved for officers. The equipment in my visor identified the caller: General Theodore Mooreland.

"You're in charge of this one, Ted? They must think I'm real dangerous to send in a veteran like you." I called him Ted. Why not? We were both generals.

"Nice of you to drill my men," he said.

"War games are one of my specialties," I said.

"So, is she here?" Mooreland asked. That meant he was keeping the locals out of the fight. He would not have needed to ask me about Ava if he had talked to Doctorow.

"Please, tell me you did not come all this way just to impress Ava."

Mooreland laughed. "No, Harris, I came for you."

"I'm flattered, Ted, really I am. But, um, I'm spoken for."

"Speck you, clone."

"Ted, I just told you, I'm not interested."

"We were going to give you twelve months to prepare, did you know that? We were going to give you a year to get your men ready, but you blew it. You shouldn't have attacked our battleships. Did you really think we'd look the other way?"

I did not say anything.

The sun started to rise in the east. Pockets of yellow, gold, and white appeared over a horizon of rolling desolation. The ruins of the city looked like a desert in the first light of the morning. If Mooreland was in command, the intruders had to be Marines. They would be wearing combat armor. They would use tactics like ours.

"You're an interesting man, Harris. I'd love to continue this chat, but my men came to fight," Mooreland said. "Are you ready?"

"Sporting of you to ask," I said. "We're as ready as we're going to get." I tried to sound confident, but I knew Mooreland meant business. He was showing me the cat–bird courtesy of a commander who knows he owns the field. But how could he be so confident with only three thousand men? I wondered what I did not know.

"Well, good luck, Harris," Mooreland said. He signed off.

I stood there on the roof of that enormous government complex, as insecure as an ancient ruler waiting for the Huns to pillage his city.

"Why haven't they attacked yet?" Thomer's question brought me out of my thoughts.

"Courtesy," I said. "They were giving us a moment to say our prayers."

CHAPTER
FIFTY-FOUR

Somebody else noticed the lights before me. Watching the world through my night-for-day lenses, I stared right at and through the scene without noticing the subtle change in luminescence. One of Thomer's snipers noticed, however.

The sniper alerted Thomer, and Thomer told me.

"There's light coming from the enemy camp, sir."

"Light?" I asked.

I switched to tactical view. At first, I thought they had fired up the shields on their transports. Patches of golden glow lit up the air. "What is that?" I asked, in a whisper directed at myself, but Thomer picked it up over the interLink and answered.

"It looks like they have the shields up on their transports," he said.

"The light isn't coming from the transports." I could see that much. Using my telescopic lenses, I zoomed in on the glow. I could not see what the light was coming from, but it wasn't the transports. I had a clear view of the tops of several U.A. transports, and their shields were down.

"Oh, shit," I said.

"Sir?" Thomer asked.

Thank God for the commandLink, it enabled me to bring Hollingsworth in on the conversation. He was in the garage, blind to the world above him. Using my Link, I showed Hollingsworth and Thomer what I saw.

"What is that?" Hollingsworth asked.

"Shields," I said.

Thomer started to say something, but I interrupted him.

"The shields aren't on the transports," I said. I shifted my focus to show the sleeping birds.

"Then what are they shielding?" Hollingsworth asked.

"Shielded armor," I said.

The patch of glowing light moved as the first of Mooreland's Marines began their march into battle.

"Hang on," I said. I ripped off my helmet and picked up a sniper rifle. The other snipers had had enough time to program their scopes to their armor so that they could look through their visors and aim their rifles. Since the visor in this suit was not yet calibrated, I had to aim the old-fashioned way. I pressed the scope against my eye and homed in on the front echelon.

We had built our strategy around waiting for Mooreland to meander into our trap, but tactics be damned. If we were about to fight men in shielded armor, the rules had just changed.

Looking through the scope, I picked out a man and studied him. His armor looked a lot like mine—the same helmet, the same chest plates and shoulder pads. It appeared to be a rich, dark brown in color, but that might have been an optical effect. Viewed through the golden glow of the shields that shone from the plating, the dark green of my armor would probably appear brown.

I steadied my rifle against my shoulder, aimed at the Marine's head, and pulled the trigger. The crack of my rifle was no louder than the sound of a man giving a single, hard clap of his hands, but it echoed. My armor absorbed the recoil of the rifle so that I felt only the slightest nudge against my shoulder. Eight hundred yards away, my bullet had about as much impact on the new Marine as a sparrow might have flying into a skyscraper.

The Marine saw or felt the bullet, or perhaps his equipment reported the shot. The man pointed to the spot where the bullet hit. I imagined him laughing as he reported the wasted attack to his platoon sergeant.

I put down my rifle and slung my helmet over my head. "Rifles are no good," I told Thomer and Hollingsworth.

Hollingsworth answered first. "Speck!" Thomer gave a similar response.

"Let me try one more shot," I said.

Aiming with the telescopic lenses in my visor, I chose another target, aimed at his helmet, and fired. My first shot went wide. The next three shots hit. The bullets showed only as momentary white flashes against the golden glow of the man's shields. I fired four more shots, hitting the son of a bitch in the chest, the stomach, the crotch, and the knee.

I had a sinking feeling of defeat as I replaced my helmet. We had signed up for a fight we would not win. Even as I thought this, my combat reflex started, filling me with confidence, clearing self-doubt from my thoughts, and turning fear into comfort. I smiled a ghoulish smile as I realized just how little the terms "impregnable" and "invincible" had in common.

"Hard on the outside, soft on the inside," I said to myself. Then, I opened a channel to Thomer, and said, "General, withdraw your snipers and reposition them in the top two floors of the garage."

"Aye, aye, sir," Thomer said.

"And Thomer, tell them to leave their sniper rifles here. We're sticking with particle beams and rocket launchers from here on out."

"But . . . Sir, the garage could cave in on us," Thomer said.

"I certainly hope so," I said, knowing that what I had in mind was the military equivalent of threading a needle.

Thomer figured out what I had in mind immediately. He said, "You evil son of a bitch," sounding more like the old Thomer than he had since New Copenhagen.

"But we'll be buried," Hollingsworth said.

"Not if we slip out the back door," I said.

"The train station," Hollingsworth said. He should have remembered it; he was the one who helped Doctorow's men drag explosives through the tunnel. "If you can't beat them, bury them. I specking love it."

"You just make sure your men do a good job rigging the garage," I said. "I don't want Mooreland digging himself out."

"Aye, aye, sir," Hollingsworth said. "It's going to take a few minutes."

"We'll buy you whatever time we can," I said. "You got that, Thomer?"

"Yes, sir."

"Thomer, have your men rig the buildings to blow on their way down. That goes double for any stairs and elevators that lead into the garage."

"Yes, sir," said Thomer.

"And remember, keep your Link chatter short. You never know who might be listening," I said.

I doubted there were any demolitions experts stationed at Fort Sebastian. Trained demolitions men could make buildings blow so precisely that they imploded in on themselves, folding in on themselves like origami figures. Our guys did not have that kind of skill, but that would not stop us from achieving our objectives. We were Marines—when we lacked the skill, we compensated for with sheer will and a large supply of explosives. The garage wouldn't exactly implode, but it would sure as hell come down. We just needed to make sure that it caved in from the top down and that we made it to the train tunnels before the world came down around us. This was war—nobody would give us extra points for neatness.

Thomer ordered his snipers to abandon their rifles and report to the first floor of the garage. By the time Mooreland's men entered sniper range, Thomer no longer had anyone on the roof to shoot them. I remained on the roof a moment longer to observe the enemy.

The shine of their shields gave Mooreland's men a godlike appearance in the frail dawn light. Had their aura shone brighter, the light from the various suits would have meshed; instead, each man had his own, personal, tea-colored glow.

As they approached, they broke into smaller formations. A couple of companies tried to fan out and flank the brigade, but that failed. Hollingsworth's FOCPIG preparations funneled them back. If they meant to chase us down into the armory, they would need to pass through two bottlenecks—the first created by our transports and the second by the entrance to the underground garage.

The last man on the roof, I took a final look at the high-velocity sniper rifles we'd abandoned in our wake. They lay spread across the concrete like sticks dropped from a bundle. In a fair fight, we might have been able to eliminate Mooreland's entire regiment with those rifles. Letting the door close behind me as I started down the stairs, I tried to remember the last time I saw a fair fight and came up dry.

"Thomer, make sure your men know this is the foreplay, not the sex," I said over a new frequency, as I left the stairwell and joined my grenadiers.

The third floor of the building looked like a breezeway. In preparation for the fight, we had knocked out the windows. The wind howled as it blew through broken casings. Hundreds of men in combat armor knelt along the wall, rocket tubes in hand. We had the high-ground advantage, nearly bulletproof cover, numerical superiority, and possibly even the element of surprise; and still, we could not afford to wage the war from this spot, not against an enemy dressed in shielded armor. Unless we found a way through their shields, Mooreland's men would make our cover cave in around us.

For this mission, my grenadiers had orders to fire a few shots and retreat to the garage. If everything went according to plan, these men would lead the way into the train station. That was, if everything went according to plan. In the heat of battle, entropy dissolves plans into chaos, and Marines sometimes forget their orders. Some become heroes, lingering to fire one final round, when they have been told to pull back. Others lose their nerve and abandon their posts.

Looking over my troops, it occurred to me that I might be going to the well one time too many. By the time we finished this battle, I would have pushed the same damn tactic three times: fighting the Avatari; destroying the battleships that followed us into the Mogat Fleet; and now, I was using it against the Unified Authority Marines. Coaxing a dangerous enemy into an ambush is a fine tactic, and there was no way these guys could know that we had used it on the Avatari and the battleships, but overused tactics have a way of coming apart on their own.

If I made it out of this, I told myself, I would ditch Nietzsche and start brushing up on military strategy. If I made it out of this alive, I would be smarter in the future.

"That which did not destroy me would make me stronger," I said to myself, citing the battlefield wisdom of Friedrich Nietzsche.

Mooreland's scouts stepped into the kill zone between the wings of the government buildings. The first of the four men entered the zone slowly, showing no more confidence than a mouse leaving its hole. The rest of his fire team followed.

These were the men on point, the sacrifices. They stepped onto a walkway, stopped, and examined the buildings. One of them pointed to the broken window casings. They knew what we had planned.

"Hold your fire," I said over the interLink.

"Hold your fire. Hold your fire," Thomer told his men. He crouched below a broken window, his first grenade launcher out and ready to fire. "Those are just the scouts. Save it for the ranks."

Waiting for Mooreland, peering over a casing, I got a close look at the new armor. The shielding glowed no brighter than a candle, but it covered the entire suit in a single continuous sheen.

"Once the shooting starts, fire one shot, and leave," I whispered over an open frequency. "One shot, no heroics." Mooreland might well have been listening. I didn't care. The information would do him no good.

Down in the kill zone, Mooreland's scouts timidly made

their way toward the two outstretched wings of the building. They came within a hundred feet of the entrance and stopped to wait for the rest of the brigade to catch up.

The point men moved forward until they were right below me. I peered over the windowsill and watched them. To me, they looked like a team of confused spirits haunting the battleground before the war even began.

Something caught my eye—their weapons were inside their shields, built into their armor. Inch-wide barrels ran along the outsides of their arms, ending just shy of the fingers on their gloves. The barrels did not look wide enough for bullets. The bastards were probably packing fléchettes, the same deadly needles we used in our S9 stealth weapons.

Dozens, then hundreds, then thousands of men appeared at the head of the buildings. They did not walk right into our gauntlet. They waited, surveying the area, filling our view with glow and bodies. One minute passed, then another. They had to know where we were hiding, but they did not fire blindly to flush us out. Watching them mass, I considered beginning our evacuation. Just as I started to issue the command, Mooreland ordered his men in.

The space between the buildings was twice the length of a football field and just as wide. Mooreland could have fit three thousand men in that space, but it might have been tight. His first wave broke into a wedge formation, facing out, arms up so they could return fire when we emerged from our painfully obvious hiding place.

"Fire!" Thomer yelled. "Shoot and run. Shoot and run. Shoot and run!"

Along the long hall, men jumped to their feet, fired a single rocket into the courtyard, tossed their empty launcher tubes aside, and ran for the stairs. The rockets hissed and flashed out of their tubes, leaving a thin smoke trail behind them.

On the ground below, the glow of the shields faded in a storm of smoke and explosions. The blasts created a strobe-light effect. In the start-and-stop motion of an ancient movie, Marines fired weapons, ran along the hall, and vanished down stairwells. Flash, five men ran crouched along the inner wall of the corridor. Flash, the first reached the door to a stairwell and wrenched it open. Flash, the third man in the line threw his hands over his head as the first two disappeared through the door. Flash, tiny holes and fine drops of blood appeared on the wall as the man crumpled to the floor. Flash, the fourth and fifth men in the line jumped over the body and disappeared down the stairs.

Sharp as needles and harder than steel, the fléchettes pierced combat armor, leaving a pinprick entrance hole on one side and a pinprick exit hole on the other. The lethal darts bored into the concrete walls as if they were made of cloth. They burrowed into the ceiling above us, vanishing into soft tiles and shattering light fixtures.

In the courtyard, our rockets were about as effective as a strong wind. The blasts threw Mooreland's Marines off their feet and cast them aside like toys, but their shielded armor protected them from shrapnel.

"We can't hurt the speckers!" somebody called on an open line.

"Shoot and run! Shoot and run! Shoot and run!" Thomer shouted, as he moved up and down the hall, his voice as dry as desert sand.

Men were dying. I watched one of my men stand, aim, and fall before he could fire; fléchette holes dotted in his helmet, his chest plates, and his shoulder plates. He fell on his back, and thin streams of blood leaked out of the holes. The man next to him sprang for the window, tripped over the body, and was shot in the head at least five times before he could steady himself.

I prepared to fire my first rocket. Taking a deep breath, I slid up to the edge of the casing, aimed the launcher into the crowd, and pulled the trigger. I did not wait to see what I hit. The moment I fired, I dropped down to safety. Dozens of fléchettes struck the spot from which I had fired. By the time they hit, I had already pulled my second rocket launcher and moved to a new spot.

As I lay on the floor, I looked across the darkened hall. Dead men in armor lay in odd poses along the floor. The waist-high window casing protected us as long as we stayed down waiting to shoot, but they left our heads and chests unprotected when we stood to fire. I saw men with shattered visors and men with holes in their helmets, men with blood leaking from so many holes in their armor that they looked like they were covered in sweat.

I climbed to my knees, peered out from behind the casing, and fired my second rocket.

"Harris, where are you?" It was Hollingsworth.

"I'm still in the building," I said.

"You need to get out of there, sir. If we don't blow those charges now, the Unifieds are going to enter the building," Hollingsworth said. He was polite, respectful, a nice guy. In a deferential way, he had just told me to get my ass out of the building.

Looking around the hall, I realized I was the last man there. In the time it took me to fire my second shot, everyone else had left or died. As I crawled toward the stairs, I saw a man rolling on the floor. He held an armored hand against his left shoulder as he rolled from side to side. My visor identified him as Corporal James Mattock.

"Mattock," I said on an open frequency, "we need to get out of here." I saw three separate streams of blood running down his arm. "Mattock," I repeated.

He did not answer. He just lay there, writhing like a dying snake. I reached a hand under his arm and pulled him with me. When we reached the stairs, I heaved him over my shoulder in a fireman's carry. The Unified Authority did not necessarily make the fléchettes the new Marines used out of the same depleted uranium we used in our stealth weapons. It occurred to me that the uranium they used could even be enriched.

If Mooreland's men were using hot uranium, the damage to his shoulder would be the least of Mattock's problems. Shooting heavily radioactive materials through your enemies was a good way to make sure they died no matter where you hit them.

Mattock did not sag like a dying man; he rolled and twisted and tried to put a hand over his wound. Holding him tight so that he would not roll out of my grip, I started down the stairs. Along the walls, I saw the charges Thomer's men left behind. Wires wound around the corners, leading from one bundle of explosives to the next.

"Are you clear, General?" Hollingsworth asked.

"Still on the stairs."

"You better hurry, sir. They're already entering the garage."

I clattered down the stairs as quickly as I could with Mattock over my shoulder. Jumping a couple of stairs, I overshot a landing and slammed into the wall. Somewhere along the line, Mattock's hand dropped from his wound and he hung limp and lifeless along my back. Hating the situation and loathing myself for doing what I had to do, I dropped the inert body and ran.

Skipping the top floor of the garage, where the fighting had already begun, I sprinted down to the second floor. "Clear!" I yelled, as I crashed out of the stairwell, slamming the door behind me.

The explosion was a classic example of Marine Corps overkill. The blast caved in the stairwell and the surrounding walls. The door I had just slammed closed came flying out of its jamb like a cork from a champagne bottle.

CHAPTER
FIFTY-FIVE

Doctorow and his men had enough weapons on the second level of the garage to launch a minor world war. Racks of M27s and particle beam cannons lined two of the walls. Crates of grenades stood in stacks that reached the ceiling. Preparing to fight the Avatari, the Unified Authority had sent three million men with enough munitions to wage a prolonged war. Now, only their surplus gear survived.

Hollingsworth's men rigged charges around the tops of the pillars. Using my night-for-day lenses to look into the shadows, I spotted the wires, but the emergency lights were bright enough to keep my visor switched to tactical lenses. Without night-for-day vision illuminating the shadows, the charges were invisible.

The garage rang with the echoes of gunfire and explosions. One floor above me, war had gone full scale. Glare and shadows flashed on the wall along the ramp out. I picked up battle chatter on every frequency as I scanned the interLink.

I contacted Hollingsworth and told him to begin evacuating the garage. I contacted Thomer and told him to retreat.

Marines started backing down the ramp in a trickle. These were the men at the back of the battle, men who might not have fired a single shot. They ran down quickly, hid as best they could, and turned to cover the ramp. They hid behind pillars and corners. A few fools hid behind crates of grenades; the wooden sides of the crates would offer little protection against fléchettes.

I ran to the side of the ramp and pulled out my particle beam pistol. The little gun would probably have no more effect against shielded armor than an M27, but I had to try.

More of my men retreated down the ramp, now in a steady stream. Some men backpedaled, firing up at the enemy as they came. Some ran and dived for cover. From my hiding place, I watched as swarms of fléchettes turned men into mist. Men hit while running for cover fell and slid along the floor. Men hit while returning fire collapsed where they stood. A few toppled over the side of the ramp.

One man fell in front of me. He was gut-shot, but not dead. He landed on his back on the concrete, his hand over the lower part of his stomach. He squirmed, his movements getting slower and weaker. I wanted to save him, but I couldn't. I wanted to kill him and put him out of his misery, but I could not bring myself to do that, either. A few moments passed and his squirming stopped. Blood trickled from holes in his armor.

My men continued their retreat. The ramp was wide and open, offering no chance of cover or concealment. When I peered over the edge, I saw more of my men falling than reaching the bottom. The screams and sounds of panic I heard over the interLink left me numb.

I opened up a channel to Thomer and yelled, "Get them moving, Thomer. Get them down to the third floor! Get them into the tunnels. They're dying up here!"

The combat reflex was in such full flow in my veins, it was almost joyous. I watched men retreating past me. They no longer stopped to fight. Sprinting across the concrete, they hit the bottom of the ramp, rounded the corner, and continued deeper into the garage.

One man came limping past me. He had streams of blood pouring out of three holes in his leg, but he kept going. In another minute, poisons from the fléchettes would kill him, but the man kept going.

Time had become as transparent as glass to me now. Seconds had no meaning as I prepared to fight and kill.

More of my men backed down the ramp, firing particle beams up as they went. As they walked past me, three men hiding along the base of ramp opened launched grenades.

"Get them out of here!" I called to Thomer.

"Fall back," Thomer gave the order even before I finished. The glow of shielded armor spilled over the ramp as Mooreland's men started down. I waited, holding my particle beam pistol ready.

Fléchettes flitted through the air, scratching chips from the concrete walls and pillars, drilling through crates and racks of weapons, forcing men from positions they had already been ordered to abandon. The tiny metal darts drilled into walls. Some banked off the concrete, making the tinkling noise of breaking glass as they dropped on to the ground. Over my head, an exposed pipe burst and light bulbs shattered. More of my men fell as they retreated.

Wanting to see what a particle beam would do at close range, I shot out of my hiding place, stood along the side of the ramp, pressed my pistol right up against the knee of an advancing U.A. Marine, and fired. The sparkling green beam struck his shielded armor and disappeared. The man did not even flinch.

And then I felt pain, a sharp and brilliant jolt. My fingers flew open. My hand went numb and I dropped my pistol. There was a moment of dead silence in my head. Then, I felt the fire in my skin. When I drew back my hand, I saw holes in my armor. Blood trickled out over my forearm and palm. I had been shot twice.

First, I felt dizzy and then confused. The warmth of my combat reflex comforted me for a moment and then it faded.

The shielded Marines reached the bottom of the ramp. Having seen the rest of my Marines in retreat, they must have expected to find the level empty. In the moment it took them to spot me, I dived behind a stack of crates and tried to roll to safety. Fléchettes ripped through the air around me. Crates shattered in a storm of dust, darts, and splinters.

"Harris, where are you?" Thomer asked.

"I'm coming," I said, the words slow as they rolled from my lips. "I'm on the second . . ."

The blood from my hand and arm did not stain my armor; it beaded and rolled across the slick, dark plating the way raindrops roll down a well-waxed car. My forearm burned, my hand was numb. My injured arm dragged as if it had fallen asleep. I tried to make a fist with my right hand as I used my left to crawl toward the next ramp down. I could not even make a fist, my fingers would not cooperate.

So many fléchettes hit the box beside me that the wood disintegrated and grenades rolled to the floor. I tried to pick one up with my right hand and could not close my fingers around it. I picked it up with my left and realized I would need my injured right hand to pull the pin.

"Are you hit?" Thomer asked.

"My arm," I said. The slurred voice in my helmet did not sound familiar to me. It sounded as if it came from a drunk man.

Bringing myself up in a sitting position, I slumped across the ledge overlooking the ramp to the next floor down. There was a ten-foot drop. I managed to thread my right pointer finger through the loop of the grenade pin, and held my right arm steady as I pulled the grenade away with my left hand. As the pin broke free, I saw men in glowing, shielded armor coming around the corner. The bastards looked like angels in the darkness. My head filled with mist and cobwebs, I bowled the grenade in their direction.

The bastards fired back at me. Fléchettes hit the rail around me, glancing off the metal in a dance of sparks and chips. One dart struck me in the leg as I swung it under the rail and rolled over the ledge. The grenade exploded. I did not see what it did to the bastards. I dropped ten feet to the concrete below, landing on my back.

I felt pain. My thoughts were disjointed. The fall must have knocked the air out of my lungs. I had to fight to breathe. My chest felt crushed.

"You're not the toughest man in the Marines, just the luckiest," Ava had told me the last time that I saw her. I did not feel so lucky now. When I tried to get up, my body ignored me.

I kept expecting the combat reflex to revive me, but it didn't. I felt cold and powerless, the weight of my body holding me down. Wondering if it was shock or radiation, I managed to roll onto my left side. I tried to push myself up with no success.

The world seemed to have left me behind. I thought I heard men fighting all around me, but the gunfire and explosions seemed far away. I reminded myself that I was in a garage, but my thoughts had become a slippery stream of images that never quite came into focus.

"I've got you, Harris," somebody said. Whoever had grabbed me did not give me a chance to stand up on my own. He pulled me along the ground first, and then threw me in the air.

I could feel knots twisting in my stomach. I was upside down, the blood rushing to my head.

"Harris, I'm getting you out," the voice said. A virtual dog tag showed in my visor, but I could not focus my eyes sufficiently to read it.

Slung over the man's shoulder, I could barely breathe. My head cleared for a moment, then I vomited. *You can drown in your own vomit,* I thought. Warm liquid ran into my nostrils and into my eyes.

I tried to remove my helmet, but my arms would not cooperate. They hung like ropes as I wrestled with the acrid-sawdust taste of bile in my throat.

The man carrying me came to a stop. Moving slowly, he lowered me onto my back. A moment later, my helmet came off. I tried to stand up, but my body ignored me. The world was dark and cold around me. Nobody spoke.

The last thing I remembered was an explosion, a thunderous, pulverizing sound followed by a rush of smoke and grit that choked out the last of my breath.

"Did we get them?" I asked.

Nobody answered, as the remaining shreds of my consciousness spun into nothing.

GHOSTS, GRAVES, AND DISHONOR

1

I had always prided myself on walking away from battles on the same legs that brought me in. That time, it didn't happen.

I was already on the mend by the time I woke from an induced coma. A civilian doctor had me make a fist and curl my toes. He poked my fingers with pins and asked me if I could feel the pressure. I assured him I could.

My head hurt. From the moment I opened my eyes, it felt like someone had tried to split my skull in two with an ax.

"You, General Harris, are the pinnacle of genetic engineering. No human could have survived what you went through."

I wanted water. I was hungry, my head ached, my entire body ached, I felt weak and dizzy and unhappy; but above all, I wanted water. "Can I have some water?" I asked, my voice a gravelly croak.

"Not just yet, General," the doctor said. I heard the man and saw his blurry silhouette, but I could not get my eyes to focus. The light from the window made my head hurt all the more.

"We still have tests to run now that you are awake." He sounded young and peppy, excited to run tests on a new patient who should already be dead.

As my head cleared, I became aware of the slings holding my arms and the tubes poking into my flesh. Someone had elevated the back of my bed so that it kept my head raised higher than my feet.

"I was shot," I said.

The doctor corrected me. "You were shot five times."

"I got hit in the arm," I said.

"Two shots pierced your right arm, and three pierced your legs. The darts went right through."

That accounted for why I was in the hospital, but it did not explain why I felt so sick. Maybe if I took one to the kidney. Something was wrong with me. Then I remembered that the fléchettes were made of uranium. "Am I hot?" I asked.

"You have a fever, but that's expected after a full blood transfusion. Fortunately, finding blood supplies wasn't a problem. You have the same blood type as every man in your command."

"Am I radioactive?"

"Radioactive? No. The darts weren't radioactive, but they were poisonous. The men you were fighting had a neurotoxin on their darts.

"You were the only one who survived being hit. The poison killed everyone else in a matter of minutes; but you, they hit you five times, and it still didn't kill you. There was so much adrenaline in your blood that the poison didn't spread the way it was supposed to." He sounded excited as he told me this.

"How many men did we lose?" I asked.

As if he did not hear me, the doctor continued raving about my genetic engineering. Then he said, "You are going to have to be more careful next time. We damaged the gland that produced all of that adrenaline when we swapped out your blood. The gland should heal, but I'm not sure how long it will take. Until then, you will need to put up with normal mortality."

With my eyes out of focus, I saw the world as a fuzzy mixture of bright light and dark colors. I could not see the doctor clearly, but it no longer mattered. I wanted to be alone. I felt tired. All I wanted to do was sleep.

"I need to rest," I said.

"But we have tests . . ."

"Later," I said.

"General Harris, you are not out of the woods just yet. We need to . . ."

"I'll take my chances," I said. I shut my eyes and pretended to sleep. The doctor stood mute, not knowing what to do. I felt his gaze and heard him breathing. Finally, he left the room.

What was I? If the gland that produced my combat reflex was out of commission, I was no longer a Liberator. I did not have the gland for the death reflex, so I was not a general-issue military clone. I was not a natural-born.

I turned to my old friends the philosophers for an answer, but Nietzsche, Hobbes, Plato, and Kant had nothing to say.

2

My Marines did not come to visit me while I was in the hospital, but other people did.

"Maybe I was wrong about you, Harris. It turns out you are not the luckiest man in the Marines, after all," Ava said.

She looked beautiful but not glamorous. She wore next to no makeup.

"I don't feel lucky," I said. I tried to sit up. Blood rushed to my head, leaving me dizzy.

Ava gently placed her hand on my shoulder, giving it a barely perceptible squeeze. "Honey, you and I were meant for each other. We both know what it feels like to be out of luck."

I wrapped my left arm around Ava's tiny waist. She leaned down and kissed my forehead. "We'd better be meant for each other, 'cause we're stuck here now," she whispered. "El says the whole fleet was destroyed." El, of course, was Ellery Doctorow.

That was the first time anybody had even mentioned the war since I woke from my coma. The doctor must have decided I was in no shape for bad news. He always pleaded ignorance. Doctorow visited me once, but said he had to leave for an "urgent appointment" when I asked about my men. I had no idea what had happened to Thomer and Hollingsworth.

"The entire fleet?" I asked.

"That's what El said," Ava told me. She frowned, then reached down and smoothed my hair. This was a new side to Ava. Now that she had a reason to nurture, it came naturally to her.

"There were over a million men up there," I said. One million men wiped away in a single day, the thought of it made me sick. One million clones killed in a training exercise.

"How about my Marines?" I asked, scared of what Ava might tell me. If she said they were killed, that would mean I was alone. If she said they were alive, then I would wonder why they had not come to visit me.

I reached for the little plastic pitcher of water that sat on the table beside my bed. Ava stopped me. She poured the glass for me. Did I love her? I thought that I might. I also thought she was right. We were stuck with each other.

"They're out at the base."

"Some of them survived?" I asked, feeling both glad and lonely. "Do they know I'm here? None of them have come to see me, not even Thomer."

"I'm not supposed to tell you any of this," Ava said. "If Doctor Feeney knew I was doing this, he'd kick me out of the hospital." She wanted to tell me something, but she was fighting the urge. I could see it in her face. She looked nervous. For a professional actress, she was awfully easy to read.

"I was here when one of your men came to see you," she whispered, looking back toward the door to make sure no one was near.

"Was it Thomer? Did you see him?"

"Hollingsworth," she said. "Doctor Feeney says he was the one who brought you here."

"Hollingsworth," I repeated. At least he was alive.

"He left when he saw me," Ava said, and immediately a thousand fractured pieces fit into one ugly picture. I had a girl. It would not matter whether I had smuggled her to Terraneau on the ship or met her on the job. I had some scrub hidden away while they were confined to the ship. They had a right to hate me. Just like a natural-born officer, I ignored their needs because my needs were met.

That was how Hollingsworth would see it.

3

"What are you doing here?"

"I'm the highest-ranking officer on Terraneau, that makes me king," I said, trying to sound more confident than I felt.

I didn't look fit for command. The doctor would not check me out of the hospital unless I left in a wheelchair, but I abandoned the wheels the moment Doctorow pulled out of the parking lot. Now I was on crutches. My head spinning, my legs weak, sweat forming on my face and running down my back, I tried to pretend like I was healthy. It was a good thing I had the crutches to lean on. I could not stand for more than a few moments at a time.

Hollingsworth shook his head, and said, "Go home. We don't want you here."

The showdown took place just outside the door to the administration building, both Hollingsworth and I glaring at each other in frosty silence. Several gawkers had come to see what would happen.

For a moment I thought it might come down to a fight. That would have been bad. Hollingsworth looked young and strong, and I felt about ready to faint. All I wanted to do at the moment was go into the admin building and sit down; but Hollingsworth was in my way, and he showed no inclination to let me pass.

Until that moment, I had never realized what life would be like without a combat reflex. I was staring into a fight and the only thing running through my veins was blood. I missed the shock of testosterone and adrenaline pumping through me giving me mingled feelings of comfort and invincibility. I should have felt strength and hate and calm. Instead, I felt weak and scared. If my arm and leg never healed, I would learn to live with it, but I wanted that gland to heal on the spot.

Summoning everything I had, I said, "Step aside, Hollingsworth. That is an order."

And he did.

He looked at the crowd that had gathered around us, then he lowered his head and stepped out of my way. Respect for authority was in his programming. He even held the door open for me as I hobbled up the stairs.

"What the speck do you assholes want?" Hollingsworth asked the people who had come, expecting a fight. Then he followed me into the building.

I made it to the empty reception desk, then dropped into the empty chair. My head swimming, my eyes watering, I turned to watch Hollingsworth coming in behind me.

"You look like shit, Harris."

"Don't be fooled, I'm running a double marathon this weekend."

Hollingsworth did not laugh. He did not even smile.

"I heard you brought me to the hospital," I said. "Were you the one who hauled me out of the parking garage as well?"

Hollingsworth hesitated. "Yeah."

"Thank you," I said.

"Was that really Ava Gardner in your hospital room?"

I wanted to tell him it was not what he thought, but my relationship with her was exactly what he thought it was. "That's her," I said.

"So the whole time you were telling us to keep it zipped, you were already getting yours. Fahey was right about you. You're worse than any of the natural-borns. You're a traitor to clones."

He waited for me to say something, but I had nothing to say. He was right.

"How long have you had her?"

"I brought her with me," I said. "She's a clone. They dumped her off at Clonetown."

"Son of a bitch," he said. I could not tell if he was calling me a son of a bitch or commenting on my luck. In Marine-speak, "son of a bitch" can be both a compliment and an insult.

"What is the situation over here?" I asked.

"We're basically screwed," Hollingsworth said. He sounded sullen and angry. "Most of the men blame you for everything. They think it's your fault the Unifieds attacked. They think it's your fault we're stuck here."

"You were already stuck here when I arrived," I pointed out.

"Stuck on the planet. We're trapped down here. They blame you.

"If you plan on running the base, you better watch your back; there are a lot of Marines who want to put a knife in it."

I didn't bother pointing out that the Navy would have attacked us no matter what happened. He knew. He had to.

"Have you established contact with the fleet?" I asked, hoping to derail the showdown I felt coming my way.

"There is no fleet," Hollingsworth said. He sat there, staring at the floor as he spoke, his body unmoving, his voice devoid of emotion.

"They destroyed every last ship?" I asked.

"Maybe," said Hollingsworth. "We can't account for every last ship. From what we can tell, there are less than a hundred dead ships out there. Most of them are ours. Nobody knows what happened to the rest of the fleet."

"What do you mean, 'nobody knows'? The rest of the ships were either destroyed or they weren't."

"They're not up there," he said. "All I know is that we can't reach them. That makes them dead in my book."

The conversation was getting us nowhere. Hollingsworth was too angry to listen. "Where is Thomer?" I asked.

For the first time since I arrived, a flash of sympathy showed on Hollingsworth's face. He sighed, and said, "Outer Bliss."

4

The video feed was taken one week after the U.A. attack, while I was still in a coma.

The video feed shows the interrogation room in Outer Bliss as seen through the hidden camera in the ceiling. Thomer is sitting at the table when the door opens, and the guards lead Senior Chief Fahey into the room.

If I had not known that Thomer asked for Fahey, I might not have recognized the man. He is not wearing makeup. His hair is long for a sailor but not for a civilian. It hangs over his ears.

Thomer tells the guards to wait outside, but they refuse. They tell him it is against regulations to leave visitors alone with prisoners. He believes them and does not argue the point.

One of the guards leads Fahey around the table and pulls out a stool for him. Even with his hands cuffed together, he has a snakelike fierceness. He looks incensed that Thomer has come. He leers at Thomer and says nothing. Nearly a minute passes before Thomer breaks the silence.

"A lot of good men died because of you," he says.

Fahey laughs, and says, "You don't know what you are talking about."

"You're a spy," Thomer says. "You reported everything we did to Admiral Brocius."

"Was that something that Harris told you, or did you come up with it yourself?"

"Is it true?" Thomer asks.

"Of course it isn't true. How would I have gotten information to Brocius?"

"I'm betting you sent it back to Earth with the natural-borns when they transferred home."

"Get specked," says Fahey.

"And I'm betting that you left holes in the blockade when you set it up so that the U.A. could place a spy on Terraneau. We located their spy. His name is Freeman."

This time Fahey does not say anything. He licks his lips, starts to say something, decides against it.

"Once you got yourself thrown in this stockade, the spy listened in on your conversations with the fleet. You knew he was out there, and you furnished him everything you knew by chatting with your friends on an open frequency."

"Bullshit. That's all bullshit," says Fahey. He looks at the guards to make sure they believe him.

"After the Unifieds landed here, they took all the prisoners back to their fleet . . . all of the prisoners except for you. Why did they leave you behind?"

A subtle shift is taking place. Now Thomer has the snake-like confidence and Fahey seems to shrink. He forces a smile, and says, "They wouldn't have left me here if I was their spy."

Thomer says, "Sure they would. You're not one of them," and he stands up and reaches into his pocket. One of the guards draws his pistol, but he only pulls out a pocketknife.

"What are you doing?" the guard asks.

"I want to try an experiment," he says to the guard.

"What are you up to?" Fahey asks.

Thomer slides the knife across the table. "Senior Chief, give me some of your hair."

"What?" Fahey asks.

"Give me a lock of your hair," Thomer repeats.

"You're joking," Fahey says.

Thomer sits down, and says, "Humor me."

Thomer is fully in control now. He is, after all, the only man in the room with an active field commission. When he gives orders, the other clones will obey them unless they have standing orders to the contrary. It's in their programming.

Fahey cuts off a lock of his hair. He gives the hair and the knife back to Thomer, who uses the knife to cut off some of his own hair.

Thomer's hair is less than an inch long. Fahey's hair is nearly four inches long. Since they are both clones of roughly the same age, they have identical brown hair except for the length; but Fahey sees his hair as blond. That, too, is in his programming. Thomer, who is aware of his synthetic nature, knows his hair is brown.

"Now for the experiment," Thomer says. He takes his own hair in his right hand and Fahey's in his left and puts both hands behind his back.

From my bird's-eye angle, I see things Fahey cannot see. Thomer drops the hair from his right hand and replaces it with some of Fahey's hair. Then he holds out both hands so only the ends of the hairs are sticking out from under his thumb.

"Whose hair is this?" he asks. "Yours or mine?"

Fahey sneers because to him the answer is obvious. The hair is brown. "It's yours," he says.

Without saying a word, Thomer rolls his hand so that the palm is facing up. He spreads his fingers revealing a twist of long hairs. "They left you behind because you are not one of them, Fahey. You're a clone."

Until that moment, I had never seen a death reflex.

Fahey stares at Thomer's open hand. He starts to rise to his feet, his entire body trembling, he remains mesmerized by the hair in Thomer's hand. His skin turns pale as he mouths words that do not escape his lips. There is a slight shudder

*of the shoulders, a quick twitch of the head, and Fahey falls
facedown on the table, a thin stream of blood leaking out of
his ear.*

5

"They hung Thomer the next day," Hollingsworth said.

"But Fahey was a spy." It didn't make sense that Thomer
should die for executing a spy.

"The guards were from the *Washington*. Everyone from
Outer Bliss came from the *Washington*, Harris. Besides,
Thomer didn't care. I offered to come get him so he could
stand trial. He didn't want a trial."

He'd already been through too many trials, I thought. He'd
convicted himself. He was guilty of surviving New Copenhagen when all of his friends had died. For him, that was a
capital offense.

6

Hollingsworth drove me out to see the place where the
ghosts had been.

"They're gone now," he said. "The last one died a few days
ago. The bastard hung on for fifteen days. Fifteen days."

"What about Mooreland?" I asked.

"He didn't even last the week," Hollingsworth said. "I
think he might have broken something when the building
came down on him. Maybe he got gangrene or something."

A long chain-link fence ran the border. Four Marines in
combat armor stood at the gate. Hollingsworth drove our jeep
up to the fence and parked. We both climbed out. He waited
as I pulled out my crutches and struggled to my feet.

Beyond the guards, the scene looked no different than most
of Norristown. Rubble covered the ground. The partial walls
of the government building stood as jagged as knife blades. If
anything, we had not been as thorough as the Avatari would
have been. The area of the building over the garage entrance
had crumbled to nothing. The far wall of the building still
stood.

"Hear any voices?" Hollingsworth asked the guards.

"Silent as a tomb," the man replied.

They traded salutes.

"Did you ever hear them?" I asked.

"Every day," Hollingsworth said.

The admitted us through the gate. Buildings like the ones we had demolished still stood on every side of the lot, but we were in a vast field of concrete and steel. Where the building once stood, a twenty-foot mound rose from the ground with girders and concrete blocks poking out. A strong wind blew across the destruction, causing half-buried papers to flap. Two ten-foot strands of rebar jutted from a concrete slab. They jangled in the breeze.

"They spoke to us over the interLink. The first few days, they tried to bargain with us," Hollingsworth said. "They wanted us to dig them out, but they wouldn't promise to surrender.

"Thomer was still here at that point. He was the only officer with the authority to negotiate . . . him and you. We didn't know if you were going to make it. Anyway, Thomer left orders for the men guarding the grave to leave their helmets back at the fort. He didn't want us talking to them. He was afraid Mooreland would order some clone to dig him out . . ."

Leaning heavily on my crutches, I walked to the edge of the rubble, knowing exactly where I was. This was the area between the two wings. It was our gauntlet. This was the spot the scouts entered first. They came this far, then they stopped.

"A few days later, Thomer was gone, and I was in charge. I put on my helmet, and that was the first time I heard them. They were begging for help by then. Some of them had already died.

"I only heard Mooreland once. He wanted to talk to you," Hollingsworth said. "He sounded as good as dead already. I think he knew his time was up."

"The locals never heard about this?" I asked.

"Hell no," Hollingsworth said. "That's why we posted guards. Thomer thought they would try to dig Mooreland out if they knew he was down there."

He was right, they would have.

The whole building had been turned into a mass grave.

Maybe all of Terraneau qualified as a mass grave. The Unified
Authority used the planet to bury its clones, trapping them in
the far end of space. Then we returned the favor, burying their
new Marines under their own government building.

"This isn't over," I said in a voice so soft I was sure that
Hollingsworth would not hear it. "This war is not over."

Where do ideas come from?

No man is an island, but some authors seem to be. Some authors can shut themselves off from the world for a month and emerge with masterpieces. I am no such magician.

I had just completed the first draft of this book in August, when I stumbled across an interesting review of my second novel, *Rogue Clone*, on goodreads.com, in which the reviewer called my book "dudely" and pointed out that the first female character to have a name did not appear until the forty-fifth chapter of a fifty-three chapter book.

The romance with Ava Gardner already existed in this book before I read that review. In fact, if you must pin the blame on someone for young Harris in love, pin it on Anne, my amazing editor at Ace. I started *The Clone Elite* with the line, "Until the first half of humanity was gone, all anybody wanted to talk about was the actress Ava Gardner."

I liked that line because I thought it begged all kinds of questions, not the least of which was, "What the heck was Ava Gardner doing in the twenty-sixth century?" Anne told me that I could only use the line if I gave Ava more of a role than simply appearing in an opening sentence. Since I had just signed a deal for three more Harris books, I asked if I could put her in the next series.

The Goodreads reviewer went on to comment that my clones were oddly restrained when it came to sex among themselves. Brown Betty on Goodreads, Perry Fahey owes much of his very existence to you.

And speaking of idea generators, I want to thank the disembodied voices of SadSamsPalace.com, my website. I have a crew of usual suspects who haunt my blog and often give me good ideas. Aaron Spuler, whose son Kaleb will have been born a few months before this book comes out, reminded me how much I like it when old characters make cameo appearances in novels.

Nope, Freeman's brief appearance was not Aaron's idea. I knew from the start that Freeman had to show up sooner or later. As both John Thorpe and Mark Adams put it, "Harris may be optional in a Wayson Harris novel, but Freeman is mandatory."

Expect a lot more Freeman in the next two books. In fact, I had toyed with the idea of creating a graphic novel called *Freeman Stories*. Then I read *Watchmen* and gave in to deep-seated feelings of inadequacy.

Harris will face a new kind of threat in the next installment of this series, and I wanted to thank a few guys for coming up with this idea. Kit Lewis, another constant customer at Sad Sam's, first proposed the idea. I have left his posting up, but you are going to need to do a lot of digging to find it.

Kit's idea had never ever occurred to me, and it made a lot of sense. Thanks, Kit.

And thank you to KillerBit. Once Kit came up with the idea, KillerBit did a little digging and fleshed it out with a little scientific fact-finding.

One last note about my blog . . . When *The Clone Elite* came out, Chris Nobles (aka Sniperae) was one of the first guys on my blog to finish the book. He could have simply called it "a masterpiece." I would have liked that, actually. Instead, he gave me mild grief about ending the book too abruptly.

I did not like that, especially because I knew he was right. Chris, I apologize. It won't happen again. (Until Chris brought this up, this novel had a very abrupt ending as well.)

On the positive side, Jon (Jaffe) said he liked the time line I put at the beginning of *The Clone Elite*. I originally updated the time line and included it in this book, then removed it, then put it back again following Jon's advice.

BTW—you may have noticed that I only refer to this novel as "this novel" in the author's notes. There is a perfectly good reason for that. As of this writing, the book is called *Clones Have Ghosts*. Anne, my brilliant and kind editor whose advice reigns supreme, has asked me to change the title.

Today is November 28, and I have eighty pages to finish proofreading before I submit the book to Ace. I will send the manuscript to the long-suffering and very wonderful Anne on Wednesday along with a letter of apology. I am not a diva, at least I do not think I am. Of course, what diva ever thinks of himself/herself as a diva?

As of this writing, Christian McGrath has not begun work on the cover for this book; but once he finishes, I know it will be magnificent. I want to thank Anne and Cam and the people at Ace who spend so much time cleaning up my work.

Before beginning my career in fiction, I spent fifteen years as a freelance journalist covering the video game industry. When I first started, *Penthouse* magazine always had a booth at trade shows for some interactive product. There were posters of three models on the walls of the *Penthouse* booth, and those same models sat at a table, signing autographs. The thing is, if I had not known that the women in the pictures were the same ones signing the autographs, I would never have guessed. The makeup, the lighting, the lenses, and the photo editors transformed those normal three women into goddesses.

Rachel Johnson, Jordan Green, Anne, and Cam have achieved an even more magical transformation on my behalf. Readers, you have no idea what this book looked like when they received it.

I need to thank Richard Curtis, my agent and adviser. Jeez, this sounds like I'm giving an acceptance speech at the Academy Awards, and I haven't even gotten around to thanking my wife and parents. Mom, Dad, Brooke, thanks.

My biggest thanks go to you, my readers. I hope you enjoyed this book.

Steven L. Kent
November 28, 2008

AUTHOR'S ADDENDUM

In 1984, when I was a student at BYU Hawaii, I met a poet from Wales named Leslie Norris. Two years later, when I transferred to the Provo, Utah, campus of BYU, he became my mentor.

Leslie Norris was a kind man, a fine man, a man of infinite patience, which I often tested. He passed away in April 2006, at the age of eighty-four, and I miss him deeply. He left behind a legacy of literature and people who counted themselves fortunate to have known such a great man.

After his passing, I kept in touch with Catherine, his widow. Kitty was strong and kind, and always a fine hostess. She was a woman who spoke her mind when she disagreed with you, but she was always especially gracious. A great person in her own right, Kitty relished the role of being "Leslie's wife."

Today, after finishing the notes you have just read, I called Kitty to wish her happy holidays and learned that she passed away.

Life is precious, make sure to spend it with the ones that you love.

SLK
November 28, 2008

WILLIAM C. DIETZ

AT EMPIRE'S EDGE

In a far-distant future, the Uman Empire has spread to the stars and beyond, conquering and colonizing worlds, ruling with a benevolent—but iron—fist. The Pax Umana reigns—and all is well...

But on one planet, the remnants of a violent, shape-shifting race called the Sagathies are confined, kept captive by Xeno cops, who have been bioengineered to be able to see through their guises. Jak Cato, a Xeno cop, is returning a fugitive Sagathi when things go horribly wrong. Now he must figure out who betrayed them, recapture the Sagathi, and exact revenge.

"When it comes to military science fiction, William Dietz can run with the best."
—Steve Perry, author of the Matador series

THE CLONE ELITE

"If you enjoy military science fiction, then this is the book for you . . . fast paced and hard-hitting. Punches, bullets, and nuclear bombs are not held back. The characters face hard choices and don't regret them after they are made."   —*SFRevu*

THE CLONE ALLIANCE

"Offers up stunning battle sequences, intriguing moral quandaries, and plenty of unexpected revelations . . . [a] fast-paced military SF book with plenty of well-scripted action and adventure, [and] a sympathetic narrator."   —*SF Site*

ROGUE CLONE

"Exciting space battles [and] haunting, quiet moments after war has taken its toll . . . Military SF fans looking for stories that combine mystery, action, espionage, politics, and some thoughtful doses of humanism in exploring their not entirely human characters would do well to add Steven L. Kent to their reading lists."   —SF Reviews.net

THE CLONE REPUBLIC

"A solid debut. Harris is an honest, engaging protagonist and thoughtful narrator, and Kent's clean, transparent prose fits well with both the main character and the story's themes . . . Kent is a skillful storyteller, and the book entertains throughout."
     —*Sci Fi Weekly*

"The first sentence gets you immediately . . . From there, the action begins fast and furious, with dark musings, lavish battle scenes, and complex characterizations . . . *The Clone Republic* feature[s] taut writing and a truly imaginative plot full of introspection and philosophizing." —*The Village Voice*

"A character-driven epic that understands that the best war stories are really antiwar stories . . . a smartly conceived adventure."   —SF Reviews.net

Ace Books by Steven L. Kent

THE CLONE REPUBLIC
ROGUE CLONE
THE CLONE ALLIANCE
THE CLONE ELITE
THE CLONE BETRAYAL